ACE MAGNETS

A Small Town Romance

GIULIA LAGOMARSINO

Cover Design courtesy of T.E. Black Designs

www.teblackdesigns.com

WANDER AGUIAR Photography

Forest H.

❀ Created with Vellum

A huge thanks to Donna for helping me with this! Your motivation and enthusiasm kept me going and pushing to get this book done. Writing it was such a joy thanks to you!

CORDUROY

How the hell had I ended up consoling this woman again? I helped her off the ground, staring down at the disgusting dead squirrel that she somehow thought she murdered. It was the squirrel's fault. Everyone knew that. The bastards couldn't make up their minds where to go, and inevitably always got hit by cars. But of course, this woman was sympathetic to the mangy bastard.

She sniffled as I pushed her into her car. "Just follow me back to your place, okay?"

She nodded. "Just don't drive too fast. I tend to get lost easily."

I wanted to roll my eyes. In a town of less than three-thousand people, there was no reason she should ever get lost.

"I promise, I'll drive slowly."

I shut the door and gritted my teeth as I headed for my police car. I wanted to say I was upset because I had to deal with this woman, but the truth was, I was upset because I really liked her. In the six months since she'd come to our small town, I'd seen her around, but always tried to ignore her. She was too tempting. She was so damn petite compared to my huge frame, and I didn't even think I was all that big, but compared to her, I was a giant. Every time I saw her, she always had something strange going on with her hair. It was either in a weird twisty thing on top of her head or braids. Hell, one time she even wore it in knots on top of her head. And I'm talking multiple tiny knots. I wasn't sure what to make of it. Somehow, it was all endearing.

I started my car and pulled out of the parking lot, watching in the rearview mirror every few seconds to make sure she was still behind me. The drive to her place took forever. How the hell did she still get lost after all this time? She had to be the worst driver known to man. That was one of the many reasons I hadn't asked her out since the first day I met her. She was a menace on the road, and I was the deputy-sheriff. I had a reputation to uphold. How could I date a woman that was such a disaster?

Pulling into her driveway, I intended to just wave her off and leave, but when she got out all chipper and waving at me, I sighed and got out. She rushed around the car in her long, flowy skirt and grabbed my hand. Shocks of desire sparked, but if she noticed, she didn't let it show.

"Thank you so much for helping me. I can't understand why I have such a hard time finding my house. You would think it would be simple, right?" she laughed.

I laughed along too, but for different reasons. "Hey, everyone has something."

"Anyway, do you have a minute? I just made my world famous cupcakes and I'd love for you to try them."

I scratched at my chin, contemplating my options. "I don't know. I usually go to Mary Anne's for breakfast."

"Oh, come on. It's just one day. And you've been so nice to me. I'd really like to repay the favor."

"Well...I do love cupcakes."

"See?" she said brightly. "It was meant to be."

She spun around and headed for the door, leaving me standing there pondering my potential demise. If this woman baked like she drove, I might end up dead. Still, it was a chance I was willing to take. I followed her to the door where she was digging through her purse.

"I know I brought my keys with me. I mean, I had to, right? Because I wouldn't have locked the door and left my keys inside."

I nodded, glancing past her and sighing. Her keys were sticking out of the lock on the bolt. "Um...they're in the door."

"What?" she asked, still digging through her purse.

"Your keys...you left them in the door."

She glanced up, stared at the keys, and then started laughing. "Oh my gosh. I'm such an idiot." She slapped herself on the forehead and unlocked the door, heading inside with the keys still in the door. I shook my head and removed the keys, placing them on the side table as I shut the door.

Inside was nothing like I had expected. Of course, with this woman, I never knew what to expect. I suppose I should have seen this coming. She was strange for sure. But this...crap, I needed to get out of here.

"What do you think?" she asked, smiling brightly at me.

"It's...cozy," I went with, hoping she wasn't offended by that. Luckily, she beamed up at me, and motioned for me to take a seat.

"Just sit wherever you want."

Where? I mouthed, looking at the seating arrangements.

It was like a hippie's paradise. A fluffy, cream rug with blue accents covered the floor, and where there should be seats, instead there were gigantic blue and brown cushions on the floor. Pillows of all shapes and sizes were spread out around the room. There was even a beanbag chair sitting in the corner. Books were stacked all around with candles on top, along with potted plants. Soft blankets were tossed all around the room, but I wasn't sure if it was decorative or if she was a slob. There were even Chinese lanterns hanging from the ceiling.

I ran my hand over my face, baffled at what I was seeing. How could I be attracted to this person? And then I glanced up and saw what I thought were astrological symbols on blankets, and they were attached to the vaulted ceiling. Slowly closing my eyes, I tried my best not to freak out. It wasn't like I was dating her or anything. I just helped her find her way home. I was in no way committed to her.

With that in mind, I took a deep breath and laughed to myself. I was freaking out way too much. I walked over to the brown ottoman cushion and sat down, jumping up when something screeched beneath me. A cat scampered out from underneath me. I hadn't seen it because of the massive amount of fur on the animal. He ran off into the other room, hissing at me as he turned the corner.

Shaking off the terrifying cat incident, I sat down on the ottoman again. It wasn't uncomfortable, but there was nothing to lean back against. I ran my hand over my face, wondering how long I had to stay here. My eyes started watering and then I sneezed hard. What the hell?

Abby came rushing into the room, her skirt billowing around her legs. Smiling, she set down a tray with some tea on the rug in front of me. There were also four gigantic cupcakes in front of me. I could do this. I could spend time with her in the name of cupcakes. It was just one time.

"I made you this peach tea that is so amazing, and I added a little sugar. I hope you like it."

"I'm sure I will," I said, lifting the cup. I didn't want to taste it. Who drank peach tea? Taking a hesitant sip, I was surprised that I actually liked it. It definitely wasn't my morning coffee, but it was delicious. "Mmm," I nodded. "It's good." My eyes were still watering, and I could feel another sneeze coming on. "Do you have a tissue?"

"Of course." She grabbed one, then smiled brightly at me, gathering her skirt as she sat down beside me, taking her own tea cup in hand. "I'm glad you like it."

I blew my nose, wondering why I suddenly felt like I had a cold. "So, are you working today?"

"Well, I work every day. There's always something my company needs done."

"You never have a day off?"

"Well, there are days that I just check in and other days I work all day."

"And what made you decide to be a virtual assistant?"

"Well, I don't like working with people."

I glanced around the space and frowned. She seemed like such a people person.

"Aren't you going to try the cupcake?"

I nodded and picked it up, tearing at the paper. This felt so wrong, like I was going against Mary Anne. Putting it to my mouth, I practically moaned when I tasted the moist, sweet goodness. It wasn't overly sweet, but it had this flavor that I couldn't even describe. It was amazing. In only two more bites, the cupcake was gone and I was licking my lips for more.

She smiled sweetly at me and pushed over another cupcake. "Go ahead. You know you want to."

"I do," I said, snatching up another one.

"I could make you muffins tomorrow. I have this recipe I've been wanting to try, but..."

"But what?" I asked around another bite.

"Well, I don't bake very often because it's just me, and if I ate all my baked goods, I would be as big as this house."

"You should definitely bake more of these. You should have opened your own bakery."

She waved me off. "What's the fun in that?"

"Um...this delicious goodness that I'm shoving in my mouth?"

"I know, but it's no fun if it's a job."

I dipped my chin, understanding what she was saying. Taking another sip of the tea, I found myself drinking it much faster than I would my coffee. There was no bitter taste, and there was just enough sugar to add some flavor.

"Whew," I said, standing up and rubbing my belly. "That was very good. Thank you so much."

"Any time," her eyes sparkled. She stood up and twisted her fingers together nervously. Was she attracted to me? She blushed slightly the longer I stared at her. Crap, I needed to get out of here before she asked me to go out or something.

"Well, thanks for the cupcakes," I said, sneezing again.

She blushed even harder. "Thank you for getting me home. Oh, and for not arresting me for murdering a squirrel."

"Yeah," I sniggered. "We don't actually do that."

I headed for the door, determined to get out of there before she said anything else to me. I sneezed again, wiping my nose on the tissue still in my hand. Crap, I must be allergic to her cat. As much as I wanted to find that one woman for me, she wasn't it.

I STOPPED at the pharmacy on the way to the station, picking up some antihistamines, popping them in my mouth right away. The last thing I needed was to feel like my head was swelling. I walked into the station and over to my desk, tossing my hat down as I took my seat.

"How's Penny?" Jack asked, staring at his paperwork. He was back to hiding. Just one person getting in an accident had him all torn up inside. I didn't want him shrinking back into the hateful man I'd seen over the past few years.

"She's recovering. She didn't look too good, but that's to be expected."

"And Nathan?" he asked, his gaze finally meeting mine. "Are they back together?"

I grinned at him. "Well, I worked my magic."

He shook his head, huffing slightly. "Of course you did. You know, one of these days, people are going to catch on to what you're doing."

"Hey, I bring people together. There's nothing to be upset about."

"You know, some people don't like you interfering in their business."

I leaned forward, resting my elbows on my desk. "Name one person that hasn't benefited from my interference."

He frowned. "Well, I don't know that they didn't benefit, but I'm sure Robert would have preferred you didn't hit on Anna quite as much as you did."

I glanced away from him. Anna was the one that got away. I always wanted her, but she always wanted someone else. In high school when she was dating him, I had been just a few days late on asking her out. If I had gotten the courage to ask her out just a few days sooner, she might have ended up with me. At least, that's what I told myself. But in all honesty, I knew she was never meant to be with me. She always had eyes for him.

"Anna was special and he didn't see it. I needed him to get his head out of his ass."

"But why? It's not like it would have affected you in any way."

I shoved back from my chair and busied myself with getting coffee.

"Did you like her?" Jack asked incredulously.

I didn't answer. I just sipped my coffee. Except, now that I'd had Abby's tea, this tasted like shit. I poured it down the drain.

"Oh my God. You never told me," Jack said, standing up. "Why didn't you say anything?"

"Because I loved her, okay?" I finally turned around and faced him, feeling ashamed that I was admitting it to someone after all these years. "It was never meant to be with us, but yeah, I loved her. I loved her since she was in my English class in high school. She sat right in front of me, and I was madly in love with her."

He frowned. "Did she ever know?"

I grunted low in my throat. "Not unless she caught me staring at her every second of the day."

"But why didn't you say anything?"

"I was trying to work up the courage to tell her, but I was too late. Robert beat me to it."

"But they broke up. You had your chance for years."

I shook my head. "She never wanted me. Trust me, I watched her all these years. She never wanted anyone else."

"But you never tried."

"Because I knew there was no point. Sure, I might have ended up with her, but she wouldn't have wanted me the way she wanted him. And where would that leave me? Loving a woman that would never love me as much? It doesn't matter anyway. She ended up with the man she was supposed to. I've moved on."

He stared at me, but then his eyes widened and he pointed at me. "That's what all this matchmaking is about. You don't want others to miss out on what you did."

I snorted in amusement. "Sure, that's why I do it."

"It makes total sense. You're an ass to all of them. You blatantly hit on women that you know are taken. It's like penance for not having the balls to do what you should have done all those years ago. And at the same time, you're helping people get together when they should have never been apart to begin with. You're cupid."

My brows pinched together in disbelief as I took my seat. "Don't we have work to do?"

"I don't know, Cupid. Are there any women out there in desperate need of your assistance?"

Abby's beautiful face flashed in my mind, the way she helplessly sat on the ground as she stared at the squirrel. Something about her was just so damn intoxicating. But she was a nut job—No pun intended. I was supposed to end up with someone more like Anna, more put together and self-reliant. Abby was a mess, and I didn't know what to make of her strange living arrangements. No, she definitely wasn't the woman for me.

"Who is she?" Jack asked, bringing me out of my inner musings.

"Who?"

"The woman you're going all googly-eyed over."

I waved him off. "I don't know what you're talking about. I'm not googly-eyed over anyone."

"Right, you just got this far off look in your eyes that I only see when you're dating someone new."

"Well, then you're wrong, because I'm not dating anyone."

"You don't have to be to appear that way. So, it's someone you've met, but you're not with," he nodded to himself as he started walking around the room. "And it can't be someone you've already dated, so that knocks out half the town."

I rolled my eyes at him. He placed his hand against his chin, scratching at his jaw as he thought.

"And it can't be someone from out of town, at least, not that far out of town, because you hardly ever leave town."

"This is ridiculous."

"You were just at the hospital. It's possible you met someone there."

I held my breath, wondering if he would guess who it was.

"But you're not the type to fall for a damsel in distress. You've always liked women that could watch after themselves. Like Anna," he grinned.

He would definitely never guess Abby then. She was the opposite of Anna in every way.

"So, it's got to be someone new to the area, someone that you're interested in, but since you haven't actually asked her out, there has to be something holding you back."

He stopped his pacing, snapping his fingers at me. "That new chick." He snapped his fingers as he tried to come up with a name. "Abigail. Yes, that woman you hugged in the middle of the street. That's who it is, isn't it?"

Crap, I was so screwed. "Why would you think it's her?"

"Oh, come on! You were hugging a woman!"

"Yeah, because she was upset."

"And you don't like to comfort women. That's not your MO at all."

"Exactly," I said, hoping he would disprove his own theory.

"And that's what it is about her. She's good looking, and despite the fact that you don't like weak women, you like her."

"She's not weak," I argued, giving myself away. I closed my eyes, shaking my head as he laughed.

"Holy shit. So, what is it about her?"

"Nothing. There's absolutely nothing about her. It's not her."

"It's gotta be the whole damsel thing. The question is, what makes her different?"

"I just said it's not her."

"Right, which means it is."

He rushed over to his computer and started typing.

"What are you doing?"

"Checking her background."

"Why?" I asked, rushing over to his side.

"Because I want to know more about her." He pulled up her name in the system, laughing at what he found. I sighed, rubbing at my eyes. "So, not only is she a damsel in distress, but she's a very chaotic damsel, and that's what you like about her."

"I never said I liked her!"

"I should have known it. The moment I saw the footage of you holding her in the street, I should have known you were going to fall for her. Of course, I'm surprised it took this long. But now that I think about it, whenever we go out—"

"The people always shout," I interrupted, hoping to throw him off, but he kept going.

"—you're always looking around, like you're watching for someone."

"Bullshit. You're seeing what you want to see."

"No, I'm finally paying attention. So, tell me about her."

"There's nothing to tell," I argued. "I don't know anything about her."

"You must know something," he laughed, "otherwise you wouldn't be so wrapped up in her."

I walked away from him, sitting down at my desk with a huff. "I'm not wrapped up in anyone. I don't like her. I don't know her, and I definitely am not the man for her."

"So you do know something about her. Because if you didn't, you wouldn't know if you were the right man for her or not," he said, jabbing a finger in my direction.

"Fine, you want to know about her? She's some kind of hippie. She has a living room filled with fluffy pillows, no furniture, and weird tea."

He nodded, grinning at me the whole time. "Did you drink the tea?"

"Fuck off," I said, storming out of the station, his laughter floating behind me.

2

ABBY

Checking the time on my wall clock, I had just enough time to deliver the muffins I made for Carter to the station. I bit my lip as I tried to decide what to wear today. I was partial to wearing flowy skirts in the summer, but it was quickly morphing into fall. I wouldn't be able to wear them too much longer. I liked feeling free as a bird. I pulled on a white skirt with a blue peasant top and quickly looked in the mirror. My hair was a mess today, flowing in weird waves over my shoulders. During the day, when I was bored, I would do all sorts of weird things to my hair. It became a bad habit of mine.

But I was so behind this morning with making the muffins, that I didn't have time to do anything to my hair. Blowing a rogue strand from my face, I decided it would just have to do. I slipped into my sandals and grabbed my crossbody bag, pulling it over my shoulder. Running for the door, I suddenly remembered the muffins, the whole reason I was leaving to begin with. Racing back to the kitchen, I snatched them off the counter and quickly headed for the door.

Pteheste was sitting right in front of the door. She was a beautiful tiger cat with a white shield on her chest. She was also my guard cat. She was always at the door waiting for me, unless she was too busy with her afternoon nap. Luckily, none of the cats came out yesterday when Corduroy was here. That was something I wasn't ready to explain to him yet. I glanced around the living room for any cats that might try to sneak out, but didn't see any other than Pteheste.

I went to grab my keys, but they weren't there. It didn't really matter. I would only be gone for a half hour tops. And this was a safe town. It wasn't like I had to worry about break-ins. It took me a few wrong turns to finally find my way into town, but once I was on Main Street, I was good to go. Now I just had to figure out what to say to him.

"*Hi,*" I said breathily. "God, that's horrible. I sound like a love-struck idiot."

Blowing out a deep breath, I tried to think of another winning opening line.

"*Hey, Carter. It's so good to see you. Muffin?*"

I laughed to myself. "Yeah, like he won't see through that one. *I just happened to show up with a container of muffins, and it has absolutely nothing to do with you.*"

Grunting in frustration, I turned the wheel and stepped on the brake pedal as I pulled into a spot in front of the sheriff's station. Except, the car didn't slow down. Instead, it sped up and jumped the curb. I slammed both feet down, finally hitting the right pedal, but it was too late. I hit the sign on the sidewalk that said Law Enforcement Only. The metal from the sign crunched against my car and I cringed.

Shoving the car into park, I took a few breaths, trying to calm my racing heart. Good lord, that was close. If I hadn't stopped in time, I would have hit the building. I put the car in reverse just as Carter came racing out of the building with Jack.

"This is so bad," I whined to myself. When the car was off the curb and back in place, I shifted into park and turned off the car. Carter came racing to the driver's side door, yanking it open.

"Are you okay?"

"I'm fine," I laughed lightly, like I hadn't just almost killed myself in a single vehicle incident. "I just accidentally stepped on the wrong pedal."

He stared at me in confusion. "How did you do that?"

I had no idea. "Two left feet, I guess."

I tried to laugh it off, but it came out awkward and stupid even to my own ears. Clearing my throat, I grabbed the muffins off the passenger seat and got out, shutting my door. Straightening my shirt that was now all cock-eyed, I smiled brightly at him.

"I brought you some muffins."

He frowned down at the container, almost like he didn't want to accept them.

"Muffins?" Jack asked.

I'd only met the sheriff twice, but I liked him well enough. Stepping past Carter, I figured maybe the best way to get in his good graces was through his boss.

"Blueberry," I said cheerfully. "I brought them because Carter helped me out yesterday, and I wanted to say thank you. There are plenty in there."

He frowned down at the container also. "Hmm...I don't know. If Mary Anne finds out about this..."

"They're just muffins. I'm sure they're nothing compared to hers."

In fact, I knew they were better. I'd heard everyone rave about her baked goods, and while they were excellent, I thought mine were better. Maybe I was being slightly biased, but I'd learned from my mother, and she was an excellent baker.

I held the container out for him, and he hesitantly took it. "Well, I guess it would be rude not to at least try them. Right, Carter?"

"Uh...yeah."

He didn't sound very convinced, but he followed Jack inside the station. Not knowing what to do, I followed. As soon as Jack was under the cover of the station, he tore into the container and snatched his first muffin, moaning as soon as he shoved it in his mouth.

"Good God, woman. This is amazing." As if he realized what he just said, he turned and glared at me. "Not a word to Mary Anne."

I made the motion of zipping my lips. "I won't say a word."

"They can't be that good," Carter muttered.

I was slightly offended by that. Like my muffins couldn't be as good as Mary Anne's? They were better.

He took one and shoved it in his mouth, chewing and pretending he didn't like it. I didn't understand. Why was he acting like he didn't like them? He liked my cupcakes.

"Yeah, they're okay."

"Okay?" I said incredulously. "They're just okay?"

"Yeah," Jack said around a mouthful. "What planet are you on?"

Carter shrugged. "What? I have to like everything someone puts in front of me?"

Confused, I took a step back. I thought yesterday he liked me, that he was interested in me, but now he was treating me like I was somebody he didn't even know. Not that he knew me that well anyway, but I made him cupcakes! That had to mean something.

"Um…" Embarrassed now that I had obviously made a huge error in judgement, I brushed my hair back behind my ear. "Well, I really need to get back to work. I just wanted to thank you again for all your help. So…"

I turned and fled before they could see the mortification on my face. This was so damn embarrassing. I ran to my car, slamming the door as soon as I got in and put the car in reverse, flying out of the space and right into a car that I didn't see. My car jerked to a stop and I closed my eyes, mortification times ten running through me.

Dropping my head to the steering wheel, I rolled my forehead back and forth across it. "Why? Why? Why?"

Sighing, I shifted into park and prepared to go beg whoever I ran into to not completely lose their shit on me. Opening the door, I ignored Carter, who stood on the sidewalk and stared at me in disbelief.

"I'm so sorry," I said as I approached the woman in the car.

She opened her door and sighed. "Dammit! I didn't want a new car."

I frowned. "The damage isn't that bad."

At worst, she had a banged up bumper.

"Yes, but when I tell my husband that I got in an accident, he's going to insist that I get a new car."

"And that's a bad thing?" I asked.

"Some girls like jewelry and pretty things. I just don't."

"Oh, I—"

"Anna, are you okay?" Carter asked, rushing over to her. "I didn't know it was you."

My jaw dropped as I watched him rush over to her side of the car and practically fawn over her. A married woman!

"I'm fine, Corduroy."

"You're sure? That was a hard hit."

"It was a tap at best. Look, there's hardly any damage to my car."

I couldn't believe it. Was I seeing things? What was going on here? Maybe I had made up the whole attraction in my head. Maybe he didn't really like me like I assumed. Which meant all the time I spent making him muffins was a gigantic waste of time.

"Um...I have to get back to work. Do you want to exchange insurance?" I asked, interrupting Carter's barrage of questions about her well-being.

She snorted. "Are you kidding me? This car is older than me. I won't waste my time filling out a report."

"You know Robert won't like that."

"Robert can kiss my ass. It's a car, and if I file a report, her insurance will go up. It's not worth it over a tiny dent."

He sighed, running his hand through his hair. "Alright, if that's what you want."

Feeling like the third wheel of a very strange situation, I decided it was time for me to leave. I walked back to my car, hoping she would move hers so I could flee the scene. I caught Jack's eye just as I was slipping inside my car. He was frowning as he looked at Carter, and then back at me. I wasn't sure what that was about, but I wasn't going to sit here and dissect it.

Luckily, the woman drove off and I was able to leave, but not before Carter knocked on my window. Great, just what I needed right now.

I rolled down my window and glanced at him unwillingly. "Yes?"

"You need to be more careful. You could have hurt her."

"Yeah," I nodded. "I got that."

He frowned. "Okay, well, I'll see you around town."

"Not likely," I muttered under my breath as I rolled the window back up. Once he stepped back from the car, I checked the street behind me and backed out of the space. I somehow made it home, which was strange because I always managed to go down the wrong street. I walked inside my unlocked house and tossed my purse on the ground. Walking over to my sanctuary, I plopped down on one of the cushions and sighed. Maybe moving here wasn't a very good idea. Now I would have to see a man I had a crush on around town, but he would be crushing on someone else.

৩৯৫৩

TWO HOURS LATER, I was woken up on my cloud of pillows by a cat licking my face. Brushing the cat away, I sat up and rubbed my eyes. Smiling at Yoda Bear, I pet his long, caramel fur, loving the way he snuggled up against me under the blanket.

"Hey, buddy. Are you coming to snuggle with me?"

His purring intensified as he rubbed his head against me. He was my most lovable cat, always sleeping under blankets with me. I'd never had a cat do that before.

"I guess you're getting hungry, aren't you?"

He jumped up and ran to the kitchen, letting me know he was ready for food. I pushed up out of my cushions and trudged to the kitchen. I was supposed to be working, but it was hard to get motivated when I felt so crushed. I wasn't even sure why I felt this way. Carter was just another man. He hadn't said anything to lead me on, but I'd somehow gotten it in my head that he liked me.

It was silly to think he'd want me. He was tall and muscular. He looked damn good in his uniform, and his hair had these blonde streaks through it that were just so darn perfect. Everything about him was perfect. And I was the weird woman with six cats.

Sighing, I got up and pulled out the cat food, walking over to the six cat bowls on the floor. Whistling loudly, a herd of wild cats came running into the kitchen, tripping over each other to get to their food.

"Habanero, be nice to your brother," I scolded my black cat. Picking him up, I held him back so Pimento could get in. It was like this every day. The Red Hot Chili Peppers as I called them, were always fighting for their spot in the line of cat food dishes. Jalapeño was the only one that tended to hold back and wait for everyone else to get in place.

My computer dinged in the other room, letting me know someone was trying to get ahold of me. "Behave yourselves," I said sternly as I headed into the other room.

I had messages stacked up from earlier, and since I took a two hour pity nap on my cushions, I was behind on my workday. I spent the next two hours working, then stopped for lunch. I did my absolute best not to think about Carter at all during the day. It was clear he wasn't interested, so there was no point in dwelling on him.

By the end of the day, I was exhausted. My back was killing me and I desperately needed a trip to my chiropractor. Sitting all the time at a desk was throwing my whole body out of whack. I spent the night on the floor of my living room, flipping through channels on the TV and eating popcorn. Every show I tried to watch didn't hold my interest. Turning the TV off, I stared at the six cats laying around me on the carpet. God, I was turning into an old cat lady. One day I would die, but no one would know until I didn't complete my tasks online. Eventually, a search party would go out for me, and the cops would find me on the floor, half-eaten by my starving cats. Perhaps it wasn't a good idea to have so many of them.

I went around turning out all the lights and got ready for bed. Slipping into my silk pajama top and shorts, I climbed into my round bed and adjusted the covers. I hated the typical bed. I liked to be able to move around and face different directions when the mood struck. The round bed just seemed like the obvious solution.

It was sometime in the middle of the night when something woke me up, jolting me from my sleep.

"Temperganda?" I called out.

She was my feisty cat, always getting into trouble. Slipping from the bed, I yawned and went in search of her. All the cats were laying scattered around the house, but I couldn't find her. She was my little slut, always getting knocked up, and then I had to find homes for the kittens. It wasn't like I could keep every litter she had.

The curtains over the kitchen window were blowing with the breeze. I was pretty sure I shut all the windows before bed, but I must have missed one. I grabbed the top of the pane, but when I started to shut it, I noticed the screen was missing.

"Oh shit," I groaned. The little whore got out, and now she was probably on the prowl for her next male victim. I ran over to my junk drawer and pulled out the flashlight. Slipping out the back door, I ran the light over the backyard, watching for her eyes reflecting in the light.

"Temperganda," I hissed. Of course, she didn't answer. She was a cat. I listened intently for any meowing, but didn't hear anything. "Temperganda! You come back here now," I whisper-hissed.

Her low meow sounded somewhere near the neighbor's house. Walking over to the fence, I peeked over it, but didn't see her. Running the flashlight along the bottom of the fence, I saw the destruction of the little wench. She had dug a hole under the fence. I crept around to the gate, hoping it was open and I could just slip inside and get her. But it was locked and too tall for me to climb.

Luckily, at the back of the neighbor's property was a wall of ivy they put in place of a fence. I headed to the back of my property and then to their back yard. The ivy was attached to some sort of wire fencing, but I couldn't see where any of the wire was because the ivy was so thick. However, I knew there was a place that used to have a gate. If I could just find that, I could slip through the ivy and get into the back yard.

3

CORDUROY

My phone rang in the middle of the night, and that never happened. Ignoring it, I rolled over and tried to go back to sleep, but it kept ringing.

Groaning, I picked up the phone and looked at the time. Midnight. "Fuck, what do you want?" I asked Jack.

"We have a disturbance call."

"What?" I asked, still groggy. "Who?"

"The Freedman's house. Someone's in their back yard."

"It's probably an animal," I mumbled, just wanting to go back to sleep.

"I need you to go check it out. I don't have anyone to watch Brody."

Sighing, I swung my legs over to the edge of the bed and sat up. "Alright, I'll head over now. Just text me the address."

"Thanks, man."

I grunted and hung up the phone. Snatching some jeans out of my dresser, I pulled them on and grabbed a long sleeved t-shirt. It was chilly out now that fall was moving in. I walked over to my safe and grabbed my gun, even though it was very unlikely I would need it. A text came in from Jack with the address. When I read it, something about it seemed familiar. Why did I know that address?

And then it hit me. It wasn't the address, but the street it was on. Fuck, that was Abby's street. I ran out the door and got in my car, hitting the lights as I tore out of my driveway. My heart was racing in my chest, but I couldn't figure out why. It wasn't like I had a thing for her. But the thought of her getting hurt sent chills down my spine. Was it a burglar? Maybe a rapist? Fuck, I had to get there fast and make sure she was okay.

I turned down her street and pulled into the Freedman's driveway, noting it was just one house over from hers. I needed to check on her, but the call came from this house, so I had to check in with them first. The door swung open and Mr. Freeman answered in his plaid robe with a scowl on his face.

"It's about time you got here."

"It's the middle of the night."

He grunted and walked away. "Two minutes later and I would be dead."

"Where's the intruder? Did you see him?"

"Him? It's not a him. It's a her. And she's out back."

I headed for the backdoor, flipping on the light, but I didn't see anything back there. "Did you see where she went?"

"Of course I did. What do you take me for? Some kind of idiot? Son, in my day, law enforcement used deductive reasoning."

I did my best not to roll my eyes at him. "Could you point out which way she went?"

"Well, she didn't go anywhere. She's stuck in my ivy."

I frowned. "She's what?"

"She tried to break in through my ivy in the back, but she got all tangled up."

"Wait, so you don't know if it was a burglar?"

"Well, who else would it be? Do you know many people that go running through other people's back yards in the middle of the night?"

It probably happened a lot more than he thought, especially with teenagers. And that was most likely what happened here. "Alright, I'll go check it out, but I'm sure it's just a teenager trying to play a prank."

He grunted at me before shuffling off to the kitchen table and sitting down. I opened the back door and headed out, walking straight for the ivy at the back.

"Hello?"

A squeak followed by the rustling of leaves told me exactly where she was.

"Ma'am, I'm going to have to ask you to step out of the ivy."

There was a pause and then a very familiar voice. "Carter?"

Tossing back my head, I stared up at the night sky and wondered why the hell it had to be me. "Abby?"

"Yeah," she answered grudgingly.

"What are you doing in Mr. Freedman's ivy?"

She huffed and then rustled some more. "Chasing down a bitch," she muttered.

"I'm sorry?"

"I was trying to get my cat. She escaped and dug a hole under the fence. I think she's coming over here for some midnight pussy."

I covered my mouth with my hand, trying not to laugh. "Um...she's what?"

"She's a whore, okay? She's gets knocked up all the time!"

"And you thought the middle of the night was a good time to come sneaking over?"

"Hey, if she gets knocked up, I have to deal with kittens! I don't have room in my house for any more cats."

I frowned. "How many cats do you have?"

"Six," she said quietly.

"Six? Isn't one enough?"

"Hey, I didn't ask for six. They just kind of...happened."

"How do six cats happen?"

She huffed in irritation. "Can we talk about this after I get out of the ivy?"

"I would love to finish this conversation. In fact, I'm dying to know why anyone in their right mind would have six cats."

Not that I was sure she was in her right mind.

"I need your help."

"With what?"

"I'm stuck."

Laughing under my breath, I stepped toward the ivy and felt around for her, accidentally grabbing something very soft and round.

"Hey! That's my boob!"

I cringed, hating how much I loved the feel of her breast...the little that I got to feel. "Sorry...It was very nice."

There was silence for a moment and then she sighed. "Thank you." She rustled some more and then yelped. "I'm stuck on the wire."

"It would help if I knew how you were stuck."

"I think one of the wires is stabbing me in the ass."

"You think? You're not sure?"

"Well, based on what feels like blood dribbling down my leg, and the fact that it hurts when I move, I would say it's a very good possibility."

I bit back my laugh. It really wasn't funny. She'd probably need antibiotics and possibly stitches. Still, she wouldn't have a wire in her ass if she hadn't come out to look for her cat in the middle of the night.

"How about you stick out your hand for me and I'll work my way toward...your ass."

After some rustling, she finally broke through the thick ivy and held out her hand. It was covered in dirt and scratches from the vines. I took her hand in mine and slowly ran my hand up her arm. Once I found her shoulder, I worked my way down her side, pulling at the vines keeping her tangled up. Once I got to the fence, I could see where the wire was piercing her in the ass.

"Um...I'm gonna have to rip your shorts so I can see where the wire is going."

She groaned in mortification. "Fine, but...don't look at anything you're not supposed to."

"I'll keep my eyes closed," I said jokingly.

"No! Don't do that!"

"I was joking. I promise. I'll be very clinical."

But as I tore at the fabric, I knew that would be impossible. The silk ripped easily, and then I was staring at her ass cheek, her very firm, beautiful ass cheek. I was going to kill Jack for sending me out here tonight. It was like he did it on purpose, though I knew that wasn't true. Pushing the fabric aside, I did my very best to assess the situation and figure out how to extract her from the wire. But the more I probed, the more I saw. And damn was it a good view.

"Carter? What do you think?"

"Very nice," I croaked out.

"What?" she screeched.

"I mean...it's in there very nice. Um...I need to further assess the damage."

She moaned. "Hurry up. I'm hanging out."

"Relax, no can see you but me."

She let out a loud sigh and rustled some more, moving around in the ivy.

"Stop moving. You're pushing the wire around."

"I can't keep standing like this. It hurts."

Against my better judgement, I reached into the ivy and pressed my hand against her very firm butt cheek to see how bad it was. Clearing my throat, I did my best not to cup her as I slid my hand down further.

"Um...I think we might need the fire department out here."

"No," she cried. "Please, I can't have people seeing me like this."

"Unfortunately, the wire is in kind of deep and I'm worried about... extracting it properly."

"Carter, I will make you muffins for an entire year if you just get this damn wire out of my ass without letting everyone in town know what's going on!"

I winced, knowing that wasn't possible. Twenty minutes later, the fire department was gathered around her, all staring at the predicament in front of them. Neighbors had formed a small circle around the property, all of them trying to get a better glimpse at the woman stuck in the wall of ivy. I tried to hold them back, but Abby didn't want me to leave her side. Not that I could blame her. As the lights swirled in the dark, I knew the town wouldn't stop talking about this for years to come. And they hadn't even seen as much as I had.

4

ABBY

I winced as I shifted slightly. The wire digging into my ass was painful, but the fact that half the town was staring at me, waiting for me to be extracted was more painful than anything.

"Abby, you have to stop moving."

"Carter, if you tell me that one more time, I'm going to pull you in here with me and shove a wire in your ass."

He chuckled at me, acting like this was one funny incident that would easily be forgotten.

"Ms. Hall," one of the firemen said as he bent over to look at me in the vines.

"Abigail," I corrected. "Or Abby." Sighing, I let reality wash over me. "Or cat lady, woman eaten by vines, woman with a wire in her ass... take your pick."

He chuckled slightly. "Abby, I'm Shane Finnegan. I'm gonna get you out of there."

I laughed slightly. "Thank God, I thought for sure I was going to be stuck here all night."

I heard a saw start up and my heart rate skyrocketed. "What the hell is that?"

"We're gonna have to cut you out of the vines."

"With a saw?" I screeched. "Are you kidding me?"

Carter appeared at my side and grabbed my hand. "Abby, they're not going to cut right next to you. They just need to move some of the fencing and the vines so they can extract you."

God, this was so embarrassing. I held on tight and squeezed my eyes shut as the saw started breaking through the vines and wire. I heard Shane shout a few times to hold up or to move a certain direction. And all of this was because of my whore of a cat.

"So, any luck finding my cat?" I asked, trying to distract myself from what was happening.

"Mr. Freedman found her hanging out under his porch."

I snorted. "Figures. He has that stray that he always feeds. Temperganda's had her eye on him for months."

"Temperganda?"

I narrowed my eyes at him. "What?"

"Nothing," he said, smothering a chuckle. "It's just an interesting name."

"Well, she has a nasty temper, but I didn't want to make her sound terrible."

He nodded, his nostrils flaring as he held it all in. "It totally makes sense."

"You're an ass. And I'm not making you muffins."

"You already promised," he said indignantly.

"You have Mary Anne's muffins. What do you need mine for?"

He glanced around and then leaned in close. "Don't tell her, but yours are better."

That made me feel slightly better, but still...he was so different earlier today. He was fawning over a married woman. What was wrong with me? Why didn't men fawn over me? I was a good catch. I made awesome baked goods. I was nice and always helpful. I made good money, so what the hell?

"So, I thought cats didn't do the dirty when they were fixed."

"Temperganda isn't fixed."

"Why not?"

"Well, she was a barn cat when I took her in. A lot of barn cats aren't fixed. And when I adopted her, I just couldn't put her through that."

"Why? She's a cat."

"With feelings! How would you like to be fixed? That's just mean."

"It's population control and a way to stop the spread of diseases."

"The same could be said for humans, but you don't see us castrating people."

"That's hardly the same thing."

"No, it's not the same thing, but it's still cruel. Besides, can you imagine having a decreased sex drive all because someone decided you should be fixed? Could you imagine not wanting sex anymore?"

He seemed to think about that for a minute. "Okay, you may have a point, but I'm not saying I agree with you."

"It doesn't matter. You'll never convince me that any of my cats should be fixed."

"Right, all six of them," he muttered. "So, tell me about them."

I was grateful for the distraction, so I smiled and told him about them. "Well, Pteheste is kind of a firecracker—"

"I'm sorry, what did you say?"

"Pteheste. It's a Native American game where you slide a buffalo horn across the ice. I don't really understand how you play."

"And you named your cat this," he said slowly.

"I wanted a unique name."

"You have very unique names," he muttered.

"Alright," Shane shouted. "We're going to extract the wire now."

"Do you think you could say it a little louder?" I asked over my shoulder. "I'm not sure the neighbors one block over heard you."

"Yeah, I'm not gonna lie to you," Carter grimaced. "This is most likely all over the town page already."

"Are you serious?"

"As a heart attack."

I sighed and hung my head. "Just get it over with," I muttered.

Ten minutes later, I was laying on my stomach on a gurney as a paramedic bandaged my ass. I was absolutely mortified, but the worst part was when they wheeled me out to the ambulance and the neighbors started taking pictures.

"Sorry, I told them to go home and stop taking pictures, but there's only one of me."

"It's fine," I muttered. My humiliation was complete. It wasn't like there was any escaping this now.

"If you want, I can go with you to the hospital."

I wanted to tell him to go leap off a tall building. After the way he treated me this morning, he was the last person I wanted around. On the other hand, he was the only person I really knew in town, so telling him to fuck off would be counterproductive at this point.

"Fine, but no staring at my ass."

He chuckled slightly, "Yeah, I can't make any promises."

AFTER GETTING CHECKED OUT, stitched up, and shot up with antibiotics, I was finally on my way home. Of course, I had an escort in the form of the very sexy deputy-sheriff, and he couldn't stop grinning at me. As I sat on my donut in the passenger side of his car, I couldn't help but pout. This was not the way to make a good impression on a man. Not that I was trying to impress him. I would never admit to liking a man who obviously had a thing for another woman, let alone a married woman.

My humiliation was already complete with a bandage on my ass and a donut that I would need to sit on so I didn't hurt my ass further. We pulled into my driveway, and luckily, it was late enough in the morning that most of my neighbors were already at work. Carter rushed around to my side of the car and opened the door for me, pulling me out gently. After shutting the door, he rested his hand on my back, guiding me to the house.

I would not swoon over the way he was helping me.

"I wasn't able to lock up your house last night. I couldn't find your keys."

I pointed to the top of the molding around the door. "I keep a spare up there."

He sighed, rubbing at his eyes. "You're joking, right?"

"Why? Is that bad or something?"

"Well, it's just about the worst hiding spot for a spare key. Anybody could find that."

"You didn't," I said challengingly.

"Right, but I also didn't think anyone still considered hiding a key above their door a good idea."

"Well, maybe it's making a comeback."

"Let's hope not. We'll have burglaries all over town."

He pushed the door open and guided me over to the cushions on the floor, frowning slightly. "Are you sure about this?"

"About what?"

"Sitting here. It's a long way down."

Nodding, I had to agree. "You're right. I should just go to bed. I didn't get much sleep last night."

"Lead the way."

"You know, I think I can take it from here."

"You probably can, but I've seen you leap out of a car because of a spider, jump a curb, and get your ass stuck on a wire, so I think I'll stick around to make sure you survive the trip."

I rolled my eyes at him and headed down the hall. Pushing the door open, I looked at my comfy bed and sighed.

"What the fuck is that?" he asked from behind me.

"It's a bed," I said, wondering what he was talking about.

"It's round."

I nodded slowly. "I'm beginning to question your deductive reasoning skills."

"Who has a round bed?"

"People that are fun."

He slowly turned to look at me, his face twisted in confusion. "So, you're saying that roughly seven and a half billion people are boring."

"No, I'm saying there are many people that sleep on round beds. We have more fun, we're more relaxed, and psychologists say it makes people feel more secure."

He looked at the bed and shook his head. "How? It would be too easy to roll out of it."

"Not at all. The mattress is extremely comfortable and it allows you to sleep in whatever direction you feel like."

He waved his arm at the gauzy material I had hanging from the ceiling, adding a sense of privacy to the space. "And what's with the drapes?"

"It's to help me sleep."

"I don't buy it. There's no way that's comfortable."

"You haven't tried it, so how would you know?"

"Because...because it's fucking round! No sane person would sleep on a round mattress."

My eyebrows shot up in surprise. "Well, I guess I know how you feel about me."

"That's not what I'm saying. It's just...look, you have this weird vibe going, between the cushions and the furry throw pillows and now the circle bed..."

"Why don't you lay down on it first and tell me what you think?"

"No, hell no. I'm sorry, but you're not drawing me into this weird..." He motioned to the bed like it was diseased.

"Fine, if you're really that scared you'll like it," I smirked.

"It's not that. I don't even know you. I'm not going to lay down on your bed."

I snorted in amusement. "That's funny, considering you spent all last night staring at my ass."

"That was different. I was doing my job."

"Uh-huh. Try it or don't. It doesn't matter to me either way. You're the one that can't handle trying something new."

"Fine," he kicked off his boots. "I'll lay on the damn bed, but it doesn't mean anything."

"I never said it did."

"And I don't want this getting out."

I nodded sagely. "Right, your reputation to uphold and everything. We wouldn't want anyone around town thinking you like weird things like round beds."

"Exactly," he stepped forward, resting his knee on the bed. He tilted his head to the side, looking at the bed, almost like he was trying to figure out how to use it. "So, I just..."

"Just what?"

"Like...I just lay anywhere?"

"Well, that is kind of the idea."

"This is fucking crazy," he laughed to himself. Then he lowered himself down on the bed and twisted to stare up at the ceiling.

"So, what do you think?"

"I think I feel like I'm facing the wrong direction."

"Why would you have to face a certain direction?"

"Because...when you lay in bed, your head should be against a wall. I'm lying diagonally."

"Are you really? Or are you just not sure you're facing the way society tells you to sleep?"

He lifted his head and glared at me. "What does that mean?"

I kicked off my own shoes and laid down on my belly. "I'm just saying, it sounds like you're way too worried about what everyone else thinks about the way you sleep. You shouldn't worry about other people so much."

"Says the woman that was freaking out last night about others seeing her."

My eyes blinked heavily as I sighed into my pillow. "That was different. My ass was sticking out."

He grunted sleepily. "It's a nice ass."

5

CORDUROY

A scream jerked me awake. I sat up disoriented, unable to figure out where I was. But the scream was real. Then I remembered I was at Abby's house and I had laid down on her damn circle bed. I must have fallen asleep. Shit, was she hurt? I rolled to the side of the bed, only since there was no straight edge, I fell off the bed, getting wrapped in the drapes. I heard a tearing sound as I fell to the floor and all the fabric came billowing down around me. Wrestling with the material, I finally extracted myself from the mess and ran toward the attached bathroom, where I was assuming the scream came from.

I flung the door open, stopping dead in my tracks when I saw a very naked Abby standing in front of me, just reaching for a towel. Her eyes went wide before she squeaked and snatched it off a hook, but it was enough time to see everything I needed to. And it was amazing. Those perfect tits would be embedded in my memory for the rest of my life. They were medium sized, perky, and those rosy nipples were hard as hell, probably waiting for me to suck on them.

"Carter!"

I stopped staring and slowly peeled my eyes away. Well, I tried to, but my eyes seemed to be half swollen shut. "Uh..." Clearing my throat, I remembered why I came bursting in here. "Is everything okay?"

"Why wouldn't it be?"

"I heard screaming."

She rolled her eyes. "That was nothing."

"People don't scream for no reason."

She tucked the towel around her body, but not before I examined every inch of her. She didn't seem like the runner type, but she had the legs of one. Muscled and toned, I could already imagine them wrapped around me as I was fucking her. Preferably not on the round bed.

"I was pulling my Turbie Twist off the doorknob and something hit me in the chest. I thought it was a spider."

Shaking my head, I went over what she said again and tried to focus. "Sorry, what's a Turbie Twist?"

She pointed to the towel thing on her head.

"And what hit you?"

"It was a hair tie, but it got caught on the towel and it flung itself at me. All I saw was black and then felt something hit me. I thought I was under attack."

Christ, I had to get out of here. This woman was so strange. Running my hand over my face, I tried to get my head on straight. "So, you're okay."

"Of course, I am."

I shook my head. The insanity that she brought into my life was getting to me. I'd never met a woman so crazy in all my life. And I knew all the Cortell wives personally.

I rubbed at my eyes. They felt like they were ten times larger than normal. My nose was stuffy, and my head was pounding. "Christ, I think I'm allergic to your cats."

"Is that why your eyes are all puffy?" she winced.

"Serves me right for staying over here," I muttered.

"What's that?"

"I should get to work. I didn't mean to fall asleep on your bed."

"It's fine," she brushed it off. "I have to check in with work too. I'm not sure they'll buy my story of getting my ass stuck to a fence as a reason for not being on time today."

"Do they know you?"

She looked at me funny. "Of course they do."

Well, that flew right over her head. I grabbed my shoes and headed to the door, turning back to her one last time. "Are you sure you're okay?"

"Nothing a rubber donut can't fix," she laughed.

My eyes widened in disbelief as I headed out. I couldn't explain the attraction I felt for her. It had to be purely sexual. She was crazy, and I wasn't a man that fell for crazy. I liked sensible women that had a plan and knew what they wanted and needed out of life.

I really needed more sleep, but I had to at least check in with Jack and see what needed to be done today. I took some more anti-histamines, grateful I had left them in the car. I pulled up to the station and parked, laughing when I saw the dented sign. That woman was a menace. I nodded to Jack as I walked in, ignoring the grin on his face.

"What the hell happened to you?"

"Cats," I muttered, still rubbing at my watering eyes.

"Like a herd of them or..."

"Abby has six of them."

He barked out a laugh, tossing his head back. "So, wire fencing, huh?"

"Did you see the video?"

"Oh, I saw part of the video. In particular, one very zoomed in image of you practically grabbing her ass."

I shot him a scathing glare. "I wasn't grabbing her ass."

I also had to figure out which video that was, because as far as I knew, no one got close enough to actually get any real footage. Which meant that someone had been lurking.

"Right, and where were you this morning?"

"I was at the hospital with her until she was released."

He bit back a grin. "And she needed you there to hold her hand."

"I didn't hold her hand. I waited until she was released and then drove her home."

"And?"

"And what? I didn't sleep all night. I got a few hours and then came in," I said, walking over to the coffee pot.

Pouring myself a cup, I was just taking a sip when he said, "Yeah, I drove by your place and you weren't home."

I choked on the coffee, barely avoiding spitting it all over the place. He got up and slapped me on the back a few times. "So, you stayed with her."

"I didn't stay with her," I grumbled. "I passed out on her bed."

"Nice," he grinned.

"It wasn't like that. I fell asleep. That was it. No funny business. She's not the woman for me."

"You know, you say that, but you've held her in your arms countless times, you caressed her ass, you drove her home, you slept in her bed... Need I go on?"

I pinched the bridge of my nose and sighed. "It's not like that. It's... an attraction, but it's nothing more."

"Right, that's what they all say. And then they're walking down the aisle and popping out kids. Face it, you're just one more hug away from putting a ring on her finger."

I minutely shook my head at the ridiculous idea. "Yeah, that's not going to happen. She might make some awesome muffins, but that's not a reason to get married."

"Ah, the muffins," he nodded. "I forgot about those. Just another point in her favor. Now, if only there was a way you could find out if she was a good cook," he said, tapping his chin. Then he snapped his fingers. "I know, you could tell her that your buddy, that would be me, hasn't had a home cooked meal since his wife died. Then you tell her you don't know how to cook, and you just wish there was some way you could help said buddy out."

"You want a free meal?" I asked incredulously.

"Well, I can't ask her. That would be rude."

"But it's not rude for me to basically con her into giving you a free meal?"

"For your benefit," he added. "Remember, this is all part of the interview process."

"What interview?" I snapped.

"The interview to be your wife. Geez, keep up."

I gritted my teeth in frustration. "There's no interview because I'm not considering dating her. She's a mess. She sleeps in a round bed! She has six cats, each one with a weirder name than the last. It's not happening!"

"Alright, geez, you don't have to bite my head off. I'll leave it alone."

"Thank you," I said, taking my seat.

I started going through my messages and looking at the paperwork Jack set on my desk. I just had to focus on getting through this day. Then I could move on as if none of this ever happened.

"So, is that a no on the whole dinner thing?"

I BACKED out of my parking space, ready to head home. The few hours I worked had been pretty much pointless. I couldn't get Abby out of my head, no matter how hard I tried. I found myself wondering if her ass was sore, if she'd had any more encounters with fake spiders, and if her cats had eaten her alive yet.

"Fuck it," I muttered to myself. I pulled out another antihistamine, deciding to be proactive this time. "I'll just go see if she's okay." Then I laughed as I contemplated someone finding her key and slipping inside. That woman really needed a lesson in safety. That was the real reason I was going over there. As an officer of the law, it was my responsibility to ensure all citizens were safe, no matter how weird they may be.

I pulled into her driveway a few minutes later and walked up to her front door. I rang the bell, but she didn't answer. Concern for her well-being grew and I found myself grabbing the doorknob and pushing inside. I bristled in irritation at the fact that her door wasn't even locked.

It was dark in the house because she had most of the curtains drawn. Maybe she was trying to get some more sleep.

"Abby?" I called out, waiting for her to answer. Looking around, it was clear she wasn't anywhere in the main part of the house. I headed for her room, thinking she was probably asleep, but when I stepped inside, the drapes were pulled back and she wasn't lying in bed. She had managed to rehang the drapes I'd gotten caught up in earlier.

Her car was in the drive, but she was nowhere to be seen. She was probably out back searching for her cat. I headed down the hall, tripping when something ran right under my feet. A cat screeched, then swatted at me, taking a chunk of skin out of my arm. I hissed at it, hoping it would run away, but instead, it growled at me.

"I hate you," I glared at it. "You're nothing but a furry menace to my allergies." Pushing to my feet, I headed for the back door. To my surprise, she was in the back yard on her knees doing gardening or something. I slid the glass door open, stopping when I heard her talking.

"I really hope it wasn't a relative of yours that I ran over."

I frowned and took a few steps to my left, squinting to see who she was talking to. A squirrel. She was talking to a fucking squirrel.

"Here you go, Herman. I know nuts don't make up for the loss of your comrade, but we need to fatten you up for the winter."

The squirrel took the nuts from her and scurried off to a tree. She smiled and brushed off her skirt, stopping when she turned and saw me standing in her house. Maybe I should have been more concerned about the fact that I was in her house uninvited, but all I could think about was the fact that she was talking to a fucking squirrel.

"Carter, what are you doing here?"

I shook my head in disbelief. "I was just...stopping by to make sure you hadn't...I don't know, impaled yourself on something else."

"Nope," her shoulders shook slightly. "Just hanging out in my back yard."

"With a squirrel," I said, still not believing what I just saw.

"Oh, Herman," she flashed me an amused grin. "Yeah, he's my buddy. I've been feeding him for six months now. About two weeks ago, I finally got him to come hang out with me."

"So, you're making friends with squirrels. You talk to them and... you don't hope they talk back, do you?"

She quirked an eyebrow at me, crossing her arms over her chest. "You think I talk to Herman like he's a human?"

I ran my hand through my hair, blowing out a harsh breath. "I wouldn't be surprised at this point."

"Herman is a squirrel. A very cute squirrel, but still a squirrel. And yes, I know that he doesn't talk back."

I nodded once and took a step back. "Well, now that I know you're fine, I should be going."

"Well, feel free to let yourself into my house anytime you want."

I frowned at that. "Are you serious?"

"No, I was just hoping you would catch my subtle hint that most people don't do that."

I didn't even bother defending myself. There was nothing to say. I had let myself in without her permission, and now I was treating her like an idiot. I was such an ass.

"I'll see you around."

"Carter," she called out. "Thanks for checking on me."

I nodded and left. I needed to get my head checked.

❧ 6 ❧

ABBY

After a week of sitting around the house on a donut, I really needed to get out. My whole body was stiff from laying around, so I decided to walk to the center of town instead of drive. I needed some breakfast and I was too lazy to make anything for myself this morning.

I was a little disappointed that Carter hadn't contacted me again after he left, but was I really expecting him to suddenly want to spend time with me? It was clear he thought I was weird. And even though he was hot, I wasn't so self-destructive that I would chase a man that thought so little of me.

The walk to town felt great, and my muscles were finally starting to work themselves out. Now that fall was creeping in, the brisk air didn't allow for my long skirts or my summer tops. So, I headed into town in skinny jeans and a jacket, but I still wore my sandals. I just couldn't give them up yet.

Pulling the door to the bakery open, I was a little shocked when all heads turned to me and then stared. Seriously, didn't these people have anything better to do than stare at the new girl? And I wasn't even that new. I had been in town for six months. Surely they had something better to gossip about now.

A bigger woman came walking up to me with a smug look on her face. "I'm Carrie," she said, almost with a southern twang. "I'm the local therapist. I saw that video on the town page of you getting stuck in all that ivy. If you ever need to talk, you just give me a call," she said, handing over her business card.

I stared down at the card and then back up at her. "Um...I don't need to talk to anyone, but thanks."

She pursed her lips. "That's what they all say, dear. But when a woman gets herself in a situation like that where she needs to be rescued, it just reeks of desperation."

"Carrie, shut your mouth before I shut it for you," a brunette snapped as she walked over.

Carrie turned to the woman and rolled her eyes. "Oh, Anna, if only I had just five minutes of your time. You're one puzzle I'd love to figure out."

"Well, guess what? I don't need or want to be figured out, especially by someone with more problems than the whole town combined."

I stared in awe at the woman in front of me. Anna, and then it clicked. She was the woman I hit last week with my car. And she was coming to my rescue. She was so badass.

"At least I didn't have to have my mother-in-law drag me down the aisle."

"That would require you to have someone that was actually interested in marrying you first," Anna snapped.

Carried pressed her hand against her chest, feigning shock. "Why, I never!"

"Yep, you never, and you're never gonna get a man with that self-righteous attitude. And stop chasing Joe. He's married and not interested."

"I'm not chasing anyone."

"Right, you're just delusional enough to think he wants you because he said you were curvy. Guess what, he accidentally called his wife fat and he was trying to figure out how to make it better. It had nothing to do with you, other than not wanting to insult you."

Carrie's nostrils flared and her face turned beat red. "Why, you little bitch."

"Better a bitch than a whiny brat that has to chase down other people's husbands!"

Carrie's hand snapped out and slapped Anna hard across the face, but Anna just laughed at her. "Is that the best you've got?"

With a banshee cry, Carrie tackled Anna to the floor, yanking on her hair. After the woman defended me, I couldn't let this woman attack her. She was practically a friend, even though we'd never actually exchanged pleasantries.

"Carrie!" I shouted, moving around them and trying to find a way to intervene in some way. "Um...perhaps you want to get off her before you smother her."

Anna yelled and spun, straddling Carrie now. I shook my head, not sure what to do. This was insane.

"You're such a bitch!" Anna shouted. "How did you even get to be a therapist? You don't help anyone!"

Carrie grabbed Anna, then bumped into a table, knocking it over. All the dishes that were still on top crashed to the ground. The chairs screeched as they slid across the floor. It was mayhem.

I turned around helplessly, hoping to find someone that would help, but everyone was just standing there filming it. Mary Anne came running out of the back with cans of Reddi-whip. She yanked the cap off one as she ran up to the women and started squirting it on them. Whipped cream streamed out of the can, covering both the women as they continued to fight, only now they were slipping in the cream as they yanked at each other's hair.

Mary Anne tossed the first can and popped the lid on the second, starting to squirt them again.

"What are you doing? That's not helping!"

"Well, I don't have a hose!"

"So, you're spraying them with whipped cream?" I shrieked. I grabbed the can, but Mary Anne refused to let go. "Give it to me! Spraying condiments is never the answer!"

"This isn't a condiment," Mary Anne argued.

I gave one more firm tug and ripped the can out of her hands, tripping over feet as I stepped backward. I fell hard, my elbow connecting with someone's face. I rolled off the women and shook my head rapidly as Carrie laid on the floor holding her eye.

"Oh my God! I'm so sorry—"

Her hand shot up and she grabbed my hair, pulling me down. I yelped and shoved the can in her face, pressing on the white tip to spray whipped cream in her face.

"Let go! I'm a tiny woman!"

"You hit me in the face!"

"You attacked Anna!"

But the woman was too big for me and she tossed me off with ease. I crashed into some chairs, but as Carrie stood up and glared down at me, Anna tackled her to the ground again. They wrestled around for another minute, and I had no idea what to do, so I slipped off my sandal and ran over to Carrie, crying out as I started smacking her with my shoe.

I had never been a violent person, but with Carrie, I saw red. The woman was insane. So I stood there, beating the snot out of her shoulder with my sandal. The release was cathartic, making me feel in charge of my life for the first time in years.

"Ho!" a male voice shouted over all the racket.

The three of us stopped and looked up, fully covered in whipped cream at this point. Jack and Carter were standing in the doorway, staring around the bakery in disbelief.

"What the hell is going on here?" Jack snapped.

I wiped the cream off my face, letting it drip to the ground from my fingertips.

"Abby?" Carter asked. "What the hell are you doing?"

Clearing my throat, I stood as demurely as I could while covered with melting white cream. "We were just having a difference of opinion."

"She attacked me!" Carrie shouted, pointing at Anna.

Jack gave Anna a disappointed look, but Anna just crossed her arms over her chest and glared at him. "Oh, it's okay when the guys start fights in here, but not us?"

"She's got a point," Carter said. "And they're covered in whipped cream."

"But why?" Jack asked.

"They did it!" Mary Anne pointed at us.

I gasped at the ridiculous statement. "You came running out of the back with the cans!"

"Yeah, but I was trying to break up the fight, not encourage it."

"I doubt that," Carter muttered under his breath.

"Alright, all three of you, we're going down to the station to sort this out. Stand up."

"I have footage," Mary Anne said cheerily. "You know, in case you need the finer details."

"Of course you do."

"It's already been live streamed to the town page," a man said. "Man, you should see the comments coming in already."

"Ladies?" Jack said, motioning for us to go with him.

"Thanks for having my back," I said to Anna as we walked toward the door.

"Any time. That woman pisses me off."

I limped out the door with my one sandal, only stopping to put it on when we were out of sight of all cameras.

"Beating someone with a sandal?" Carter asked. "Really?"

"She started it," I said irritatedly. "You weren't there."

"She hit me in the eye!" Carrie screeched.

"I tripped over your feet!"

"Ladies! Let's save it for the jail cell," Jack said, huffing in irritation as he headed down the sidewalk.

"Shouldn't we be cuffed or something?" I whispered to Anna as we walked down the sidewalk.

"Do you want to be handcuffed?"

I shrugged. "I've never been arrested before. I think being cuffed is only fair. After all, we did cause a lot of destruction at the bakery."

"Don't worry, Mary Anne makes a lot of money off fights happening in her bakery."

I GLARED at Carrie from across the room. She was cuffed to one side of the jail cell, then me a little further apart, and finally Anna was on the other side of me. They had put us all in one cell, but all that did was start another fight.

"So, do you ladies want to tell us what this was about?" Jack asked, leaning against his desk.

"I simply tried to help Abby with her situation," Carrie said primly.

"Bullshit," Anna snapped. "You were being a bitch."

"Yeah, what she said," I added with my own glare, flicking my sandal off my foot at her. It fell about a foot short, leaving my attempt at getting back at her slightly anticlimactic. "It was supposed to hit you," I grumbled under my breath.

"Having trouble attracting attention?" she asked with a smirk.

"You're such a bitch," I seethed.

"Hey, it's not my fault you had that video made the other night." Carrie smirked at me. "If you weren't trying to get attention, you never would have ended up all over the town page."

"I wasn't trying to get attention! I was trying to get my cat back."

"Right," she nodded. "It was all over some pussy."

Jack sighed. "Carrie, I hardly think that's helpful."

The doors to the station burst in and six angry men glared at Jack and Carter. "Really, Jack? Arresting my wife?"

He held up his hands in defense. "Hey, I had nothing to do with this one. If you don't believe me, check out the town page."

I obviously knew which one was Anna's husband, but who were the other men?

"Are they part of a gang or something?" I asked.

"No, that's my husband and his brothers."

I sighed. "I wish I had a horde of men coming to my rescue."

"Trust me, it's not as sexy as you'd think."

"Joe, I'm so glad you're here," Carrie sighed.

"I'm not here for you," he said incredulously.

She batted her eyes at him like a crazy person. "I know you can't say anything in front of them. It's okay. Our love is nobody else's business."

"Your love?" one of the brothers asked.

"Good lord, someone shove a sock in her mouth," Anna grumbled.

"You're just jealous because you got the prick brother," Carrie snapped.

"Hey! If I wasn't cuffed to a jail cell right now, I'd shank you, bitch!"

"Yeah, snitches get stitches," Anna snapped.

Jack leaned over to Carter with a grin. "I think I like her."

"Baby, that doesn't even make sense," Robert sighed, rubbing his eyes.

"Which one?" Carter asked, shaking his head.

"Abby. She's feisty in a tiny kitten sort of way."

"I'm not a tiny kitten," I argued.

"Joey," Carrie pleaded. "Tell them what a bitch she is. You know I would never attack someone that didn't deserve it."

Joe stared at her, obviously not knowing what to say. Shaking his head slightly, he backed toward the door. "I...uh...sorry, man. I'm out. I can't even..."

He turned on his heel and stormed out of the station.

I glanced over at Anna. "He can't even what?"

She shook her head, like it wasn't worth explaining, but now I was dying to know what he couldn't even...Damnit, this was going to bother me all day. And I couldn't ask him, because he was gone now.

"Look, you ladies can't just start a fight in the middle of the bakery. Whipped cream or not, it's not cool," Carter said. "And while we all appreciate the visual that came along with it, Mary Anne has a huge mess to clean up now."

"None of this would have happened if Carrie had just kept her mouth shut," Anna snapped.

"Hitting someone is not the answer," Jack said.

"No, but it sure did make me feel better."

"Ooh, me too," I agreed. "I've never actually hit someone before. Not that I meant to hit Carrie. It's more that I tripped over her feet and landed on her, but seeing her eye well up like that sent a rush through me."

Carter cleared his throat. "Maybe keep that little bit of information to yourself."

Jack stepped forward and unlocked Anna's cuffs. "Let's keep the peace around here from now on. Remember, sticks and stones..."

Anna rubbed her wrists and walked up to Carrie with a smirk on her face. "Yeah, sticks and stones may break some bones, but hollow points expand on impact."

She turned and walked over to Robert, who stared at her incredulously. "Who are you and where is my wife?"

"What?" she shrugged. "Carly has some very useful information sometimes."

"You don't...you don't have a gun, do you?" he asked, swallowing hard.

"No, but I might consider getting one if this bitch keeps running her mouth."

Jack sighed as he came to unlock me. "I'm going to pretend I didn't hear any of that."

After I was unlocked, I snatched my sandal off the floor and slipped it back on, sticking my tongue out at Carrie before I walked away.

"Thank you for standing up for me," I said to Anna as I joined her and her horde of men.

"No problem. We have to stick together."

"Still, after I backed into your car—"

"This is who backed into your car?" her husband asked. "And you defended her?"

"Hey, she was getting picked on for that video. All of you have had a little too much attention on Facebook. Are you seriously telling me you wouldn't want me to help her?"

All of them were silent, nodding grudgingly.

She turned back to me, one eyebrow quirked. "Friday night, girls night. I'll text you the address."

And then she walked out, leaving me alone with Carter, and Jack, who was trying to explain to Carrie that Joe was a taken man.

"I'm assuming you don't have a ride home," Carter said.

"How did you know?"

"You didn't bring your purse. No keys. Which means you also just left your house keys laying around outside your house."

I shrugged. "On top of the door."

He sighed and grabbed me by the arm, pulling me toward the door. "Alright, let's get you home before you cause any more trouble."

"Hey, I'll have you know that I didn't instigate any of that. I just walked into the bakery."

"But you hit her."

"Not on purpose," I muttered. "Although, I'd like to think I'm awesome enough to hit someone."

He chuckled derisively and opened the passenger side door, practically shoving me inside. He walked around to his side and got in, slamming the door. He stared out the window for a moment, but I wasn't sure why we were just sitting here.

"Is something wrong?"

"You just—You get into so much trouble, and I'm an officer of the law."

"Okay," I said slowly.

"You have too many damn cats and I'm allergic to them, and you leave your house keys right the fuck on top of your door."

I nodded, but I wasn't sure what he was getting at.

"And let's not even go over that fiasco last week with the ivy."

I frowned, trying to figure out where he was going with this. "If you're trying to tell me something, you're going to have to spell it out."

He sighed and started the car, then backed out of the space, not saying a word. We drove in silence back to my house, and when we got there, he shoved the door open and came around to my side. I really had no idea where to go with this.

I unlocked my door, ignoring the irritated sound he made, and walked inside. "Well, thanks for—"

He shoved his way inside and slammed the door behind him. "You can't just go around pulling shit like that."

I nodded, thinking I was about to get a lecture.

"You know, people get in serious trouble for the shit you pull. You're lucky we live in a small town. Trespassing is a serious offense."

"I was just getting my—"

"And jumping out of a car because of a spider? You could have killed someone."

"It could have killed me!"

"And now starting a fight in the bakery!"

"I didn't start that!"

"No, but you finished it. And if this were to go before a judge, who do you think would get in trouble?"

I frowned, biting my lip. He had a point. I was the new girl. Carrie was a therapist, and though she seemed like a pretty shitty one, a judge would probably take her side over mine.

"I hear you."

"Do you? Because you need to understand that your actions have consequences."

I nodded. "I know, and I had some time to think about it. Prison's changed me."

"You weren't in prison," he snapped. "And you weren't even technically behind bars. You were cuffed *to* the bar! And you were only there for about five minutes."

"Right," I continued to nod, "but it really made me think about my actions. How my life could all go up in flames. Being in cuffs like that really changed me. It hardened me to the outside world."

"Christ," he muttered, rolling his eyes. "I just want to..." He grunted and made a throttling motion, like he was going to choke me. But then he grabbed me by the shoulders and pulled me against him, pressing his lips to mine. "You're such a pain in the ass," he muttered against my lips.

"I know," I said, but I wasn't sure why as I slipped my tongue inside his mouth and kissed him passionately. I knew now what it was like to lose all my freedom. I needed to feel alive again, and Carter could give me that. I grabbed the front of his shirt, ready to tear it off. I was having a moment of temporary insanity when he grabbed my wrists and pulled me off him.

I looked up at him through dazed eyes, my lips swollen from his rough kiss.

"God, I fucking want you."

"I want you too."

"But I can't have you."

I swallowed hard. "Because I'm a criminal."

He huffed out a laugh and stared up at my ceiling. "Fuck, what am I going to do with you?" he asked, right before he turned and walked out my door.

7

CORDUROY

"Are you sure you don't want to come to poker night?" I asked Jack as I shut down my computer.

"With Antonio? No thanks. I may be turning over a new leaf, but I haven't totally flipped it over."

"You need to let off some steam. Have you uh..."

When I stopped talking, his eyes flicked up to mine. "Have I what?"

"You know," I motioned. "Found someone new to fulfill that need since Natalie."

"Are you asking me if I'm screwing someone?"

"Well, I was trying to be delicate."

"Next time just fucking ask. You sound like a pussy."

"Fine, have you been fucking anyone else?"

"No," he said shortly. "It's not like I just got over my wife and decided to get laid."

"Maybe you should."

He stood up angrily, shoving back his chair. I held out my hands, only now realizing how insensitive that sounded.

"I didn't mean it like that. I just meant...maybe you need to just go fuck some random chick and get it over with. Maybe it'll help you to move on."

"Like that would make me feel better?"

"Well, it might."

"Or it might make me feel like complete shit. My wife was everything to me. And I've never just gone out and fucked random women, so I don't see how doing that now will solve anything."

I felt bad for my friend. I wanted to be able to help in some way, but he needed to help himself too.

"Look, we all loved Natalie, but it's time to move on. She's gone."

"Yeah, like you've moved on from Anna?"

"I never had Anna."

"Yeah, and you never tried either. You were so fucking in love with her, but you never even tried. And then Robert came along and you just handed her over. You didn't even fight for her."

"Because she was never supposed to be mine," I argued.

"And what about this girl, now?"

"What girl?"

"You know who I'm talking about. The one that has you running all over town just to catch a glimpse of her. You're crazy about her."

"No, she drives me crazy. There's a difference."

"Yeah, she's not the woman you thought you would end up with. It must really suck to be attracted to a woman that isn't perfect."

"This isn't about me. I'm not even interested in dating anyone."

"You never are. You want to talk about someone not moving on? Look in the fucking mirror," he said, right before he stormed out of the station.

As MUCH AS I hated to admit it, Jack had a point. I had been a pussy when it came to Anna. But he was dead wrong about Abby. I wasn't interested in having a relationship with her. Hell, I barely understood her. She was this weird woman that said and did all these things that drove me insane, and I hadn't even known her that long.

If I were to take her out, even just for a good time, I would probably end up in knots, but not the good kind of knots. I would be so frustrated by the end of the night that I might end up killing her. She was not the woman for me. Hell, she wasn't even on my radar. Except that she was really hot. I couldn't deny I was attracted to her.

Driving out to Eric's house, I tried not to think about her. I had stayed away from her for a week, and the moment I saw her again, it was because she was getting in a whipped cream fight. She was an absolute mess of a woman.

I wasn't about to let her think that I was interested in her. I wasn't. She was totally wrong for me. It was going to be hard to stay away. I'd already had several dreams that all featured her. And I swore I saw her around town from time to time, and then I found myself chasing her down, even though it wasn't her. Luckily, no one seemed to notice.

Pulling into Eric's driveway, I saw that pretty much everyone was already there. I didn't bother knocking on his door, since no one else bothered to. Jerking my chin at them, I took a seat at the table, sighing heavily.

"What's wrong with you?" Robert asked, shuffling the deck.

"Nothing, just work."

"Yeah? Are those donuts getting heavy?" he smirked.

I laughed mockingly. "Oh, you're so funny."

"I know," he retorted. "So, what's with you and Abby?"

"Why do you ask?" I said quickly.

He stopped and stared at me. "Um...I was just making conversation."

Narrowing my eyes at him, I shook my head. "What did you hear?"

He glanced around at the other guys, a look of confusion on his face. "What are you talking about?"

"Is this because of this afternoon at the station? Well, nothing's going on there. She's just a woman, that's all."

"Um...okay. I was just talking about the fact that you drove her home. I thought maybe you were friends."

"Right," I scoffed. "You thought we were friends."

"So, you're not friends?"

"Christ, I just drove her home. Why does that have to mean something?"

He shook his head. "I'm so confused."

"Don't play stupid with me. I know what you're doing."

"And what's that?"

"What you guys all do to each other. You mess with each other until someone admits something they don't want to admit. Like you think you're going to get me to admit that I like Abby, even though I don't. She's not at all for me. She's weird and...It's never going to happen."

"What's going on?" Eric asked, sitting down at the table with a beer.

"I'm not sure. Corduroy apparently thinks I'm trying to get him to admit his feelings for a woman named Abby."

Eric pointed at me. "The woman from the station. Wasn't she also the chick you were feeling up in the video?"

"I wasn't feeling her up!"

Robert's eyes went wide. "That chick was Abby? Holy shit, she was hot. If you're not fucking her, you should be."

"Right, make it sound like you have no idea what I'm talking about. I know how you guys all do this. It's not going to work on me."

"What's not going to work on you?" Antonio asked as he pulled up a chair.

"They're all trying to get me to fuck Abby."

Antonio heaved a sigh and picked up his cards. "Is this seriously what it's going to be like every time we play poker? It's like a goddamn therapy session."

"Maybe we should get Phil to come one of these nights," Robert laughed.

"Who's that?" Antonio asked. "Is he some kind of assassin?"

Eric shook his head. "He's a therapist. Relax. Put away your guns."

"I think Corduroy secretly wants to date this woman, but he's ashamed of her."

"Why would you be ashamed of her?" Eric asked.

The door swung open and Joe walked through, yelling at Andrew. "I'm not a fucking chubby chaser!"

"Carrie seemed to think differently."

"Carrie's off her fucking rocker."

"Listen, do whatever you want, but nothing gets back to Sofia."

"Whoa," Eric stood. "You're encouraging him to have an affair?"

"Not a good idea," Robert said. "It always gets back to the woman."

"I'm not encouraging it, but if he can't keep his dick in his pants, he has to find a way to hide it from Sofia so she doesn't get hurt."

"For the last fucking time," Joe shouted. "I'm not into Carrie. Until six months ago, I'd never even spoken to the woman."

Antonio grinned. "So, that's when the affair started."

"No! I'm not having an affair. You know Sofia. Why would I cheat on her?"

"That's what I'm trying to figure out," Andrew snapped.

Joe pinched the bridge of his nose and sighed. "She's delusional. She's formed some kind of attachment to me, but I don't like her. Hell, I don't even know her, and I don't want to. In fact, now that I know she has psychological problems, I don't want her anywhere near me. Sofia is the only woman I want."

"See, you need to take advice from Joe," Robert pointed at his brother. "Sofia was a little out there when she first came to town, and look at her now."

"Abby isn't a little out there. She's a fucking weirdo. She has cats running all over her house, a round bed, she got stuck climbing through ivy, and I caught her talking to a squirrel last week!"

Andrew leaned on the table. "Like...she was expecting it to talk back?"

"She said she knew it wouldn't, but I'm not so sure."

"You know what your problem is," Antonio snapped. "You like her, but you don't want to like her, because she doesn't fit the perfect mold you have in your head."

"That's not true," I shot back.

"Oh, he's right," Robert nodded. "Remember when you were trying to get Anna?"

"I was just trying to get you two together."

"Yeah, but we all know you were in love with her."

"Maybe he still is," Eric said, drinking his beer. "Maybe that's why he can't date this woman. She's the opposite of Anna."

I snorted. "That's an understatement. She left a key on the top of her front door in case she got locked out."

"She sounds exactly like Anna," Robert muttered.

"I'm a cop. What would that say about me if I dated someone like her?"

"You mean, someone hot?" Joe asked.

"She hit a light pole escaping a spider. She jumped the curb in front of the station, and then backed into Anna's car."

"And you went running to Anna's rescue," Robert cackled.

"I'm not in love with your wife," I stressed.

"No, but you hold everyone to this standard you expect them to have. Anna was strong and resilient. She didn't rely on anyone. Your woman is a chaotic mess, and if you date her, you'll be seen as the man dating the crazy lady."

I thought that over, wondering if he was right. But it didn't matter because I didn't want to date her. The problem was, they were all pointing out the exact same things that Jack just said to me before I headed over here, and that had me wondering if they were on to something I wasn't.

"You don't have to date her," Andrew said. "Just fuck her and get it out of your system. Chances are, you don't actually like her as much as you think you do. Once you fuck her, you'll feel better and move on."

I perked up at that. I liked where this was going. "You think?"

"Don't listen to him," Eric said, slapping his brother on the back of the head. "If you like this woman, do not under any circumstances try to sleep with her just to get her out of your system. It won't work, and then you'll have slept with her and you'll still want her."

"I don't like her like that," I insisted.

"Look, Corduroy," Eric said, leaning in across the table. "I don't want to be the one to point it out, but you do everything possible to make sure everyone else gets together with the person they're supposed to be with. Yet, you neglect your own personal life. When was the last time you got laid?"

"What does that have to do with anything?"

"You're deflecting, focusing on everyone else so you don't have to face the cold, hard truth. You're lonely and you're looking for the right woman. And now that this woman has come into your life, you're terrified that you'll mess it up. So, you're picking her apart and finding all her flaws so you don't have to actually take a chance that she's the one. Which just makes you an idiot. If you like her, then take her on a fucking date and stop being a pussy."

"I'm not a pussy."

"You're all a bunch of pussies," Antonio muttered. "Christ, I've never heard so many guys sit around and talk about their feelings before."

"Let me point out where you're wrong," I told Eric. "First, I'm not lonely. I have a very fulfilling life. Second, I'm not looking for the right woman, let alone any woman."

"Which means his hand is getting a workout," Joe laughed.

I rolled my eyes and continued. "Third, I'm not scared of anything. If she was the right woman for me, I wouldn't be running from her. Fourth, I'm not picking her apart. She just naturally lets all her flaws shine for everyone to see. And that's not my fault. Fifth—"

Andrew groaned, rolling back his head. "Fuck, how long is this going to take? It's like listening to a woman tell you all the reasons you're wrong. You've turned into a woman. Are you happy now?"

"I'm not—"

"Yes, you are," Eric laughed. "I hate to side with Andrew on this, but you're fucking up big time. If you like her, but you don't want a relationship, then tell her straight up. Just tell her you like her, but you're not looking for anything serious. But if you think there's even a chance you might seriously like this woman, then you need to think about all your options before you blow the whole thing sky high."

Everyone at the table nodded in agreement with Eric. Fuck, I hated it when everyone agreed. I was so desperate for a different answer that I turned to Antonio.

"Don't look at me. I live with two women, two dogs, and a cat."

Sighing, I picked up a beer. I didn't know what to do, but now they all had me second-guessing myself.

The door swung open and Will walked in, grinning like an idiot. "Please tell me you're fucking the whipped cream woman."

8

ABBY

I couldn't stop thinking about Carter. That kiss yesterday...I had to take care of a few things last night so I could fall asleep. I didn't understand it. The man acted like he hated me, but then he kissed me like that, making me think he wanted something more. And where did we go from here? Did he want me or did he just have a momentary lapse of judgment?

He told me all the things that were wrong with me, like I didn't already know. But then he kissed me like he needed me, and I felt for the first time in my life what it would be like to be with a man that passionate.

Looking back on my life, I couldn't say I'd chosen men well. There was Jerry. He thought he was a comedian, but he wasn't funny at all. And when he started turning those jokes on me, I was out of there. Bill wasn't terrible. At least, not until I found out he was a serial cheater. I only found out because he was sleeping with my roommate at the same time as me. I moved out the same day. That was how I ended up here. So, not really a big pool of guys to judge from, but it wasn't exactly a winning pool either.

Carter seemed like a good guy. He was nice, handsome, had a good job, and as far as I knew, he wasn't a cheater. Wouldn't the whole town know about that? Hell, they gossiped about everything else. Why not that? Granted, he wasn't always nice to me. He liked to point out everything that was wrong with me, but I got the feeling he was more fighting some inner battle than actually taking out his frustrations on me.

There was only one way I would find out if he liked me or not. I was going to have to be bold and talk to him. I could break the ice by making him some scones. I already knew he liked my baking, so bringing him something would be a good way to stay on his good side. Not to mention, I could totally pull it off as a thank you for helping me out after the whole bakery situation.

Getting to work, I whipped up a batch of scones and then got some work done while they were baking. It was a slow day for me, so I had plenty of time to take a morning break and bring them in to him.

After packing them up, I headed to the station, only missing the turn once. I was proud of myself for not getting lost nearly as frequently as I used to. As I pulled in, my stomach fluttered in anticipation of seeing him. I wondered if he would kiss me again. Maybe he would ask me out on a date.

I pushed open my door and stepped out, cradling the container under my arm. Taking a deep breath, I headed into the station.

"I'll be right with you," he said with his head still down as he read something. Running my fingers through my hair, I hoped I didn't seem too chaotic today. I hadn't bothered to do much with myself this morning, and then I was so eager to see him that I kind of forgot about looking at myself in the mirror. I ran my tongue over my teeth and cringed. Oh God, was that scone in my teeth? I had to taste test them before I brought them over, but I should have brushed my teeth. Now if he kissed me again, he'd get scone in his mouth. It would come loose and fall onto his tongue and he'd be disgusted.

"Abby?"

I jerked my head up, feeling my whole face flush red. "Yeah?"

He narrowed his eyes at me. "Is there something I can do for you?"

I tried to suck the crumb out, but it wouldn't come out. "Um...I brought you scones."

"Why?"

"As a thank you for not keeping me in prison."

"Jail," he corrected. "And I'm not even sure what I would have held you on."

"Disturbing the peace, inciting violence, assault, terrorist threats..."

"Huh?"

"The list goes on and on."

"Are you trying to get me to arrest you?"

Images of him locking me up with cuffs while I was naked flashed in my mind and I laughed nervously. "What?" It came out all squeaky and weird. "Of course not."

He stood and walked over to me, his swagger so damn sexy. His hand slowly reached out to me. He was going to hold my hand. My heart started to pitter-pat until it was thumping wildly in my chest. This was it. I slipped my hand in his and gazed up at him with what probably appeared to be stars in my eyes.

"The tin?"

"What?"

"Are you going to give me the container?"

I stared down at the container and then at my hand in his. My eyes slipped closed in embarrassment. I was holding his hand after I just offered him scones. I was such an idiot.

"Right," I laughed, slapping myself upside the head. "Doh!"

I handed the tin over and tried to pretend like I wasn't the most awkward person in the world. I didn't understand it. I wasn't like this around him before, but then one kiss from him had me acting like a complete lunatic.

"Is everything okay?" he asked.

"Of course. Why wouldn't it be?"

"You're just...Is this about yesterday?"

Suddenly, all my confidence flew out the window. I wasn't the girl that went up to guys and asked where we stood. What would I even say to him? And if he said it was nothing, I would be crushed and run out of here, probably getting in another accident. I wasn't even sure I liked him!

"The kiss? Is that what you mean? No, not at all. It was a nice kiss, but it was just a kiss, not like...something big."

"Like?"

"Like what?"

"You said it wasn't something big. Like what?"

I laughed, my shoulders shaking up and down in this wild way that I knew made me look like I was having a seizure or something. I forced myself to stop laughing and focus on him.

"It was just a kiss. It wasn't an invitation for sex or anything."

He frowned, staring down at the scones.

"Did...did you *want* to have sex?"

"No," he said quickly. "No, it was just like you said, a kiss."

"Right," I bobbed my head. "A kiss. It meant absolutely nothing. Zero. Zilch. Nada."

I took a step back, fully aware that I had now crossed the line from slightly crazy to bordering on psycho. I was that girl now. I showed up and made an idiot of myself over a kiss. And not even that good of a kiss! Okay, that was a lie. It was a magnificent kiss, but he obviously didn't see it that way or he would be begging me to kiss him again. And he wasn't doing that. He was just staring at my scones.

"You should really try them. It's one of my favorite recipes."

He popped the tin and peered inside. Grabbing one, he bit in and moaned. "Oh yeah, that's amazing."

"Really?" I blushed.

"This rivals Mary Anne's scones."

"What rivals Mary Anne's scones?" Jack asked as he walked up behind me. He peered into the tin and then snatched one, taking a huge bite of it. Moaning, his eyes rolled back. "Heaven. It's...there are no words. Can you make these every day? I'll pay you."

"You don't have to pay me," I said quickly.

"She's not making you scones," Carter snapped.

"Why not? I like her food."

"What would Mary Anne say?"

"Oh, I don't want to cause any problems with Mary Anne," I said quickly.

"These are amazing. Who taught you to bake? First muffins and now scones..."

"Um...well, my grandma. She was the baker in the family."

"So, what do we look forward to tomorrow?" he asked.

"Nothing," Carter snapped, "because she's not making us anything."

"Speak for yourself."

"I could make them," I said uncertainly. "It's no big deal. I love to bake."

This was probably a really bad idea. I was so wrapped up in Carter that now I was offering to make him baked goods every day. I would have to see him, smell him, but never taste him.

"Are you sure?" Carter asked, his eyes shining down at me.

"Of course," I said breathily, staring up at him. I couldn't tear my eyes away. He was just so damn magnificent looking. "I'll go home right now and figure out what to bake tomorrow."

"She's amazing," Jack grinned, slinging an arm around Carter's shoulders. "Isn't she something?"

"Yeah," Carter said gruffly, sending tingles down to my lady parts. He thought I was amazing.

"Okay," I giggled slightly. "I'll make something and bring it in tomorrow."

"We look forward to it," Jack tipped his hat at me. I lifted both hands and did this really weird double hand wave. And it just kept going. I couldn't seem to stop it. As if an invisible force was trying to save my dignity, my hands dropped and I turned tail. I never left a building so fast in all my life. I had to leave before I made things even worse than they already were.

9

CORDUROY

"What the hell was that?" I snapped at Jack, snatching the container from him. At some point, he took it from me, trying to eat my scones. She made them for me, not for him.

"That was me helping you out."

"How did that help me out? You saw that, didn't you?"

"Yeah, she's cute."

"She's awkward and..."

"Cute," Jack grinned.

"She's probably going to get in an accident on the way home, or get lost!"

"Maybe you should chase after her and find out."

"Not a chance in hell. That woman is not my responsibility. She's just a woman I know."

"A woman you like," he pointed out.

"Okay, she may be a good kisser. I'll give you that—"

"Whoa, hold on. When did you kiss her?"

Sighing, I plopped down in my chair and shoved a scone in my mouth. "Yesterday, after I drove her home," I said around a mouthful of the most delicious thing in the world.

"Was it scone-worthy?"

"Fuck," I rolled my head back. "It was...better than any kiss I've ever had."

"Then what the fuck are you doing here? Why aren't you out wooing her?"

"Wooing?"

"Yeah, get her to fall in love with you. Get her to bake more for you. Bring me some more damn scones."

"Right, because this is all about your eating habits."

"Damn straight, and if you knew what was good for you, you would realize that my win is your win."

"She's psychotic!"

"She's a little on the quirky side."

"She's more than quirky. You should have seen her when she walked in here."

"You should have seen you when I walked in here."

"What?"

"Uh-huh. Love struck puppy. That's what I saw."

I burst out in laughter. "There is no way that's what I looked like."

"Would you like me to take a picture next time? I gotta say, I haven't seen you look at any woman like that."

"Like I'm going to puke?"

"I just can't figure out why you're pushing her away if you like her so much."

"Because she's not the woman for me."

"I beg to differ. These scones beg to differ." He shoved the rest in his mouth and brushed off his hands. "I wonder what she'll bring me tomorrow."

I narrowed my eyes at him. "What she's bringing *me* tomorrow. The only reason you're getting anything is because of me."

"That would be incorrect. If you'll recall, she said she would bring you more food after I suggested it. If I left it up to you, we'd be eating Mary Anne's baking tomorrow. Not that there's anything wrong with it," he said, scanning the room like someone was spying on us.

"I would take Mary Anne's over Abby's any day. She's going to start thinking this means something."

"It does. It means we get good food."

"And she's going to think I want to date her."

"But you do."

"I do not."

"Then why did you accept her scones?"

"Because you practically shoved them in my face and begged her to make them for me!"

He nodded slightly. "I can see how you'd think that."

"The truth is, this is all your fault," I said, standing up and pacing. "I was working on getting her out of my life and then you stormed in and pushed us back together."

"You could have told her no."

"Yeah, and then I'd be the asshole that broke her heart."

"Only if you were a jerk about it. You could have kindly denied her baked goods. Who knows, maybe tomorrow's treats will come with a side of something else."

I shook my head at his grin. "You just love this, don't you?"

"What? I don't know what you mean."

"Yes, you do. Meddling in people's lives and trying to push a woman on me. Someone could get hurt."

He nodded seriously, tapping his chin. "You're right. There's someone else in this town that likes to do that. Now, who would that be?"

I rolled my eyes as he held up his finger.

"I've got it! It's you. *You* like to meddle in people's lives."

"Yeah, but I know what I'm doing. You just shoved me at a woman I have no interest in."

"No interest at all?"

"Do I look like I'm kissing her right now?"

"No, but I saw the way you were staring at her. Can you honestly tell me that you don't want to see her naked?"

"I already have," I muttered.

He burst out laughing, slapping his knee. "When?"

Sighing, I pinched the bridge of my nose. "The morning after the ivy incident. When I fell asleep in her room."

"Oh man, you're in worse than I thought. You've already seen her naked and you're accepting her scones. You are so screwed."

I glared at him, pointing my finger at him. "This is all your fault, and when things go sideways and her heart gets broken, I'm sending her to you."

I stormed out of the station as he shouted. "Just don't forget my baked goods first!"

OKAY, I had to admit the baked goods were really good. She brought them every morning like clockwork, smiling up at me like I was the most magnificent man in the world. It made me feel like the most amazing man and the biggest piece of shit at the same time. And of course, Jack was loving all of this. He was waiting for me to tell her not to bring any more baked goods because I didn't like her, but every time she walked through that door, I just couldn't make that smile disappear from her face.

And today she brought lemon cake. I didn't even like lemons, but I had to admit this stuff was amazing. And that only got me thinking about what her cooking would taste like. Was she one of those women that could bake really well, but was crap at cooking? Or was she like Martha Stewart? God, I really wanted to find out, but I wouldn't give Jack the satisfaction.

"Are you going to poker night tonight?"

I glanced at the calendar, pissed the town poker night had snuck up on me and I hadn't even noticed. Sighing, I tossed down my pen. "What is it this week?"

"1940's," he grinned. "Zoot suits."

"Thank God. I don't have a zoot suit, so I guess I get out of going."

"Yeah, I'm gonna need you to go."

"What? But I just said I couldn't."

"No, you said you didn't have a costume, which isn't going to be a problem if you show up as security for the night. Just wear what you're wearing now."

"And why can't you go?" I asked accusingly.

"Because I have a date."

My jaw dropped. "You do?"

"Yes, my son asked me to take him to a movie."

"Oh."

"So, while you're watching all the town make idiots of themselves, I'll be eating popcorn and watching a movie."

"Sounds perfect," I grumbled. "Can't you say you need me there too?"

"Well, first, that would be lying, and the Cortell women can always tell when one of us is lying. Second, you saw how rowdy it got last week. The last thing we need is a jail cell full of women."

I shrugged. "It could be interesting."

"Carter, if I come home and you've let the whole town go crazy, I will personally make sure that you see to booking every single person, doing all the paperwork, and following up on them at every single poker night for the rest of the year."

I winced, not liking the sound of that. "Fine, I'll be there."

"Good. Oh, and I told Abby this morning you would take her. She's never been to a town poker night and she didn't feel comfortable going alone."

"What?" I whined. "You can't be serious."

"Carter," he regarded me seriously. "As a member of the county sheriff's department, it is our duty to ensure all citizens feel safe and protected. Now, she's been nice enough to bring us baked goods every morning. The least you could do is escort her to the town poker night and help her to feel included."

I glared at the fucker. I really wanted to throat punch him right now. What a manipulative bastard.

"If I do this, I'm not going to another town poker night for at least four months."

"Two months."

"Three months."

"Two months," he countered.

"Three."

"Two, and if you don't stop trying to make me go higher, I'll make sure you take her next month also."

My nostrils flared as I stood and grabbed my jacket. "Fine, but I'm not going to have any fun, and you can't make me."

"Just make sure you have her home by midnight." I flipped him the bird as I headed for the door. "And make sure you use protection! We don't need you showing up at the school to talk about sex safety after you've knocked up a chick!"

⚜ 10 ⚜

ABBY

I was at the town thrift store, trying to find something to wear tonight. What did someone wear to a town poker night? And the theme was the 1940's. I had no idea what I should wear. I shuffled through the dresses, each more hideous than the last. Most looked like prom dresses, which wasn't something I was going for.

"Hey, you didn't show up for poker night."

I spun around, seeing Anna glare at me.

"Sorry about that. I was...busy."

"You were busy?"

I shrugged. "Well, Temperganda was getting into fights with Yoda Bear, and it was this whole fiasco where I ended up chasing them around the house all night, and when I finally separated them, I had to lock them in different areas of the house so The Red Hot Chili Peppers didn't get involved. Because once they get involved, Pteheste goes a little crazy."

She stared at me like everything I had said was Greek. "I think I need a drink after that explanation."

I nodded. "I'm with you. I drank like...two beers that night."

"Wow," she said, her eyebrows climbing. "You need a girls' night more than I anticipated."

I snorted. "Tell me about it."

"So, what are you doing here?"

"Oh, Carter's taking me to the town poker night tonight, and I guess it's some kind of theme night, but I have no idea what to wear."

"Carter's taking you?" she grinned.

I cocked my head uncertainly. "Is that a problem?"

"Why would it be a problem?"

"Well, because...because of his...feelings for you."

She burst out laughing, gripping my shoulder. "Oh my gosh, are you serious?"

"Well, I heard he was sort of in love with you."

She swiped at her eyes and sighed. "Carter was in love with the idea of me. Sure, I guess he had feelings for me at some point, but it was never actually love."

"How do you know?"

"Well, I was here for ten years and he never made a move. I didn't even really know he existed. I was lost in my world and our lives never really crossed paths. He told me when I was dating Robert that he was in love with me, but honestly, I can only guess that if he never gave it a shot, it's because he knew he didn't actually love me."

"But those feelings obviously didn't just go away. When I hit you with my car, he ran up to you and practically fawned all over you."

She waved me off. "That's just Carter. He's like this really good guy that cares about everyone and wants to make sure everyone is taken care of. Of course, you can't see it that often because he pretends to be an ass."

"He's always an ass to me," I muttered. "He has these moments where I think we're really connecting, and then he shoves it in my face that I'm an idiot."

"Yeah, he's deflecting."

"In what way?"

"It's obvious, isn't it?"

I shook my head and she sighed heavily.

"Carter loves to get involved in everyone's lives. He's always looking out for people. The fact that he's getting so upset over what happens with you tells me he really likes you."

"That's what you get from that?" I asked incredulously.

"Duh. You're the first woman that he actually likes more than for just a good time. But he doesn't know how to handle that. He's scared."

"I'm pretty sure that's not what's going on here. I'm pretty sure he just thinks I'm an idiot. Even when he kissed me, he told me he wanted me, but then stormed out of my house and acted like it never happened. And like the idiot I am, I've been making baked goods for him every day, thinking each morning that today's the day he'll kiss me again or tell me he wants to take me out."

"But you said he's taking you to the town poker night."

"Yeah," I said with exasperation. "Because Jack is making him. I'm a pity date. Or a pity pick up. Technically, it's not even a date. He's only taking me so I don't have to go alone."

A wide grin spread across her face and she took me by the hand. "Well, we'll just have to fix that, won't we?"

"How?"

"You just leave that to me. Right now, we need to get you a killer dress. Oh, and text Corduroy to tell him you have a date tonight."

"What?" I shrieked.

"Well, you don't want him showing up at your house."

I knew she was right, but still...it just seemed mean. "Couldn't I just do this another time?"

"No, and the fact is he thinks this is an obligation, so you should have no problem letting him out of it."

Sighing, I sent the text and waited for the fallout that would come. I really hoped she knew what she was doing.

"I LOOK RIDICULOUS."

"You do not," Anna burst out laughing. "This is amazing! Now, the thing to remember tonight is that you're just there to have fun. Don't worry about Corduroy."

"But I thought I was supposed to be getting Carter's attention?"

"Trust me, you will."

I sighed and stared at myself in the full-length mirror. My hair was done up all fancy and I was wearing a black dress that showed off my cleavage, but also curved around my waist and then flared out to show off my legs. It wasn't really my style, but then again, this was a theme night. I wasn't supposed to look like myself.

"And this guy, you're sure he's on board with this?"

"Of course. I told him exactly what was going on."

"What's his name again?"

"Jake."

"Jake," I repeated, taking a deep breath. "Okay, I can do this. No problem."

"Just think of it as hanging out with a friend."

"How do you know him?"

"He works for Eric. He's a good guy. Trust me, I've met him many times."

"Right, good guy. Not a serial killer."

"Not at all. Do you really think Robert would let me around a guy he didn't trust?"

"I suppose not."

The doorbell rang and my nerves shot through the roof. Was I really going to do this? I followed Anna into the other room and hesitantly peeked around her at the man standing in the doorway. I almost burst into laughter, he looked so ridiculous.

He had blondish brown hair, but it was covered up with a black fedora. He wore a black and white plaid zoot suit with black and white shoes. It was actually pretty cool. But it was those gorgeous eyes admiring me that really captivated me. I swallowed hard, choking down a nervous giggle.

"Abigail?"

"Yes," I squeaked. "Or Abby. Either one works."

"I'm Jake." He stepped inside as a handsome smile split his lips. He wrapped his large, warm hand around mine, sending tingles down my spine. Good God, this man was hot. Under the scruff on his jaw, I saw a sexy dimple peek out that made him look even more devilishly charming. I almost started fanning myself.

"Um...Anna tells me you work for Eric?"

"Yeah, I just moved here about six months ago."

"Me too," I bobbed my head way too much. "It's quite a change from the city I came from."

"Yeah? Where's that?"

"A suburb of Chicago. This is definitely slower."

He nodded. "I just moved here from Pennsylvania. I've been moving around for a while."

"Well, you two should head out. I'll meet up with you there," Anna said, shooing us out the door.

I followed Jake out to his truck. He was a gentleman, opening the door for me, and even helping me when my dress was hanging out. After shutting the door, he got in and headed for the community center.

"So, how did you get roped into going tonight?"

"Well, Jack sort of set this up with Carter, but I knew he didn't want to take me."

"Ah," he grinned. "So, I'm your backup."

"No! It's nothing like that!"

"Relax," he smiled. "I'm not offended or anything. I had no plans for tonight anyway. Besides, I don't mind showing a lady a good time when another man can't see what's in front of him."

"So, you know about the plan?"

"Of course I do. Anna called and told me what was happening. I was all over that."

"Why? I mean, I'm grateful, but why?"

He shrugged. "The fun of it? Back in Pennsylvania, I have this friend, a woman, and her husband is a jealous bastard. I liked to screw with him whenever I could."

"Because you liked the woman?"

"Because we were friends and he was being an ass."

"Are they still together?"

"Yeah, they got married, had some kids." He frowned slightly, like something was bothering him.

"What is it?"

He shook his head. "She runs this bed and breakfast, and she urged me to come out here when this opportunity came up. See, I helped her fix up the bed and breakfast, but when that was done, there wasn't a whole lot of work coming in. I was getting restless. So, her husband works with one of the Cortell brothers, and he knew Eric needed another project manager. The pay was good and so was the job. As much as I didn't want to leave, I also had to find something more inspiring than just being a handyman."

"So, what's the problem?"

"I haven't heard from them in a while. Usually Lindsey calls me and tells me what's new, but it's been a while. Months actually."

"Did you try her bed and breakfast?"

He nodded. "They don't know where she is. In fact, it looks like it'll have to shut down. They can't keep running it without her."

"Well, where's her husband?"

He shook his head slightly. "No one knows. The whole company disappeared. I tried to get something out of Eric, because his brother's missing too, but he says he doesn't have any more answers than I do."

"That's weird, isn't it?"

"Definitely."

"Did you think about going to search for them?"

"I wanted to, but honestly, they're a security company. There's not much I could do to find them. If they don't want to be found, I'm not going to. So, I just keep waiting to hear something, hoping something terrible hasn't happened."

I didn't know what to say. He seemed almost resigned over the whole thing.

"I hope you hear something soon."

"Me too," he said, turning his head to smile at me. "But anyway, let's just have a good time tonight, yeah?"

"Yeah."

11

CORDUROY

I was so relieved when Abby told me she had a date tonight. It took all the pressure off me to perform in any way. Like I needed that kind of pressure from a woman I wasn't interested in. I was slightly irritated that she'd waited until the last minute to tell me. It was almost like she was going out of her way to find another date so she didn't have to go with me. And why wouldn't she want to go with me? I was a good catch. I was handsome and I made good enough money. I was a stable choice. So, why the sudden change of heart?

Maybe she met someone and just decided to go with it. It wasn't like I was trying to get her attention. In fact, I'd been pretty good about keeping my distance over the past week.

Heading over to the community center, I took up my position at the bar, only drinking water as I watched everyone come in. Some were dressed up in 40's attire, while others were just wearing regular clothes. What shocked the hell out of me was when Nathan walked in with Penny and his dogs in tow. And the one dog was wearing a fucking vest and fedora.

Strolling up to him, I stared down at the dog and frowned. "What the fuck is this?"

"Theme night," he cocked his head.

I slowly shook my head as I sneered at him. "You're supposed to dress up, not the fucking dog."

He shrugged, grinning at me. "You have to admit, it's a good look for him. Besides, Gimpy can be a bastard, so I slipped a shock collar around him. Now, every time he gets rowdy, I zap him," he laughed.

"You're a little fucking crazy," I said, checking out his *outfit*. "And you're dressed like a doctor."

"Well, I wasn't about to dress up for this thing. But my dogs, now that's a different story."

Laughing at him, I leaned in and kissed Penny on the cheek. "You look beautiful tonight."

"Thanks, Corduroy. You look the same as usual."

I winked at her. "That's a compliment, right?"

"Always."

I heard a gasp and turned around, my jaw practically hitting the floor. Abby walked in, a vivid image of beauty. She was fucking beautiful, all dressed up with her makeup done and the most killer heels on. And on her arm was that fucking plaid bastard, dressed in a plaid zoot suit.

I didn't even realize I was growling under my breath until Nathan pressed his hand against my chest. "Dude, calm down. What are you getting so upset about?"

"*That's* her date?"

"Why? What's wrong with him?"

My jaw clenched in anger as I watched him wrap his arm around her waist and guide her down the steps onto the main floor. Everyone was gushing over her, telling her how beautiful she was. At least, I assumed that's what they were doing. She was absolutely breathtaking. And when she smiled up at him, it was like he was everything to her. That smile was supposed to be for me. Was she baking him tasty treats now too?

"Calm down, Corduroy. What's the big deal?"

"She was supposed to come with me."

"Okay, but you were here before her, so...did you forget to pick her up?"

"No," I ground out. "She texted me that she had a date."

"Ouch," Penny winced. "That's harsh. That takes some nerve to back out of a date and then show up with someone else."

"It wasn't a date," I admitted. "Jack set the whole thing up. He was trying to force me to go out with her."

"Wait, you didn't even want to go out with her?" Nathan asked.

"Well..."

He laughed and clapped me on the back. "Sounds like you waited too long and lost out. She's moved on, and I gotta tell you, they're a good couple."

"What makes you say that?"

"Well, just look at them. They're good together. And look how happy she is. She hasn't stopped smiling since she walked through the door."

My head whipped around and I glared at Nathan. "Fuck off."

I stormed off to the bar and ordered a whiskey. Goddamnit, I wasn't supposed to feel this way. I didn't even like her. She was just the annoying chick that brought me food. So why the hell was I so pissed she showed up with him?

I leaned back against the bar and watched as he led her over to a table, pulling out her chair for her. She beamed up at him as she sat down, even blushed when he leaned in and kissed her cheek.

I huffed out a laugh. "Putz."

"Who's a putz?" Eric asked as he stood beside me, waving down the bartender to get a drink.

I nodded over to the plaid zoot suit. "Jake," I said in a pissy tone.

"Jake? What's wrong with him?"

"Look at him," I jerked my chin at him. "He's pulling out all the stops tonight."

"Oh, you mean with Abby?" He took a sip of his drink, pretending to not know who I was talking about. "I guess you missed out on that one."

"I didn't miss out on anything, because I wasn't trying to get her to begin with."

"Then why are you so pissed?"

"Because she can do better. He just moved to town. What do we really know about him?"

"Actually, Derek told me all about him. I guess he's a pretty good guy. And he's a hell of a foreman. You know, since I hired him, jobs are getting done faster and more efficiently than when I just had RJ running the show. And, he has all these connections from traveling around—"

"Yeah, I get it. He's a fucking unicorn."

"What?"

"You talk about him like he's some magical creature or something. He's just a guy. And what's with all the fucking plaid?"

Eric chuckled as he took a drink. "Ice, that's one of the guys Derek works with, calls him Plaid Man because of all the plaid he wears."

"What's with that? What kind of psycho wears that much plaid?"

He shrugged. "I don't see anything wrong with it. So he likes plaid. What's the big deal?"

"Yeah, but to like it so much that you wear a zoot suit made of plaid? I'm sorry, but there's gotta be something wrong with him."

"Or, he's just a normal guy that likes plaid," Eric said slowly.

"Sure, take his side," I said, snatching my drink and walking around the room.

I did my job, making sure there was law and order while everyone was gambling, but my eyes kept drifting back to her. She just looked so damn happy. And Plaid Man kept laughing with her, and showing her how to play poker. It just pissed me off. Who was he to step into my territory and take over? She was my responsibility and had been since the day she crashed into that light pole.

I set my drink on the bar and headed over to him, but Anna stepped in my path, her arms crossed over her chest. "Just what do you think you're doing?"

"I'm going to talk to the Plaid Wonder."

"Why?"

"Because he's here and I'm the deputy-sheriff. I'm perfectly within my rights to go talk to anyone I choose."

"Yeah," she nodded, "but if you're going over there to pick a fight because he came here tonight with Abby, then you need to walk away."

"And why would I do that?"

"Because you're not an asshole, Carter. She's having a good time tonight. Why can't you just let her have that?"

"Because she's mine," I snapped.

Her eyebrows shot up and she laughed humorlessly. "So, she's yours now that she's all dressed up and wearing beautiful clothes. But when she gets into trouble and dresses like a hippie, you want nothing to do with her."

I frowned. "What are you talking about?"

"You make her feel like an idiot. Let me tell you, she's really nice. Yeah, maybe she's a little out there, but she's nice. You're just jerking her around. I know about those baked goods. You know she does that because she likes you, yet you've got zero balls and can't even tell her you aren't interested."

"Who said I wasn't interested?"

"If you were, you would have made a move already. You spend enough time with her, but you don't actually want to date her, so let her have fun and leave her alone. You're no good for her anyway."

"Why would you say that?"

"Because I know you, Carter. You're self-destructive. You make sure everyone else is happy, but you won't fight for your own happiness. So tell me, how are you going to make her happy?"

I studied Abby and frowned. She was laughing hard as she leaned across the table and pulled all the chips in front of her. She had won the hand. And it wasn't me beside her, cheering her on and making her feel good. It was Plaid Man. He was the one making sure she had a good time.

Turning, I headed back for the bar and ordered another drink. Swallowing it whole, I ordered another. I hated that Anna was right. I was stuck in this self-destructive pattern of ruining everything I could have going for me. The only thing I truly cared about was my job. And now that I found a woman I was actually attracted to, I didn't have the balls to date her.

I wasn't sure how long I sat at the bar drinking, but the more I drank, the less I cared about what I was supposed to be doing here. Like anyone really needed a sheriff to watch over the town poker night. I snorted into my drink and swallowed it all. The room was starting to spin slightly. Fuck, I shouldn't have drunk so much. I tossed down some money and stood, almost falling off my bar stool. When I stood, the first thing I saw was the Plaid Wonder leaning into Abby and whispering in her ear as his hand lightly gripped her neck.

Anger rushed through me and I stormed across the room, stumbling and running into chairs along the way. I walked right up to Jake and slammed my fist into his face, sending him flying out of his chair. Abby screeched and pushed back out of her chair, crouching down beside Jake.

"What the hell are you doing?" she yelled.

I seriously had no fucking clue. I only knew that he was touching her and it pissed me off. Hands gripped my arm and I swung around, hitting someone else. When I saw Eric crash into the table, I knew I was really fucked up. Hell, I was acting like an idiot, but I couldn't seem to stop myself.

Someone tackled me from behind and I fell face first onto the floor. Then I felt my arms being wrenched behind my back and my own fucking cuffs clicking into place. I saw Abby shaking her head at me in disappointment, and then I was hauled up and someone was marching me out of the building.

Twenty minutes later, I was sitting in my own fucking jail cell. Eric and Robert were glaring at me as they sat in Jack's chair and my chair. Fucking hell, this night had gone to shit. And then Jack walked in, marching right up to the cell and glaring at me.

"When I told you not to let anyone cause any trouble, that included you."

12

ABBY

"I'm so sorry," I apologized to Jake for the tenth time since we left the community center. I pressed an ice pack to his face as we sat in my living room on my cushions.

He pressed his hand over mine and smirked. "I told you, I'm fine."

"But he attacked you for no reason."

"Not for no reason. It's obvious the man likes you more than he thought."

I shook my head, denying what he was saying. "If he liked me, there are other ways to go about letting a girl know."

"Yeah, but jealousy is a powerful motivator."

I stood and walked to the kitchen to pour some water. "Well, I don't want a man to realize he likes me because I was with another man."

"So, that's it? You're not going to give him a chance?"

"After tonight? No way."

He tossed the ice pack down and walked over to me. "So...does that mean you're up for seeing other people?"

My gaze shot up to his and I stared at him in shock. "You...you want to date me?"

"Why not? You're gorgeous. You make me laugh. Why wouldn't I want to get to know you?"

My mouth dropped open as I tried to figure out what to say. "I'm a mess," is what came out. "I mean, I'm always embarrassing myself and I'm a terrible driver. I think I've been in four accidents in the last year, two in this town. Three, if you count me jumping the curb in front of the sheriff's station."

"Okay, so I'll drive. You can just sit in the passenger seat."

I smiled at him. "Did you see the town video?"

"Of the ivy? Totally hot."

I covered my face and sighed. "Are you sure about this?"

"Listen, if this is about Carter, if you still like him and want to see if things go anywhere, I won't be upset."

"Really?"

He shrugged. "I'll have missed out. It's happened before."

I bit my lip, kind of excited that he was asking me out. I hadn't planned on going into tonight with this kind of outcome. I just went from one man sort of interested, to two men fighting over me. I had to say, that really boosted my ego.

"Okay, say we did go out. Where are you thinking?"

"Anything you want to do. Movies, dinner, skinny dipping…"

I laughed. "It's a little cold for skinny dipping."

"I can warm you up," he said, his voice husky as he gazed down at my lips.

And just like that, lust was racing through me, begging me to just kiss the man and say to hell with it. But I wanted the date, and I couldn't rush this. Taking a step back, I fanned my face and grinned sheepishly at him.

"Okay, one date. You choose what we do."

"Alright. Tomorrow night?"

The smile that spread across my face gave away everything I was feeling, and he could see it all.

"I'll pick you up at seven."

"Alright."

He stepped up to me, his body brushing against mine. His lips pressed a soft kiss against my cheek, but he didn't move away right away. I swallowed hard when he finally stepped away.

"See you tomorrow."

He turned and walked out my door, leaving me standing like jello in my kitchen. I grabbed a glass of water and started drinking, but it did nothing to cool me off. I filled it again, only this time I poured it down the front of my dress. Pressing my hands to the counter, I took in deep breaths. Wow.

The doorbell rang and I quickly ran over, thinking maybe it was Jake and he forgot something. Unfortunately, it was Anna grinning at me like an idiot. She shoved past me and spun around.

"So? What happened?"

I shrugged like nothing had happened. "He brought me home and he left."

"Yeah, I was outside the whole time. He was here way too long to have just dropped you off."

"Okay, he stayed so I could put ice on his face."

"And?"

"And what?" I played it cool.

"You know what! Stop messing with me and tell me what else happened!"

I clapped my hands and squealed. "And we're going out tomorrow night!"

Her face fell and she plopped down on a cushion. "You're going out with Jake?"

"Yeah." I sat down beside her. "I thought...what did you think was going to happen?"

"I assumed you were going to plot out your next move to get Corduroy."

"Wait, this is a good thing. Jake's a good guy."

"Well, obviously he is, but Corduroy is the guy for you."

"How do you figure?"

"Did you see how jealous he got over you being with Jake?"

"Any man can get jealous. That doesn't mean I should date the guy."

"But this is Corduroy," she argued. "The guy that helps you get home and cuts you out of ivy in the middle of the night. He's the guy you've been baking for."

"Right, he's also the guy that's ignored me for weeks until the night I showed up with another guy."

"Okay, I can see how you'd be a little pissed about that, but..."

"But what, Anna? He doesn't like me like that."

"He does. He just needs a little push."

"Is that supposed to make me feel better? A guy can't decide that he likes me for me, so he needs someone else to make a move first? I have more respect for myself than that."

She sighed, nodding to me. "I know, I get it. It's just...I would hate for the two of you to miss out on this."

"Why do you care so much about this? You and I barely know each other. And Corduroy..." My eyes widened in surprise. "This is about making sure Corduroy is happy."

She slumped down in the cushions and stared up at the ceiling. "This stays between us, okay?"

"Okay," I promised.

"There was this moment when Robert and I were getting fake married. It was because of a case he was handling, and the woman trusted him because she thought Robert and I were engaged. And then she showed up at the wedding."

"Wait, you had a wedding for a fake engagement?"

"It was supposed to be Kat and Eric's wedding, but we hijacked it. Anyway, it was this rush of getting everything switched around. Of course, all of his family was already there, but I didn't have any family there. I had no one to walk me down the aisle. And it shouldn't have mattered because it was all fake, but it really sucks to know no one is there for you. Anyway, Corduroy stepped in and said he would walk me down the aisle."

"That was nice of him."

"That was more than nice of him. You know how I told you that he doesn't really love me?" I nodded. "Well, I don't think he realized it at the time. I'm pretty sure he still thought he was in love with me. And knowing how much it would hurt him to walk me down that aisle, fake wedding or not, he stepped in and he did that for me. He hurt himself because he didn't want me to have to do it alone. I think it was his way of finally letting me go."

By the time she finished, I had tears in my eyes, and I was wiping my cheeks furiously. The guy she was talking about sounded like one of the best guys on the planet.

"So, when I tell you he's a good guy, and he's just standing in his own way, I'm saying it from experience. If you think Jake is the guy for you, then go out with him. But if you think there's even a chance that you still think Corduroy is someone you could be with, please don't do that to him. He's doing enough to hurt himself."

She stood and headed for the door, slipping out without another word. I laid there trying to decide what to do. I felt like I understood a little better what she was talking about, but the man she was talking about, and the man I saw were two different people. I felt like he was hanging around me despite his unsure feelings of me, like Elizabeth Bennet and Mr. Darcy in *Pride and Prejudice*.

But then there was Jake, who openly admitted to liking me and wanting to spend time with me. I would be foolish to turn a man like him away. There really was nothing to decide. One man liked me while the other tolerated me. I had to do what was best for me, and in this case, that was going out with the man that actually showed some desire for me. That decided, I smiled and headed for bed.

I WAS A NERVOUS WRECK. If I thought meeting him the first time was scary, this was even worse. The man was gorgeous and made me feel like a princess. But I hadn't been on a real date in over a year. I changed my outfit ten times, each time thinking I looked just a tad too strange. But in the end, I decided to go with something that made me feel just like me. After all, he would understand who I was soon enough. Better that he see the real me sooner rather than later.

It was still a little warm out for fall, but I knew the night would be cool. I dressed in my skinny jeans and a fun, colorful top that I found at a thrift store and paired it with a scarf my grandmother made. It was burnt orange and blue, something that most people would find ridiculous, but I loved it. I pulled on my jacket just as the doorbell rang. There was no going back now.

I opened the door and smiled, hoping he didn't immediately look at me with disgust. Instead, his eyes burned and reached out to touch the scarf.

"I like this."

"Really?"

He nodded. "It's quirky."

"Well, I'm quirky."

"Good."

Holding out his hand, I took it and pulled the door closed behind me, but Carter's constant nagging about locking my door filtered into my mind.

"I just have to lock the door." Pulling the key down from the top of the door, I quickly locked up and almost slipped the key back on top of the door.

"It's just about the worst hiding spot for a spare key. Anybody could find that."

Deciding to hide it in a better spot, I slipped it inside the planter next to my door. It would probably get lost in the dirt, but at least nobody else would find it either.

"So, where are we going?"

"Go Kart racing."

"Seriously?" My face lit up.

"I thought it would be fun. And now you can hit things when you're supposed to. Maybe it'll help you avoid the other cars on the road."

I laughed at his humor. "I doubt that, but it's worth a try."

After pulling out of my driveway, we talked the whole way to the racetrack. Every second was so easy. There was no tension between us, and it felt like I was hanging out with an old friend. Was that a bad sign? I shook that thought from my head and just focused on having fun.

We bought our tickets and raced over to the track. Most of the people there were teenagers, but I didn't care. I was going to have fun and not worry about anything else. I got in my car and strapped myself in. Jake smiled at me and quirked his eyebrows in challenge. It was so on.

When the green light flashed, I pushed the pedal all the way to the floor and screamed as I raced down the track. When Jake was just a little too close, I slammed my car against his, laughing when he almost hit the wall. There was another kid just ahead of me, so I swerved to his side and cut him off on the next turn. It felt like I was going to tip over, but I came through it alright. If only driving every day was like this. I was so close to the finish line when Jake caught up, smirking at me like he had an ace up his sleeve.

"Towanda!" I shouted, jerking the wheel and driving him straight into the barricade. Of course, I also ended up in the pit of stacked tires, neither of us winning the race in the end, but I'd never had so much fun in all my life.

Taking off my helmet, I was laughing so hard I was sure I would pee my pants. Jake ran up to me and wrapped me in his arms, laughing along with me.

"That was so awesome!"

"I know! I haven't had that much fun in so long!"

"What the hell did you scream before you hit me?"

Taking a deep breath and calming down, I finally explained. "Haven't you ever seen *Fried Green Tomatoes*?"

"No," he laughed.

"Well, there's this part where these young girls take this older woman's parking spot at the grocery store and then laugh at her. So, she gets her revenge by smashing her car into theirs over and over again, and she shouts *Towanda!* And then she says to the girls, *Face it, I'm older and have better insurance*. And then she drives off laughing."

"Okay, I get it."

"No, you don't, but you should watch the movie."

"I would watch it with you," he smiled, wrapping his arm around me.

"We could go back to my place. I could cook dinner and we could watch it."

His eyes sparkled as he stared at me. "I think that sounds like a good plan."

It didn't take long after we got back to my place for my nerves to kick in. It occurred to me on the way home that I may have perhaps invited him back to my place for sex without meaning to. And judging by the way his eyes perused me, sex was on his mind. I wasn't a girl that just slept around, so he would be disappointed at the end of the night.

I made dinner, avoiding his touch every time he tried to rest his hand on my back. I didn't want to send off the wrong signals. But as dinner was cooking on the stove, I found myself being spun around and backed up against the counter. He caged me in, pressing his body against mine as he leaned in close. I wanted to push him away, but he was just so damn sexy and I wanted to be kissed again. But just as he was leaning in, Corduroy's face flashed in my mind. I pressed my hands against his chest and pushed him slightly.

He stepped back, frowning. "Did you not want me to kiss you?"

"I do...I just...freaked out or something."

His lips tilted up. "But you *do* want me to kiss you."

And just like that, his smooth voice melted me and I found myself nodding. His lips slid across mine, his body pressed tightly up against me. I could feel his erection digging into my belly. My mouth opened and his tongue slid inside and...

We both broke apart, shaking our heads as we spit out in disgust. I chanced a look, happy to see it wasn't just me.

"I'm sorry," I apologized. "That was..."

"Weird," he nodded.

"Exactly."

"But we have so much in common. We have so much fun. Why..."

I shrugged. "I have no idea. Two minutes ago, I was ready to...well, to do things I shouldn't want to do."

"I know!" He shook his head and sighed. "Maybe it was a fluke."

"Maybe."

"Should we...try again?"

What could it hurt? Better to know for sure than throw something away on a bad kiss. "Let's do it."

He laughed. "I like the sound of that."

His fingers trailed down my face, brushing against my neck before he skimmed my waist and gripped me hard, pulling me against him. His lips crashed down on mine and his tongue slipped inside. I slid my fingers through his hair, tugging at the strands, hoping to make something spark. A full minute went by with both of us trying to make something out of nothing. Finally, we broke apart and grimaced at each other.

"I'm not even hard anymore," he muttered.

"Yeah, nothing going on here either."

"Should we try a third time? I mean, just to be sure?"

"I don't think three times a charm works here."

He nodded. "So...fucking then?"

I laughed and slapped him on the arm. "That would be pretty hard when you can't get it up. No pun intended."

He laughed and pulled me in for a hug. "Well, at least we'll still have Paris."

I laughed against his chest and hugged him back. It wasn't going to happen for us, but at least I still had a friend out this.

13

CORDUROY

Two days later and I was still fighting off the remnants of my hangover. I hid out in my house all day yesterday, mortified by my behavior. And if it wasn't bad enough to replay it in my head, it was plastered all over the town page. How could I have been so stupid? But now I had to go to work and face Jack. I knew he would be pissed at me. From the little bit that I remembered from the other night, angry would have been putting it mildly.

I parked outside the station, keeping my sunglasses on despite the cloudy weather. My head was still pounding, but that was probably because I didn't normally drink whiskey, and definitely not to the extreme I had the other night. The door slammed closed behind me just a little too loudly for my liking. I winced and walked inside, hoping Jack wouldn't say anything and just let me work off my hangover in silence.

"Nice of you to show up to work today," he shouted.

I grimaced and held my head, but he didn't care.

"Brody was pissed that I had to cut our movie night short because my deputy got drunk and had to be dragged down to the station. I expect you to apologize the next time you see him."

"Of course," I mumbled, still trying to beat back the ringing in my ears.

"So, you couldn't handle bringing her to the poker night."

"I didn't bring her at all. She canceled because she had a date."

"So then what was the fight about?" he shouted.

Sighing, I rubbed my temples. I needed some food, something with carbs, but as I looked around, I didn't see anything. I bet Abby made great hangover food.

"She showed up with Plaid Man."

"Who?"

"Jake, the guy that works for Eric."

"Christ, does everyone in this town need to have a nickname?"

"Hey, I didn't give it to him. And he wears a lot of plaid."

"That's besides the point. You got pissed because she showed up with someone else. You didn't even want to take her!"

"Could you stop yelling?" I asked.

"No! Because you're a fucking dumbass. You want her. You don't want her. Make up your fucking mind!"

"I don't know what I want! I want to kiss her and sleep with her, but a relationship? I don't think I'm up for that. And I wouldn't care if she was dating someone, but...fuck! Why does it have to be him?"

"What's wrong with him?"

"He's...good-looking and fun. You should have seen him staring at her. And the way she stared back at him, like the world revolved around him. And now he's probably going to get her baked goods!"

Jack sat up and stalked over to me, grabbing me by the collar. "You go over there and apologize. I don't care what you have to say to her, but you make things right with her. I want those baked goods back and I want them now. Do you understand me?"

I nodded and pried his hands from my shirt. Taking a deep breath, he walked over to his desk and sat down, composing himself once again. I shook my head and started sorting through messages.

"What the fuck are you doing?"

"Working?"

He pointed to the door. "Baked goods!"

I tossed down my things and grabbed my keys. "Fine, I'll go apologize now. It's not like I have any work to do."

"If you come back here empty-handed, you're fired!"

I rolled my eyes and walked out of the office, then headed over to Abby's house. This was ridiculous. I didn't even know if she would accept my apology. I had been an ass. For all I knew, she was with Plaid Man now. Still, I had to at least try.

I pulled into her driveway and parked, hoping maybe she wasn't home and I could do this another time. Walking up her steps, I tried to think of something I could say to make this right. I would just say I was sorry. That was really all that could be done at this point.

Knocking on the door, I waited for her to answer. When the door swung open and her face fell, so did my hope of making this right. Jack was going to kill me.

"Hey," I said. Worst opening line ever.

"Hey." She crossed her arms over her chest and stared down at the ground.

"Can I come in for a minute?"

"I don't think that's such a good idea."

"I swear, I'm not drunk."

Sighing, she opened the door wider and let me in. As she stared at me, I begged the words to come, but still, I got nothing.

"This would be the part where you say you're sorry for being an ass."

I nodded. "And I am. I just...suck at this."

"Clearly."

I nodded again and looked around her place. "I know I can be a jerk. I don't mean to be, but I saw you with...Jake," I bit out, "and I just lost it."

"I don't get why. You don't even like me."

I huffed in amusement. "I do like you. Fuck, I think about you in the shower and when I'm jerking off..." Her jaw dropped and I winced. "Sorry, still just a tad hungover."

"Maybe you should go—"

I rushed forward and grabbed her by the arms, pulling her against me. "Don't make me go. There's something between us. I can feel it. Can't you?"

Her face softened and she seemed to collapse in my arms.

"Look, whatever this is...we should see where it goes. I mean, you're weird as shit and you have way too many cats. And let's not even talk about your driving skills. But I like you and I want to fuck you. So... let's just get this out of our systems so things can go back to normal."

The absolute anger on her face should have warned me about the incoming slap, but somehow, I still missed it.

"You want to fuck? What is it with me? Two in one week!"

"Two?" I frowned. "Who else propositioned you?"

"It doesn't matter," she snapped. "Seriously, does no one want to actually date me or am I only good enough to fuck." I opened my mouth, but she beat me to it. "Don't answer that!"

Running her hands through her hair, she started walking around the room, muttering to herself and laughing every now and then. Was this another new thing she was just picking up, or did she always do this?

"You need to leave."

"But...where do we stand on the whole sex thing?"

"Out!" she shouted, pointing at the door. I flinched and practically ran for the door. I was just about to close it when I peeked my head back in.

"So, does this mean no more baked goods?"

She grabbed the door and flung it shut, giving me just a second to remove my head from being smashed into the doorframe. Staring at the ground, I shook my head.

"I don't get it. I thought she wanted to sleep with me."

As I walked into the station, Jack frowned at my empty hands in utter disappointment. "You didn't get them?"

"I...I think I made it worse."

"How could you have possibly made it worse?"

I winced. "I said we were attracted to each other and we should just fuck and get it out of our systems."

He stared at me incredulously, and then he exploded. "You said what?"

"I may have also said she was weird and insulted her about a few other things."

He grabbed the morning paper off his desk and rolled it up, then came charging at me, slapping me over the head multiple times. "I said apologize!"

"I know! It just came out."

"You're lucky I can't shoot you!"

I held up my hands placatingly. "Just remember, I'm your friend."

"Yeah, but I'm also your boss."

He walked over to the jail cell and opened it. "Get your ass inside."

"What?"

"You heard me. If you're going to behave like an idiot, you'll get treated like an idiot."

"Jack—"

"Don't fuck with me. Those baked goods were one of two things going right in my life and now they're gone. You sit in there and think about what you've done."

Trudging into the jail cell, I sat down on the bench as the door slammed shut. Pouting, I rested my chin on my fist and wondered what the hell I was going to do in here all day.

Jack tossed a pad of paper and pen into the cell. "I want thirty different apologies, and you're not getting out until it's done."

"Are you serious?"

He glared at me, so I picked up the paper and got to work. Damn, it was hard coming up with thirty ways to apologize to a woman.

❧ 14 ❧

ABBY

I was finished with my work, but still had to stick around for another hour. I sat at my computer and twirled my hair around just for something to do. I dug small ponytail holders out of my drawer and decided I might as well have some fun while I waited. Sectioning out my hair into small pieces, I started putting braids all over my head. I was about halfway through when someone knocked on my door.

"Shit," I swore, staring at myself in the camera on my computer. Pushing my nose up against the screen, I studied my hair, trying to determine how bad I looked. I quickly started to undo one of the braids, but when the knocking came again, I knew I didn't have time to take it all out.

Getting up, I grabbed a scarf off the back of my chair and wrapped it around my head. There. Even though I looked like an idiot, no one would see how bad it really was. Putting a smile on my face, I swung the door open.

Anna's eyebrows shot up as she gaped at my head. "Cold?"

"Um...something like that."

She nodded and pushed past me. "So, what happened with Jake?"

I shut the door and headed for the kitchen, but as I walked past her, she tore the scarf from my head. I screeched and grabbed for it, but I was too late. She already saw the worst of it.

Staring at me in shock, I snatched the scarf back and rewrapped it. "What is that?"

"I was bored," I snapped, going back to the kitchen.

"Well, don't walk around with a scarf now. I've already seen it."

Sighing, I took off the scarf and stared at her. "Happy?"

She snorted with laughter. "I'm sorry, but that isn't the best look on you."

"I wasn't doing it to look good. I was bored and needed something to do. I'm a fidgeter."

I pulled open the fridge and offered her a water, then grabbed one for myself.

"So, what's with all the cushions and candles and shit?"

She took a seat, bouncing around slightly to get comfortable.

"I don't know. I saw it in a magazine and it looked comfortable. I like eclectic things."

"I can tell."

"Why? Is there something wrong with it?"

She shrugged. "As long as you like it. So, not to be nosy, but I'm going to be nosy. What happened with Jake? Did you go out with him?"

"As a matter of fact I did, and we had a great time."

Her face fell. "So, you really like him."

I nodded. "I do. We really got along so well. It was really natural, you know?"

"Yeah," she grumbled.

She looked so sad about everything that I decided to put her out of her misery. "If it makes you feel any better, he kissed me and it was terrible."

She perked up at that, her eyes widening in surprise. "Really?"

"I'm sure he's a good kisser, but it was gross for both of us."

"How so? Too much spit?"

"No, it wasn't that."

"Too much tongue?"

I thought about it and shook my head. "No, it wasn't that either."

She grimaced. "Not passionate enough?"

"It wasn't that either," I sighed.

Rolling her eyes, she stood and placed her hands on her hips. "Well, if it wasn't that, then what was it?"

"Well, part of the problem was that when he went to kiss me, I thought of Carter." She grinned, motioning for me to go on. "Honestly, it was like kissing my brother or something."

"But you said you liked him."

"I know. It was so weird. We both had this great time, and the chemistry was there. He was even hard," I said, making my eyes go wide. "But then we kissed and it was just...wrong."

With a satisfied grin, she took her seat again. "So, that means Corduroy still has a chance."

I grimaced, shaking my head. "I'm afraid not. He came over here to apologize."

She groaned, her head rolling back. "No, he didn't."

"Yes, and it was...the worst apology I've ever heard. Well, I guess at first it was good. He said he was sorry, and that was the good part."

"I'm afraid to hear the bad part."

"He said there was something between us."

"That's good."

"And then he said I was weird, but we should sleep together and get it out of our systems."

She slapped her forehead, shaking it slightly. "God, why are men so stupid?"

"If I knew that, I might not be single." Then again, maybe he never intended that. "Do you think maybe he accidentally said it?"

"Did it sound like it was an accident?"

I shook my head. "No, I think he just wanted to sleep with me and that's it. What is it with men? I just don't understand. Don't men understand that women don't just want a cheap thrill?"

"See, I don't think he does want a cheap thrill."

"Oh, come on. Not this again. The man asked me to fuck him and get it over with. He couldn't have been clearer."

"Yes, but he also got really upset when he saw you with Jake. That has to mean something."

"Yeah, Jake was about to get laid and he wasn't. Besides, what are his options? There can't be that many single women in town. Unless he wants to take Carrie off Joe's hands," I laughed.

"I swear, if I ever get within ten feet of that woman again, I'm going to throttle her."

"Then you'd end up in jail again," I pointed out.

She flicked her hand at me. "Like that actually means something. You know, what we need is a plan."

"For what?"

"To get you with Corduroy. Have you been listening to anything I've said?"

"Anna," I begged. "Let it go. I've had enough humiliation to last a lifetime. The last thing I need is another plan that'll go south. It's over. He doesn't like me like that, and that's fine. I don't want someone that thinks I'm weird anyway."

She stared at me for a moment. "You know, we need some coffee. You're driving."

"What?" I asked as she popped up and headed for the door. "Anna, look at my hair!"

"It's fine. Besides, we're just getting coffee. Who cares what your hair looks like? You're not that vain, are you?"

I frowned. "No, but—"

"So, let's go."

Sighing, I pushed myself up and grabbed my keys. "Why can't you drive? Wouldn't it make more sense?"

"Either way we have to come back here. Trust me, it's better if you drive."

I had no idea why I had to drive, but I went along with it and got in my car, reaching into the backseat for a baseball cap. Shoving it down on my head, I did the best I could to hide my erratic hair.

When we got to the bakery, I had flashbacks of my stint in jail. It wasn't something I wanted to repeat anytime soon. Luckily, there were no signs of Carrie today, so that fiasco would be avoided.

"Hey, Mary Anne," Anna said cheerily. "We need two coffees to go."

"Latte?"

"You know it!"

They were interacting as if we hadn't just destroyed her bakery days ago. Mary Anne didn't scowl at her or threaten her if she ever stepped in the shop again. It was weird.

"That's it?" I leaned over and whispered to Anna. "Why isn't she more upset?"

Anna waved me off. "Mary Anne lives for our crazy stunts."

"Why?"

"Exposure. Every time something happens in her shop, more people come by, just waiting for one of us to come in and do something crazy."

"Don't people have better things to do with their time?"

She shrugged. "You would think so."

"Here you go, ladies. Whipped cream?"

Mary Anne smirked at Anna and they both burst out laughing.

"That's a good one!"

"How are sales?"

"Booming," Mary Anne said excitedly. "Can't wait for the next episode. I mean—the next time you come in."

Anna winked at her and grabbed our coffees, handing mine over. She headed for the door, walking back to our car. She was watching down the street for something, but just as quickly looked away.

"We should go back to your place," she said, hurrying to my car.

I didn't get a chance to see whatever she was watching. "Why are you in such a rush?"

"Um...I have to pee."

"There are bathrooms in the bakery."

"Right, but...I have to go number two. I can't do that in public."

Rolling my eyes, I got in. "By all means, feel free to use my bathroom."

"I will," she grinned. She glimpsed out her side. "All clear from this direction."

I put the car in reverse and started backing out.

"Hurry!" Anna shouted. "I'm about to shit my pants!"

I pressed the pedal down, backing out much quicker than I would have liked. The car lurched back and then slammed to a stop as I hit something. "Shit!"

I closed my eyes and rested my forehead against the steering wheel. "Why? Why? Why!"

"We'd better check out the damage," Anna said, flinging her car door open. I pushed my door open and stepped out. "Oh, Corduroy. We didn't see you."

I slowly turned and stared at the man who just last night had told me he wanted to fuck me out of his system. But he obviously wasn't thinking about that right now. No, right now, he was bent over and staring at the front of his car. I wanted to slink away and pretend none of this ever happened. When he raised his eyes and saw me, he shook his head in disappointment.

"Really?"

"I—"

"Just one fucking day. That's all I'm asking!"

"It wasn't my fault!"

"Who hit who?"

I stomped my foot in frustration. "Anna had to go number two. I was trying to hurry!"

"Did you bother to look before you backed out?" he snapped.

"Anna said—" I stopped and glowered at Anna, who was looking anywhere but at me. "You set me up!"

"I did not," she said indignantly. "You were driving. Tell me how I set you up."

"You told me to back up!"

"If I told you to jump off a bridge, would you do that?"

My jaw dropped open, but I had nothing to say. As the driver, yes, it was my responsibility to make sure I wasn't about to hit anyone. But this reeked of a setup. She wanted me to hit Corduroy. That must have been who she saw when we stepped out of the bakery.

"You little witch! You did this!" I shrieked, running at her. I slammed her into the car, setting off the alarm when we hit it. We fell to the ground, rolling around as we pulled each other's hair.

"You should have looked where you were going," she shouted, pulling at my hat and rolling over me.

"You should stop trying to set me up with men that don't want me!" I yanked her hair in retaliation and flipped her back over.

"He's the man for you," she snapped, this time yanking my hat off as she pulled at my hair.

I gasped and grabbed at the mess on top of my head, glaring down at her. "You bitch! You did that on purpose!"

"You're damn right I did!"

I was pulled off Anna just a second later, but I struggled to get back to her, pushing away from Corduroy. I knew it was him by his scent. "Get off me!" I shouted. Then I pointed my finger at Anna. "I'll get you for this!"

She smirked at me. "*You* hit another vehicle. *You* attacked me. And now *you're* going to jail."

I hated her. I'd never hated anyone in my life, but right now, I seriously hated her. And as the door to the jail cell slammed shut, I glared over at her on the bench beside me.

"How did that plan work out for you?"

She huffed and leaned back against the wall. "Well, I wasn't supposed to be thrown in jail."

15

CORDUROY

"You need to get your woman under control," Robert snapped at me as we stood outside the station.

"*My* woman? What about your woman?"

"Anna was an innocent bystander."

"Bullshit," I snapped. "There's nothing innocent about Anna. She knew exactly what she was doing today."

"Are you accusing her of causing that accident?"

"No, I'm flat out saying that she manipulated Abby to try and get us back together."

He frowned at me. "*Back* together? When were you together the first time?"

"That's not important. You know what Anna's doing."

"Yeah, and you should be thanking her. Do you really think you would have seen Abby again if it weren't for Anna? She's trying to help you."

"I thought you said she was innocent," I grumbled.

"Okay, well, not completely innocent. But she cares about you, so cut her some slack and let her go."

"Christ," I said, rubbing my hand over my face. "This is ridiculous. I don't even like Abby like that."

"You know what your problem is?"

"Please, enlighten me," I said sarcastically.

"You've got a really hot chick in there that likes you, but you're too stubborn to see it. And now that you've fucked it up, it's too late. And in just a few days, you're going to start missing her quirky attitude and her baked goods."

My jaw dropped in shock.

"Yeah, that's right. Jack told me about your baked goods. And now they're gone. What are you going to do about it?"

"I'm not going to try and date her based on baked goods."

"It shouldn't take you long to figure out that's not all you're missing out on."

He walked inside, leaving me outside the station. Fuck, what was I going to do? I did like Abby, but well enough to put in that much effort for her? I barely knew her. Okay, she was unusual to say the least. She wasn't like any other woman I knew. She was kind of funny, and definitely a hazard to anyone she met. But she also wasn't obsessed with herself. Maybe I was making a huge mistake by not taking a chance and getting to know her. What was the worst that could happen?

I walked back inside just as Jack was letting Anna out of her cell. "Try not to cause any more accidents today."

"Do I get to leave also?"

Jack looked over at me, but when I didn't say anything, he nodded to her. "Try not to hit anyone else today."

She walked out of the cell and sighed. "My car insurance is going to go up again."

I wanted to grab her as she passed and pull her into my arms, but I just couldn't bring myself to do it. She didn't even try to meet my eyes as she walked out of the station. I had a feeling whatever I had going for me before was now long gone.

"Nice going," Jack muttered. "You fucked up again."

"Let it go, Jack," I said defeatedly, walking over to my desk.

"That's it? You're not going to go after her?"

"And what would I say? I hit on her last night and now I'm going to pretend like I'm not a bastard and I want her for real? She'd never believe it."

"Then make her believe it. Stop dicking around and be a man."

"Would you let this go? It's over. I fucked it up and it's time to move on."

He sighed and plopped down in his chair angrily. It seemed that both of us were having trouble moving on.

By the end of the day, I was ready to get the hell out of here and just sulk in a beer, but Jack had other plans.

"Hey, poker night tonight."

I frowned. "It's not Friday."

He shrugged. "The guys called an impromptu poker night."

"And you're going," I said slowly.

He sighed, and I could see the indecision on his face. "I've got to move past this, right?"

The crinkle of his eyes and the way his shoulders sagged told me that he really wasn't ready to move on, but the fact that he was willing to try said a lot about him.

"Yeah, I could go for a poker night," I lied.

"Good," he nodded. "That's good. Do you want to drive together?"

It almost sounded like a desperate plea. He wasn't sure if he could do this. Maybe I could be like his wingman, there to save him if he was struggling tonight. I could make up some excuse about needing to leave so he didn't have to admit he wasn't ready for this.

"Yeah, save on gas, right?"

He looked so relieved, it almost broke my heart. We got in my car and headed out to Eric's house. We'd just had poker night here, so I wasn't sure why he was hosting again, but that was fine. Eric's house was more neutral ground, so hopefully it would be easier on Jack. On the other hand, Natalie had been killed at his house, so that was a point against it.

"So, you're sure you want to do this?"

"Yeah...you were right. I can't just spend my time wallowing. I need to move on."

"Does that mean you're going to start dating?"

He barked out a laugh. "Yeah, I'm thinking it's still too soon for that."

I pulled down Eric's driveway and parked. As we walked up the steps, I grinned as I remembered my fight with Robert after I baited him on Thanksgiving a few years back. Those were good times.

"What are you grinning about?"

"I was just remembering showing up here on Thanksgiving and pushing Robert and Anna together. We ended up in a huge fight."

He grunted. "Yeah, I remember the bruises all over your face. I still can't believe he kicked your ass."

"He may be a fancy suit, but he's still strong," I said defensively.

He knocked, unlike the rest of us, and waited for Eric to answer. "Jack, you showed up. It's good to see you."

"You see me in town almost every day," he retorted.

"Yeah, but...this is good, man." He pulled Jack in for a hug against his will, slapping his back. Jack pulled back and cleared his throat.

"Yeah, well, let's not get too excited. It's a poker game."

"Do I get a hug too?" I said jokingly.

He glared at me, motioning for me to come in. Everyone else was already there, sitting around the table, including Antonio. I was surprised when Jack sat down and didn't say a damn word to Antonio. He didn't even glance in his direction.

"So, five card draw?" Eric asked, shuffling the cards.

"Sounds good to me," Robert nodded, scooting back to walk over to the fridge. He grabbed a round of beers and handed them out before taking his seat again. We played a hand, but I could tell something was off.

"You suck tonight," Joe muttered to Andrew.

"Yeah, well, that happens when you piss off your woman."

"What'd you do this time?"

He snorted. "What didn't I do? I swear to God, I was just sitting there and she threw a knife at me. She said it slipped. Like that really happens."

"Are we back to thinking Lorelei's a murderer?" Will asked.

"Hell, I don't know."

"What actually happened?" Robert asked. "For legal purposes."

Andrew winked at him, pointing his finger. "I gotcha, Hunty." I heard a low growl come from Antonio, but Andrew didn't even notice. "So, I was sitting at the kitchen island and she's chopping up vegetables for dinner.

Something outside banged and she fucking threw the knife at me. Of course, I ducked because I didn't want to get hit by the knife, and that's when she started yelling at me for still thinking of her as a murderer."

"Do you?" Eric asked.

"Well, I didn't admit that to her," Andrew laughed. "I don't have a death wish. We had one too many close encounters when we first met."

"So, she got scared by a noise and you accused her of trying to kill you?" I asked.

"No, see I didn't *say* anything. She came to that conclusion all on her own."

"But you didn't correct her either."

"Well...no, but sometimes I still wonder. It's a legitimate concern of mine."

"You dumbass," Eric snapped, tossing a chip at him. "Now she thinks you don't trust her."

"Well, how do I fix that?"

"Earning back a woman's trust is hard," he sighed. I listened more intently because I had a feeling that whatever he was about to say might help me with my situation with Abby. "See, you have to prove to her that you're not scared of her. So, the next time she does something that freaks you out, stand your ground and prove to her that you think she's perfectly normal."

"Wait," I interrupted. "Does that apply to all kinds of trust issues?"

Eric frowned. "I guess generally speaking. That depends. You wouldn't pretend to not be afraid if, say...you fucked up the laundry."

I could see what he was saying. But how would I apply that to Abby? She didn't even want to see me.

"Okay, so as long as we're doing this whole sharing thing," Antonio grumbled. "Let's say that..." He cleared his throat, shifting in his seat. He obviously wasn't used to opening up. "Let's say that you asked a girl to marry you."

He glanced around at all of us. Josh had a huge grin on his face, but the rest of us were waiting for the doom and gloom part of the story.

"So, let's say you ask her to marry you, but you don't have the best of intentions."

"How does marrying someone not have good intentions?" Josh asked.

He shrugged slightly. "Perhaps the question was asked as a way to keep that person around."

Will burst out laughing. "Oh God, I wish something like that would have worked on Charlie."

"But it didn't?" Antonio asked.

"Charlie is the last person in the world that would accept a marriage proposal like that."

"Well, she was very understanding—"

"They always are," Eric said, "until they're not. You're not out of the dog house yet."

"So, how do I fix it? I already got her two dogs and a cat."

I frowned. That wouldn't work for me either. Abby already had six cats, and while she would probably take in another, I was pretty sure that her house just wasn't big enough for another. A dog on the other hand might eat all the cats and leave me with only the dog to contend with.

"What are you smirking about?" Jack asked.

"Nothing," I said quickly.

"You can't fix it with cats and dogs," Robert sighed. "Trust me on this one. Women can't be bought. Well, most women. I tried that with Anna, thinking if I bought her pretty things or showed her my pent-house, she would love that. But she would rather live in her shitty trailer than be bribed with everything I had."

"So, you had to show her that you just wanted her," I said, catching on to this whole relationship thing.

"Well, that and sing her a song in front of the entire town."

"But what about when you've done nothing wrong?" Joe asked. "Sofia's got it in her head that I'm after this Carrie woman. She threatened me with divorce if I ever saw her again! I didn't even do anything wrong. I said this woman looked good, but what was I supposed to say? I didn't want to say she was fat!"

"Did you explain that to her?" Will asked.

"And then some. I need some way to make it up to her. You know, sometimes guys just say stupid shit. It happens. But how do you take that back?"

I internally chastised myself. That's what I wanted to know.

Jack took a sip of his beer and finally joined in the conversation. "You just have to admit to her how you feel. Women don't respond to bullshit excuses. You can't tell them you didn't mean it or that you were an idiot. You have to be honest and open yourself up to her, even if it means you might get hurt."

I narrowed my eyes at him, suddenly realizing what this was all about. I tossed down my cards and glared at him. "You set this up, didn't you?"

Jack's brows crinkled in confusion. "What are you talking about?"

"This last minute poker game. Wanting to drive together. Getting along with Antonio," I snapped. "And suddenly you all have problems that you need answers to. *Woman problems*. You did this so I would figure out how to work past my issues with Abby."

He didn't say anything. I looked over at Andrew. "Did Lorelei really throw a knife at you?"

He swallowed hard and shook his head. "No, but she really does scare the fuck out of me."

"And you," I said, turning to Joe. "Sofia doesn't blame you at all, does she."

"No," he said sullenly.

I shoved back from my chair, shaking my head. "Christ, you're something else, Jack."

"Hey, I really did propose to Ciara to get her to stay," Antonio said as I stormed out the door.

16

CORDUROY

I couldn't believe what Jack tried to pull last night. I was up half the night thinking about his master plan to make me think of how to fix my relationship with Abby, my non-existent relationship. Well, screw them all. I didn't need their made-up advice. It wasn't like any of it was useful anyway. I didn't have anything deep and meaningful to tell Abby, I didn't need to get her any animals, and there was no trust to rebuild because there was never any to begin with. Hell, if anything, *she* needed to earn back *my* trust.

Since Abby's baked goods were no longer an option for me, I decided to just head to Mary Anne's and get something from there. Her food was really good, it just wasn't Abby's. I walked through the door and tried to put a smile on my face like I always did, but I just wasn't feeling it. I had fucked up big time, and it wasn't just the pastries I was missing out on.

When I pulled Abby off Anna yesterday, and got a mouthful of her half-braided hair, I couldn't help but notice how good her body felt against mine. It reminded me of that kiss. There was so much passion in her, but it was hidden under all that weirdness. Damn, I had to stop thinking about her. But as I walked into the bakery and smelled all the delicious food, all I could think about was that first taste of her cupcakes.

"Hey, Corduroy!" Mary Anne said cheerily. "I haven't seen you in over a week!"

"Uh..." Crap, I couldn't tell Mary Anne that I went somewhere else for her baked goods. I patted my stomach. "Trying to lay off the sweets."

Her face lit up. "You know, I have just the thing for you. I've got this new line of gluten-free scones and gluten-free muffins! You'll still get that flavor you want without all the sugars."

I gave her what I hoped was a smile. "That's great."

"I'll just package up some of your favorites. Do you need some for Jack too?"

"Yeah," I grinned. "The gluten-free stuff. We're going on a diet together."

"I just love that, you boys supporting each other."

She finished bagging it all up and handed it over, along with coffee. "Now, I know you and Jack like sugar and cream in your coffee some-times, so I'll make up a special drink for you today. This is made with heavy whipping cream and a sugar replacement."

"That's...perfect."

I walked with my faux-baked goods down to the station and plopped a coffee down on Jack's desk. "Mary Anne made it special for us today."

He looked up and frowned. "Why would she do that?"

"Because I couldn't tell her the real reason I haven't been getting her baked goods, so I told her I was on a diet." I tossed the bag of food on his desk. "It's gluten-free. And the coffee has cream and replacement sugar."

He grimaced and opened the bag. "What the hell is gluten-free?"

"No sugar, no carbs, no fun."

He shoved the bag back to me. "No thanks. I think I'll just go hungry until lunch."

"It can't be that bad. Mary Anne made it."

He leaned forward and stared at me. "Did you hear the no sugar part?"

I shoved my hand in the bag and grabbed a snack. "It can't be that bad."

"Then by all means, be the first to try it."

"I will," I said, stuffing a whole mini-scone in my mouth. It tasted like saw dust. There was no sweet flavor, no moisture to it...It was disgusting. Picking up his garbage can, I spit it out. I grabbed the coffee and chugged it, barely able to swallow it.

"How is it?" Jack asked.

"The coffee is better than the scone."

He picked up the cup and sniffed it. "It doesn't smell like it normally does."

"Well, she didn't use the same creamer."

He took a sip and grimaced. "Not my favorite, but not terrible."

"You'll need it to wash down the scone." I picked out a muffin, thinking that might taste better. "What the hell, I still need to eat, right?"

I stuffed the muffin in my mouth and chewed for what felt like ages. Jack did the same, both of us taking long sips of our coffee to wash it down. Neither of us were spitting it out. It was like a contest to see who could last the longest. After finishing my muffin, I swallowed down the rest of my large coffee and tossed the cup in the garbage, making a sour face. Jack did the same.

"What are we going to do tomorrow?"

"We could go to the diner," I suggested.

"Or you could go apologize to Abby."

"And what would we do about Mary Anne?"

"Look, this is like getting a new girlfriend. Eventually the old one finds out about the new one. There's no way around it."

"I'm not doing it. Your trick didn't work on me."

"Yeah, well, it didn't work for your shitty attitude either," he snapped. "Do you see me? I'm angry all the time now, and it's your fault. You ruined a good thing I had going for me."

"Yeah, it was all about you."

I sat down at my desk, but I was too angry to work. I needed to get out around town. But if I walked around town, I might run into Abby, and that would just ruin my day. So, I stayed at my desk for as long as I could, making up any excuse not to leave.

My stomach rumbled loudly, but not in a good way. My stomach muscles tightened painfully as a cramp tore through my abdomen. "Oh hell," I muttered under my breath. "What did she do to us?"

Jack shook his head. "I think it was the coffee."

As I struggled through the pain, I saw Jack in pretty much the same position as I was. And then it struck, that overwhelming feeling of needing to go right now or it would all come out in a fiery explosion. I shot up from my chair and raced around my desk, but Jack was faster. I dove for him, catching his shoe and making him trip. He fell to the ground and I started army crawling over him, just to get to the bathroom.

"Oh, fuck, get off me."

"I need the bathroom," I moaned.

"So do I, and if you don't get off me, you'll be wearing what's about to come out of me."

"That's fucking disgusting," I groaned, pulling myself to my feet. I hobbled over to the bathroom door, squeezing my butt cheeks together so nothing came out. Pain flashed through my stomach again and I doubled over, giving Jack just enough time to slip inside. He slammed the door in my face and then I heard him moan loudly. I banged on the door as loud as I could.

"Let me in!"

"Oh God, this is horrible!"

"It's about to be horrible out here!"

"Use the bathroom in the jail cell," he shouted.

It was just a urinal, but a drain was a drain at this point. I hobbled over to the cell and slammed the door shut, like that would give me a modicum of privacy. I pulled down my pants and sat down on the urinal as best I could. The relief came all at once, flying out of me like a water slide. My face was sweating and my heart was pounding, but the end was in sight. I hung my head as the pain finally ended.

"Holy shit. What is that smell?"

My head jerked up just as I saw Joe walk in. He stopped when he saw me sitting on the urinal and grimaced.

"Dude, what the fuck are you doing?"

I covered myself as best I could and pointed my finger at him. "This better not end up on the town page."

⁂

EVERY DAY AFTER THAT, I avoided Mary Anne like the plague. But after three days of no tasty treats, Jack was hounding me like crazy. He was going insane without his sugar fix.

"Look, we just walk in there and say that we're not on a diet anymore."

He laughed, slapping me on the shoulder. "I don't have to say shit. It's not my ass on the line."

He started to walk in, but I grabbed him by the jacket and pulled him back. "Do you really think that? You honestly think there'll be no blowback if you go in there and admit that you were sneaking someone else's baked goods?"

He winced, pulling my hand off his jacket. "Poor choice of words."

I nodded, remembering what happened the other day. "Good point."

Jack stormed through the doors, leaving me to chase him. I grabbed him again and lowered my voice. "We can just say that we're craving the sugar. She'll never know that we prefer someone else's muffins."

"Who's muffins?" Mary Anne's voice drifted over to us.

We both slowly looked up at the red-faced woman standing not ten feet away, glaring at us like she would kill us if we answered wrong.

"Who's what?" I stuttered out, actually in fear for my life even though I was the one with the gun.

"You've been eating someone else's muffins?"

I stared at her with my mouth in an O, completely unable to speak.

"No," Jack scoffed. "Of course not."

She narrowed her gaze on him. "You haven't been in here either, which means that both of you are getting your baked goods elsewhere."

"No, I swear—"

"Who is she?"

"How do you know it's a she?" I croaked.

"So there is someone else!"

Jack slapped me. "Way to go, asshole."

"What? She asked!"

"It's that woman you were seeing, isn't it? I heard she was showing up every morning at the station. I just assumed it was because you were seeing her. I didn't think you were hiding her from me like some dirty little secret!"

"Mary Anne, you know no one bakes like you do."

"Then why did you taste her muffins?"

My mouth was moving, but nothing was coming out. "I...She...I couldn't tell her no."

Her nostrils flared in disapproval. "I want a bake-off."

"A what?" Jack asked.

"You heard me. This weekend. High-noon. Right here. And if she doesn't show, I'll know that she's a gutless coward."

"It's just a muffin," I said, huffing out a laugh. "It's not worth getting this upset over."

Jack shook his head and groaned. "You really don't understand women, do you?"

I turned to him, shaking my head. "No! Why do you think I'm single?"

"Well, now you get to go tell Abby that you just got her into a bake-off."

"I can't tell her that! What the hell would I even say? And why would she agree to it?"

Mary Anne's lips turned up in a smile. "It's a matter of pride. She won't turn me down."

Jack spun me around to face him. "Carter, this is your in."

"My what?"

"Tell me honestly, do you like her?"

I shook my head, ready to deny it, but he slapped me across the face.

"Stop fucking around here. You like her. I know you do. Stop being the guy that only helps others get together, and go be the guy that gets the girl."

I swallowed hard. "I don't know how."

"Yes, you do. I already fucking told you."

17

ABBY

A pounding at my door woke me up way sooner than I wanted. I didn't have to work as early today, so I stayed up late binge-watching my favorite shows. But I was paying for it now.

"Go away," I muttered against my pillow.

"Abby! I know you're in there!"

I groaned and shoved my face into my pillow, drowning out all the noise. I flipped the sides of the pillow up to cover my ears and pretended Corduroy wasn't at my door. What did he want anyway? It wasn't like I would give him a booty call at whatever-the-hell o'clock it was.

I heard my front door open and then boots stomping down the hall, but still I didn't move. My comforter was keeping me so nice and warm, and there was no way in hell I was leaving this bed.

A gush of cold air hit my body as the covers were torn from me. I screeched and curled up in a tight ball to ward off the chill.

"What the hell are you doing?" I shouted.

"You didn't answer your door."

"So you let yourself in?"

He knelt next to the bed and held up my spare key. "It wasn't hard to find it in the planter."

I scowled at him. "You're mean."

"I'm mean?" He started laughing. "I told you to find a better hiding spot."

"Well, I moved it from the top of the door."

He nodded. "Yeah, and no one will think to find it in the planter. What were you planning on doing when the flowers die off in another week?"

"I would have found a new spot."

"I'm sure you would have, but I don't have time to talk to you right now about your terrible hiding skills."

"Why's that?" I asked, almost regretting it the moment I asked.

"Because you have a bake-off to prepare for."

I peeled an eye open and stared at him. "What are you talking about?"

He sat on the edge of the bed, but I shoved him off. He fell to the ground and glared at me.

"Was that really necessary?"

I laughed into my pillow. "It was funny. Serves you right for waking me up so early."

"It's eight o'clock."

"I didn't have to work until this afternoon. You're ruining my morning of sleeping in."

"I'll make it up to you."

"How?"

"By taking you out on a date," he grinned.

I coughed on my own spit, sure I had heard him wrong. "Why would you take me out on a date? Just to have sex?"

"No, because...because I miss you."

My eyelids blinked rapidly as tears filled my eyes. Sighing, he ran his hand over my face. "You know—"

Unable to hold it in, I started laughing so hard that my stomach cramped up. He watched me warily, which only made me laugh harder. "I'm sorry. It's just...you're so funny."

His brows pinched together. "What are you talking about?"

"Oh come on. You miss me? I know you better than that."

"You don't know me at all," he grumbled.

"And whose fault is that?" I asked, wiping the tears from my cheeks.

"I know I'm not the most...open person in the world, but—"

"Where is all this coming from?" I interrupted.

"Excuse me?"

"A week ago, you wanted nothing to do with me. Now you miss me and you're acting all...regretful."

"If you must know," he said, his voice softening. "I had a sort of... revelation at poker night."

I sat up and wiped at my eyes. "Oh, this I have to hear."

He gestured to the bed. "May I?"

"For this, you can lay down."

"Sitting is fine," he said, taking a seat beside me.

I didn't miss the way his eyes trailed over my bare legs as he sat, or the way he stared at my nipples for just a few seconds too long. And I didn't feel at all guilty for it. Let him eat it up. He wouldn't be touching me. He lost that chance.

"Well, the guys were talking about how they screwed up with their wives. One of them said he lost his wife's trust. And I sort of figured that I couldn't have lost yours since I never had it to begin with. That being said, I also realize I may have led you to believe I wanted more with you."

My eyebrows shot up. "This is fascinating."

"Can I finish?" I nodded. "So, then another one said that he proposed to his girlfriend, but that he only did it so she would stay. Obviously, that part doesn't apply, but he mentioned that he got her two dogs and a cat, but you already have six. So, bringing you more animals isn't going to do me any favors."

"I happen to love animals," I said, just to contradict him.

He shot me a look that told me to shut up until he was finished. "So, the last guy accidentally told another woman she was hot. He didn't actually like her, but he didn't want to hurt this other woman's feelings. Jack said that he should apologize to her and tell her how he really felt. He said that women don't believe the whole 'we're idiots' excuse."

"True."

"So, he said the guy had to be real with his wife."

I narrowed my eyes at him. "Is any of this true?"

"The whole damn thing. Well, technically, two of them were bull-shitting me. Jack set it up so I would have some revelation on how to apologize to you so you would take me back."

"Do you want me to take you back?" I asked skeptically.

He shrugged. "The most honest answer I can give you is that I really like you. I think you're hot, which you already know. I'm definitely attracted to you. That kiss..." He blew out a breath. "Best kiss I've ever had. And I would love to sleep with you."

My eyes popped in shock. "Wow, a winning compliment."

"And I know that if I want to find out if what I think I feel for you could go anywhere, I need to stop acting like a jackass and do what every other guy in the world does. So, I want to take you out on a date and see if maybe you'll not only forgive me for being a jerk, but also if this could actually go somewhere."

"If you're talking about it going to the bedroom—"

He grabbed my hand, linking our fingers. "I'm talking about us dating, seeing where things go, and possibly being in a relationship. If you don't run me over with your car first."

I tried to bite back my laugh, but it slipped out. "And sex?"

"I'm really hoping you'll want to have sex, I won't lie. But we'll see how things go. I won't expect it."

I frowned, biting the inside of my cheek. I wasn't sure where to go with this. Did men really have a massive revelation like this? It just seemed so odd.

"Is this just because you want me to do this bake-off thing?"

He lifted his shoulder in a half shrug. "No, I don't have to worry about that. Mary Anne said you would do it."

"How is she so sure?"

"She said it was a point of pride."

I was pretty sure I wouldn't win against a professional baker. She did this for a living. I just did it for fun. And I always screwed up when the pressure was on. Hell, I was a mess when things were on the line. Which meant that I would most likely lose.

I smiled at him. "I'll make a deal with you. If I win, I'll go out on one date with you."

"And if you lose?" he asked, his eyes searching mine.

"Then we don't go out on a date and we pretend that amazing kiss was just an amazing kiss."

He laughed slightly, looking down at our joined hands. "I guess I'll have to take my chances then."

❦

IT WAS the morning of the bake-off and I was so nervous. Technically, it was midnight. We were given all morning to bake as much as possible for today, though I wasn't sure why we needed so much food for just Jack and Carter.

My stomach kept flip-flopping, making me feel like I was going to throw up. It shouldn't matter if I won or lost, but somehow it did. If I won, I would be going out with Carter on a date, and I didn't know how to feel about that. I liked Carter, despite his asshole tendencies. If I lost, I wouldn't be going out with him. Also, somehow, I had it in my head that Mary Anne needed to win this bake-off. It would be bad for the town if she lost. Her bakery was the heart and soul of this community.

I ran to the bathroom, sure I was going to throw up. I leaned over the sink and took deep breaths to calm myself. "You can do this. You just need some sort of guidance." My gaze shot up to stare at my reflection in the mirror. "I need a list."

I ran out of the bathroom to my desk and grabbed a pen and paper. Making two columns, I started a pros and cons list. "Okay, pros."

1. Sexy

2. Charming

3. Caring

I tapped the pen against the paper and tried to think of anything else I could put under pros. The problem was, he was constantly making me change my mind. Yes, he was caring, but he was also completely insensitive. So, did that count as a pro?

4. Protective

5. Good kisser

I nodded and moved onto the cons list.

1. Complete ass

2. Insensitive jerk

3. Insults me constantly

4. Doesn't understand relationships or women

I stared down at the list and frowned. The pros outweighed the cons, but the cons were way worse than the pros. Although, I could really wrap all four cons into one major con. They were all basically connected.

Grunting in frustration, I tossed the paper down and stared up at the ceiling. I had to leave within fifteen minutes to get to the bakery, but I still didn't know what I should do.

Pimento jumped up into my lap and rubbed against me. I ran my hand over his back as I tried to come up with the answer. "I just have to see how things go throughout the day."

"*Meow*."

"You don't agree? You think I need to make a decision now?"

"*Meow*."

"Well, I can't just assume that I'm going to win or lose. But if I try to lose, then I already know how all of this turns out."

Pimento jumped off my lap and flipped up his tail at me. "Oh, like you have such good ideas?" I snapped.

Shaking my head, I sighed. "Great, I'm arguing with a cat. Thank God Carter isn't here to see this," I laughed to myself.

It didn't really matter at this point. I needed to leave, and sitting here thinking everything over wouldn't give me any more answers than what I had last night. I rushed out the door and headed to the bakery. In the dark of night, I could see the lights on in the bakery, indicating she was already there and prepping.

I rushed into the bakery and smiled at Mary Anne, but she didn't look happy. "Hey."

"So, you think your baking is better than mine?"

"Uh, I didn't say that. I like to bake, but I'm sure there's a lot I can learn from you."

"Well, I guess we'll find out at noon who the town favors."

"Wait," I stopped her. "The whole town? I thought this was just a Jack and Carter thing."

She burst out laughing. "Are you kidding? The minute I posted about this bake-off, the town page had an event posted and invitations were sent out. Practically everyone in town is coming. Why did you think we were coming in so early?"

My eyes widened in surprise and terror. "I have no idea. But...I don't bake for dozens of people. I only bake for me."

Her face softened and she jerked her head to the back. I followed her as she spoke. "Don't worry about it. I can be competitive, but honestly, this is bringing in a ton of business for me. Besides, it'll be nice to have someone else help me with stocking the bakery this morning."

"So, how do we do this? Do I make certain things and you make certain things?"

"No, we both make the same thing and then the town will vote on it."

"Okay. I guess we should get started."

She handed me an apron and grinned. "May the best baker win, but let's put on a good show for the town."

Over the wee morning hours, Mary Anne and I worked side by side, sharing tips and tricks for each of our recipes. She showed me how to quickly whip up large batches of baked goods instead of making just small batches at a time. I gave her my secret ingredient for my muffins, not caring at all when she slipped it into her own recipe. We laughed and cranked up some music to sing along with. It was actually pretty fun.

And when it was time to start the bake-off, I had come to my final conclusion. I needed to throw the bake-off in some way. Mary Anne was a great person and vital to this town. They needed her, so whether or not I wanted to go on a date with Carter, I had to lose for the sake of the town.

"Alright, are you ready to do this?" Mary Anne asked.

I nodded, then acted like I forgot something. "Oh! I didn't add the confectioners' sugar!"

I rushed into the backroom and sprinkled salt on all my baked goods, effectively ruining all of them. Then I went back up front and joined Mary Anne for the big announcement. The bakery was too small to host the event, so Main Street had been shut down and lined with tables for the baked goods. Crowds filled the sidewalks and the streets on either side of the tables. I hoped we had enough food for everyone. This was ridiculous.

"Ladies and Gentlemen," a loud, booming voice said over the loud-speakers.

I shifted in the crowd so I could see who was speaking. It was the man everyone in town had told me was aptly named Chili Man, though I wasn't sure why.

"Today marks the very first year for the town bake-off! Not many people would be daring enough to go up against Mary Anne and her famous baked goods, but today, we have a contestant that could knock Mary Anne out of her top spot, according to the sheriff's department! Honestly, I think a chili cook-off would have been better, especially since it's fall and that's more tempting than—"

"Shut it, Chili Man!" someone shouted.

"Yeah! We want the muffins!"

The crowd started screaming for food. Mary Anne looked at me and jerked her head for the back. Apparently, there were already helpers signed up to carry trays from the back of the bakery to the tables. We gave directions for what to take and where to take it, then stepped outside again and waited for the first taste testing.

"Just remember," Mary Anne leaned over, "make this good for them."

I frowned, not sure what she was talking about.

"Now," Chili Man said. "Before we begin, let's get a few words from our bakers."

Mary Anne beamed and stepped up to the mic. "Welcome every-one! It's so great for you all to come out and support us today. Although, I think in the end you'll wish this day never happened." She held her hand up to her mouth like she was going to tell them a secret. "I'll let you in on a secret...She forgot the butter."

The town gasped, as did I. I stomped my foot and walked up to her. "You know I didn't forget the butter. You handed it to me!"

She threw her head back and laughed. "You wouldn't know butter if you ate a whole stick."

The town started laughing, but I just stared at her. I didn't get the joke. Her eyes widened and she motioned discreetly for me to say something.

"Who would eat a whole stick of butter?"

She rolled her eyes and turned back to the crowd. "I've always been told I'm a plump woman. But it's just so hard to stop eating when I make such delicious food." Then she gestured to me. "You should never eat food from a skinny chef."

I shook my head, grabbing the mic. "I have a high metabolism!"

She pulled the mic away and whispered in my ear. "You really suck at the trash talk."

I jerked back and then leaned in to whisper in her ear. "That's what you wanted?"

"I told you to put on a good show."

I nodded slightly, letting her know I was on board. She held the mic up to her mouth again and continued.

"When we got started this morning, she couldn't figure out how to set the timer on the oven. I told her, *Just press the on button, dear.* I'm guessing that's not the only button she has trouble finding."

"Ooh," the town collectively said, like that was some kind of burn.

I scrambled to come up with an insult, but I was one of those people that never knew a good insult until ten minutes after it was needed.

"Yeah, well...you wouldn't...know a good muffin if you...ate it."

I frowned, running that through my head again. The town just stared at me, as did Mary Anne. Shaking her head, she turned to the crowd. "Let the bake-off begin!"

People started shoving at each other to get to the tables. Everyone had already tasted Mary Anne's baking before, so they instantly went to mine. I held back my smile as I saw people take their first bites. One by one, the grimaces formed on their faces and they started spitting out their food in the nearest trash cans. A few of them started shouting about how terrible my baking was, and this wasn't even a fair bake-off because there wasn't a good challenger.

Mary Anne leaned over to me. "Do you want to tell me how we made some of the same exact recipes, yet yours are disgusting and everyone is flocking to mine?"

I shrugged. "I have no idea what I could have done."

"Strange, isn't it?"

I nodded.

"What did you do to the muffins?"

I pretended to think it over. "Um...I know I added all the mix, and I put in the pinch of salt like you said—"

"You what?"

I tilted my head at her. "What?"

"You added salt?"

"Didn't you say to add salt?"

She pinched the bridge of her nose and sighed. "Why would you add salt?"

"Oh," I said, like a lightbulb came on. "That was for the Russian Spice cookies."

She shook her head at me. "You threw the bake-off, didn't you?"

"That doesn't sound like something I would do. Look at all these people, standing there making fun of me. Why would I purposely do that to myself?"

A small smile split her lips before she pulled me in for a hug. "You conniving bitch."

I chuckled against her shoulder. "I assume that's a term of endearment."

We both started laughing, but when I looked back at the crowd, I saw Carter frowning up at me. His shoulders were slumped in defeat, and then he turned and walked away, his head hanging low. I had saved one thing in this town, but ruined another.

❧ 18 ❧

CORDUROY

She lost. I couldn't believe it. I assumed she would win the bake-off. Her food was so good, so why was everyone spitting it out? I snatched one off the table and bit into it, but it was terrible. I spit it out, glaring at the offending piece of food. And then it hit me. She had been sabotaged. But by who? Would Mary Anne be so petty that she would ruin someone else's baking? I wasn't buying it. But maybe someone else didn't want us together.

"Are you alright?" Jack asked as he walked up to me.

My shoulder jerked as I laughed slightly. "I thought she would win."

"Yeah, so did I."

"I was counting on her winning."

He shrugged. "What's the big deal? So the town doesn't like her baking. More for you and me."

"You don't understand," I snarled. "I made a bet with her. If she won, she was going to go on a date with me."

"And if she lost?"

I shook my head, still unable to believe it. "We agreed that our great kiss would remain just a great kiss."

"Yeah, but you don't buy that, do you?" He laughed slightly. "I mean, no one would really choose not to date you based on a bet."

"You don't get it," I bit out. "I laid it all out there for her. I took your advice and told her how I felt, and she still didn't want to give me a chance. This was the only way, and now it's gone."

I ran my hand through my hair, angry at myself for thinking this might actually work.

"Why the hell did I listen to you? If I hadn't said anything, I would never know."

"And that would be better?"

"Than feeling like this? Fuck yes. You know, you had me thinking that if I pulled my head out of my ass, I could finally be happy," I said in frustration. "You made it sound like it would all be okay if I could just admit that I like her. Well, now I've done that. You're fucking right. I do like her, a hell of a lot more than I ever knew. The moment I told her how I felt, it was like...fuck, I don't know—"

"Like you knew you had to see if this was the woman for you," he said quietly.

I nodded, realizing that must have been how he felt about Natalie. "I'm such a fucking idiot."

"You're not an idiot."

"I knew I was attracted to her," I sighed. "I knew I wanted to kiss her, to sleep with her. How is it possible that I didn't see what I see now?"

"What *do* you see now? What changed?"

I didn't even know how to explain it. "She's...she's caring and sweet. She's funny and awkward, but..." I took a minute to think about it. "She makes me want to be the man for her, you know? When I think of her going home and leaving her door unlocked, I want to go check and make sure she's okay. And it's not because I want to protect her, but...I want to be the one there for her. Does that make sense?"

Jack grimaced. "In a twisted and idiotic way, yeah, it does. So, what are you going to do?"

"I don't know."

"You need to talk to her. You need—oh shit."

"What?" I asked, frowning as I looked in the same direction as him. My jaw clenched and my fists tightened as anger surged through me. That plaid jackass was on the stage with her, holding her and rubbing her back like he had a right to. And maybe he did. He didn't treat her the way I did, so maybe he was better for her. But as I watched them together, I knew there was no way in hell I could walk away from her, not even for a man more worthy.

Before I knew it, I was running at them. I'm pretty sure I was even screaming. I had lost my mind, running at the Plaid Wonder like I was about to murder him. I saw the moment he turned and his eyes went wide. He shoved Abby off to the side right as I tackled him to the ground off the platform. We landed on a table of fruit pies and I picked one up, upending it right on his face and then squishing it in.

Abby tugged at my arm, begging me to stop. "Carter, what are you doing? This is insane!"

Her words filtered into my mind long enough to tell me this was way beyond wrong. I got off him and stood there heaving like a jackass.

"You were supposed to be mine," I shouted, slamming my fist into my chest. "I know I fucked up, but you were supposed to give me a chance to make it right. He's not the one for you. I am!"

"Carter—"

"No, you don't get to do this to me. After I came to you and laid my fucking heart on the line, you don't get to act like we have nothing."

"Carter," she lowered her voice. "Can we talk in private?"

"So you can humiliate me alone? I think here is fine."

She huffed and pulled me away from people, hoping to gain some semblance of privacy. "I'm not seeing Jake."

"It sure as fuck didn't look like that to me."

"I'm serious. We went out and we had a great time. He's an amazing guy—"

I nodded. "Right, more amazing than me. I get it."

"You don't get it," she snapped. "It didn't work. We kissed and it was...like kissing a shoe."

"Hey," Jake said, sounding offended. "At least try to make me sound like a good kisser."

Abby heaved a sigh. "He was amazing. He did all the right things and it was passionate, but it's not like either of us enjoyed it."

"That's a little better," Jake grumbled.

"So, you're not with Jake?"

"No."

"Then...why did you make that bet?"

"Honestly? I wasn't sure you were really serious when you came to my house the other day. I know you meant well, but you could have changed your mind."

I narrowed my eyes at her. It was all beginning to make sense now. People spitting out her food when I knew damn well that her baking was better than Mary Anne's. And now she was admitting that she wasn't sure about me. Fuck, I was an idiot.

"You threw the bake-off."

"I did, but not for the reasons you think," she whispered.

"Then why?"

She glanced around and then back at me. "Because Mary Anne's bakery is a huge part of this town. I didn't want anything to happen where she might lose business."

My eyebrows shot up in surprise. "So...you didn't lose because you don't want to date me."

She dropped her gaze and sighed. "Carter, this was never going to work between us. I know you think you want it to, but that's just not who you are."

"You don't know anything about me," I seethed.

"I know that you want to fuck me. I know that's all you see when you look at me. You never took the chance to get to know me. You judge me based on the decorations in my house or the number of cats I have. Tell me, what about that should make me think you seriously want to date me?"

I stood there, unsure of what to say. She was right. I had totally fucked everything up, and I didn't even know it.

"Goodbye, Carter."

I watched her walk away, feeling like my whole world was crashing down. Not because she was walking away, but because I realized I had done this to myself over the years. I had distanced myself from any relationship just so I didn't have to feel anything. I hadn't thought it was important. But now the one woman I wanted was walking away, and it was because I had shown her I couldn't be real with her.

"Are you okay?" Jack asked as he walked across the street.

I shook my head. "What the hell am I supposed to do?"

"You go after her. You prove to her that you want her."

I scoffed. "I already tried that, Jack, and look at where it got me. I'm standing in the middle of the street and she just walked away from me because she doesn't think I actually want to be with her."

"So, go prove her wrong."

"What for?" I snapped. "So she can spit in my face again?"

"So you don't lose out on something good. Trust me, you don't want to miss this opportunity."

"Oh, is this the part where you tell me about how much you loved Natalie and how now it's all gone? I know that already, but I'm not you and Abby's not Natalie."

He nodded, shoving his hands in his pockets. "No, you're right there. Because Natalie and I just let it flow between us. We weren't cowards. You're letting her walk away and you're throwing up your hands without even fucking trying. Do you really think relationships aren't work? You have to fight for her with everything you have."

"I already fought," I said defeatedly. "And I lost."

I WAS ROUGHLY GRABBED from my bed at some point in the night. I didn't know what the hell was going on, and since I had gotten drunk before I came to bed, I was out of it for way too long. I felt my hands jerked together and tied with rope before my brain kicked in that something was wrong. I struck out with my foot at my assailant, but it was no use. Both of my legs were quickly grabbed and tied together also, and then the ties at my feet and hands were roped together.

And it was only after I was tied up that I realized something like a bag was over my face. I could smell the alcohol on my breath, filling the small amount of air around me as I was tossed over someone's shoulder and hauled out of my house. The sharp shoulder dug into my stomach, making me feel like I was about to throw up everything I drank. I had to sober up. There was no way in hell I could fight off these fuckers if I was still drunk.

"Put him in the trunk," a gruff voice said.

I winced as my shoulder hit the edge of the car before I was not so gently set in the trunk of a car. If I had to guess, I'd say it was a mid-size car based on the interior size. The trunk slammed shut and then tires kicked up gravel as we pulled out of my driveway.

I wiggled my head around, trying to get the damn sack off my head, but it must have been tied on me or something. And the more I moved my head, the dizzier I felt.

"Fuck," I grumbled as my stomach roiled. I really hoped I didn't throw up in the trunk.

I needed to focus. I couldn't get out of here, but I could try and figure out who the hell took me. I was just a small town deputy-sheriff. Who the hell would want to take me as a hostage?

The mafia.

Fuck, the mob must have found out about Carly or Antonio staying in town, and now they were after us, but why? Was this for our part in helping Carly out when she first came to town? Her family was dead. Antonio was the last living family member, so if this was mob-related, it had to be because of Antonio. Unfortunately, I didn't know much about his business, and now I was regretting it. Maybe if I knew a little more about what happened with him, why he came here, I would know who the fuck had kidnapped me.

I squeezed my eyes shut and tried to remember anything about the time Antonio came here. I knew he left Jo here and took off with Ciara. And she was part of the mafia too. It was entirely possible this had to do with her, but again, what the fuck did that have to do with me?

The longer we drove, the more I realized just how wide-spread this could go. If they took me, they most likely wanted to get rid of the law enforcement presence, which meant they took Jack also. Fuck, I hoped he was okay. And what about Brody? Did they have him too, or did they leave him behind? How long would it take for someone to realize we were missing and Brody was all alone?

I sighed and rested my head against the floor of the trunk. Thank

God Abby had turned me down last night. She might have been with me, and then she would be wrapped up in this too. I never thought what I did for a living would affect her in any way. We were from a small town. Shit like this just didn't happen around here. Not until Josh disappeared. It all started then, and since that day, our town was plagued with tragedy.

The car slowed to a stop and the trunk popped open. If I had any way to fight, I would have, but instead, I was lifted out of the trunk and tossed on the ground. What I wasn't expecting was the car to drive off and leave me here tied up. Silence filled my ears, letting me know I was truly alone.

"Hello?" a small voice cried out.

Frowning, I shifted around on the ground, trying to figure out where it was coming from. "Who's there?"

"Carter?"

"Abby?"

"Oh my God, what's going on?"

I had no clue. Why the hell would anyone take both of us? It didn't make any sense. I could hear it in her voice that she was on the brink of a breakdown. I had to keep her calm so I could get us out of this. But I didn't even know what this was.

"Are you okay?"

"Yeah," she cried. "I'm tied up. I can't...I can't..."

"Abby, just stay calm, okay? I'm gonna work my way over to you."

"I got the bag off my head. Just follow my voice. I'll help you get over here."

I started wiggling across the ground like a worm to reach her. Every once in a while she would tell me to move a little to the left or right. It felt like it took forever, but when I was finally there, I was just relieved I was with her.

She nuzzled her face against my chest, or what I assumed was her face... "Abby, can you get the bag off my head?"

"I'll try."

She shifted until she was higher up against my body. Her teeth nipped at the bag, and then my skin. I flinched back.

"What the hell are you doing? I said take the bag off, not try to bite my neck."

"Well, it's not exactly easy with my hands tied behind my back."

I huffed in irritation, but not at her. I was just pissed we were taken. She tugged at the bag, finally getting it up over my chin, but then jerked too hard and it caught on my nose.

"Ow, ow, ow!"

"Sorry. Okay, let me move some more."

She wiggled up further and then grasped the bag between her teeth again. Finally, the bag was off and I could see her tear-streaked face. She instantly pressed her lips to mine, which took me by surprise. But then I realized she was just happy to be alive and it had nothing to do with seeing me.

"What happened to you?" I asked calmly.

"I was just sleeping and then I heard a noise, but I'm a light sleeper, so that's not uncommon. And it was like there were footsteps in my house. I mean, humans attached to the footsteps, and then they were walking toward my bedroom. I grabbed the lamp on the table, but Temperganda jumped at the guy and grabbed him by the balls with her teeth. And then another man ran in the room, and he tripped over the guy on the floor and I swung the lamp at him, but I tripped on the cord before I could hit him. Then I was being tied up and all the cats attacked, but it must not have been enough," she said in one long-winded breath.

"Did you see their faces?"

She shook her head furiously. "No, they had on face masks."

"What about a scent? Maybe cologne or something?"

"Why would I know that?" she screamed hysterically. "Do you think I stopped to smell them so I could buy you a bottle?"

"No, I was thinking you might have recognized their scents so we could identify them," I snapped back.

"What? Am I a dog? Am I going to track them with my nose?"

I sighed heavily and tried to refocus. "Okay, we just need to think. They took both of us, which must mean that we saw something."

"Wait, who saw us?"

"The mafia."

She gasped, staring at me with wide eyes. "You think the mafia took us? But I don't even go downtown!"

"Abby, Antonio and Carly used to be part of the Italian Crime Family in Chicago. Someone must have realized they were here. Up until now, everyone thought they were dead."

"But...if they were after Antonio and Carly, why would they take us?" she asked in confusion. I really hated explaining things to women.

"Because I'm the deputy-sheriff. For all we know, Jack was taken to a separate location. Or they could be on their way with him now."

"And what about me?"

"They must have seen us together and decided to take both of us, in case you knew something you weren't supposed to."

"But I didn't even know they existed until you just told me!"

"Would you like me to go flag them down and explain that to them?"

"Yes!" she shouted.

"Abby, we've been taken by the mob. They don't care if you saw anything or not. They've taken you and now they can't let you walk away. Do you get that?"

She stared at me for a moment and then said, "No!"

Taking a calming breath, I refocused. "We need to get out of these bonds. If they come back here and we're still here, we're as good as dead."

"But why didn't they just kill us to begin with?"

"That's something I intend to find out," I said with as much steel in my voice as possible. "This is going to be easy, okay? We'll get out of these bonds and then we'll hike out of here."

"But we don't know where here is!"

"Abby, you have to stop shouting. The more you do that, the more likely it is that someone will come to shut you up." She sniffed back some tears and nodded. "That's a good girl."

I looked her over, seeing how she was tied up at the feet with her hands behind her back, while I was tied in the front. "Alright, Abby, I need you to use your teeth to try and undo the rope around my hands. Then I can untie you."

"Why don't you untie me and then I can untie you?"

"Because if they come back, one of us needs to be able to fight them off."

"Do you have your gun on you?" she asked.

"No."

"Then logically speaking, I have just as good a chance as you do."

"I'm bigger than you."

"I'm scrappier than you."

"You don't have your cats with you," I countered.

She shut her mouth and sighed. "Fine."

I stood up as she got to her knees and pressed her mouth against the rope on my hands. She breathed hard as she struggled to free my hands, but the longer her mouth was near my crotch, the harder I got. She started rubbing her chin against me as she worked, each time she moved, my cock pushed harder against my boxers.

"You know, I think you're right. I think I should undo your hands first," I croaked out.

"Why?" she mumbled against my hands. "It's hard, but I'm getting there."

I rolled my eyes and shifted slightly. "Abby—"

She shifted again, rubbing even more against my cock. "I've almost got it. Just another minute and I'll have you free."

I squeezed my eyes shut and prayed that she finished soon, or I would be finishing right in her face.

"Got it!" she shouted, pulling the rope out of the loop. With a few more tugs, the rope was loose enough that I could finish pulling the ropes off. I sat down and pulled them off my ankles. I was fucking freezing out here in just my boxers.

"Alright, turn around."

"I'm the one tied up. How about you walk around me," she snapped.

"Geez, no need to get testy. We have a long night ahead of us."

I knelt down and started on her hands, but then noticed she was wearing one of those sexy negligées that only came down to right past her ass. My hand skimmed her leg...just to see.

"Abby, why the fuck did you wear a thong?"

She huffed. "Seriously, was I supposed to stop and ask them to let me change my underwear first?"

"Yes!" I snapped, even though I knew it wasn't logical.

"If I had known I was going to be kidnapped, don't you think I would have put on something warmer?"

"Like your orange scarf?" I muttered.

"Hey, I like that scarf."

"Well so do I!" I growled.

I finished undoing her hands and undid the rope around her feet. Finally, free, I grabbed her hand and started running toward the trees.

"Shouldn't we be running to the road to flag someone down?" she asked.

"Only if you're hoping the mafia won't be driving on it."

"They can't be the only ones out," she muttered.

"Abby, it's the middle of the night. We're in the middle of fucking nowhere. I don't have my phone. I don't have a GPS. So, I'd like to go into the forest and take my chances in there instead of taking my chances that we'll get a bullet if we go to the street."

"But why did they keep us alive? If they took us, and this is the mafia, then wouldn't we be fish food by now?"

I ran my hand through my hair and sighed. "Fuck, I don't know. Maybe they needed to question us."

"In the middle of nowhere?" she asked incredulously.

"Look around you. Do you see all the possible burial spots? Hell, they wouldn't even have to bury us. They could just dump us in the woods and a coyote would eat us by morning."

"Well, that certainly makes me feel better about going into the woods!"

She stomped off by herself, looking all over the ground for something.

"What are you looking for?"

"A stick."

"For what?"

"To make a spear, of course!"

I scratched my head, trying to understand her logic. "Is this for the coyote or the mafia?"

"Either one. The way I see it, if we come across a coyote, we'll just stab it to death. And if we come across the mafia, same principle."

"Except the mafia has guns, and a coyote has forty-two teeth that could tear us to shreds."

"Well, it's better than standing here completely defenseless and just hoping I don't get killed."

19

ABBY

I ignored Carter and headed off to find more sticks. I didn't care what he said. I was getting as many sticks as possible to defend myself with.

"We should be finding a way out of here, not looking for useless weapons."

"You said we couldn't go to the road because the mafia might find us. Okay, I'll agree with you on that point, but there is no way I'm going into the woods without a gun or a machete or…a steak knife!"

He grabbed me by the arm as I bent over to pick up another stick. "Listen to me," he jerked me hard in his grasp. "This is serious. You don't know what it was like the last time we had to deal with the mafia. We don't have time to mess around. We have to find a way out now or we'll die out here."

I nodded, not really because I believed that it wasn't important to have weapons, but because he seemed so adamant. "Alright. We'll do this your way."

"Good. Now, if we head east, that should take us further away from the road, assuming the road doesn't curve in that direction."

"And deeper into the wilderness where we might get eaten by a coyote."

"I'm in boxers and you're in lingerie. I'm thinking coyotes are not our biggest problem right now. It's cold and as soon as the adrenaline wears off, we're going to feel the cold a hell of a lot more than we are now. We need to keep moving."

"Why don't we just take this road here? It's a dirt road, so it's not a main road."

"It's still a road. Will you just let me do the thinking?"

"Lead the way," I swept out my hand.

I followed him as he cut his own path into the woods. Call me crazy, but I just didn't think this was the smartest idea right now. If anything, it seemed like a good way to get ourselves killed. On the other hand, I wasn't exactly a country girl. He had to know a lot more about surviving than I did.

"Do you think they got to Jack?" I asked after a few minutes.

"I hope not. His kid has been through enough."

"Ow!" I shouted when I felt something sharp dig into the bottom of my foot. "Holy monkey balls, that really hurt!"

"Will you lower your voice? We're trying not to draw attention to ourselves."

"Well, maybe if you offered me a ride on your back, I wouldn't have stepped on the really sharp stick, proving my point that sharp sticks hurt people!"

"But they don't hurt coyotes!"

"Now who's shouting?"

"Fuck," he swore, turning around to continue walking. "Let's just keep going."

"Fine."

I was freezing and my feet were killing me. Whoever these assholes were that snatched us were going to get a serious can of whoop-ass unleashed on them. Not by me, but they'd still get their comeuppance.

I tried my best to keep up with Carter, but damn, even in just boxers in the freezing cold, he moved like we were just going for a hike. It was annoying. I started blowing out breaths of air just so I could watch the puffs float around in front of me for entertainment. I watched as they moved off to the right on the slight breeze blowing through. And that's when I saw it.

It looked like a light of some kind. "I spy with my little eye—"

"You're not serious right now, are you?" Carter snapped.

"Don't you want to know what I see?"

He spun around and scowled at me. "No, what I want to do is find a way out of here."

"You know, for someone that practically spouted his undying love to me yesterday, you sure are being a dick now."

"Well, that tends to happen when a woman stomps on your heart."

"I didn't stomp on it. I didn't even do a tap dance on it," I laughed. "You only wanted sex!"

"I wanted you!" he snapped. "Why is that so hard to believe?"

"Does it really matter? I think we have more important things to think about than whether or not you really wanted me."

"You're the one that brought it up."

"Whatever."

"Just keep your mouth shut and let me figure this out."

"Right, because only a man could get us out of this."

"Better than leaving it to you."

"And how exactly did you end up here anyway, Mr. Lawman?"

He scowled at me, obviously irritated that I pointed out the obvious. "I was drunk."

"You were drunk? That's your great excuse?"

"And what's yours?"

I shrugged. "I have no idea how they got in. I put my key in a really good hiding spot this time."

"Yeah? Where's that?"

I crossed my arms over my chest and smirked at him. "I hid the key in my light fixture."

He barked out a laugh, throwing his head back. "Did you turn the light on to check if it could be seen?"

"Of course I did!" I said indignantly. "How else was I going to make sure I could see it if I needed it?"

"But you didn't stop to think that others could see it too, did you?"

I opened my mouth to argue with him, only to realize he had a good point.

"Yeah, they walked right into your house. They didn't even need a key."

"Well...at least I'm not...you know what? You suck!"

"Great comeback. I'll have to write that one down."

"Ugh!" I stomped past him. Now he could find the damn light himself. Why was it that men always thought they were so much smarter?

"Where are you going?" he shouted.

"This way!"

"You don't even know where you're going," he chastised.

Spinning around, I got in his face. "I know exactly where I'm going, and if you weren't so bullheaded, you would have listened to me earlier when I was trying to tell you. But no," I said dramatically. "You're a man and you couldn't possibly listen to a woman."

"Not a woman that can't find her own house, or leaves her keys in the most obvious places!"

"Then tell me how such a woman could find a house," I goaded, pointing to where I had seen the light on just a few minutes ago, "with a light shining in the window if she was so stupid!"

His gaze shifted in the direction of my finger. I watched with pride and a little bit of glee that I had pulled one over on him. His head tilted slightly as he squinted into the night to see the light in the distance.

"That's what you..."

"I spy with my little eye? Yeah, that's what I was trying to tell you."

He cleared his throat as he looked at me sheepishly. "Well, that was a good find. We should get there before we freeze."

He strode past me as if I hadn't just proven what an ass he was. "That's it?"

"Yep," he said without turning back.

I shook my head in disbelief. "What an ass."

"OH, THANK GOD!" I shouted in relief when we broke the tree line and the house appeared in front of us. "Do you think they'll let us in dressed the way we are?"

"It'll be hard to convince them I'm a deputy-sheriff dressed this way, but I'll do whatever I have to. My balls are freezing."

"My nipples feel like they could cut glass right now."

"Don't remind me," he muttered. "Why do you think I've been walking in front of you the whole time?"

"Um...because you knew the way?"

He turned to me and grabbed me by the arms, pulling me against him. My eyes widened as I felt his erection pressing against me. "Because even in the cold, my body still wants you. I couldn't stand to walk behind you and see your ass swaying in front of me without doing anything about it."

I swallowed hard, a little turned on by the situation. "Oh."

"Oh," he nodded. Then, as if it pained him to do so, he released me and stepped back. "Let's just go see if they'll let us in. Or at the very least, use a phone."

I followed him to the door and waited as he knocked. Now that we weren't walking, I was feeling the cold seep into my bones more and more. He pounded on the door again, but still no one answered.

He stepped back and walked around the house, then came back to my side. "No one's home."

I groaned, rubbing my hands up and down my arms. "I'm so cold," I whined.

He tried the doorknob and looked at me in surprise when it was unlocked. We hurried inside, shutting the door behind us. I rushed over to the fireplace, holding my hands out in front of me.

"They must not have gone far. No one would leave a fire burning out here."

"I don't care why they did it. I'm just glad they did."

He walked over to the counter and picked up some food off a plate, sniffing it. "This is fresh."

"Where do you think they went?"

"I have no idea, but I'm guessing they're not going to like it when they show up and find two half-naked people in their house."

"Then they shouldn't have left the door unlocked."

"Let's see if we can find some clothes in the bedroom."

I nodded and followed him through the house, looking into different rooms until we came across the bedroom. When he opened the door, he stopped immediately, making me run into him.

"What's going on?"

"I'd like to know," he muttered.

I ducked under his arm and went into the bedroom, my eyes wide as I took in all the candles that were lit and the rose petals on the bed. In the center was a giant heart with the letters C and A.

Slowly turning, I stared up at Carter with all the affection in the world. "Did you do this for me?"

"What?" he snapped.

"C and A. Carter and Abby. Did you do this?"

"You think I got us kidnapped as a romantic gesture?" he asked incredulously.

"Well, how else do you explain this?"

"I have no fucking clue."

I smiled as I walked over to him. He was so sweet, even if he did something really insane to get my attention. "I can't believe you created this whole fiasco just to get me alone."

"I didn't do this!"

I nodded at him, knowing he probably didn't want to admit to being such a romantic. "Well, whoever did really set the mood for us. Rose petals on the bed, candles lit all around the room..."

"It's a fucking fire hazard."

I gasped when I spotted the champagne chilling on the side table. "You even got champagne!"

"Abby, how many fucking times do I have to tell you? I didn't do this!"

"Well, who else would do this? You really expect me to believe that a random person set this up with our initials?"

"Maybe it's for someone else," he argued.

"Or it's for us," I encouraged.

"Who the hell would kidnap us, drag us out to the middle of fucking nowhere, drop us at a location where we could easily get lost, only to hope we would find this cabin that they left a fire for us and rose petals on the bed?"

"Don't forget the champagne."

He threw up his hands angrily. "Yes, let's not forget about the champagne!"

"It's so sweet," I said, still grinning like an idiot. "You know what would have made this perfect?" I ran my hand up his chest, leaning in to whisper in his ear. "Chocolate covered strawberries."

"Yeah, that would have been perfect. Maybe you should talk to our kidnappers about that."

"I can't believe you're still denying this."

He grabbed me by the arms and shook me. "Abby, listen to me. Why would I have myself kidnapped almost completely naked and dropped off in the middle of the wilderness in the cold? This is a coincidence! A really bad coincidence, but it's still a coincidence. I didn't lay out these candles, and I wouldn't do that anyway because it's a fire hazard. And these petals," he stormed over to the bed, grabbing a handful. "I didn't do this either. In fact, I fucking hate flowers. What man in his right mind would want to fuck on flowers? They'd get stuck in all the wrong places! And no man drinks champagne."

"But...you did it for me."

"I hate to break it to you, but no man does anything like this for a woman. This is insanity, and whoever did this was most likely a woman, but I'm telling you, none of this is for us."

I frowned, a little disappointed at this turn in events. "So, you really didn't do this for me?"

"No!"

"So, we really are on the run from psychos?"

"Yes!"

"And this is just some beautiful...setup that we stumbled upon?"

"Yes!" he shouted, like he was relieved that I finally got it.

My shoulders drooped in sadness. "For a moment, this was a really beautiful thing you'd done."

"I didn't do it!"

"You still didn't have to ruin it," I muttered, walking out of the room. I didn't want to see my fantasies become someone else's reality.

It was so depressing. Walking into the kitchen, I grabbed a piece of food off the plate and shoved it in my mouth.

"What are you doing? You don't know if that's safe to eat."

"I'm eating away my feelings," I mumbled around my food.

He snatched a folded piece of paper off the counter and frowned. "What's this?"

"I don't know. Maybe it's a note from whoever lives here, taunting us with their romantic notions and good food."

He opened the folded note and read through it, shaking his head. "Fuck," he whispered.

"What? What does it say?"

He shoved it into my hands.

WORK SHIT OUT. *I'll pick you up in two days.*
   Jack

"WAIT...WHAT DOES THIS MEAN?"

He started pacing the room, angrily swiping his hand through his hair.

"Carter, what does this mean?"

"It means that the mafia isn't after us."

"They're not?"

"No, Jack was behind this."

"He kidnapped us! But...but he's the sheriff. That's illegal!"

"Not only that, but he stranded us out here."

"Well...at least we don't have to worry about murderers, right?"

His glare cut through me like knives. "I would have preferred the murderers."

20

CORDUROY

Fuck, why had I said that? Her face dropped, making this situation even worse. It was bad enough that I ruined her fantasy, but then I had to go and throw gasoline on the fire. I was such a shithead, but I was hungover and still pissed that she threw away my attempts to actually try to date her.

"Wow, okay. I guess I'll just be in the other room and leave you alone to wallow."

"Probably for the best," I muttered under my breath as she stormed past me.

Then she spun around and pointed her finger at me.

"Or not," I said, getting ready for her onslaught.

"You know, I'm a good catch, and if you weren't such an ass, you would have seen that from the beginning. You thought I was good enough to sleep with, but apparently, I'm just too stupid for you."

"I didn't—"

"Don't even deny it. All those little jabs at me were just mean. And still, I thought there was a decent man under this...slab of beef."

"Slab of beef?"

"Yes, you have a nice body," she said snottily. "I don't think I need to tell you that. It's obvious, okay? All the girls in town know what a catch you are."

"Really?" I grinned cockily.

"Yeah, and there's that stupid smirk that I want to slap off your face. That right there is why I wouldn't give you a chance."

"Because I smirked you wouldn't give me a chance?"

"Because of that and your stupid, hot body," she said, almost prowling toward me. "You think you're so hot. You *know* you're so hot, and therefore, you don't need to consider that you might hurt someone else's feelings."

"That's not fair."

"Really? So, if I were to kiss you right now, you could take my feelings into account? You could do the decent thing and tell me no because you know it won't go anywhere? Or would you sleep with me and then drop me like a hot potato because you could have someone better?"

I wrapped my arm around her and pulled her against me. "I would fucking kiss you and then take you in that bedroom and fuck you hard. But I wouldn't let you go after that, and I wouldn't walk away out of decency."

"Just like I thought."

I growled at her. "You still don't listen. I wouldn't let you go because I can't." I slammed my mouth down on hers, kissing her hard. Tearing my lips from hers, I slid my hand down to her ass.

She tore herself away from me and walked over to the wall, resting her hands and head against it. I watched as she warred with herself, not wanting to give in to me, but also needing to know what it could be like between us.

"I don't just want to fuck you. I want all of you, lost keys, bad directions, crazy cats, and all," I said as I stepped up behind her and slid my hands onto her waist. I slowly slid them up her body, taking her negligée with me. She didn't lift her arms like I hoped. She needed more convincing that I just wanted her.

Pressing myself against her, I pulled her hair off her neck, slipping it over the other shoulder. A burning need filled me as I pressed my lips to her neck, sucking her perfect skin into my mouth. She hissed, pressing back into me, inviting me to take more. Sliding my hand up, I cupped her breast as I slid my tongue along the curve of her neck. She tilted her head to the side, making me crave her even more. I felt her hands on my hips as she guided the fabric down my legs. I yanked my boxers the rest of the way down and pressed my cock against the seam of her ass.

She rocked back against me, moaning as the flame between us grew. I was drowning in desire for her, needing to feel my cock inside her wet pussy, ready to feel the pressure mount as my cock filled her. Gripping the fabric between her breasts, I tore it from her body. She gasped, tossing her head back as her breasts pushed out. I cupped her breasts, pushing the head of my cock between her ass cheeks, sliding in and out of her wetness.

I nuzzled my face against her cheek, whispering how much I wanted her. Her eyes fluttered shut as she spread her legs, allowing me to slip inside her. Her body quivered as I slowly pumped in and out of her. I was falling hard, reveling in the feel of her wrapped around me. She grasped my hands, squeezing them around her breasts.

Her breathing became ragged as I thrust inside her. I could feel her body shaking as she struggled to stay upright. I wrapped my arm around her chest, pressing my other hand against the wall as I started fucking her harder. She intertwined her hand with mine, bracing herself as I slammed into her. Sweat slickened my chest as I pressed against her back, surrendering to what my body needed. Every thrust, every quiver of her body sparked more desire inside me.

She tossed her head back, biting back a moan as her pussy clamped down on me. I roared as I came hard inside her, slamming into her as my cum filled her.

"Carter!" she cried out, her voice ragged as she squeezed my hand.

I was shaking by the time my cock went soft. Pressing my face to her back, I kissed down her spine, pulling myself from her body. I slid my hand up her leg, catching my release, then sliding it through her pussy. She started rocking against my hand, shuddering as I flicked her clit. I could feel my cock swelling again, ready to slide inside her once more, but this was about her. I thrust my fingers inside her, pumping in and out torturously slow. With her hands pressed against the wall, she panted harder, pushing back even more, taking what she needed from me.

I grazed her clit again, and that was all it took for her to gush in my hand. Her legs shook as she panted hard, falling into my arms from her orgasm. I caught her and scooped her up in my arms, carrying her into the other room. Laying her down on the bed, I slid between her legs, looking into her eyes as I pushed inside.

Her hands framed my face as she stared at me in confusion. "What happens when this is over?"

"Who said anything about this being over?"

IT DIDN'T FEEL like any of this was real. After a whole night of fucking, we slept the morning away, only getting up when we needed to eat. I finally had her where I wanted her. Now I just had to figure out how to keep her. If there was one thing I realized after last night, it was that I had completely destroyed her trust in me. I sort of felt like she was two sides of the coin at any given time. One minute she was naive and quirky, and the next, she was this seductress that awakened something inside me, leaving me needing more from her. I had a feeling there was some sort of balance to her. I just hadn't found it.

"Look," she waggled her eyebrows as she walked back into the bedroom, holding a tray. "They did leave chocolate covered strawberries."

My eyes trailed down her body that was covered only with a sheet wrapped tightly around her chest. She lifted the fabric enough to kneel on the bed. Grabbing the tray from her, I wrapped my arm around her and pulled her into me, kissing her hard as I blindly set the tray on the bed, hoping it didn't fall to the ground. Rolling her over, my lips slid over hers as my fingers caught in her tousled hair.

My cock pressed against her hip, longing to slide inside her again, but with the sheet between us, I couldn't get to her and she seemed to need the break. Smiling down at her, I brushed the hair away from her face.

"So, do you believe me now?"

"About what?" she asked, her eyes burning into mine.

"That I want you," I said, leaning down to kiss her. "That I'm not walking away." I pressed another kiss to her lips. "That I need more than a night with you," I whispered as my lips skimmed down her neck. My tongue traced the curve of her breasts, single-minded in its pursuit.

She chuckled, trying to pull my head out from between her breasts. "Yeah, that's really convincing."

"Hey, it's not my fault that you have such a nice body. This slab of beef has no choice but to go after it's favorite toppings."

"Oh God," she groaned. "You're terrible."

"When Jack picks us up tomorrow, I need to know that you're not going to pretend none of this happened."

"Why are you so concerned about this?"

"I have this feeling you're going to push me away, because you think I'm not serious about this."

She sat up, essentially pushing me off her as she held the sheet to her chest. "What are you expecting out of this?"

"I don't know," I shook my head. "I'm not sure it'll go anywhere."

She scoffed, pushing her legs off the bed, but I pulled her back by the waist. "Don't start putting words in my mouth. I'm trying to be honest and realistic here. We got off to a weird start. I want a chance with you, but we both know that we can't just make a relationship out of this weekend."

"So, you want to date."

"Exactly. And I haven't really done that in a long time, so I'm going to need some help on that."

"Wait," she laughed. "You're asking me for help?"

I shrugged. "Well, I figure that we both have our strengths. Mine is knowing how to get to your house and where to hide your keys—"

"And killing spiders," she interjected.

"Is that a requirement of dating you?"

She scoffed at me. "You'd better believe it. If I call you because there's a spider, you'd better drop everything to come save me."

"Even if I'm in the middle of arresting someone?"

"Even then."

"What if someone's having a heart attack?"

"Call the paramedics and then haul ass over to me."

"Hmm," I nodded thoughtfully. "So, basically you're saying that spiders are your trump card."

"Exactly. And not showing up when I call breaks our dating contract."

"Now we have a contract?" I laughed.

"Think of it like marriage vows."

I ran my hand through my hair, blowing out a harsh breath. "But we're not actually taking vows." I just needed to be sure we were on the same page.

"Of course not. You're just making this vow that you'll show up if and when I need you to kill a spider."

"And what do I get out of it?"

"What do you want?"

I thought about it for a minute. There were a lot of things I could ask for. Sex was a good one, but too superficial for her. And we weren't at the point in our relationship where I could ask for anything too serious.

"I want three strikes."

"Three strikes of what?"

"You know, baseball...three strikes and you're out? I get three strikes before you break up with me. And they have to be good strikes. Not like...you were late picking me up, or you said something stupid."

She watched me for a moment before holding out her hand. "I can do that."

"Then we have a deal."

"We have an accord."

I quirked an eyebrow at her.

"What? I always wanted to say that."

WHEN JACK PULLED up the next day, I was actually a little disappointed. I'd been having fun being holed up in the cabin. But then when he stepped out of his car, I remembered what he'd done to us.

Marching out onto the front porch, I stomped down the steps.

"Hey, did you guys—"

I swung hard, punching him right across the jaw. His head jerked to the side and he stumbled slightly. That was when I really attacked. Flinging myself at his torso, I tackled him to the ground and punched him again.

He kicked me off him, getting to his feet as he took up a defensive stance. "I take it the weekend didn't go as planned."

"It was fucking fantastic."

He straightened, tilting his head in confusion. "Then why the fuck are you hitting me?"

"That was for kidnapping us and leaving us out here in the fucking wilderness."

The door opened behind me and Abby ran down the steps, pulling on a sweatshirt. We'd found a change of clothes in a suitcase in the closet. At least he had been nice enough to do that much.

"I didn't leave you in the wilderness," he argued. "I left you at the end of a driveway. You had to walk a whole two minutes to get to the cabin."

I frowned, not understanding. "What?"

"Wait," Abby laughed. "You mean that dirt road next to where you dropped us was the driveway for this house?"

"Yeah," Jack said exasperatedly. "What? Did you think I just took you out here and dumped you?"

Abby was laughing hard at this point. I glared at her, but it only egged her on.

"Wait, if you didn't take the road, how did you get here?"

"It doesn't matter," I muttered. "The point is, you're an ass."

"Did you walk through the woods?" Jack asked, biting back a laugh.

"Shut up," I seethed.

"Good detective work."

"Don't be mean, Jack. He was drunk."

"Yeah, I was drunk," I agreed with Abby.

Jack looked between us and grinned. "So, I take it you worked your shit out."

"Do you want a medal?" I asked irritatedly.

"I have to admit, after seeing you do this for so many years, it's nice to see you on the other side of things."

"Whatever. You're here now, so you can take us home."

"That's it?" Abby asked, frowning at me.

I stepped closer to her so only she could hear. "You know that's not it. But right now, I want to get home. We need to figure this out away from the cabin."

She nodded, looking a little uncertain.

"You trust me, right?"

"Of course."

"Alright, lovebirds, let's get you home. Am I taking you to one house or two?"

"Two," I said at the same time Abby said, "One."

I turned to her and frowned. "You want to go home with me?"

"Well, we just talked about making this work," she said hesitantly.

"Right, but I thought you would want to go check on the cats."

"Well, yeah, but I can do that and then go home with you."

I wrapped my hand around her waist and pulled her against me. "No, we're not just jumping into this. We're going to go out on a date and I'm going to show you just how amazing I am."

"I think I already got a pretty good preview of that."

"Ugh," Jack muttered, shaking his head. "I should have sent Andrew or Joe to get you. At least then I wouldn't have to listen to this."

"Hey, how did you kidnap both of us anyway? You couldn't have done it yourself."

He winked at me. "You're right. I had Antonio and Josh grab you while I grabbed Abby with Joe." He turned to Abby. "He says he never wants to see your cats again."

"Serves him right for attacking me in my own home. I hope his balls bled."

"How the hell did you get Antonio to help you?"

"Easy," Jack waved off my question. "I pulled him over doing thirty-two in a thirty mile an hour zone. I told him I'd let him off if he helped me."

That didn't sit right. "I'm surprised you'd even ask for his help."

"Well, Josh was with him. He's the one I really wanted."

"So, are things good between the two of you now?"

He quirked his head in thought. "Let's say that I don't feel like pulling out my gun and shooting him when I see him."

He slapped me on the shoulder and headed back to the car. Abby leaned in to me and whispered, "Remind me not to get on his bad side."

21

CORDUROY

I was walking to the bakery after my weekend off. It was nice to get back to the daily grind. As much as I loved being wrapped up in Abby, I would get bored if I just stayed home in bed all day. Eventually, I'd crave some excitement. Not that Abby wasn't exciting, but everyone needed a break from sex once in a while.

When I opened the door, I almost turned around and walked back out. Plaid Man came walking up to me, a smirk on his face. I wanted to smash it in. Just knowing that he had kissed Abby pissed me off, even if it was a terrible kiss.

"Carter," he nodded. "Are we good?"

"Well, I got the girl, so I'd say we're good."

He held out his hand for me to shake and I hesitated, smelling a trap. "Look, I like Abby. She's nice, but I know it's not going anywhere. I just wanted to wish you luck."

I nodded and reluctantly shook his hand. "So, this amazing date you took her on...where did you go?"

"Go Kart racing."

"Seriously?" I asked, a little shocked by that.

"Yeah," he shrugged. "I just wanted to have fun. Maybe some girls like to be wined and dined, but I want someone that wants to have fun with me."

"So, every day's a party."

"Not at all. But would you want to sit through a boring dinner where you're trying to figure out what the fuck to say?"

He had a point. I was terrible at small talk. And there was nothing like the pressure of the first date, saying the right thing and making sure you didn't fuck it up.

"Anyway, have fun. She's a great woman."

I nodded my thanks, but I was already trying to figure out what I could do that would be more fun than Go Karts. Heading to the station, I hoped Jack was in so I could talk to him. Luckily, he was there, along with Eric, Will, and Joe. That gave me a good round perspective on things.

"I need an idea for where to take Abby on our date," I said, my voice slightly panicked.

"To dinner," Eric said, frowning slightly. "Where else would you take her?"

"Well, Plaid Man took her Go Kart racing, and apparently they had a great time. Now I need something equally as awesome or she'll think I'm boring."

"That's bullshit," Jack said. "Eric's right. Take her to dinner and do it right. Make sure she knows that you want to spend the money on her."

"Chicks don't care about money," Joe said. "I had one of the richest girls and all she wanted was a guy that actually paid attention to her."

"It's not about showing her you have money," Will cut in. "It's proving that you're willing to sit through all the boring shit to get to the good shit."

"Wait, why does it matter if you sit there through the boring shit? Does anyone really have a good time with that?"

None of them said anything.

"Alright," I started pacing the room. "So, ideas, people. Places I can take her, things we can do."

"Ooh!" Joe snapped his fingers. "Moonlight walk on the beach. That's romantic as hell."

"We don't have a beach," I said.

"Right, that could be a problem."

"Dinner at Marcello's," Eric added. "It's romantic. It's got candle-light. You'll be setting the stage for a beautiful evening."

"A beautiful evening?" Will mocked him. "Are we in the early 1900's? Are we courting women?"

"We should be," Eric grumbled.

"What if I take her to an escape room?" I suggested. "It's fun and you're actively doing something together instead of just staring at the person across from you."

"You want to lock her in a room with you to solve a mystery?" Joe asked. "And that's supposed to lead to sex?"

"Well...I could wear my handcuffs. It could be sexy."

"And if you end up hating each other, you're locked in an escape room until you can solve the crime or the time runs out."

I nodded. "Good point."

"On the other hand, if she's not into the date, but you are, at least you get something fun out of it," Will added.

Another valid point.

"Trust me on this," Jack said, "Go to a restaurant. You don't want anything too fancy, but don't take her to Red Lobster either. You sit down and get to know her. Women eat that up."

"But I suck at small talk. How do I do that?"

"Oh, that's easy," Will grinned. "You answer every question with a question."

"What?"

"Okay, so say Eric is Abby—"

"Why do I have to Abby?"

"Because you're acting like a girl with all the romantic bullshit. So, anyway, Abby asks you a personal question."

Eric stared at Will, and when Will motioned for him to say some-thing, Eric sighed.

"Fine, um...Do you have any brothers or sisters?"

"And then you would answer with *I do, but I want to hear more about your family.* See what I did there?"

"Interesting."

"Right? So, the key is to always keep them talking. Women want to feel like you're interested in everything they have to say. Don't you dare break eye contact and don't pretend like there's something better to do than sit there and listen to her. You need to be quick and sharp with your answers."

I groaned, throwing my head back. "But that sounds so exhausting," I whined.

"It is, but after you get through that first date, it leaves you open to actually having fun. You need her to get comfortable with you, so she needs to know you're listening."

"Does that mean I always have to listen?" I asked. "Because being on like that all the time sounds like too much work to put in."

"Well, you have to redirect to conversations that could be interesting to her. So, if she wants to talk about last year's flower show, you give her a little, telling her what you liked about it. Then you swing that conversation around to something better."

"Like what?"

"Tell her you think after the success of the flower show, it would be cool to have a car show."

I nodded, liking where this was going. "So, basically, this date is all one big misdirection."

He snapped his fingers and pointed at me. "Exactly! Just keep bouncing around, always keeping her on her toes. She'll think you're interesting and smart, and then she'll want to fuck you when you get home."

"Yeah, but I want to take this slow."

"Slow?" Joe asked. "Why would you want to do that?"

"We started out backwards. We fucked first and now we're dating. I don't want her to think that I'm taking her out on a date just so I can sleep with her."

"But you are," Jack said.

"Yeah, but I don't have to act like that."

"I took it slow with Kat," Eric shrugged.

"Yes," Will groaned. "We all know about you and your magical love affair with Kat, and how the whole world should look to you as an example."

"There's no need to be rude," Eric huffed, crossing his arms over his chest.

"Alright, I can do this," I said, blowing out a breath. "It's like a con. I can be a conman."

"Right," Jack laughed. "And I'm a serial killer."

"Hey, I've had dreams about that."

22

ABBY

"Wow," Carter said as I opened the door. His eyes skimmed my body, taking in every inch of me. I hadn't left much to the imagination. I wanted to tempt him tonight. Ever since we returned from the cabin, he was all about doing things right. He didn't want me to stay with him, because he wanted the chance to prove to me that he could do the whole dating thing.

My dress hung in a loose V down my front and was backless with the fabric just scraping my ass dimples. The rest of the dress was tight, just hitting at mid-thigh. I thought I might be overdressed...or under-dressed, depending on which way you looked at it.

He swallowed hard and took a step back, clearing his throat. "You're just...wow."

"Thank you," I said, pleased that my plan worked.

"I'm not sure I can take you out in that."

"Why not?"

"Because people are going to think I paid for you."

My face fell. "Excuse me?"

His gaze shot up from my legs to my face. "No! I didn't mean it like that. I meant that you look so hot and I'm not at all...You're out of my league, so people are going to think I had to pay you to come out with me. Not that you look like a hooker."

I bit my lip as I laughed. "Okay, that sounds a lot better than what I thought you meant."

He cleared his throat again and motioned behind him. "Should we...I mean, are you ready?"

"Yeah, just let me grab my keys."

"Not leaving them above the door?"

"Or in the potted plant."

"So, where are they?"

"I can't tell you that. Then you could break into my house."

He chuckled slightly. "You were listening."

"Well, I listened to this really smart man that was trying to keep me from being murdered in my sleep."

"Or during the day," he said seriously. "Not all crime happens at night."

"I'll keep that in mind," I grinned.

As he held the car door open for me, I suddenly realized what a bad idea this dress was. I could barely get in without showing off everything. And Carter seemed to realize that because he stood right in front of me, blocking anyone that might be watching.

I brushed the hair off my shoulders and checked my lips in the mirror one last time, making sure I didn't have lipstick on my teeth. I never wore it, so tonight would be interesting.

"So, where are we going?"

"Marcello's," he said, glancing over at me with a sexy grin. "Does that sound good?"

"Perfect."

Marcello's was expensive as hell. I'd never eaten there, but I'd heard amazing things about their food.

"So, you look beautiful."

"You already said that," I laughed.

"I believe what I said was *Wow*, and then I swallowed my tongue."

"Don't worry. I know CPR and the Heimlich."

"Thank God for that."

He chuckled slightly and then it got quiet. Small talk was never my thing, and I assumed it wasn't his either, which was why I was surprised when he said he was taking me out to a nice restaurant. He didn't seem like the type of guy that wanted to go anywhere he would feel trapped.

"Can I ask you a question?"

"Of course."

"Why did you want to go out to dinner?"

"Because I wanted to spend some time with you. I want to get to know you, just like I said."

Well, it wasn't like I could beat him up over that. He was trying at least. I was quiet the rest of the drive, not knowing what to say. When we got to the restaurant, he pulled out my chair and sat across from me, looking only slightly nervous.

"How often do you take girls out to dinner?"

"Um...not often. What about you?"

"I never take girls out to dinner."

His lips quirked up. "So, how often do you have dates?"

"Well, Jake was my first and only since I moved here."

"And you like it here?"

"It's nice. What about you?"

"Well, I work here." He cleared his throat, his brows pulled tight. "So, you left your last place..."

I nodded.

"Why?"

"Well, my boyfriend was cheating on me with my roommate. I didn't really feel like sticking around to listen to them screwing."

It was silent again, and I still had no idea what to do. So, I turned the conversation back on him, hoping he would be a little more forthcoming with information so I didn't have to fill in all the silence.

"So, do you have brothers and sisters?"

"Uh...a brother. What about you?"

"Two sisters. They live in Tennessee."

"That's cool. What do they do?"

"One's in real estate. The other is in politics," I cringed.

"What made you decide to become a virtual assistant?"

I was surprised by the question. We'd already covered this. "It's the way business is moving. Remember? We talked about it?"

"Right," he said, nodding too much. "I just thought you might like to expand on that."

"In what way?"

"Um...so you have cats."

"What?"

"Do you like dogs?"

"They're okay."

"And birds? Do you like them?"

"I guess. So, tell me, what made you decide to go into law enforcement?"

"Job security. Tell me more about these cats."

I shook my head slightly. "What's going on here? Why do you keep asking me about animals?"

His face morphed into shock and he started sweating profusely. "I just...you like animals and I wanted to know more about that."

"About me liking animals?"

"Right. And anything else you want to tell me."

"About what?"

"Anything at all. The sky's the limit."

I took a deep breath and leaned back in my chair. "Okay, what's really going on here? You're asking me weird questions. This isn't a conversation. It's an interrogation."

"I could see how you'd think that."

"So, what's going on?"

He grabbed his water glass and chugged it. "Look, I'm terrible at small talk. Now, if we're just out and about, I can talk to you no problem, but now we're in this restaurant and there's all this pressure to talk. And everyone's watching us. They know we're on a first date and they're probably gambling on whether or not we're going to make it. See that couple over there? They've been married for at least seven years. The spark is gone, yet they come out to dinner because it's date night. Who has fun just sitting at a table on date night? Why not do something you enjoy? This isn't a date. This is a prison camp."

He leaned back in his seat and blew out a breath.

"You were the one that suggested this."

"Right, because this is what's expected."

I leaned forward slightly so only he could hear. "Do you want to know something?" He nodded. "I hate dates too. I think they're totally pointless. You don't truly know anything about the other person unless you're in their space or doing something with them. Why do all that bullshit of being polite at dinner and answering certain questions that are deemed socially appropriate for a date? Why not get down to the important stuff?"

"And what's the important stuff?"

"Do you put the laundry in the dryer right after it's done washing, or do you wash it three more days in a row until you remember to switch loads?"

"Most of the time I switch it right away, but I've been known to wait a day or two."

"How many dryer sheets do you use?"

"One," he said, looking at me funny. "Only a psycho would use more than one."

"Right? Because otherwise the fabric is too soft and almost moist or something."

"Exactly. And no self-respecting guy walks around smelling like flowers."

"Air freshener or fan in the bathroom."

"Both. Use it or go home to take care of business."

I nodded, grinning. Now this was a date. "Do you sleep with socks on?"

"No, do you?"

"No, but my feet get cold."

"I draw the line at cold feet. I'm sorry, but it's like having a fish on me. If you're cold, put some damn socks on."

"Fair enough. Last question. Was there room for Jack on that door?"

"There was more than enough room. And let me tell you right now, I would have shoved her off the damn door and taken it for myself. Selfish bitch."

I threw my head back in laughter, loving how this night was turning out. He took my hand in his and leaned forward.

"Wanna get out of here and go to an Escape Room?"

"YOU'RE SERIOUSLY the worst at finding clues," Carter chuckled as he walked me to my door.

"Hey, I'm not a detective!"

"I know, but some of those clues were really easy. There's no way you should have missed them."

"It was my first time. Give me a break," I laughed, turning to face him at the door. "So, can you guess where I hid my key this time?"

"Well, you said you moved it from the potted plant."

"Yep."

"And I'm guessing it's not in the siding."

I laughed out loud. "Well, that would be silly."

He looked around the small porch, trying to find anywhere I might have hid it. "It would need to be someplace you could easily access because you usually have your hands full."

I opened my mouth to protest, but he held up his hand.

"And you're catching on to places that are easily spotted, so you wouldn't put it under your welcome mat." Glancing down at the cats all over the mat, he looked up at me with a raised eyebrow. "As scary as that mat is."

"Maybe I didn't actually hide a spare key. Maybe I just want you to think I did."

He nodded. "Very possible, except that you always forget your keys, so I'm going to say that's not true."

"Maybe it's on me. Maybe hanging on a chain around my neck."

He stepped closer, unbuttoning my jacket at the top. "I didn't see any chains around your neck tonight, so if you were wearing one, it would have to be hanging indecently low on you. And you wouldn't have wanted to distract me with a key hanging around your neck."

I hated his deductive reasoning skills. "Fine, then where is it?"

He reached past me to the mailbox attached to my house and lifted the lid. I watched in shock as he tore the taped key from the inside of the box and grinned at me.

"How did you know? I hid that really well!"

"I'm very observant."

"No, it can't just be that. You cheated in some way."

"Me?" he asked, pressing his hand to his chest. "You wound me. I would never cheat."

"So, you're not going to admit it?"

"You would have to prove it first."

I crossed my arms over my chest and smirked at him. "That's fine. If you don't tell me, I just won't go out with you again."

"Who says I want to go out with you again?"

"Well...I'm fun and...you like me!"

He nodded and started undoing the rest of the buttons on my jacket, sliding his hands inside around my waist.

"You're right. I do like you, but I'm still not telling you how I knew your key was hidden there." He leaned in and whispered in my ear, "I have to keep some of my secrets."

My breath caught as his hands slid over my skin. My eyes slipped closed as his hand gripped my hip slightly. Memories of our fun at the cabin flitted through my mind, and all I could think about was taking him inside and getting him naked.

"Why don't you show me some of them?" I slipped my hand over the doorknob and pushed it open. His lips crashed against mine. Before I knew it, he was hiking up my skirt and lifting me up. I clasped my legs around his waist and kissed him hard, my fingers gripping his hair tightly.

"Are you going to be okay with the cats?" I asked, moaning as his lips kissed my skin.

"I always take something now," he muttered.

After we stumbled down the hall, he kicked open the bedroom door, pressing me up against the wall. His lips grazed over my neck. I gasped, clutching his hair in my hands as tingles rippled through my body. I could feel his erection pressing against me as the flames ignited. My head dropped to his, my senses filling with his intoxicating cologne. He pulled away the fabric that clung to my breasts and laved his tongue over my nipples.

Every touch was overwhelming. He had a way of sending my whole body into overdrive, like I was in a seductive sex scene. He started rocking his body against mine, every touch claiming me until I was consumed by him.

He spun me around and lowered me to the bed, his body covering mine as he spread my legs and thrust his erection against the thin material covering my pussy. I surrendered to the feel of his cock fucking me without entering me. I cried out as he bit down on my neck, sending shocks down my spine.

"Oh God!"

"Yeah," he moaned, sucking in a large breath, then coughing. He was suddenly sitting up, choking or something.

"What's wrong?"

His face was turning red as he coughed uncontrollably. "Water."

He bent over and started coughing like he was trying to hack up a fur ball. I ran out of the room for water as the sounds grew more disgusting. When I got back to the room, he was in the bathroom, throwing up. Grimacing, I covered my mouth.

He rested his hand on the toilet lid and sighed. "That was disgusting."

"What happened?"

"I think I sucked in a lump of fur."

I burst out laughing, but when he turned to me, I knew he wasn't joking. "You're serious?"

He nodded, bracing himself against the sink. I covered my mouth, so embarrassed by this. I kept the house really clean. I had to with six cats, but since we'd been gone all weekend, I hadn't really been able to clean up as well once I got home.

"I am so sorry," I said, feeling absolutely horrible.

"It's okay."

"Are you feeling better?" I asked, handing over the glass of water.

He nodded, drinking the entire glass. "I had to get it out of my throat." He gagged again, like just the thought of it would make him throw up.

"Um...do you want to...go to your place?"

He shook his head. "You know, I'm not feeling it anymore."

I winced slightly. "I'm really sorry. I promise, this won't happen again."

"How about we leave the fucking for at my place?"

I agreed. What else was I supposed to do? I almost suffocated my boyfriend with cat fur.

23

CORDUROY

Another night of fun. Another night of really seductive outfits. Another night that she drove me completely insane. Every swipe of her tongue against her lips, every brush of her hand against mine was like torture. I wanted to skip the fucking dates and just take her home, but I had to do this right. If it were up to me, I would take her home and fuck her all night.

As much as I loved how much she dressed up for our dates, I was starting to miss the woman that ran around with the crazy hair and weird outfits. As odd as it was, I was used to her quirky side. I missed those floofy skirts and burnt orange scarves. I wanted those back.

I pressed her back against my front door, resting my hand above her head. I could take her right now, push up her dress and fuck her hard against the door. But as a law-abiding citizen, someone that was supposed to be an example to the community, I just couldn't do it.

"Should we take this inside?"

She bit her lip, nodding at me in such a way that I was tempted to say fuck it and take her right here. Growling under my breath, I opened the door and let her inside, flicking on the lights.

"Oh wow," she said, walking further inside in awe. "This place is..."
I grinned, knowing my place was pretty awesome. "Stale."

I cocked my head to the side, confused by her assessment. "It's what?"

"I'm not judging. It's just so...there are no blankets or books. Where are the comfy seats?"

"I have a leather couch right there," I said, pointing to the luxurious couch in the living room.

"Yeah, but..."

"This is a man's house. Sorry, but you're not going to find any cushions on the floor or blankets draped over chairs."

"The couch is really throwing off the whole feng shui of the house. Have you thought of maybe not having it?"

"Then where would I sit?"

She walked over to me, wrapping her arms around my waist. "Where do I sit?"

"You're not going to convince me to give up my couch. I love that couch."

"What about adding in some drapes for a soft feeling?"

I sighed, knowing what was coming. "You're going to have my house redecorated by the weekend, aren't you?"

"I promise not to touch anything without your permission."

"Yeah, and then I'm going to wake up in a circular bed."

"Speaking of which...I think you promised me a night of fun."

"Then what the fuck are we talking about furniture for?" I asked, picking her up in my arms.

⚜

I RAN my hand over the other side of the bed, only to feel cold sheets. Rolling over, I sat up and searched the room for any signs of Abby, but she was gone. I flopped back and sighed as I stared up at the ceiling. I couldn't believe she left.

Wait. I sat up suddenly. She couldn't have left. I drove her here. Flinging off the sheets, I pulled on some pajama pants and headed for the door. That's when I noticed her clothes were folded in a neat pile on the bench at the foot of my bed. Grinning, I went searching for her.

The minute I stepped into the hallway, I smelled something that sent my stomach grumbling.

"Jeremiah was a bullfrog! Dun Dun Dun! He was a good friend of mine!"

I stared in amazement as I watched from the living room as Abby twirled around my kitchen, mixing something on the counter as she sang. She was wearing a t-shirt of mine and it looked damn sexy on her, stopping just below her ass.

She spun around, whisk in hand, flinging batter across the room. "Shit," she swore, rushing over to the sink to grab a wet rag. I crept into the kitchen to see what she was doing, laughing to myself when all she did was smear the batter that had landed on the back of my cloth kitchen chair.

"Oh crap. Come on." She scrubbed even harder, but all it was doing was rubbing it into the material. I didn't really care. I'd gotten them at a garage sale when I bought the house, but seeing how worked up she got over it was so cute.

"Great, just perfect! You spend the night at his house one time and you ruin his chair. Now he's going to think I did this on purpose to get rid of his furniture!"

I slowly walked up behind her and pressed my hand over hers. She gasped and jerked back against me, those big blues watching me sheepishly.

"This is not what it looks like."

"It looks like you're trying to wipe batter off my chair after you flung it on there as you were dancing around the kitchen."

She frowned. "Okay, it's exactly what it looks like. Hey! How did you know that?"

I shrugged, pulling her to her feet. "Good guess."

"That was an oddly specific guess."

"I used my deductive reasoning skills," I grinned.

"I hate that you have those. I'm really sorry about the chair. I'll take it to get dry cleaned or something."

"You don't have to. I got them at a garage sale."

"Still, it's your furniture and I just ruined it."

"You didn't ruin it. I'm sure there's a very simple way to get batter out of material." Prying the whisk from her other hand, I set it on the counter and took the cloth and tossed it in the sink. "Besides, I think we can do something more fun than clean furniture." I skimmed my hand under her shirt and up her back. "Don't you think?"

Her palms slid up my chest as she raised her eyes to meet mine. "Well, to be honest, there was something I really wanted to do."

"Yeah? What is it?" I asked, pulling her in closer so she could feel how hard I was for her.

"I really want to hold your gun."

I chuckled, grinning at her as I stepped back. "Baby, you can hold my gun any time you want." I started pulling down my pants, but she shook her head.

"No, I actually want to hold your gun."

I tried to hold back the horrified expression on my face. "Have you ever held a gun before?"

"No, that's why I want to."

"Baby, I'm sorry, but I don't think you and guns would mix very well."

She rolled her eyes, laughing at me. "I didn't mean that I would hold a loaded gun. I just want to see what it's like, maybe try on your gun belt too," she said, waggling her eyebrows at me. '

"You want to wear my gun belt?"

"Why not? Don't you think it would look sexy on me?"

Images of her in my belt, holding a gun were...terrifying. But she wanted to try it. "*If* I let you do this, you're not allowed near any ammo."

"Of course not."

"And you have to listen to everything I say."

"Scouts honor," she said, holding up her hand.

She didn't even know what the Scout sign was. "Alright, let's go."

She followed me back to my room and waited as I unlocked the gun safe. Then I pulled out the belt and tried to wrap it around her waist, but it was too big for her. It kept sliding down her waist.

"It's okay. I'll just hold it."

She gathered the two ends of the belt and held them in place, grinning up at me. "So, what do you think?"

The belt pulled at the fabric of her shirt, showing off more than she intended. With this view, I could see everything underneath. And she wasn't wearing panties.

"I think I need to cuff you," I said, reaching for the belt.

"Ah, ah, ah! You made me a promise."

"I did," I sighed. Unloading the magazine and ejecting the live round from the chamber, I considered if I really wanted her to get a taste of this. Holding onto the barrel, I slowly handed it over. "This isn't loaded, but at no time should you point this at anyone you don't intend to kill."

"What if I want to maim them?"

"Do you know someone you want to maim?"

"Well, we don't know yet how this will all turn out," she smirked.

I nodded. "Just don't point it at anyone and we're good."

She took it from me and her eyes widened. "It's so heavy. I didn't expect that."

"What were you expecting?"

"Well, the only gun I've ever held was made of wood, so I don't have much to go on."

"This is most definitely not made of wood."

She turned to the window and raised the gun. Her stance was all off, along with the way she was gripping the gun, but I didn't have time to correct her this morning. Not if I wanted to fuck her before we left for work. Stepping up behind her, I slid my hands along her arms until they were over hers on the gun.

"What do you think?"

"I think...you look sexy as hell."

"Yeah?"

"And you definitely need to go to a gun range for lessons before I ever let you hold a gun again."

She huffed out a laugh and released the gun into my hands. "You're no fun."

"No, I'm just not up for getting shot."

"I would never shoot you."

"No, but you wouldn't intentionally hit a light pole either."

She stuck her tongue out at me. "Fair point."

"Now, about that shirt..."

She put her hand up against my chest. "Sorry, we don't have time for that this morning. I have to get home and shower before work. I have an early meeting."

I groaned, nuzzling my nose into her neck. "But I'm so horny for you."

"Then you'll have to wait until we both get off work."

"Or I could come see you on my lunch break. Then we can both get off."

"I like the sound of that," she mumbled against my lips right before I kissed her. Her fingers threaded through my hair as my hands wandered all over her body. I started walking her back toward the bed against her protests.

"I have work," she panted as I pulled up her shirt and kissed her nipples.

I slid my pants down and pushed her legs open. My cock was instantly coated in her arousal. I shoved inside and kissed her hard, swallowing her moans.

"I'll be late."

I pinched her nipples as I thrust inside her over and over.

"Fuck it. I'll tell them I had car trouble."

❦ 24 ❦

ABBY

"I'm going to be so late," I said as I rushed around Carter's house and picked up all my things. I almost forgot my phone and had to go searching for it. I swear, he was hiding things from me so I wouldn't leave.

"These muffins are so good, baby," Carter said from the kitchen. "Will you make these for me every day?"

"Do you not see that I'm running around trying to find my stuff?"

"I know, but, baby, I just can't stop eating these. Jack will kill me if he finds out that I get your muffins and he doesn't."

"Fine, I'll make them for him. Can you just help me find my phone?"

He walked up to me with a grin on his face. "I hid it on me."

I pursed my lips, holding out my hand. "I need to leave, so hand it over."

He narrowed his eyes at me. "Just go with it. You know you want to."

"I know I want to get home so I'm not late," I snapped. God, I was freaking out.

"Baby, you said your meeting doesn't start for another hour."

"I know! But I'm never late to a meeting. You don't understand. I hate it when people say they'll be somewhere at a certain time and then they're not."

"I'll keep that in mind."

"It's just a thing I have," I said, holding out my hand.

"If you stick that in my pants, you'll get what you're looking for."

"If I stick my hand in your pants, you'll be in a lot of pain."

He grimaced and shoved his hand down his pants, pulling out my phone. Plopping it down in my hand, he pouted. "You take all the fun out of everything."

I held it up with two fingers and grimaced. "I'm going to have to have this sanitized."

"Hey, you had your mouth all over me last night."

"That's different. This is going to be against my face all day. I'll feel like I constantly have your dick in my face."

"Now that's something I can get behind."

I rolled my eyes at him and headed for the door. "Let's go."

He grabbed his keys and strolled to the door like he had nothing better to do.

"Can we leave today?"

"Alright, alright. I'm coming. Hold your horses."

"If you pick up the pace, I promise to make you baked goods every morning."

"Now, that's a deal I can get behind."

I kissed him quickly on the lips as he pulled into my driveway, not even bothering to say goodbye. I was so late. I still had to organize all my files, even though I was meticulous about how everything was laid out for work. Deep down, I knew I was ready, I just didn't like not triple checking everything first. I might be a mess in real life, but at work, nobody could accuse me of not being on top of stuff.

The meeting droned on for hours, but luckily, I was great at multitasking at work. I got pretty much all my work done for the day during the meeting, while also providing the information needed when I was called on. By the time everything was wrapped up, I had a few hours to relax before I had to check in at the end of the day.

I started browsing the internet when I came across an ad for antihistamines. It was like the internet was spying on me. I clicked on the ad, but everything was so chemically produced. If I wanted Carter to stay with me at my place, I needed to find a remedy for him that would ease his allergies.

I got lost in a rabbit hole of research. By the time he showed up at my house, I already had a list a mile long. I just needed to grab a few plants to make some of the remedies. There were also a few pills we could try.

"Are you done with work?" he asked as he walked through the door.

"Yep, all done for the day. I just need to check in one last time, but nothing ever comes through."

"So, what do you want to do tonight?"

"Actually," I said, pushing back my chair as I stood. "I was doing some research and I came up with all these natural remedies to help with your allergies."

"Baby, I have antihistamines. I'll be fine."

"I know, but you shouldn't take that long term." I grabbed his hand and pulled him to the kitchen. "Here, you need Vitamin C." I pulled out a glass and orange juice, pouring a full glass for him. "Here, drink up."

"Really, I think I'll be fine."

"Please," I pouted. "I really want to try this and see if it helps."

"So, I just have to drink the O.J."

"Well, and I'll try some other things too."

Sighing, he tipped back the glass and took a sip. "Tasty."

"I know that," I said irritatedly. "But you have to drink the whole glass."

"Abby, I don't need more Vitamin C. I'm sure I get plenty."

"It doesn't hurt to try more. And I also have these Emergen-C packets you can try."

I took his glass after he finished drinking and poured two packets in a glass, then filled it with water.

"Shouldn't it only be one packet?"

"Better safe than sorry," I grinned, handing it over. "Drink up."

"But I just drank a whole glass of orange juice. I'm kind of full."

I gave him pouty eyes that I knew he couldn't resist. After a big sigh, he drank down the second glass, grimacing as he finished it. "That's disgusting."

"Well, I did load you up with two packets. Maybe it was too much."

"You think?"

"I wanted you to get better," I huffed. "I was being caring."

He smiled and pulled me into his arms, running his hand up and down my back. "I know, baby. And I appreciate it."

"This is just the beginning," I said, tilting my head back so I could look at him. "We need to go to the store and pick up an air purifier, an indoor natural neutralizer, cat shampoo, a HEPA filter, a bag of oranges, eye drops, extra hand wash, and something called nettle tea."

"Don't you think you're taking this thing just a little too far?"

"Not when it comes to your health."

"You could just get rid of the cats," he muttered under his breath.

I stepped back with a gasp. "You want me to get rid of my cats?"

"Like it would be a hardship. Temperganda humps everything in sight. Pteheste attacks me every time I walk in here. And I still don't know about the Red Hot Chili Peppers."

"And Yoda Bear?" I asked, my chin quivering.

He sighed, rubbing at his eyes. "Okay, I like Yoda Bear. He's cute."

"And he looks like Yoda."

He nodded, rolling his eyes. "Yes, he looks like Yoda."

"See? There's no way I could get rid of them."

"We could just stay at my place more often."

"We could, but then the cats would think I'd abandoned them. They might start peeing all over the place."

His shoulders sagging in defeat, he jerked his thumb toward the door. "Let's go shopping."

❦ 25 ❦

CORDUROY

My stomach roiled as I sat at my desk. I wasn't sure what end it was coming out, but one way or another, I was going to be in the bathroom for a while. I groaned, dropping my head to my desk.

"What's your problem?" Jack asked.

"I feel like shit."

"Too bad. I need you to head out to Antonio's place."

I groaned again, holding my stomach. "I can't. I won't make it."

"What the hell is wrong with you?"

"Abby...she made me drink all these Vitamin C packets."

"How many?"

"Fuck, I don't know. She shoved them at me and put me on a schedule."

"For what?"

"My allergies to her cats."

I burped in my mouth, grateful nothing came up. This was worse than when I drank the coffee Mary Anne gave us.

"Why is she giving you Vitamin C?"

"Because she wants me to be able to go over to her house without taking antihistamines. She said they're bad for me."

"And this is better?"

I shot up from the desk and raced to the bathroom, slamming the door behind me. I was in there for a good twenty minutes before I finally felt good enough to come out. My legs were shaky and I felt like I had the chills, despite the heat being on in the building.

"Man, you look like shit," he said as he pulled on his jacket. "Maybe you should head home."

"I'll be okay," I croaked out. "As long as I just sit here and don't move a muscle."

"What good are you then?"

"I can answer phones."

"Just go home. We'll be fine for the rest of the day. Do you need me to drive you? I can drop you off on the way out to Antonio's."

"That's probably for the best," I said, hunching over as I walked toward the door. I hadn't even bothered with my jacket. It was too much work to get it. Luckily, Jack got it for me.

He shoved me into the passenger side of the car and got in on the driver's side. "Do you want me to take you to Abby's or your house?"

"My house," I said quickly. "God knows what she'd give me for this."

"Well, I guess I know what not to do when I get sick."

I groaned and pulled up my legs as best as possible, trying to curl into a ball. I was fucking miserable. I fell asleep on the short drive home, and then Jack had to help me in the house. My stomach was cramping up so bad.

"Do you want the bedroom or the couch?"

"Couch. I don't think I can make it any further."

He set me down and then grabbed a blanket and the remote for the TV. Then he grabbed a bottle of water.

"I don't think I can stomach anything right now."

"You need to flush that out of your system as soon as possible. Drink up. You'll either piss it out or puke. Either way, you'll feel better faster."

I grunted and took the bottle from him, drinking a small amount.

"I'll come back and check on you later."

"Thanks, man."

He turned to go, but then stopped. "Why did you drink all that shit? You had to know it wasn't good to take that much."

"She's trying to take care of me. I couldn't tell her no."

I heard him snort. "Pussy-whipped."

Yep, that about summed it up.

I dozed on the couch for most of the day, only having to run to the bathroom another three times before my stomach finally seemed to settle. By the time Abby showed up, I was feeling well enough to at least sit upright on the couch. She rushed through the door, tossing bags on the ground.

"Oh my gosh! Jack called me."

I was going to kill Jack. The last thing I needed was Abby here to take care of me. She was probably going to poison me with something.

"Was it the Vitamin C?"

I nodded, feeling horrible when her eyes welled up with tears. "It's okay, baby. I'm feeling a lot better."

"I just feel so bad. I shouldn't have had you take so much. But I'm going to make you the best soup ever. You'll feel great after you're done with it."

"I don't think I'm up to eating anything."

"I promise," she crossed her heart. "This is my family remedy for anything and everything."

I gave her a tight smile. "Okay, baby."

She grinned down at me and pressed a kiss to my lips. "I'll have it whipped up in no time."

She stood and walked into my kitchen and started preparing whatever she was making. And that was the moment I knew I was fucked. I actually smiled as I watched her move around my kitchen. She'd practically poisoned me with Vitamin C, and I was trying to reassure her that I was okay because I didn't want to hurt her feelings. I felt light and...happy. What was this affection? It was so strange? I wasn't sure I cared at this point. I just wanted to keep feeling this way.

AFTER A WEEK OF NORMALCY, she approached me again. I should have seen it coming. For days, she'd been scouring the internet. She was distracted when we were together, always doing some kind of research, and now I knew why.

"Baby, so I've done a lot of research and I found something that could really help with your allergies."

"You know, the antihistamines are working fine."

"I know, but I think you should try this. Like a million people swear by it."

"A million, huh?"

She nodded brightly. "They said it works better than the antihistamines, and even gives them more energy. Imagine what you could do with all that extra energy," she grinned.

Well, I liked the sound of that. "Yeah? And will this work instantly?"

"Do you need a boost?" she asked saucily.

"Not right now." I grabbed her and pulled her down onto the bed, kissing her hard. "What time do you have to leave?"

She swiveled her head to look at the clock. "Not for another forty-five minutes."

She quickly pulled her shirt over her head as I stripped out of my pants. She left the best part for me. I bent over and yanked her pants off, eliciting a yelp from her. I tossed them across the room and covered her body with mine.

Kissing her, I inhaled her scent, smiling as it reminded me of laying down in bed with her last night. She had fallen asleep in my arms and I spent the next hour just smelling her hair and touching her. I hadn't wanted to fall asleep, like I would wake up at any moment and find this was all a crazy dream.

"Baby?"

I met her eyes and smiled. "Yeah?"

"You kind of spaced out there."

"I was just thinking about last night."

She slapped my chest. "You're always thinking about sex."

I rocked my body against hers and kissed her deep. "Actually. I was thinking about how you fell asleep in my arms, and how I was thinking this was all some crazy dream."

"Crazy in a good way or a bad way?"

Smiling, I slid inside her and slowly rocked into her. "The very best way."

"Yeah?"

My lips burned a trail down her neck, devouring every inch of her skin. "I can't get enough of you," I whispered, sucking her earlobe into my mouth. Her fingers grazed across my back as my body pulsed against hers.

Needing more, I flipped her over, sitting up so she was straddling me. She wrapped her arms around my neck as she slowly tormented me, lowering herself down on me achingly slowly. My blood skyrocketed as she leaned in and whispered how good I felt inside her. I pulled her tighter against me, rocking my hips as best I could up into her. She moaned and cried as she shattered around me, but I wasn't through yet. I rolled her back over and pressed her into the mattress, pulling her legs up to wrap around my waist.

I slammed inside her, then fucked her in short, deep bursts that had her crying out and pulling me tighter against her. I could feel her body shaking against mine as another orgasm surged through her. I was panting hard, barely controlling myself with her. And then I felt her hand on my balls, squeezing me gently and I shot off. With a roar, I pumped into her a few more times and came hard, reveling in the most amazing orgasm to date.

Our sweaty bodies stayed intertwined as I kissed her shoulder, her breasts, and her neck. I couldn't get enough of her. I was falling hard for her. I didn't know what it was about her, but she made me crave her, and if I didn't have her, I would go insane. I had no idea if she felt the same way, or even thought of this as more than sex. But I was going to do everything possible to prove to her that I was here to stay.

❦ 26 ❦

ABBY

I didn't want to leave Carter's arms. I felt protected and loved right now. Whatever just happened between us was something I only dreamed of. Every girl thinks they'll meet this wonderful guy and get it all. He'll love her and protect her, he'll be a great lover, and despite men and women being so different, he'll find that endearing. That was what I felt with Carter.

I wasn't sure if he loved me. He hadn't said so, and I wasn't about to say it first. I knew how hesitant he had been when we first met. He had all these excuses why we couldn't date. I was a mess. I was a traffic accident waiting to happen, and my terrible key hiding skills were bound to cause a few more confrontations between us. I just wasn't sure how long I could keep him in this dream fantasy with me.

"I should get ready for work," he said, sitting up and taking me with him. I just wanted to stay in bed with him all day, but that wouldn't be possible.

"Do you want some company in the shower?"

He grinned at me. "I always want company in the shower."

Twenty minutes later, I was drying off and pulling out some clothes out of my overnight bag.

"You know, you can leave stuff here if you want."

My head jerked up in surprise. "You want me to leave stuff here?"

He shrugged. "Why not? It's silly for you to keep packing a bag every time you stay the night."

My jaw dropped open slightly. "Um...if you're sure."

"Yeah, I'll make sure there's a drawer for you when I get home."

I stood there for a moment as he moved around the room, getting dressed for work. "Um...Do you want one at my place?"

"That's up to you. You stay here more than I stay there."

"Speaking of which," I remembered, pulling out the pills. "Here, take two of these. It's just like an antihistamine, but it's all natural."

He frowned down at them. "Are you sure?"

"Totally."

"Alright." He popped them in his mouth like he totally trusted me and then went to the kitchen for some water. My lips turned up in a smile as I watched him move. He wasn't just hot. He actually was extremely hot, but that wasn't what I loved about him. Before, I had only seen this player that wanted sex. But now that we'd been together a few weeks, I saw this man opening up to me, trusting me and accepting me, quirkiness and all. I'd never had anyone accept me as I was.

I walked out in the living room, wanting to run just a small test to see what he would say. "So, I was thinking of maybe getting a beanbag chair or some cushions for the living room."

He looked up at me as he rifled through his bag. "Yeah? Where were you thinking? Over there?" He pointed to a cozy little nook in the corner of the room.

"Sure. Wherever it's not in your way."

He shrugged. "Do whatever you want. Just don't touch my couch," he winked.

"I would never." He kissed me and then headed to the bedroom to pull on all his gear.

"And what about maybe a few blankets? Would that be too much?"

I was surprised when he brushed my hair back from my face, cupping my cheek. "Make it your own space."

"Really?"

His lips slipped over mine and I felt a grin pull at his lips. "I want you to be comfortable here, and I know you'd rather sit on cushions than on furniture. So, make yourself happy."

He pressed another kiss to my lips and pulled on his vest, strapping it in place. My heart swelled about a thousand times. This man...he surprised me more and more every day. With a grin I couldn't wipe off my face if I tried, I finished getting ready, but when I tried to pack up my stuff, he grabbed it out of my hands and put it in his hamper.

"There. Now you have to come back."

"I was planning to anyway."

"I know," he said in a cocky tone, "but now you have to."

27

CORDUROY

I walked into the station, itching at my neck. I wasn't sure what the hell bit me, but I needed something for it or I would scratch my skin off.

"Hey, where do you want me today?"

"I have to run over to Wilton, so can you do rounds in town?"

"Sure," I said, scratching at my neck some more. "Christ, do I have a bug bite or something?" I asked, walking over to Jack.

He grumbled under his breath and stood, pulling at my shirt. "Uh... that's not a bug bite."

"It's not?"

"No, not unless you walked into a swarm of bugs and they attacked you."

"What the hell is it then?" Then I noticed the itch was starting to spread. I popped the buttons on my shirt and took it off, then removed my vest, looking under my t-shirt. "Holy shit. My whole fucking chest is red."

"Let me see."

I pulled up my shirt and his eyebrows popped up. "What did you do? Take a roll in poison ivy?"

"No, I didn't do anything."

"Well, you must have done something. Did you eat something funny?"

"No, Abby made muffins this morning."

He narrowed his eyes at me. "And you didn't bring me any?"

"I have a chest full of...hives or something, and you want to bust my balls over muffins?"

"I bet they were damn good muffins," he muttered.

"They were and I already told her you would get pissed if you found out I was getting muffins and you weren't."

"Then why the hell did you tell me?"

"Can we just focus on the fact that my entire body is turning red?" I shouted.

He cringed as he looked at my face. Leaning in close, he grimaced. "I think...I think you might need to go to the hospital."

"Why?" I ran to the bathroom and stared in the mirror. My face was forming blisters or something and my eyes were starting to swell shut. "Oh my God! What's happening to me?"

"I don't know, but sitting around here isn't going to do us any good."

I followed him out to the car, yanking down the visor to watch the rapid progression of the hives. "I just can't believe this. My lips are starting to swell!"

"I'll call Nathan."

"What if my throat closes up and I die?"

"That's highly unlikely," he said as he dialed Nathan's number. "I'm like...forty-five percent certain of that."

"Forty-five? That's terrible odds!" I shouted.

"I know! Stop yelling at me! I don't know what the hell I'm doing."

"Do we have an epipen?"

"In the trunk," he said, jerking the steering wheel and pulling us off on the side of the road. He got out and ran around to the trunk, swearing as he dug through the med kit. I stared in the mirror, touching my face as it swelled to an ungodly size.

"Nobody will ever want me when they see me like this," I mumbled, though my lips were becoming too swollen to speak clearly.

Jack yanked open the door and pulled the cap off the pen, stabbing me in the leg.

"At ucking urt!" I shouted. "I oice!" I started screaming in panic as everything started to close up. I was going to die and I had no idea why. But as the medicine took effect, slowly, I could feel my airways reopening. I leaned back in the seat as Jack ran back around and hopped in the driver's side, speeding off to the hospital. He called Nathan, asking him to meet us there.

When we arrived at the emergency room, Nathan came running out, biting back his laugh when he saw my face. "Uck ou!" I shouted.

He snorted in laughter, but helped me inside and took me back to a curtained off room.

"What did you eat?"

"Uhing! Ust Uhhins."

He looked to Jack for guidance. "He had muffins."

Nathan nodded. "What about anything else? A new drink? Did you use a new shampoo or body wash?"

I shook my head.

"What about any medication?"

I started to shake my head no, but then stopped and stared at Jack.

"Oh God," he muttered. "What did she give you?"

I shrugged. I had no idea and I couldn't explain it if I wanted to.

"Give me your phone."

I handed it over and he dialed Abby's number. "Abby, I'm at the hospital with Carter. He's having an allergic reaction to something. We need to know what pills you gave him." He pulled the phone away from his ear and winced. "Alright, I know. Just bring them to the hospital as fast as you can."

"Ell er to oo it anying!"

His brows pinched in confusion, so I mimed driving in a car and then crashing into something. Jack nodded.

"He says to drive slowly and don't crash." He hung up and sighed. "Well, I guess that's my day blown to shit."

I glared at him. "Ay. I ou ay has hit."

Jack turned to Nathan with a grin. "Can you give him something to make him stay this way? I find this version of him more fun."

"OH MY GOD! Oh my God! Oh my God!" Abby screamed as she ran in the room in a panic. "Did I do this to you?"

Nathan started to speak, but I shook my head at him. He shot me a dumfounded expression. "It's highly unlikely. We just want to be sure that nothing in there interacted with something else."

"Okay," Abby nodded, digging through her purse for the bottle. She pulled it out and handed it over. Nathan frowned as he read the label. I nodded for Jack to take Abby outside.

"Oh?" I asked Nathan.

"Yep, she poisoned you."

"At?"

"It's right there on the label. May cause hives, respiratory distress, anaphylactic shock...I could go on if you want, but you pretty much have every side effect you could possibly get from this...whatever the hell this is."

"A I oing oo e oay?"

"You should be fine. The epipen should be wearing off soon. I'll get you hooked up to some medicine to help fight this off." He leaned in and lowered his voice. "In the meantime, I would suggest not taking random pills your girlfriend gives you."

I flipped him off as he walked out of the room. A few minutes later, a nurse came in and loaded me up with medicine. It wasn't long before I was feeling better.

"Hey," Abby said as she walked into my room. "Feeling better?"

"Ractically new," I said, noting that my speech was only partly screwed up now.

"I'm so sorry," she cried. "I never thought this would happen. Everyone said it worked so well!"

Jack was standing in the doorway and could obviously see my distress. He walked over and placed a hand on her shoulder. "Hey, Nathan said it might have interacted with something else."

"But he would have been fine if I hadn't given it to him."

He shrugged. "Eh, think of it as identifying something he's allergic to."

I nodded, liking the way he was going with this.

"So, I didn't almost kill him?"

"No," he said, his brows furrowing. "Not at all. He's fine. See? He mostly just had hives."

"Really?"

"Totally. So, we'll just let him rest for a while. I'm sure he's tired."

"Okay." She walked over to me, tears still in her eyes, and kissed me on the lips. "I'm so sorry I almost killed you."

"Baby, iss okay." She started crying again and I had no idea what to do, so I grabbed her hand and brought it to my lips, kissing it lightly. "I uv you."

Her head snapped up and so did Jack's.

"What?" she gasped.

"Yeah, what?" Jack asked.

"Did...did you just say you love me?"

I grinned and shrugged. It was true. I wasn't even mad at her. She was doing this all out of trying to help me. How could I be mad at her for that?

She flung herself in my arms and hugged me a little too tight. "I love you too!"

Jack stood there with his mouth gaping, shaking his head. "I don't believe it. She almost kills him and that somehow endears her to him," he muttered, running his hand through his hair.

"Alright," she said, smiling brightly at me. "I'm going to let you rest, and as soon as they release you, I'll take you home and make you something really good for dinner."

I nodded, smiling at her like she was my whole world. She stepped out of the room and Jack walked up beside me. "Are you sure about this?"

"Compwetwy."

"So, she tried to kill you, and you love her more for it?"

I sighed dreamily. "Uv is Uv."

"I'd better call Nathan and ask for a second opinion."

28

ABBY

The weather had changed a lot over the last month. Since landing Carter in the hospital, I'd given up on trying different home remedies on him. It wasn't worth it. Seeing him in the hospital was too much for me. I stayed mostly over at his house, and went home for work during the day so the cats weren't always alone. It seemed to work for us, but it was tiring too. Just once, I'd like him to stay at my place.

"Alright, kitties. Mommy's going over to Carter's now, so be good and don't tear up the furniture."

Yoda Bear climbed up my leg, crying because I was leaving. I picked him up and pet his beautiful orange fur. "It's okay, sweetie. You get my bed to yourself," I whispered.

Setting him down, I picked up my bag and headed for the door. I had found an amazing new place for my key that even Carter hadn't found yet. I was very proud of myself.

When I pulled up the Carter's, he was already waiting outside for me. He ran up to my window and knocked. "Hey, is everything okay?"

"It's supposed to freeze tonight. Park in the garage."

"Are you sure?"

"Yeah. I'll park on the street."

"That's really not necessary."

He grinned at me. "What kind of boyfriend would I be if I let you park outside in the cold when I have a perfectly good garage?"

"Fine, but I get to run out and start your car in the morning."

"Yeah, that's not going to happen," he laughed.

I pulled into his single-car garage and shut off the car. He was already waiting for me at the garage entrance to the house. I walked into his outstretched arms and burrowed into his warmth. "You're always so warm."

"Is that a bad thing?"

"No, it's good. You keep me warm at night."

"Yeah, you and your fish feet."

"I do not have fish feet."

We headed inside and I pulled off my coat, draping it over a chair.

"We talked about this on our first date. I told you that I don't tolerate cold feet."

"Then why do you keep pulling my feet between your legs?"

"Because I'm a man, and I can't have my wife—" His eyes went wide and his face blanched. "Uh...That's not... I didn't mean."

"I know what you meant," I laughed. "I'm not expecting a ring."

"Really?"

"It was a slip of the tongue. It happens all the time. Trust me, I know."

He nodded, like he wasn't really certain.

"So, what are we doing for dinner? I'm starving."

"Burgers," he said, pulling out a package of meat.

"Ooh, I could make fries with it."

"I don't have a deep fryer."

I waved him off. "All I need is a cookie sheet. I'll make them in the oven," I said, preheating the oven.

"Are you sure?"

"Yep. They're fantastic." I started washing the potatoes as he started working on the beef.

"Okay," he said warily. "So, anything exciting happen at work today?"

"Not really. It was a pretty typical day." I grabbed a knife and started slicing the potatoes. "Oh, but I did hear this really juicy piece of gossip."

"Yeah?"

"Apparently, some higher up in the company caught his secretary stealing from the company."

"How?"

"She was using the company credit card."

"Huh. I didn't know they used them."

"Neither did I. That's way above my pay grade. I'm just a lowly virtual assistant."

"So, what happened?"

I shrugged. "I'm not sure. I heard she was fired, but then I also heard that she was hauled off in handcuffs, so your guess is as good as mine."

"I think handcuffs are a bit excessive."

I turned to him with a big grin. "That's what I told them! I said my cop boyfriend wouldn't haul anyone off in cuffs for using the company card."

"Yeah, but this isn't exactly the big city. It's a little different here."

I drizzled some olive oil over the potatoes and then seasoned them, sticking them in the oven.

"Anything new with you?"

"Chili Man started a petition for a chili cook-off. Apparently, he's still a little butt hurt over the bake-off."

"But who would do it with him?"

"I don't know, but he's all over the town page, threatening to spill secrets if people don't sign the petition."

"Whose secrets?"

He shrugged with laughter. "Beats me. No one in this town has secrets anymore."

"Maybe I'll sign up for it."

He groaned, tossing his head back. "Please don't."

"Why not? I feel bad for Chili Man. The poor guy doesn't have anyone to cook with. It's sad."

"The man is obsessed with chili. Do not participate."

"Why doesn't anyone call him by his name?"

"I don't know. Because Chili Man is easier to remember?"

"What is his name?" I felt a little bad not knowing. "Is it James?"

"No...Maybe John or Sam...I can't remember."

"Well, I think I'll enter. It's just wrong that he wants to do this and has no competition."

"Don't say I didn't warn you. And don't expect me to punch him the way I punched Plaid Man."

"Well, the difference is..." I said, walking over to Carter and wrapping my arms around his neck. "I'm not in love with Chili Man."

Carter's brows furrowed. "Are you saying you loved Plaid Man?"

"Well, I do have a thing for plaid."

He growled under his breath. "I'm not fucking wearing plaid."

⊙⧉⊚

I RAN around the kitchen island and kissed Carter. "Thank you for letting me park in the garage."

"You're leaving already?" he asked, chewing on a scone.

"Early meeting."

"You have a lot of those."

"Well, I don't schedule the meetings. Anyway, I love you. I'll talk to you later!"

I ran for the door, but then remembered something and ran back to the counter, picking up the container and setting it in front of Carter. "These are for Jack."

He narrowed his eyes at the cookies, shaking his head. "Of course they are."

"And if they don't make it to Jack this time, I'll know."

He smirked at me. "Yeah? What are you going to do about it?"

"I'll cut you off."

He chuckled in amusement. "You couldn't go a single night without my cock."

"I meant from my baking."

His face fell and he dropped his scone to his plate. Brushing off his hands, he pulled me into his arms. "I swear, they'll go to Jack."

"Thank you." I kissed his cheek and spun around. "Now I'm really going to be late!"

I ran out into the garage and started my car, hitting my brand new garage door opener that Carter gave me last night. After the door was open, I placed my right hand on the back of the passenger seat and turned so I could see as I backed out.

The sound of screeching metal had me slamming on my brakes. In a panic, I shifted into drive and pulled forward. I watched in horror as the track for the garage door was yanked from the side of the frame. I shoved the car into park just as the garage door to the house was flung open and Carter stomped out, staring at the disaster in front of him.

I opened my door and stepped out, nervous as hell. Was he going to yell at me? Oh God, this was terrible. But then I walked around the back of the car and saw just how bad the damage was. Half the track was torn off the frame and my front bumper was hanging off the car.

He stared at it in silence for a good two minutes. I tried to think of something to say, but there was nothing to fix this.

"Carter?" I said after a few more minutes.

"I just...how?"

"Well, I was looking back and I must have turned the wheel slightly as I was backing out," I winced.

"But...how?"

I stared at him in confusion. "Well...I think the car turned slightly and the bumper caught on the track."

His gaze slowly rose to meet mine. I swallowed hard, feeling like I was about to be murdered. I raised my hands slowly, like I was trying to tame a wild animal. "Now, Carter...remember you love me."

He stepped over the wreckage and slowly stalked toward me. I backed away, wondering how the hell I was going to get out of this.

"Carter...this is not the worst thing I've done."

He didn't say anything as he kept stalking toward me.

"I'll make you more muffins!"

His face turned into a scowl and then he was on me, grabbing me by the arm and dragging me to his car. He wasn't even dressed for the day yet. He was still in plaid pajama pants and a t-shirt.

"Carter! Where are we going?"

He opened the back door and pushed me inside.

"I don't have my purse!"

He stormed around to the other side and got in. I gripped the police grating and pleaded with him some more. "Carter, this is insane. You can't treat me like this!"

He was silent the whole way through town, not even acknowledging anything I said. That was how I knew he was truly pissed. When he pulled into the station, my eyes widened in shock.

"You're arresting me?"

He opened the back door and hauled me out, pulling me behind. Jake was walking down the sidewalk and nodded to us. "Nice pants," he grinned.

"Shut it, Plaid Man."

"Everything okay?" Jake asked me.

"I think he's arresting me?"

He nodded. "Well, good luck with that!"

I jerked my head around to stare at him as I was dragged through the front door. He marched me right past Jack's desk and opened the cell door, then shoved me inside. With the slam of the door, I spun around and gripped the bars.

"You can't do this!"

"What's going on?" Jack asked.

"You want to know what's going on?"

Jack looked me over and then back to Carter. "I think I need an explanation."

"It was an accident!" I shouted.

"Did you hit someone? Christ, there wasn't a spider in your car, was there?"

"No," I said to Jack. "I just tore the track off his garage."

"On purpose?"

"Why would I do that on purpose?" I asked incredulously.

He shrugged lightly. "That depends. What did he do?"

"Nothing! It was just an accident."

Carter was still pacing the station, not saying anything.

"I understand you're mad, but I have to get to work."

"Why are you in pajamas?" Jack asked.

"Because I had to haul my girlfriend into jail."

"No you didn't," I spat.

"And you couldn't stop for five minutes to get dressed? Carter, you're not even wearing shoes!"

"I had to get her off the streets. She's a menace!"

I crossed my arms over my chest, royally pissed that he was acting like this. "I'm a menace now? Five minutes ago I was the woman you loved!"

"I thought that was just part of the whole near death experience?" Jack asked. "You were serious?"

"Until five minutes ago," I snapped. "It seems love doesn't overcome all."

"Five minutes ago I didn't have a destroyed garage!" Carter yelled at me.

Jack stood, raising his hands as he walked around his desk. "Alright, I think we all need to calm down now. Carter, it was just a garage door."

"See? He gets it!"

"Now, hold on a minute there," Jack turned to me with an admonishing glare. "He's right. Christ, woman. If you can't back out of a garage without tearing out the track, we just can't have you driving around town."

My eyes bulged in disbelief. "So your solution is to lock me up?"

"She's right." He sighed, running his hand through his hair. "We can't just lock her up."

"Why not?" Carter argued. "It's better than her tearing apart my garage. Or jumping out of her car because of a spider!"

"Well, most boyfriends don't try to toss their girlfriends in jail." Then he winced. "Well, besides Andrew."

"What happened with Andrew?" I asked.

"Well, his wife was a serial killer. Suspected, but we're ninety-nine percent certain she's not."

"Wait," I shook my head at Jack. "This is Andrew and Lorelei?"

"Yep," he nodded.

"And she lives here...and you know she's a serial killer."

"Again, suspected. She may have killed someone. I don't know. It's a gray area."

"How can killing be a gray area?" I asked incredulously.

"Well, with the circumstances and who was involved," he bobbed his head from side to side. "It's really hard to say. Like I said, we're pretty sure it's all good. I mean, no one in town has died yet. Knock on wood," he laughed, knocking on his desk.

"*That* you find funny?" Carter snapped. "So, it's okay to be pissed at Josh, but not a woman you suspect of possibly being a killer."

"Hey, she explained the circumstances to us," Jack argued. "The charges were dropped against her."

"And Josh?"

"You know I'm working past that."

"Hey!" I shouted, getting their attention. "Can we focus on me getting out of here? I'm late for a meeting!"

"Carter," Jack sighed. "We can't hold her, unless you're pressing charges."

Carter's brows furrowed and he stayed silent.

"You can't be serious. You're pressing charges against me?"

"I'm thinking."

"Oh, you are so not getting laid tonight," I scoffed, turning around and taking a seat on the bench.

"Hey, I'm the one with the busted garage. I don't understand why you're so pissy."

I snorted. "You think I'm pissy, just wait until you see me tonight. This is your first strike, buddy!"

"See, this is why we don't arrest our girlfriends," Jack pointed out. "It never ends well."

"Yeah, it was him arresting me that made me so angry," I scowled. "Not the fact that he won't talk to me, or that he threw me in the back of his police car like a criminal. Yeah, it was just the jail part."

"Hey, I'm not advocating his behavior, but lady, you are a menace on the road."

I glared at Jack, pissed that he was taking Carter's side. "I'm beginning to think you really don't want my baked goods."

"Now, I think I have a way that we can work this out and everyone gets their way," Jack said placatingly.

"Take away her keys," Carter scowled.

"No, I was thinking we could make her take the EVOC course. Tyler runs it."

Carter's eyes lit up. "You know, that's not a bad idea."

"What's an EVOC course?" I asked.

"And that way, she's no longer a menace on the road," Jack said.

"What's an EVOC course," I shouted.

"Well, that's still to be determined."

"It's an EVOC course. What could go wrong?"

Carter lifted an eyebrow. "What can't go wrong?"

❧ 29 ❧

CORDUROY

"Are you sure this is necessary?" Abby asked as I strapped on her helmet.

"Baby, I've seen you drive. This is necessary for you and the safety of the whole town."

She huffed in exasperation, but Jack was right. The only way I could trust her was if she took this course.

Tyler came walking up to us, a huge grin on his face. "It's a beautiful day for some EVOC training."

"I could be doing so many other things right now," Abby muttered.

"Aw, what's wrong? You don't want to spend the day in the car with me?"

"No, I would rather be doing anything other than this. I could go hiking and get attacked by a bear and I would still have more fun."

Tyler pretended to look wounded. "That's a shame. I promise you this, by the time we're done with this course, you're not only going to be amazing, but you're going to love driving so much that you'll want to test out your new skills on the racetrack."

I held up my hands, trying to tone things down. "Let's not push it. How about we just stick to the basics and see how it goes."

"No problem. Anything for you guys," he said, winking at me and

Jack. Thank God Jack was here with me. My heart was racing out of control. We were in a controlled area in the country and Tyler was a trained professional, but still...this was Abby. So much could go wrong.

"Alright, let's do this," Tyler shouted, giving a fist bump to Abby, who limply hit his fist back. He cocked his head to the side. "We'll get you there. Hey, I have you hooked up so you can hear inside the car."

I grimaced, not sure I wanted to hear what was going on. "Great."

Abby turned to me, blowing out a harsh breath. "Don't worry. I've got this," she said nervously.

"That's the spirit. Go out there and show me how awesome you are."

She nodded repeatedly and I had to press my hand to her helmet to get her to stop. "You'll be great."

"Okay, I got this."

"That's right. You are the arrow. You are the eye of the tiger!"

She looked at me funny and slowly turned around, slinking off behind Tyler.

"This is going to be so bad," I muttered to Jack.

"Oh yeah, this is going to end badly."

"Fuck, should I just stop this now?"

His lips turned down slightly. "Nah, let's let it play out. You never know, you could get some great entertainment out of this."

We watched from a distance as Tyler went over all parts of the car with her and what they did for the driver. Then he got in the passenger side and gave us a thumbs up. The first test was driving between the cones. I'd asked him to place them far enough apart that she could easily maneuver. I wasn't sure she would pass otherwise.

Slowly, she pulled forward, making it through the first few cones with ease.

"See? She's not so bad. I really think—"

I hissed in a breath as she ran over three cones in a row.

"That could happen to anyone," Jack said, squinting as he watched her drive over the last few cones before turning around and heading back. One of the cones was caught in the wheel well, causing the car to swerve erratically. I could hear Tyler yelling at her to stop, but she screamed and then the car picked up speed and she drove full steam ahead. Tyler tried to grab the wheel, but she kept jerking it out of his grasp.

"Fucking stop!" he shouted.

She finally slammed on the brakes and they both flew forward, their belts stopping them. She shifted into park and they sat there for a few minutes just breathing.

I cocked my head toward Jack. "You know, that didn't go as bad as I thought it would."

"Yeah, you know, that could have gone so much worse."

"Right? She could have hit every cone."

We both nodded, nothing more positive to say about it. Tyler got out and slammed the door, leaning against the frame of the car, taking in deep breaths.

"Should we..."

"No," I shook my head. "Let's just let him work shit out."

"Good plan."

When he collected himself, he removed the cone stuck in the wheel well and tossed it across the parking lot. He got back in the car and slammed the door.

"Alright, Abby, let's work on driving in wet conditions."

"I hate driving when it's raining."

"That's why we're doing this," Tyler said calmly.

We watched curiously as they drove across the lot to the skid pad.

"Oh shit," Jack muttered. "This is a bad idea."

"Yeah," I said slowly. "Well...look on the bright side."

"There's a bright side?"

"She's wearing a helmet," I offered.

He nodded. "Thank God for small favors."

"I think he should have started with less water on the skid pad."

Jack had nothing to say to that, but he sighed heavily.

"Alright, now you want to go slow and don't overcorrect when you're driving on wet pavement."

He went through all the instructions with her as Jack and I listened. I already knew what he was telling her, but I couldn't listen. I was too nervous about what was going down. My heart was racing out of control and I felt nauseous.

"I don't think this is a good idea."

"Relax." Jack gripped my shoulder and rubbed it soothingly. "She's got this. Trust me, by the end of the day, she'll be a pro."

"I'm gonna throw up." I twisted out of his arm and ran to the edge of the grass, throwing up several times. Standing up, I took a few cleansing breaths and then headed back to Jack.

"Feel better?"

"Not at all."

They started out slow on the wet pavement, taking it easy through the turns.

"See? She's doing fine."

I nodded. He was right. She was doing pretty good. She made it through three rounds with hardly any problems.

"Alright," Tyler said soothingly. "That was great driving only twenty-five miles an hour, but now we're going to pick up the pace. We need to hit that skid pad going a lot faster. Let's get it up to fifty-five."

"She just had to find her groove," Jack grinned. "It just takes some people longer than others to get into it."

I laughed, slapping my leg as I watched her pull into the fourth turn. "I can't believe it. She's doing it."

She picked up speed and they hit the skid pad going well over fifty-five miles an hour. The car started to spin and she freaked out. I could see it on her face. She jerked the wheel hard, trying to get out of the spin, but instead, just sent them into donuts. The car was spinning out of control and Abby was screaming so loud we didn't need the radio to hear it. I was torn between wanting to run over to help, and trying to stay out of the way in case she accidentally headed my way. Either option, I was likely to die.

Tyler was shouting at her, grabbing at the wheel as she slammed on the brakes. The car finally came to a rocking halt and Tyler got out, throwing up right outside the passenger door. Abby sat in the front seat panting hard. I wanted to go to her, but I also didn't want to interfere.

On shaky legs, Tyler walked over to us, his face a sheen of sweat. When he stopped in front of us, he placed his hands on his hips and shook his head. "I think we're going about this wrong. I think we need to go back to the beginning with her. I'm going to take her around the track and see how she does."

"That's basically like driving down the road."

Tyler gave me a deadpan stare. "I'm aware. Let's take this one thing at a time."

"Whatever you think is necessary."

He nodded and headed back to the car.

"Do you think she can make it around the track?" Jack asked.

"God, I hope so. Otherwise, why the hell did they give her a license?"

"Maybe they passed her just so they wouldn't have to drive with her," he said thoughtfully.

We watched over the next hour as Tyler took her around the track, slowing down and speeding up. She was doing great. Even when he had her drive into the pit lane at a high speed.

"You know, I was beginning to worry, but Tyler was right. She just needed to go back to basics."

"Alright," Tyler said once they were stopped. "Now, we're going to practice driving backwards. Eventually, we'll try some J turns."

"What's that?"

"It's when you drive backward and then spin the wheel until the car turns one hundred and eighty degrees. Then you drive forward."

"Do you think I'm ready for that?"

"I'll let you know when to do it, and we'll start out slow. For now, let's just practice driving backward."

I looked at Jack, both of us appearing less than enthused about this. "It'll be okay."

"You know, you keep saying that."

I watched intently as he had her drive backward. When nothing happened, I was relieved. Then they started slowly practicing her doing J turns. She lost control a few times, but quickly corrected. I was beginning to feel slightly more at ease with this whole thing.

"Okay, are you ready to do your first J turn?"

"Yeah," she said, her voice cracking. "I've got this."

She put the car in reverse and sped up.

"Okay, you're going a little fast," Tyler said calmly. "Abby, you're going too fast."

"You want me to go faster?" she asked in a panic. "Is it time to turn?"

"Do not turn!"

"You want me to turn?" she shouted, jerking the wheel.

Jack and I watched in horror as she jerked the wheel hard. She was going too fast and the car flipped over, setting back on its tires before flipping onto the hood one more time. I raced over to the driver's side, staring at her in horror as she hung upside down from her seat.

"Are you okay, baby?"

"Oh my God! I flipped the car! I flipped the car!"

"Are you hurt?" I asked, trying to keep her calm.

"Do I look like I'm hurt to you?" she screamed at me. "I hate you for making me do this!"

Tyler released his belt, landing on his knees. Then he crawled out and tore off his helmet, throwing it on the ground. "Oh God! I can't believe you let her have a license!" His legs wobbled before he collapsed to his knees. "I never thought I would be so happy to be done with EVOC training." He bent over and kissed the ground.

I ignored him and reached in to unbuckle Abby. "Okay, I'm going to catch you. Let your knees fall so you can land on them."

She nodded and I released her belt, catching her as she fell. Pulling her out, she shoved me away, breathing hard. "You're psychotic!"

"Me?" I asked incredulously.

"I was fine driving on my own, and then you came along and...and... I hate you!"

She stomped away with Tyler, leaving Jack and me by the wreck of a car. I stared down at it, still unable to believe what just happened. And she walked away without a scratch.

Jack sighed heavily. "Well, at least it was CPD's car and not ours."

AFTER THE DISASTER at the track, I decided not to push Abby anymore about taking driving courses. So, I just decided to pick her up and take her everywhere. I told her that I didn't get to spend enough time with her, and she didn't seem to care, though I think she knew the real reason.

I hadn't heard from Tyler in two weeks, so I took that to mean that he was still pissed at me. How was I to know it would be so bad? I dropped Abby off this morning and headed into the station. I knew Jack would be out of the office this morning, so I was covering everything at the station.

"Heading out?" I asked Jack as he slipped his coat on.

"Yeah. I'm hoping it shouldn't take too long, but who knows with these county meetings."

I grunted, glad that it was him and not me.

"Did you drop Abby off again this morning?"

"Of course."

"And she doesn't care?"

"Not yet."

He laughed, completely baffled. "I can't believe you survived that. I was positive it was over after she yelled at you."

"I know, but if anything, we seem to be getting closer."

"Yeah?"

I blew out an excited breath. "I think I might ask her to move in with me."

"No shit?"

"I know," I laughed. "Who'd have thought I would ever move in with a woman."

"When are you going to ask her?"

"I have no idea. I want it to be the right moment, you know?"

He grinned, and I could see his mind drifting off to Natalie. "When I asked Natalie," he huffed out a laugh. "We had just gotten in this huge fight. She..." His eyes welled with tears slightly and he shook his head. "We'd gotten in this fight over what to watch on TV. She wanted to watch some sappy chick flick and I wanted to watch YouTube videos."

"Seriously?" I laughed.

"Yeah." He shook his head, still smiling at the memory. "I remember she said she could never live with me because I would drive her insane. And I dared her to try."

"That's not really asking her to move in."

"No, but it worked. She moved in that weekend." His smile slipped as he stared off into space. "I never watched YouTube videos after that. I was so determined to make it work with her that I stopped, and then eventually, I just wasn't interested anymore. And after she died, I couldn't bring myself to go on YouTube again. It was like I was ruining the peace of the house," he laughed.

Blowing out a harsh breath, he slugged me in the shoulder. "I'm happy for you. Just let me know when you ask her. I'll help you move her."

"That's if she says yes," I laughed.

Jack headed for the door, waving me off. I sat down at my desk and tried not to imagine what it would be like if I lost Abby. I didn't think I could bear it. The phone rang and I got to work. There was a call of an unruly driver on the road, and so my day began.

I drove out of town where the vehicle had been reportedly swerving all over the road. The caller had given me updates along the way so I knew where to go. By the time I pulled up, the guy was already pulled off to the side of the road.

"Fuck," I groaned, calling into dispatch where I was, informing them I may need backup. Jack was out, so I had to hope one of the neighboring towns could provide backup.

I opened my door and slowly approached the car, knocking on the window when I saw the guy passed out in the front seat. He jerked awake and opened the window.

"Sir, are you having car trouble?"

"What?" he said drunkenly.

"Are you having car trouble?" I repeated.

"Nah, I'z just tired."

"Sir, you can't pull off on the side of the road. Have you been drinking?"

"Only a tiny bit," he said, holding his thumb and finger together. He picked up a bottle that was hiding at his feet, showing the nearly empty bottle of Jack.

Groaning, I stepped back. "Sir, I'm going to need you to take a breathalyzer."

"I'm not taking that," he slurred.

"Then I'm going to need you to step out of the vehicle so I can give you a field sobriety test."

"A what?"

"A field sobriety test."

He shoved at the door, barely getting it open. He tumbled out onto the ground, passing out as soon as he hit the ground.

"Christ," I muttered, bending down to wake him up. "Sir?"

He jerked awake and rolled over, laughing as he pointed at me. "You're a cop."

"Sir, I'm going to need you to stand up against the car so I can cuff you."

"Yeah?"

"Yes."

"Ahight," he mumbled, stumbling to his feet. It took about three minutes, but I finally had him facing the car and was cuffing him. I read him his Miranda rights and marched him back to my car, only catching him twice on the way. I opened the back door and gently pushed him inside. Getting back in the car, I called it in and put the car in drive, but when I looked up, there was a cow in the road. I honked my horn at him, but he didn't move.

I flashed the lights and put on the siren, but this cow wasn't going anywhere. By now, there were cars lined up in both directions trying to pass. I got out and headed over to the cow, trying to get it to move. I slapped his rear, but nothing happened.

I turned to the people hanging out their windows, watching the spectacle. "Anyone know how to move a cow?" I shouted.

"You gotta walk behind her," someone shouted.

Nodding, I walked up behind her, but nothing happened. I moved back and tried again, this time running at her. She jolted and ran head first right into my car, smashing the driver's side door in. Then she ran off into a nearby field.

I looked up at the darkening sky. "Why?" I asked. This day couldn't get any shittier. Moving off the road, the cars all passed, leaving me alone with the drunk guy. I jerked on the car door, but it wouldn't open. I walked around to the other side, but the passenger side wouldn't open either. The doors had fucking locked.

Dropping my head to the frame of the car, I sighed. Then the thunder rolled and the clouds broke. Rain poured down around me as I stared at my rain gear sitting in the passenger seat.

❧ 30 ❧

ABBY

"Why are you so wet?" I asked as I ran out to Carter's car.

"You don't want to know," he grumbled, putting the car in reverse and backing out of my driveway. He hadn't come to the door today, which meant that he was already in a bad mood.

"Well, I invited the guys over tonight. I figured you might like a good poker night."

"Why would you do that?"

I flinched at his tone. "Um...because I thought you would enjoy it?"

"And who else is coming?"

"Well...the girls are coming over too."

"Perfect," he grunted.

"Do you want me to call and cancel?"

"No," he said, his hands tightening on the steering wheel. "It's fine."

"It doesn't sound fine."

"I said it's fine, didn't I?"

"Yeah, but you sound really angry. It's not a big deal. I can just call everyone and tell them not to come. They'll understand."

"No, you already made the plans," he said, trying to sound nonchalant, but I knew better.

"If I—"

"I said it was fine. Just leave it alone."

Okay, I mouthed, turning away from him. I didn't understand why he couldn't just tell me to cancel. And if I went behind his back and canceled, then he would be even more pissed. There was no way to win this. I would just try to keep things short tonight. Or maybe the guys could pull him out of this funk. Either way, it wasn't going to be a fun night.

When we got home, he stormed off to the bedroom and I got busy putting together some food for the night. By the time everyone started showing up, he still hadn't said another word to me. I just didn't understand it. This was the first time we'd truly had a fight as a couple, if you didn't count him throwing me in jail.

He was sulking in his room when Eric showed up with Kat.

"Hey, I think Carter's still getting ready. Let me just grab him. There's food in the kitchen."

"Thanks, Abby," Eric smiled.

I headed to the bedroom and walked inside. Carter was laying on the bed, his arm draped over his face.

"Is everything okay?"

"No, everything's not okay. I had a shitty day, and instead of spending it with you, I'm here to entertain half the town."

"It's not half the town. It's just a few friends."

"Right, and they're in my house, so I can't do anything until they leave."

Gritting my teeth, I did my best not to snap at him. "I told you I would cancel."

He sat up and glared at me. "And then you would have been pissed at me."

"Not nearly as pissed as I am right now. If you had just told me, I would have called everyone and said you had a really bad day. No one would have cared. But instead, you're going to sit in here and pout because you don't get your way because you wouldn't just say what you wanted. You did this to yourself."

"You did this to me. You invited a bunch of people over without even asking!"

"I didn't know I needed your permission."

"Oh, I'm sorry. Did I miss the part where you became an owner of this house?"

I flinched back, pursing my lips in anger. I didn't know what to say, so I turned and walked out of the room, closing the door behind me. With a smile on my face, I headed to the kitchen. I couldn't just leave everyone out here by themselves all night. And now I had all this food laid out and some more people showed up and were already sitting around the table. The night would have to go on whether Carter came out or not.

"Hey, is everything okay?" Anna asked.

"You know men. They can't tell you what they want or need."

"Tell me about it. They're the worst. You know, they say that we're the more complicated species. Well, I call bullshit. Half the problems in the world could be fixed if the man just opened his mouth and said what the fuck was wrong."

"I know," I whisper-hissed. "He's pissed for some reason and now he's blaming me."

"Girl, just enjoy the night and let him wallow. If he sees that his attitude isn't affecting you, it's only going to make him feel like an ass."

"Really?"

"Trust me on this. If you feed into their hysteria, they think they've won. Won what?" she asked incredulously. "Is there some prize for being an asshole?"

"I'm just so shocked. We haven't fought at all since we've been together. This is so weird."

"It's a long time coming then. Trust me, this was going to happen sooner or later. If you don't fight, you never really know what's wrong."

"Yeah, but I liked that we didn't fight."

"Well, look on the bright side, when he realizes what an ass he's being, there's going to be a lot of groveling."

"I bet he thinks he's going to get makeup sex."

She laughed. "They always think that. Makeup sex isn't a thing. There's the woman being pissed for days on end, and after days of him apologizing profusely, he gets to make it up to his woman in orgasms."

"So, you don't talk it out?"

She looked at me like I was an idiot. "Hell no. You hold out until you feel there's been sufficient groveling, and then you make him beg you for sex. It's practically a rule, and if it isn't, it should be."

She walked away just as Carter walked out of the room, glaring at me. I glared right back. I wasn't giving in to him. I picked up my drink and joined the girls, ignoring him the rest of the night.

❧ 31 ❧

CORDUROY

Who the hell did she think she was inviting people over to my house? The last thing I needed after the shit I dealt with today was a bunch of people over here invading my space. I laid on the bed in my wet clothes and refused to move. I could feel the comforter getting wet underneath me, but I couldn't care less. Fuck this bullshit.

When I heard the door open and a female voice, it almost sent me over the edge, but when she walked in here, almost demanding I go out there, that was the end for me. I finally got my ass off the bed and took a shower, but that only pissed me off even more. Didn't she realize I just wanted to spend the night with her?

Slamming around in the bedroom, I grabbed some clean clothes and tried to decide if I should go out there or not. As much as I wanted to sit in my bedroom and ignore everyone out there, I knew that would make me an asshole. So, I would go out there and she would see what a bad idea this was.

Except, when I opened the door, she glared at me once and then just ignored me. In my own fucking house, she pretended like it didn't matter if I was there or not. Walking over to the fridge, I grabbed a beer, completely ignoring her, and headed for the poker table that had been set up.

"Make yourselves comfortable," I grumbled, taking my seat.

"What's up your ass?" Robert asked as he shuffled the deck.

"I had a shitty day, and then when I got home, Abby informed me that we were having company."

"So why didn't you just tell her to cancel?"

I slowly turned my gaze on his, my eyes razor sharp. "Because that would make me an asshole."

"And what do you call this?" Will asked.

"This is me playing along," I retorted.

"Gee, thanks for playing along for us," Eric muttered. "I know I would rather sit here with your grumpy ass than be at home where I don't have to take shit from someone else."

"Hey, she started this." I leaned forward on the table and lowered my voice. "What kind of woman invites people over to her boyfriend's home without asking first."

Nathan looked around at the weird decorations and colorful curtains that now hung in my house. "I thought she lived here."

"No, she has a drawer here," I corrected. "There's a difference."

Joe burst out laughing. "Seriously? You think there's a difference?"

"Of course there is. A drawer implies that a woman is allowed to stay over and make herself comfortable, but it doesn't give her the right to act like this is her house."

"But...you let her decorate," Eric said in confusion.

"Well, yeah, because I wanted her to feel comfortable."

I took my cards, barely paying attention. I was too pissed.

"There's something you need to get straight in your head right now," Eric said seriously. "You let her into your home. She stays here a lot I'm guessing..."

"Every night," I muttered.

"Okay, and I'm assuming you don't ask her to go home."

"No," I grumbled.

"And you let her put up those decorations. In fact, I would go so far as to say you told her to do it. Otherwise, you would have freaked out a long time ago. Am I right?"

"Maybe," I said, not wanting to commit to anything.

"You need to face it. You gave her every impression that this was her home just as much as yours. And if you didn't want it that way, you should have told her."

"Should have told who what?" Jack asked as he walked up behind me. He took off his jacket and hung it over the back of his chair. "Sorry I'm late. Work was a bitch today."

"Tell me about it," I muttered.

"What happened to you?" he asked, snatching my beer from me.

"I was drinking that," I protested.

He shrugged. "Didn't look like it. Grab your own."

"That was my own," I retorted. "Jesus, what else can go wrong today?"

I glanced across the room at Abby and scowled. She was laughing and having fun, which just made me more angry. Didn't I make it clear to her that I wasn't happy? She should be over there pining over me or something.

"A beer going missing is ruining your day?" he laughed.

"No, but the drunk, the downpour, and the cow ramming my car made for a pretty shitty day."

Jack's eyebrows shot up in surprise. "A cow rammed the car?"

"Yeah, which you would have known if you had bothered to check in."

"You knew I had meetings all day."

"This is payback, that's what this is," I said, pointing at the guys.

"Payback for what?" Nathan asked, "and why are you pointing at us? I don't even live in this town."

"For taking Abby on that EVOC training. CPD's car was ruined because of her. Now God is punishing me by having a cow fuck up my car."

"Yeah, God is spiteful like that," Eric laughed.

"Whatever, you didn't see the look in that cow's eyes. She was ready to kill me."

"Were you standing in front of him?" Andrew asked in confusion.

"No, I was behind it."

"Then how do you know she was attacking because of you? Listen, I have some experience with vengeful women. If she wanted to kill you, she wouldn't have attacked your car."

I looked at my cards, smiling internally. I had a pair of Kings. The one fucking good thing that was going right today. But then the flop came and the inevitable Ace showed up on the table. If anyone else had an Ace, I was fucked. I played it out though, thinking maybe I could pull it out in the end, though it was unlikely. I just needed a little bit of luck. But by the time we got to the river, I knew I was screwed. We all showed our hands, and like I thought, Eric had a pair of Aces and Queens. I tossed my cards down on the table.

"Fuck."

"See," Jack pointed at my cards. "Ace Magnets. Story of your life."

"What the fuck are you talking about?"

"This is what you always do. Okay, you have two kings, but they usually draw an Ace on the flop, which means you're fucked. Someone else's hand beat yours."

"Yeah," I said slowly. "I got that."

"Just like in life. You're the fucking Ace Magnet. You draw in the ladies, but someone else gets them."

I frowned, not quite understanding his reference. "What the fuck are you talking about?"

"Man, poker is a game of strategy and luck, but you're treating this relationship like poker. You don't have to let someone else swoop in and steal your girl. You don't have to fold, and you sure as shit don't have to wait and see what happens."

"I'm not treating my relationship like poker," I said defensively.

"Really? Then why is she in there pretending you don't exist and you're scowling at her every chance you get?"

"Hey, she's the one that fucked up."

"How?" Jack asked.

"Don't," Robert cut in. "You seriously don't want to know. It's ridiculous."

"Man, pull your head out of your ass before you lose that woman," Jack scolded me. "You're only hurting yourself."

32

ABBY

I waved Anna and Robert off as they pulled out of the driveway. The kitchen was a mess, and I really didn't feel like cleaning it up tonight, but I also didn't want to piss Carter off any more than I already had. I still didn't know what happened today to make him so angry. This just wasn't like him. He was always in a good mood.

Grabbing the plates off the table, I started loading the dishwasher and putting the leftovers away. I had no idea where Carter was or if he was even interested in seeing me. I had never wanted my own car more than I did at this moment.

"You don't have to do that," I heard him say from behind me.

I couldn't resist. "Why? Because it's not my house?"

He didn't say anything, so I turned around to face him, my eyebrow raised in challenge.

"Look, I had a bad day and you just...took over. I just wanted to spend the night with you."

"But you didn't say that. I offered to cancel tonight."

"I know, but then you would have been pissed."

"Why are you making assumptions like that?"

"Because I know women!" he said, grabbing his hair. "You're all the same. You all get angry over stupid shit. Why do we always have to do things with other people? Can't a guy just drink beer at home alone without other people around?"

"So, now you don't want me here either? *You* picked *me* up!"

"That's not what I said."

"That's exactly what you said. You want to stay home alone without other people around. Why didn't you just tell me you wanted a night to yourself? I would have understood that."

"Oh, really?"

"There are plenty of nights I would rather be at my house," I shouted.

"Am I really that terrible to be around?"

"Tonight? You bet your ass! If this is the way you're going to act instead of talking things out with me, then yeah, I'd rather be at my house. I could sit with my cats and do the things I like without you yelling at me over not having enough time to yourself!"

"Yeah, I'm sure those cats are really going to keep you warm at night," he snapped.

"They do keep me warm, and let me tell you something, buddy. I know at least one of them is going to get way more pussy than you will anytime soon."

I turned and grabbed my coat, snatching his keys off the counter as I stormed out his front door. It was still pouring rain, but I didn't care. I marched to his car and unlocked the door. Was it stealing a cop car if the car belonged to my boyfriend? Then again, he may not be my boyfriend anymore.

I backed out of his driveway, not really paying attention to where I was going. I slammed into his mailbox as I turned, but as I stared at it on the pavement, I just couldn't bring myself to care. I put the car in drive and roared down the road. It only took me five minutes to find my house, but it was also raining really hard, so there was that.

As I approached my driveway, I turned too soon, going partway into the ditch. Screaming, I hit the brakes, which was actually the gas, and jumped back onto the driveway. The car tore across the pavement, right into the bush outside my house. I wasn't sure if I hit the brakes to stop the car or if the bush stopped it. I shoved the door open and headed for the front door, not even bothering to shut the car off or close the door.

I found my key hidden under the rocking chair and unlocked my door. My cats rushed me, instantly wrapping their bodies around my legs, which made their fur stick to me. Dripping everywhere, I walked down the hall and grabbed a towel off the bar in the bathroom and started wringing my hair out.

As I stared around my empty house, I wondered if it was really better to be here, where I wasn't arguing with Carter, than at his house arguing with him. I flicked on the kitchen light and watched it slowly flicker before dying. I was all alone again.

33

CORDUROY

"**G**oddamnit!" I shouted, kicking the door shut that she just ran out of.

Stalking into the other room, I grabbed my bottle of vodka and poured myself a glass. Why the hell had I yelled at her? Why hadn't I listened to Jack? He was right, I was doing this to myself. Abby was just trying to be nice and I yelled at her for it. So she invited some people over. Was that really such a bad thing?

I looked around my place, at the purple and orange sheer curtains that hung in my living room. They were weird as hell, but she loved that shit. Taking my glass, I walked over to her beanbag chair and slumped down in it. Her scent was everywhere, reminding me how alone I was without her.

I picked up an Astrology book sitting on top of a stack of books next to her chair. Flipping through it, I found that I was a Leo. Apparently, my strengths were that I was creative, passionate, generous, warm-hearted, cheerful, and humorous. Well, some of that was true. Then I looked at my weaknesses. Arrogant, stubborn, self-centered, lazy, inflexible. I huffed in annoyance. And even worse, it listed dislikes, which were being ignored, facing difficult reality, not being treated like a king.

I slammed the book shut and sighed. Okay, maybe I overreacted just a bit. The question was, what did I do about it now? I could wait until tomorrow, get my head on straight and go apologize to her, or I could go over there now and tell her I loved her and I was an idiot. I was pretty sure she would appreciate the second more than the first.

I got up rather awkwardly. Men were not meant to sit in beanbag chairs. I set my glass down on the kitchen island and headed for the door, but my keys weren't on the table. I searched all around, but came up with nothing. My gaze jerked to the door, I opened it and found my driveway empty.

"Aw, hell," I muttered. It made sense. Did I really think she walked home? Grabbing my jacket, I ran out into the rain. I was soaked by the time I reached the end of the driveway. It was so dark out I could barely see in front of me with the downpour. I tripped over something and fell to the ground, scuffing my cheek on the pavement. Groaning, I rolled over and stared up at the night sky. This was not how I planned on making my great apology. I swiped at my face and came away with a little blood. Just perfect. Sitting up, I looked for what I tripped over, only to find my mailbox on the ground and the post broken in half.

Sighing, I knew it had been Abby. Not that it mattered. My car had already been beaten to death with a cow today. As I stood, I was more determined than ever to get to Abby and make things right. I would not be defeated by rain or mailboxes or my own ridiculous attitude. I took off down the road, running to the end of the street when I started to get a stitch in my side.

By the time I was running down Main Street, I was seriously considering stopping for a rest at Joe's apartment. It was just down the road. I leaned against the brick building and took a few deep breaths. Fuck, running in your mid-thirties was nothing like running in high school.

I pushed off the building and half-ran, half-dragged my ass down the road. When I hit her street, I told myself I was almost there. I only had to make it to the end. I passed house after house, exhausted and drenched, but I was so close to seeing her. By the time I saw the tree in her front yard, I felt a surge of adrenaline and pushed harder. What I wasn't expecting was to see my car parked in a bush or the door hanging open. It was clear she wasn't inside, so I bypassed it and headed right for her door.

Leaning against the doorframe, I pounded on her door until she answered.

"Carter, what—"

I snatched her around the waist and pulled her into me, crashing my lips down on hers. Her arms wrapped around my neck, running through the soaking strands. With every breath, every touch, I felt more like myself again and my day drained away. I had her, and that was all I needed.

When I finally pulled away, I stared into those beautiful eyes and poured my heart out. "I'm so fucking sorry. I'm a jackass. I had a shit day, and then I took it out on you. I never should have talked to you like that. Please, say you'll forgive me. I couldn't stand it if you weren't in my life anymore."

She tilted her head, smiling slightly. "Carter, we had a fight. I'm not leaving you."

"You're not?" I asked in shock.

"No. I just needed to leave before we both said things we couldn't take back."

I nodded slightly. "Because I read in this book that as a Leo I tend to be arrogant, stubborn and inflexible."

She grinned up at me. "You read that in a book, huh?"

"Well, it was just sitting there..."

She bit her lip, but her smile fell. "Carter, I have something to tell you."

"Yeah?"

"I um...I sort of hit your mailbox."

"I know. I tripped over it."

"Is that what this is?" she asked, running her hand over my cheek.

"Yep."

"That's not the only thing. I sort of drove your car into my bush."

"I noticed that too." I sighed heavily. "I guess it's just another report I'll have to write."

"I'm really sorry about the extra work."

"Fuck it," I said, sealing my lips over hers. "I've written a ton. I'll just copy and paste."

❦

"SHOULD WE GET YOUR CAR?" Abby asked as I stumbled into her living room.

"Fuck it," I waved my hand at the door.

"Won't Jack be pissed?"

Heaving a sigh, I pulled out my phone and dialed Jack's number. "Hey."

"I just saw you. Why are you calling me?"

"I need a favor."

"Christ, what do you need now?"

"My car is in a bush. Can you have it towed?"

"Where?" he asked skeptically.

"At Abby's house."

"Fuck, is anyone hurt?"

"Nah, just the car, but with the cow, that thing was already on its last leg."

"Who was driving?"

I looked at Abby and decided it was better if no one knew that. Let them guess. "That doesn't matter."

"It kind of does. Was alcohol involved?"

"No," I said firmly. "Trust me on this."

I knew I was putting him in a tough spot and eventually I'd have to answer his questions, but they could wait for now.

"You always have to make my job so fucking hard," he muttered.

"Name one time," I countered.

"Whenever you're in the room. Fine, I'll get your damn tow truck and have it towed to Josh's garage. But you're going to have to explain yourself tomorrow."

"Yeah, I know. I'll see you tomorrow."

"Fuck, I hate you sometimes."

I grinned and hung up the phone. Leaning back against the cushion, Abby sat next to me and frowned. "What was that about a cow?"

"I was out on a call. The guy was drunk and by the time I got him in the car, there was a line of cars waiting to pass. There was a fucking cow in the road that wouldn't move. I got her to go, but she took off and rammed my car."

Abby snorted, covering her mouth. "Wait, you got in an accident?"

"I didn't get in an accident. A cow hit me. That's some kind of crazy cosmic imbalance."

"Cosmic imbalance," she repeated. "Just how much of my book did you read?"

"Not that much. The whole cosmic thing was all me."

She had this huge grin on her face and I tried to ignore it, but she was just so damn cute. "What?"

"Nothing. I just find it hilarious that the great Carter was in an accident with a cow."

"You jumped out of a car because of a spider," I accused.

"It jumped at me from my rearview mirror. It was trying to attack me. If anything, I have more of a leg to stand on because I was physically being attacked."

"Maybe, but a cow is a lot bigger than a spider."

She pressed a kiss to my lips, running her fingers over my bloodied cheek. "Are you alright?"

"Besides freezing my ass off?"

"I can fix that," she said, leaning forward, unbuttoning my shirt. I grabbed her hand and held it still.

"Can we just...sit here?"

"Tired?"

"Fucking beat. After my day, and then I ran all the way here in the rain," I said dramatically. "I don't think I could move my legs if I tried."

"Leave that to me," she said, standing and walking out of the room. She returned with some of my clothes that I'd stashed here when we first did the whole drawer thing. This was the first time I was using it. I grabbed them and then promptly sneezed. She winced and headed for the kitchen. "I have something for your allergies."

"I'll be fine," I sneezed again. "I don't think I can handle ending up in the emergency room tonight."

She returned with a box of over the counter antihistamines. She shrugged as she handed them to me, along with a glass of water. "I didn't want you to stop breathing again."

"I appreciate that."

She bent down and undid the buttons on my jeans. Pulling them off was difficult, but she somehow managed, then handed me pajama bottoms. After I was fully dressed, we snuggled into the cushions and I pulled one of her million blankets over us.

"Do you want to watch some TV?" she asked.

"You have a TV?"

"Of course I do," she laughed. She hit a button and a door opened on her cabinet in the corner, revealing a TV. "What are you in the mood for?"

"Anything. I just want to relax."

She turned the TV and the sounds of *Bad Boys* filled the air as COPS came on. I turned to her and frowned. "This wasn't what I had in mind."

"I can put on a Nicholas Sparks movie if you'd like."

"This is good," I nodded, snuggling back into her.

34
ABBY

I stared out my window at the first snow shower of the season. It wouldn't stick around. It wasn't cold enough and they weren't predicting more than a twenty percent chance of snow.

It had been nearly a month since Carter and I had our big blowup. Since then, everything had been normal. When he had bad days, he always tried his best to tell me what was going on, even if he was too pissy to talk about it. And I did my best to not invite people over without asking first, even though he insisted it was fine.

I finished up working for the day, checking off my task list I had been given. There was more work coming in, and I had no idea why, but it kept me busy. Messenger popped up on my computer, stating I was going to be receiving a phone call from the corporate office in two minutes.

That was strange. Corporate never called me. In fact, I wasn't even quite sure where corporate was based out of. It was a large company and I was just a cog in their wheel. When my phone rang, I did my best to sound professional.

"This is Abigail."

"Ms. Hall, this is Danielle Woodson from HR."

"Is everything okay?"

"Yes, everything is perfectly fine. We've had some changes around here. Mr. Donahue is currently without an executive assistant and based on your time with the company and the work you've done, he would like to meet with you to interview."

"To interview..."

"Yes, would Friday be convenient?"

I didn't even know who Mr. Donahue was.

"Um...this would be a job in an office?"

"Yes, in New York."

"Oh, I'm not interested in moving."

"There would be a substantial pay raise, along with an apartment in the city paid for six months. There's also a driver that would escort you wherever you need to go, traveling around the world, and of course, we would cover all relocation costs."

My head was spinning. That was a lot to consider. Still, I didn't even know who this guy was. "Let me check my schedule. Can I call you back in a few minutes?"

"Of course. Just call this number."

"Thank you."

I hung up and quickly searched online for this Donahue guy's name. It didn't take me long to find him. He was the owner of the company.

"Shit," I muttered to myself. This was huge. Like, way more than huge. And he wanted to interview me. That was just insane. I'd been with the company for a long time, and yes, I was very efficient with my work, but did that mean I was qualified for this position? All he had to do was meet with me in person and he would know I wasn't the girl for the job.

I called Danielle back, taking a deep breath.

"Danielle Woodson speaking."

"Hi, this is Abigail Hall calling back. I really don't think this is the job for me—"

"Abigail, may I call you Abby?"

"Sure."

"This is just a preliminary interview. It's not a job offer yet. There are other applicants that still need to be interviewed."

"I understand."

"Great, then we'll put you down for Friday and I'll send over all the flight information once it's booked."

"Wait, I wasn't agreeing—"

"Abby, this is a once in a lifetime opportunity. I would urge you to at least meet with Mr. Donahue before turning down the job."

"Of course," I nodded. That sounded reasonable. "And this won't affect my current job in any way if I don't get the job."

"No, you would resume your current position."

"Okay."

"Perfect. We'll see you Friday."

I hung up the phone mechanically and shook my head in disbelief. This was insane. Grabbing my purse, I headed out the door, almost forgetting to lock it on the way. I needed to talk with Carter.

When I got to the station, I walked inside and sat down in the chair next to his desk. He looked up at me and grinned. "Hey, babe."

"On Friday, I'm going to New York to interview with my company's CEO for an executive assistant position."

"You're what?"

"Yeah," I nodded. "I just got the call. It's not a job offer. It's just a meeting, but...what the hell, right?"

He leaned back in his chair and stared at me. "You're moving to New York."

"No," I shook my head. "This isn't a job offer. It's just an interview."

"But you wouldn't be going if you weren't considering the job."

"I guess," I said slowly.

"So, what does this mean for us?"

I laughed lightly. "I have no idea. I got the call right before I came here. I probably wouldn't get it anyway. Once they meet me in person, they'll kick me out of there. But it's a trip to New York, so that's kind of cool."

His head bobbed up and down in a sort of nod, but he didn't look happy for me.

"Is that all you're going to say?"

"What do you want me to say?"

"I don't know. That's amazing! I'm so proud of you. I know you'll get the job."

"But I don't know that you'll get the job, and while I think it's great you were offered an interview, you didn't discuss it with me first."

"But she literally just called. What was I supposed to do? Say *Let me go talk to my boyfriend before I let you know?*"

"For starters," he snapped.

"Why are you being like this? I'm about to interview for a job with the guy that runs the company out of New York. This is the best job offer I could ever get!"

"And you'd be leaving me," he retorted.

I sat back, just realizing why he was so mad. "You could come with me. There are law enforcement jobs in New York. You've been a deputy-sheriff for a long time. You could get a great job."

"Abby, I don't want to move to New York. I like my home."

"Right, but wouldn't you even consider it? I don't know if I'll even get the job, but I would consider turning it down for you. Won't you consider moving there for me?"

He sighed heavily, running his hand over his face. Then he turned to me and smiled. "You're right. We should celebrate. Whether you get the job or not, it's amazing they even called you up out of the blue like this. We should go get some dinner."

"Really?" I asked excitedly.

"Hell yeah."

I jumped up and ran over to him, plopping myself down in his lap. "Thank you. I know I won't get the job, but it's just exciting to be considered."

His hand skimmed along my leg. "Then let's make it a night to remember."

WE PULLED up to a drop-off zone at the airport. I was so nervous. I hated flying, but that was only part of the problem. I had this interview that I felt totally unprepared for, Carter and I still hadn't worked out how we were going to deal with this job if I got it, and on top of all that, I had to leave my cats for three days.

"Are you ready?" he asked, pulling my luggage out of the trunk.

I gave him a tight smile. "As ready as I'll ever be."

"Relax," he smiled, rubbing up and down my arms to soothe me. "You're going to be great."

"Yeah, but what if they don't like me?"

"Look, they called you. They must have seen something they liked. They want to know that you'll be an asset to the boss. As long as you present the woman that shows up to work every day and not the woman that leaves her keys in the door, you'll be fine."

I took a deep breath and nodded. "You're right."

"Of course I am."

He pulled me into his arms and hugged me tight. "You'll do great. I know it."

He kissed me hard and then stepped back, but I could see the hesitation on his face. He didn't want me to go.

"It's just an interview," I said, trying to reassure him.

"Exactly."

Except, we were talking about two different things.

"Send me your flight information when you get it."

"I will."

"Love you."

"I love you too."

Affection shone in his eyes before he turned and got back in his car. I headed inside, rushing to check in. I didn't fly very often, so I didn't really know what I was doing. The line took forever and when I had to find my gate, I got lost, despite having an employee give me directions. By the time I got to my flight, I was a nervous wreck.

The flight was even worse. I was so nauseous that I had to grab a puke bag and pray I didn't throw up in the middle of takeoff. After sipping on some ginger ale, I finally felt better. The man next to me looked relieved to say the least.

When I got off the flight, a limo was waiting for me, and whisked me right to the business headquarters. New York was unlike anything I imagined. I thought of this amazing city where dreams and possibilities came true. But when I stepped out of the limo, the sidewalk was crowded and people pushed and shoved to get where they were going. One man flipped me off when he almost tripped over my bag. The receptionist at the front desk was irritable and seemed to hate her job and people in general. It definitely wasn't the friendly feel I had been expecting. This was nothing like home.

I was sent up to the top floor to wait for my interview. This floor was calmer, with fewer people, who were actually smiling.

"Hi. I'm Abigail Hall. I'm here for an interview with Mr. Donahue."

She checked on her computer quickly. "Of course. You're a little early." With her eyes roaming over me, she gestured to the right where the sign for the restrooms hung. "Would you like to freshen up before your interview?"

"That would be great. I came right from the airport."

She slid back and pulled a key out of her drawer. "Go down the hall and on the right you'll find a private restroom. You can get cleaned up in there and change, if you'd like."

I took the key from her, grateful for her help. "Thank you so much."

"No problem. Just be back in a half hour for your interview."

"I will."

I took my bag and headed down the hall. The restroom as she called it was more of a lounge. There was a bathroom with a shower and a large area where I could dress without my clothes touching the floor. There were hangers and a separate vanity from the sinks where I could touch up my makeup. I locked the door and quickly pulled out my interview clothes. I wasn't sure I'd have time to change before the interview, but I didn't want to arrive in a crumpled outfit. I took the chance I would have a few spare minutes.

Finding some wipes on the counter, I did a quick sink wash so I didn't smell, then brushed out my hair and pinned it up so I looked professional. I checked my watch, cringing when I saw how much time was left. After dressing, I checked my makeup and packed everything away with five minutes to spare.

As I handed over the key, she picked up the phone and dialed a number. "Mr. Donahue, your one o'clock is here... Yes, sir." She set down the phone and gestured to the office door. "He's ready for you. If you'd like, you can leave your bag out here."

"Thank you."

I put the bag in the space she offered and headed for the door, hoping I didn't make a total fool of myself. Opening the door, I stepped inside and smiled at the middle-aged man in front of me. I had honestly been expecting someone older. He was handsome, but then, men seemed to age better than women. He had a hint of grey in his hair, but it looked good on him. And his clothes were obviously expensive. I felt cheap standing in his presence.

"Ms. Hall, it's very nice to meet you."

I was a little surprised at his friendly demeanor. He stepped forward and shook my hand, then gestured for me to take a seat. Unbuttoning his suit jacket, he sat across from me and looked at my file.

"So, it says here you've been with the company for seven years."

"Yes, sir."

"I've been going over your work with the company. You don't have any experience as an executive assistant, but you always get your work done in a timely manner, if not way ahead of schedule."

"I don't like falling behind," I admitted. "Do you mind if I ask why you wanted to interview me knowing I had no experience as an assistant?"

"Well, first, I like to hire within my company. I believe in promoting those that work hard for me. Second, I've had other assistants, and not many of them last. They like the title of the job, but not the work that comes with it. I have to tell you, this is a full time job, and then some. I expect a lot from my assistant. There are a lot of late nights, but there's also a lot of traveling to some spectacular cities. If you get the job, you'll have a credit card for expenses—"

"Expenses?"

"Clothing, jewelry, dry cleaning..."

"I don't understand. Why would you pay for that?"

He laughed slightly. "You know, you're the first person whose eyes didn't light up when I told them that?"

I shifted uncomfortably. "Well...honestly, I'm not sure why you'd provide it. Isn't it the employees job to provide clothing for the job?"

He grinned at me. "We'll be attending some charity events, dinners, client meetings. I need you to dress a certain way. You'll have a personal shopper that will ensure you have everything you need."

"Honestly, that makes me a little uncomfortable."

"You have no idea how happy it makes me to hear that."

I wasn't sure how to take that. Either he had some really crappy people working for him, or these outfits were not something I'd want to wear.

"Ms. Hall, what I'm most interested in is how efficient you are. Your job performance reviews are glowing."

"Thank you."

"So, you're not from around here. Is moving to New York something you're interested in?"

"Honestly, when I was called, I was pretty sure it was a mistake."

"And why's that?"

"Well, because I work from home with my six cats. I live in a small town where I've never even seen the inside of a place like this," I said, waving my hand around. "It's so...big and...fancy. I mean, I have cushions on my floor and astrological signs everywhere. We don't even have Uber where I live," I snorted, quickly covering my face in embarrassment. "I'm so sorry."

He chuckled, leaning forward in his chair. "It's okay. My wife loves astrology. She's always trying to tell me about what something means. Honestly, it's over my head. Give me a spreadsheet and I can break it down for you, but I don't understand the rest."

I knew he was trying to make me feel better, but the part of me that Carter told me to keep hidden was rearing its ugly head.

"Look, I feel it's only right to warn you that I'm a bit of a mess. I know I shouldn't be telling you this because it's an interview that could potentially change my life, but it feels dishonest not to say anything."

"Go on," he lifted his chin in interest.

"I always forget my keys...like everywhere I go. I hide my house keys in the worst places, I'm a terrible driver. I once got into an accident because a spider was in the car with me. I freaked out and crashed into a light pole. I had to have the car fumigated! So, I feel it's only right to let you know these things ahead of time to avoid any uncomfortable...issues if you do hire me."

A smile tilted his lips and he rested his elbow on the arm of the chair, staring at me like he found this all very interesting.

"You're going to fire me, aren't you? I mean, maybe not fire me because I haven't gotten the job yet, but you aren't going to hire me." He didn't say anything and then I realized my blunder. "Of course, you can fire me, because I do work for you, just not in this office building. But since I work so far away, I would ask that you don't fire me since you don't have to deal with me on a personal day to day basis."

"Is that all?"

I thought it all over in my head, thinking I got all the pertinent details. "I think so."

"Well, if you do get the job, I won't entrust my keys to you. And since you'll have a driver, you won't have to worry about driving anywhere." Then he leaned forward, resting his hands on the desk. "I also personally detest spiders, so I won't hold that against you."

I realized I was holding my breath and let it out in a big whoosh. "So, you're not not hiring me, but you're not firing me either?"

"I'll tell you what." Flipping the folder shut, he ran his hand along his jaw. "I have a few more people to interview, but I'd like to meet again. Why don't you set up a follow-up meeting with Janice for tomorrow?"

"Okay."

"She'll make sure your hotel is squared away."

"Thank you, Mr. Donahue."

I stood, feeling like I was being dismissed, and headed for the door. Against my better judgement, I turned around and asked, "Why me? I'm not the typical corporate person."

"And that's exactly why I like you."

I nodded and opened the door. By the time I met Janice in reception, she was already gathering up a packet for me and handing it over.

"Mr. Donahue said he'd like to schedule a follow-up interview," she smiled, handing over the packet. "This is your hotel information and

I've called a car to take you there. Now, how does tomorrow morning at nine sound?"

"Perfect."

"Alright, we'll see you then."

I grabbed my bag and headed to the elevator. When I stepped in, I leaned back against the wall and took a deep breath. I had done it. Well, I'd made it through the first round. What would happen tomorrow?

35

CORDUROY

I couldn't concentrate on anything. Every time the phone rang, I was checking to see if it was her. She hadn't texted when she landed, which worried me a little. I knew the flight landed. I'd watched for it on the arrivals board online. I knew she was busy. She had a lot to prepare for, so obviously she wouldn't have time to think about me. But it felt like she already had one foot out the door.

"Any word from Abby yet?" Jack asked.

"No, but she's probably busy. She'll call when she gets the chance."

"Carter, you know you can be honest with me, right?"

I stared at him in confusion. "I don't know what you're talking about."

He tossed his pen down and stood, walking around his desk. "The woman you love is at a job interview halfway across the country. She's thinking about leaving you and everything you have for a job. That doesn't piss you off?"

"It's a great opportunity for her."

"Bullshit. You fought like hell to get this woman to give you a date. I don't buy for one minute that you're indifferent to her plans."

Pulling at the neck of my shirt that suddenly felt too tight, I sighed. "Jack, what do you want me to say? She was really excited about this. I wasn't happy about it when I found out, and all that did was cause problems."

"So, you're just going to let her take this job? That's it?"

"What do you want me to do? Should I tell her she's not allowed to take the job? Should I blame her if this all ends?"

"Uh, yeah," he said like I was stupid. "You can't just let her walk away."

"I can't force her to stay either," I countered. "If I tell her not to go, then I'm taking this opportunity away from her."

"No, you're asking her to stay for you. You're better than some job."

"What if I'm not?" I asked quietly. "I'm not being self-pitying or anything. I'm just saying, she was really excited for this. What if this is what she needs? What if I'm not enough? If she gets the job and I tell her not to take it, she won't still think I'm wonderful. She'll think I'm the person standing in her way."

"Christ," he shook his head. "I can't believe I'm agreeing with you on this."

"It's a no-win situation," I muttered. "I just have to pray that she doesn't get the job. That way she doesn't have to make the choice."

"And if she does get it?"

I looked up at Jack, hating the words as I spoke them. "Then I'll let her go if this is what she really wants."

My phone rang and I quickly picked it up, my heart kicking into overdrive when I saw it was her. I glanced up at Jack, swallowing hard.

"It's her?"

I nodded.

"I'll leave you alone."

He walked out the door just as I answered. "Hey, baby," I said with as much cheer as I could muster. "How was the interview?"

"Oh, my gosh, Carter. You wouldn't believe New York. It's nothing like I expected."

"In what way?"

"Ugh, everyone's so rude here. Everyone pushes and shoves and gives dirty looks. It's nothing like home."

Did that mean she didn't want to go there? Hope filled my chest, but she hadn't yet said how the interview went.

"That sucks."

"Anyway, the interview was…weird. He was so nice. He was nothing like I expected. And I sort of did a blab on how I leave my keys everywhere, hate spiders, and I'm a terrible driver, but I think that endeared me to him."

I closed my eyes, leaning my head back in the chair. That didn't bode well for me.

I forced out a laugh, "Yeah? How'd he take that?"

"He said it was refreshing. So, anyway, I'm meeting him again tomorrow."

"You got called back for a second interview," I croaked out. "That's amazing. I'm so proud of you."

"I know. I never expected it. I've spent the whole afternoon studying up on the company. You know, I always work on the stuff they send my way, but I never paid attention to the other things the company is involved in. This guy literally flies all over the world. Just last week, he was closing a deal in Paris. Can you believe that?"

"That's pretty cool."

"I know, and he said that I would be traveling with him, which they already told me, but to hear it from him…it's just so surreal."

She sighed dreamily on the other end. Here I was hoping that the interview sucked so she would stay with me, and she was dreaming of trips to Paris.

"Well, anyway, I need to get off. I want to be prepared for tomorrow, so I have some more research to do."

"Of course. Call me before you go to bed."

"Will do. Talk to you later."

"I love you."

The line went dead. She didn't say it. I stared at the screen for what felt like an eternity. I didn't know what to think. I was devastated. My whole world was crumbling. She wanted this job. I could hear it in her voice. She was so excited, yet she didn't even realize how much this was killing me.

"How'd it go?"

I looked up. Jack was leaning against the doorframe. His face was pinched in concern. I laughed humorlessly. It struck me how hilarious this situation was. For the past few years, I had been there for Jack, constantly trying to keep him going after Natalie died. If Abby got this job, he would be hauling my ass off the ground.

I tossed my phone on the desk with a sigh. "The interview went amazingly well. The guy loved her and her quirky personality. She has another interview tomorrow."

"How did she sound?"

I lowered my head, my whole body sagging in defeat. "Happy. Like she'd just gotten the best news of her life."

"I'm sorry, man. That doesn't mean she'll get it, though."

"No, it doesn't. But then what happens? Will she be content to stay here?"

He sat down across from me, resting his elbows on his knees. Both of us were quiet. There was nothing to say. If she got this job, she would move on and leave me. And if she didn't, I would always be wondering if she wanted something better.

"I could have you guys kidnapped again," Jack suggested.

I WAS DREADING her flight back. She hadn't called me last night like she promised. All I heard from her was a text with her arrival time and flight information. Her head was one hundred percent with this new job. I wasn't even a background thought.

When she stepped off that plane, she would either tell me that she was staying or she was taking the job. We hadn't really had a chance to discuss any of it. One minute she was here, and the next, she was getting on that flight. I felt like the ground was shifting beneath my feet.

I waited at baggage claim for her, hoping she didn't get the job. Was that terrible of me? How could I love her and wish for her to not get this dream job? But if she got it, what would happen to us? I knew myself enough to know that a big city life was not right for me. And as much as I loved her, I just couldn't give up my life here for something I would hate. I'd end up resenting her, and in the end, we wouldn't be happy.

I saw her burnt orange scarf first. It stood out in the sea of colorless outfits walking through the airport. I raised my hand to wave to her and her face lit up. She started running toward me, jumping into my arms and wrapping her legs around my waist. I hugged her tight to me, making one last prayer that everything would go my way.

"Hey, baby. How was the flight?"

"It was fine. You know, a little turbulence, but I survived."

"No running to the bathroom?"

"No," she laughed. "I took some nausea medication before the flight."

I nodded, taking her hand in mine as we headed toward the carousel for bags. "So, what happened?"

"Well, they offered me the job," she squealed, jumping up and down.

I nodded, smiling down at her as a lump caught in my throat. "That's great, baby," I said, trying not to sound like my heart was being ripped out. It wasn't over yet. She hadn't accepted the job, so there was still hope.

"I know! I can't believe it. Imagine me working for the boss! It would be so amazing, traveling to all those different countries and seeing so many places."

"Does that mean you've made up your mind?" I asked, unable to look at her.

"Well, not yet. I haven't given them my answer. I wanted to talk about it with you first. It's a great opportunity, but I'm not sure it's something I really want."

"It's a big decision," I said diplomatically.

"So...what do you think?"

I finally turned to her, trying to keep my emotions in check. This wasn't the place for this discussion. I grabbed her hand and pulled her in for a kiss. "I think you've been gone for days and I want to get you home and into my bed."

I kissed her again, hoping to end the conversation now. When she smiled up at me, it was clear she knew what I was doing, but she let it slide.

"I'm starving. How about we pick up something on the way home?"

"Sure."

We headed out to the car, but the drive home was stiff and uncomfortable. Neither of us could think of anything to talk about that wasn't related to the gigantic elephant in the car. I tried to talk about work, but there wasn't much that was new. But even worse than driving home was actually getting home where I could no longer avoid the discussion in front of us.

We sat down to eat, but again, it was uncomfortable. Finally, she set down her fork and cleared her throat. "Are we going to talk about this?"

"Of course. What would you like to do?"

"Well, I want to know what you want."

"You already know what I want," I said, staring her straight in the eyes. "But you can't do what I want."

"That's not helpful."

"What do you want me to say? Do you want me to get down on my knees and beg you not to go?"

"Well, maybe put up a little bit of an argument," she muttered.

"Okay, how's this for an argument? If you go, you'll be destroying everything we've built. It'll be over for us. Can you live with that?"

"So, our relationship lives or dies on my decision?"

"What do you think?"

"Why won't you even consider moving with me?"

"Because it's not the life I want!" I said, slamming my hand down on the table.

"If I stay, I'm doing it to make you happy. How is that fair to me? It seems like you're the only one that wins if I stay."

I laughed humorlessly. "Wins? I don't want you to stay if you don't want to. I want you to stay because you choose me over this job. But if you think this job will make you happier, then go do it."

"You can't ask me to choose between a job and the man I love."

"Well, you're going to have to make that decision."

"This is a once in a lifetime opportunity for me," she argued. "I never dreamed something like this would come my way, but I've worked my butt off and got the chance of a lifetime."

"You've already said that."

"And the pay...I could never make that around here. I could pay off my student loans and..."

"And what?"

She shrugged slightly. "Live a different life."

"What's wrong with the life you have? And how does a New York lifestyle fit in with the person you are?"

"What does that mean?"

"New York is...fancy and corporate."

"And I'm not fancy."

"Don't put words in my mouth," I said irritatedly. "Look, it's just not who you are. Your living room has cushions on the floor and throw blankets everywhere. Hell, look at what you've done to this place," I said, waving my hand around.

"I had no idea you hated it so much."

"I don't hate it. That's my point! You fit in here. New York will swallow you up and spit you out."

She tossed her napkin down and stood, pushing back her chair. "Well, thanks for telling me where I don't belong."

Tears pricked her eyes and I sighed, hating myself for making her cry. I wasn't trying to hurt her. I loved her just the way she was. Why couldn't she see that?

"Abby, I love who you are, and I would hate to see that get snuffed out just so you fit into their world."

"And how do you figure that would happen?" she asked, crossing her arms over her chest.

"For starters, there's probably a dress code, and I would guess they won't let you show up to work in your free-spirited skirts and your orange scarves."

"I have a bigger wardrobe than that," she argued.

"Yeah, but when would you get to wear your clothes? On the weekends?"

"Plenty of people have a work wardrobe and a weekend wardrobe!"

I knew I was making stupid arguments, though part of it was true.

I just couldn't stand the thought of her moving there and being torn apart by the harsh city.

"Let's get down to the real problem," she huffed. "You don't want me to leave you behind, but you're not willing to come with me so we can stay together."

I sighed heavily. "Would you want me to?"

"Of course I would!"

I stood and walked over to her, taking her in my arms. "You'd want me to give up my friends and my family to move across the country to a big city, to a new job to protect people I don't know, while you travel for weeks on end and we barely see each other?"

Her eyes dropped to my chest and her body heaved as the first tears started to come. "I want this so bad."

I hugged her to me, rubbing my hand up and down her back. "I know you do," I whispered, feeling my heart break.

"Carter, you have to tell me what to do," she cried, fisting my shirt.

For the first time in a long time, I felt tears fill my eyes. She was going to leave me. I knew it. This was something she really wanted, and if I didn't tell her it was okay to go, she would resent me for taking this chance from her. Blinking back the tears, I composed myself before stepping back slightly. I raised her chin to look at me and smiled.

"You have to do whatever you think is best for you. I can't tell you what to do. But if you really want this job, you should take it. Like you said, opportunities like this don't come around often."

"But what about you?"

I clenched my jaw, hating what I was about to say. But when I looked into her eyes, I knew it was the right thing to do. She wouldn't go otherwise. "Don't worry about me. I love you, and that's not going to change. You have to do what's right for you."

"Maybe we could do the long distance thing," she said hopefully.

"For how long?"

Her face fell. "I don't know. But maybe I won't like my job, or maybe you'll change your mind and decide to come out to New York."

I didn't believe that was true. In fact, I was almost certain that when she got on that plane, I would never see her again.

"Abby, I think we have to face the fact that if you get on that plane, what we have isn't going to last. I'm not saying that to make you feel bad or change your mind. I'm just trying to be realistic here."

Her chin quivered as she looked up at me. She swiped at the tears streaming down her face, sniffling into her sleeve. "Carter, I don't want to lose you."

I tried my best to put on a brave face for her. "Maybe this was all the time we were meant to have together."

"You don't really believe that, do you?"

"Abby, you're going off to a new job. You've got this amazing new world ahead of you, full of adventure. But it's not the life for me. So, you go do this and find out if it's what you want. And if it isn't, I'll be here waiting."

I could see the heartbreak in her eyes as she wrapped her arms around herself. Pulling her into my arms, I rubbed her back and told her it would be okay, because if I told her what I really thought would happen, it would break both of us. In order to get through this, I needed to lie to both of us. I could fall apart once she was gone.

36

ABBY

Boxes were stacked all around me. Everything in the house was a mess as I tried to pack up the pieces of my life and fit it in all these moving boxes. I had second-guessed myself every second of packing. Was I really doing this? Was I moving across the country, leaving everyone behind for a job? It was ridiculous, but for once in my life, I wanted to do something ridiculous for me. I always felt like the klutz at pretty much everything, except my job. I knew I was really good at my job, so this was like recognition for all my hard work. I didn't want to pass it up.

I packed the last of my blankets into the box and taped it shut, pulling the tape for the next box. Temperganda and Pteheste ran past me, tangling me up in their paws. I fell backwards with a scream, tumbling into the stack of boxes I had already taped. Laying in the pile of cardboard boxes, I stared up at the ceiling on the verge of tears. This couldn't be my life. I blew at the piece of tape that dangled in my face, then reached up to pull it away. But as I did, I felt the pinch against my scalp.

Panic clawed through me as I realized the tape was stuck to my hair. "No, no, no!" I screamed, running to the bathroom mirror. The tape was stuck to the front part of my hair, and the tape dispenser was dangling from it. And we're not talking Scotch tape. No, this was one of those massive tape dispensers, and it was pulling at my scalp. As carefully as possible, I held the dispenser in one hand while trying to extricate myself from the tape with my other hand. Tears sprang to my eyes with every tug. The damn thing was stuck in there good.

The doorbell rang and I tried to yank the tape off, but it just pulled out a few hairs as it stuck to more strands. With tears in my eyes, I skulked to the front door and flung it open, ready to cry on whoever's shoulder appeared in front of me.

Anna stared at my hair, her eyes wide in shock. Robert stood behind her, backing away slightly. My face crumpled and tears started pouring down my face. I pointed to my hair, a cry escaping me as I incoherently tried to explain what happened.

Robert shook his head slightly and backed away. "You know, I think I forgot something in the truck."

"Not so fast," Anna said, snatching him by the coat and dragging him inside.

I sniffled, still crying out of control. Anna held her hands out to keep me calm. "It's okay. This is nothing. We just need to...to pull it out gently."

"I already tried," I cried. "It's useless." Spotting a pair of scissors, I snatched them and held them to my hair, ready to cut it out.

"No!" Anna shouted, leaping forward to grab them from me. "Scissors are never the answer."

"Isn't that easiest?" Robert asked.

Anna glared at him. "Only if you want to make her look worse." Turning back to me, she smiled kindly. "Okay, Robert is going to hold the tape dispenser and I'll gently pull your hair off the tape. Your job is to stay as still as possible."

I nodded slightly. "Okay."

"And I need you to stop crying. I can't work under that kind of pressure. Buck up."

Sucking in a breath, I blinked back the tears and stood still. Robert approached me like a caged lion, taking the dispenser from me.

"Okay," Anna said, blowing out a deep breath. "This is easy. Just one strand at a time."

Gently, she started peeling my hair off the tape until almost all of it was unstuck. She winced as she got to the end. "I can't get it all. I'm just going to rip it off, okay?"

"Rip it off?"

"I'll be quick."

"It'll hurt," I cried.

"No, we're going to do this on the count of three. You can do this. Ready?"

I wasn't, but I nodded anyway. I squeezed my eyes closed and prepared for the dreaded countdown.

"One." I held my breath and waited for two. "Two." I winced, knowing three was coming, but it never did. She yanked and tore the tape from my hair, taking some with it. I fell backwards from the sudden jerk, falling into some boxes.

"Why didn't you catch her?" Anna shouted.

Robert looked at her in shock. "You told me to stand here and hold the dispenser. I did my job!"

"And you didn't think you should try to catch her?"

"I might have gotten more tape on her!"

"Oh, that's a likely story," Anna spat.

"It is!" he shouted back. "Then we would have had to start over!"

Sitting in the pile of boxes, I started crying, tears streaming down my face.

"My life sucks," I cried. "Everything is so wrong! Carter's supposed to be here with me, but instead he's ignoring me. This is supposed to be one of the most exciting times of my life and I have no one to share it with," I whined.

Anna slowly knelt down in front of me. "Okay, I think you need to go take a break and get some different tape."

I swiped at my nose, my sleeve coming away with snot. "I have more tape in the other room."

"Yeah, I think you need some more."

"I'll go get it," Robert said quickly.

Anna's gaze jerked to meet his. "No, you won't." She helped me to my feet and patted my shoulder. "You need a break. Go grab a coffee or something. Just get out of here for a while. Robert and I will keep packing for you."

"I can't let you do that."

"Well, we certainly can't keep you here with the tape and scissors. Trust me on this. You'll feel better if you take a break."

Sniffling, I nodded, swiping at my face. "Maybe you're right."

"Of course I'm right." She glared past me at Robert. He must have been pissed that he had to stay here and pack while I left, but I couldn't bring myself to care. I needed the break. Grabbing my purse, I headed out, not looking back. I just needed some perspective.

37

CORDUROY

"Man, you cannot sit here moping in your Cheerios," Jack sighed as he leaned against my desk.

"I don't have any Cheerios," I grumbled.

"It's seven o'clock at night. Why are you still here?"

"Why are you?" I asked accusingly.

"Because it's obvious I can't leave you alone. You'll just sit here all night and stink up the place."

I grunted and stared at my desk. I didn't know why I was still here. I supposed it was because I didn't want to go home and be alone. Better to sit here than smell Abby all over my house and wish she was in my arms. But she wouldn't be. She was leaving me.

"Have you talked to her?" Jack asked.

"What for?"

"Oh, I don't know. To see how she is? To tell her how much you love her?"

I grunted, not liking that idea.

"She's probably just as sad as you are."

"You think?" I asked hopefully.

"I bet she's crying in her Cheerios too."

"Probably not," I grumbled. "She's probably packing with her squirrel friends and making moving clothes for her cat."

He rolled his eyes. "She's not Cinderella."

"Might as well be," I said, laying my head down on my desk. "I thought she was so weird."

"When?"

"The day I saw her talking to the squirrel. Who the fuck talks to squirrels? It's psychotic and... weird, but she was my psycho."

He sighed heavily. "She's not a psycho. You need to go see her."

"No, I don't."

He grabbed me by the arm and hauled me out of the chair. "Yes, you do. You need to go tell her you love her and wish her the best. You can't leave this the way you are. Either beg her to stay or say goodbye properly, but don't pout. It's not a good look on you."

I followed him as he dragged me out of the station. Slumping down in the passenger seat, I stared out the window as he drove me over to Abby's house. When we pulled up, I wasn't prepared for what I saw.

"Did you do this on purpose?" I asked scathingly.

He stared with wide eyes at the front window where two people were groping each other inside. I couldn't see their faces, so I didn't know who she was in there fucking, but just knowing that she was leaving and already screwing someone else was enough to set my temper off like a rocket.

"Holy shit," Jack whispered. "It's like that old song."

"What?" I snapped.

"Are we at the right house?"

"You drove us here. Of course we're at the right house."

He shook his head slowly. "It can't be." He started humming something..."Two silhouettes on the shade..."

"What are you talking about?"

"Remember that old song? The guy shows up and his girlfriend is fucking another guy, only he's at the wrong house."

I looked back at the house. "This isn't the wrong house, and this isn't a fucking song! That's my girlfriend in there, obviously fucking someone else."

I threw the door open and stormed up the driveway to her front door. Jack ran after me, stumbling in front of me, trying to stop me. "Now, just think about this, man. Don't cause any trouble. She's leaving anyway. I don't want to have to throw you in jail."

He grabbed me and tried to stop me, but I ripped his hands off me and kept moving forward. "I need to see for myself."

"Nobody needs to see that," he argued, jumping in front of me again.

"Move," I growled, ready to rip him limb from limb.

He slowly stepped aside, sighing heavily. "Alright, just...don't do something you'll regret."

Walking past him, I mumbled. "I already regret everything."

As I stepped up to her door, I thought about ringing the doorbell, but decided the element of surprise was so much better. Looking around, I found her key under the chair on her little porch. Shoving the key in the lock, I wasn't surprised at all to find the door already open. Flinging it open, I marched in.

"Ha! Caught—"

"Ah!" Anna screamed, pulling her shirt up off the floor to cover herself up.

"What are you doing here?" Robert accused.

"What am *I* doing here? What are *you* doing here?"

"Helping Abby pack," Anna shouted.

"Oh yeah, you really look like you're helping a lot."

"What the hell—"

Jack stormed in, his face dropping in surprise. "This was not what I expected."

"Yeah, it was a shock for me too," I grumbled.

"Well, you weren't supposed to walk in."

"You weren't supposed to be fucking in front of the window," I snapped.

"See," Jack grinned. "It *is* like the song. Not the wrong house, but the wrong couple."

"Thanks," I snapped. "This is so much better."

He nodded. "Right, see your old love fucking her husband must be hard."

"What? No, because I thought Abby was fucking someone else."

"Right, but this isn't Abby."

"Maybe not, but I'm still pissed," I snapped.

"What is it with you two?" Jack asked Robert and Anna. "Didn't Andrew catch you fucking at his place?"

"You know about that?" Anna asked.

"Like anything is a secret in this town," Jack grumbled. "So, you just go around screwing in other people's homes?"

"It's not what it looks like. We just...we're trying to have another baby."

"So, any old place will do," I nodded. "Seems logical. What did you have to do to get Abby out of here?" Then I looked around. "She is out of here, right?"

"I told her to go get coffee," Anna mumbled.

I rolled my eyes and sighed. I suppose this was better than the other outcome.

"Look, I would really appreciate it if you didn't tell her what you walked in on."

I narrowed my eyes at her. "It's going to cost you."

"I figured."

"You don't tell her I was here."

"Why not?" Robert asked.

"Would you want Anna knowing you stormed into her house, assuming she was fucking another man?"

He winced. "Good point."

Sighing, I ran a hand through my hair. "I have to get out of here."

Jack pointed at them. "I want this place cleaned up before she gets back, or I'll drag you down to the station for...breaking in and fucking."

"We were invited," Robert snapped.

"Not for this," Jack muttered as he guided me out the door. We shut the door and stood there for a moment. Both of us shuddered.

"I did not need to see that much of Anna," Jack muttered.

"At least you didn't see what I saw."

"What did you see?"

I shook my head. "Let's just say I saw Robert's little man."

❦ 38 ❧

ABBY

Packing up the rest of my life was more depressing than it had been two nights ago. When I got back, Anna and Robert helped me pack for three hours before calling it quits. Though, they were a little awkward when I returned. I could only assume it was because I had made it weird with my whole hair debacle and all the crying.

A moving service was coming tomorrow and I still had a lot to do. I wanted to ask Carter to help me, but that didn't seem fair. We had ended things on a sad note earlier in the week and I hadn't talked to him since.

No matter how many times I told myself to stay, I couldn't help but wonder what I would be missing out on if I didn't go. And that told me I needed to at least give this a shot. Carter said he would wait for me. I just had to trust that he meant it.

I picked up my phone, needing to take care of something before it was too late. Calling Jo, I avoided my cats' eyes as I prepared to ask for them to be relocated.

"Hello?"

"Jo?"

"Yeah, this is her."

"Um... I got your number from a friend. I just got a new job in New

York and I can't take my cats with me. I need to find them a new home."

"When do you leave?"

"Tomorrow."

"Ooh, that's short notice."

"I know. I'm sorry, but it's sort of a last minute thing."

"Well, I can get out there in the afternoon. How many cats?"

"Six."

"Six?"

"Yeah," I chuckled. "They're not fixed, but I have up-to-date vet records."

"Okay. And you don't have anyone that could take one or two?"

I wished I could ask Carter, but he wasn't exactly a fan of all my cats. "I'm afraid not."

"Alright, I'll be out there tomorrow afternoon. What's the address?"

I gave it to her and hung up. Pteheste stared at me like I was evil.

"I would bring you with if I could."

"*Meow.*"

"I'm sorry, but I can't take all of you to New York. The apartment doesn't allow pets."

He jumped off the bed, running away from me. Sighing, I plopped down on my bed. That seemed to be the general theme here. Everyone wanted to get away from me. I continued packing for most of the afternoon until I was interrupted by the doorbell. I hurried to the front door, thinking maybe Carter was here, but when I swung the door open, it was Anna.

"Oh, hey."

"Wow, so that's how you greet the friend that spent the night helping you pack?"

"Sorry," I said, opening the door for her. She took off her coat and hung it on the coat rack. "I'm just busy packing and I have so much left to do. I hoped maybe you were Carter."

She winced. "So, he hasn't come by?"

"No," I sighed. She frowned, like she was expecting a different response. "Do you want some coffee?"

"It's three o'clock in the afternoon."

"Yeah," I yawned, pouring myself a cup. "I haven't really slept well all week."

"Well, coffee isn't going to help that."

"I know, but I need something. I'll never finish otherwise."

"Have you thought that maybe the reason you're not getting sleep is because you don't really want to leave?"

"I've considered it."

"But you're still going."

I set my mug down on the counter and rested my elbows on it. "Have you ever wanted something so bad in life and you knew if you didn't take the chance you'd regret it?"

"No," she said bluntly. "Honestly, nothing that exciting has ever happened to me." She took a seat on one of the stools. "But let me tell you a little story."

"Why do I have the feeling this is going to be some story where a man and woman were separated and it was devastating?"

"Because it is. Now shut up and listen."

I took a seat and waited for her to start.

"Once upon a time, there were two high school sweethearts. One of them was from a good home and the other was basically trailer park trash. They had these big plans to go to the same college and then have this big life. But things didn't work out as planned."

"Why not?"

"Because she got pregnant."

"What happened?"

"Well, she moved in with her aunt and he went off to college."

"He left her?"

She nodded. "In all fairness, there was nothing for him to do. She was across the country. So, he went off to school, but she returned after the baby was born. She lived in that town for over ten years, working to pay off her mother's debts and tried to rebuild her life."

"Where was he?"

"He moved to a big city and became a big shot lawyer."

"Wait, are you talking about you and Robert?" She nodded. "But he doesn't work in the city."

"I very rarely saw him when he came home. But one day, I don't know, it was like we were suddenly thrust back into each other's lives. Everywhere I turned, he was there. He desperately wanted me to move with him to Chicago and live with him there, but I didn't want to go. I loved it down here. I couldn't see it working."

"Did you try?"

"I went to Chicago and even stayed there a few times and worked out of his apartment, but it wasn't for me. I didn't like all the fancy clothes and the expensive restaurants."

"But just because you live in the city, that doesn't mean you have to live that way."

"No, but it was what he was used to. He liked that stuff and I didn't. In the time we were apart, he had changed so much, but I was still that girl that just wanted to live in the country."

"So, how did you end up together?"

"I made the very hard decision that his life wasn't for me. I left and came back here to live my life. It was...possibly one of the worst decisions of my life. I was just about to run back to Chicago and give up everything for him when he showed up in town. He'd given up everything to be with me."

"That's so sweet," I said, my eyes filling with tears. "See? You guys made it work."

"Yes, but here's the thing...you can't make someone fit into a world you want."

Her words kind of shocked me. "So, you're saying things won't work between Carter and me."

"Wouldn't he be here now if he thought they would work?"

She stood and walked over to me. "I really hope this is what you want, because if it's not, you're giving up a really good guy for a job. And the sad truth is, he may not want to wait around for you."

She gave me a hug, then made me promise to keep in touch before walking out my door.

39

CORDUROY

"When does Abby leave?" Jack asked.

"Uh...tomorrow," I said, pretending to be busy with paperwork.

"Why don't you take the rest of the day off and go be with her."

"Nah," I said, focusing on the words on the paper in front of me. "She's busy packing and I have to finish this report."

He snatched the report off the desk and studied it. "A report on Chili Man causing a scene at the bakery over his chili cook-off." He looked back at me, shaking his head. "You're being an ass. This isn't something that needs to be done today."

I snatched it back and got to work.

"I don't get it. You love this woman. You busted into her house when you thought she was fucking someone else. Now you're ignoring her. Why aren't you spending every last second with her?"

"Because it won't change anything," I snapped.

He barked out a laugh. "Are you kidding me? Do you know what I would give for just one more afternoon with Natalie?"

"That's not the same thing."

"Yes, it is. You love her. Go be with her."

I shoved my chair back and leaned over the desk. "The difference was Natalie chose you. She wanted to be with you. Abby doesn't. She's leaving me for a fucking job, and I have to pretend to be okay with it."

"You don't know what's going to happen. She could be miserable and come back within a month."

"Yeah," I scoffed. "I'll bank on that, right? Just pretend it doesn't mean a damn thing that she's knowingly walking away from me. Do you know what that feels like? I love her! I was going to have her move in with me. I wanted her to marry me, but she would rather move across the fucking country for a job than stay with me. How am I supposed to deal with that?"

He dropped his eyes, his shoulders sagging. "I don't know, man. But I know that if you don't spend this time with her, you're going to regret it. Just go be with her. Soak in that time, because once she's gone, you're not going to get it back."

I didn't have any other arguments for him, so I grabbed my coat and walked out the door. I stopped by the diner and ordered two meals to go. She was packing, so she wouldn't want the mess in the house. Driving over to her house, I had to talk myself into walking through that door. I didn't want to do it, but I also needed to see her one last time before she left.

Pulling up to her house, I took a deep breath and grabbed the take out containers. When I knocked on her door, it suddenly hit me that this would be the last time I would pull into her driveway, the last time I would search the outside of her house for the hidden key. I smiled when I saw the loose floorboard on the porch. Bending over, I set the containers on the ground and pried up the board. The door swung open and there she was, standing there in all her messy glory.

I held up the key and grinned at her. "I sure hope they have better hiding places in New York."

She took the key from me, the corners of her eyes crinkling. "I'll have to get one of those fake key holders that looks like a plant or something."

"I'm pretty sure everyone knows what those are."

Her smile was still there, but it was dull and lifeless.

"I brought dinner."

She opened the door for me and I stepped through. What I saw hit me like a mac truck. It was basically empty in here. A few boxes were stacked against the wall, but everything else was basically gone.

"I thought the movers were coming tomorrow?"

"They arrived a day early, so I loaded up everything I could. I figured it would be less stress tomorrow."

I nodded, setting the food down on the counter. "What time do you have to be at the airport?"

"My flight is at one." I nodded, but continued opening the food for us. "You're taking me, right?"

I pressed my palms into the counter and shook my head slowly. "I can't do it," I said quietly. Finally looking up at her, I told her the best truth I could give her. "I love you so much, and I want you to be happy. And if this is what you need, then you should go do it. But don't ask me to put you on that plane. I just...I can't watch you walk away."

"Carter, this isn't the end. I'll call all the time and I'll fly home whenever I can. I'll be making better money, so I can afford it."

Except we both knew that she wouldn't have the time. At first, she'd be getting her footing with the job. And after that, there would be trips to take. Her life would belong to the company, and I wouldn't ever see her again.

"Abby..." I could feel the tears building in my eyes, the way my heart felt like it was splitting in two. She stepped into my arms and I held her tight, kissing the side of her face, down to her lips. I could hardly breathe as my throat closed up. This was it, the last time I would be with her. I didn't know how I would go on without her. I finally found the woman for me, and now she was leaving me.

With a shaky hand, I lifted her shirt and tossed it to the ground. I memorized every inch of her, knowing I would never see her like this again. Picking her up, I carried her down the hall to her bedroom. Her bed was still there, so I laid her down on it and slowly pulled off her clothes.

That night, I took my time, kissing every inch of her, bringing her to orgasm multiple times. With every thrust, I drew out my orgasm, never wanting it to end. When it was over, what was left for me? And when I came, I bent forward and slowly kissed her, praying she knew how much I really loved her, that she would change her mind and come home to me.

As we laid there in the early morning light, I knew I had to leave. I kissed her one last time, pretending I didn't see the tears in her eyes or the way she curled in on herself. I wouldn't be able to leave if I let myself feel her pain.

"I love you, Abby. Remember that."

Her lip quivered as she pressed her hand to my cheek. "Please don't hate me. I love you so much, Carter."

"How could I hate you?" I whispered. "I would give anything to keep you with me, but I know you need to do this. So, go do what you need to do, and I'll be waiting."

I WAS tired all fucking day. The minutes ticked by, reminding me that Abby would soon be gone. There was still time to try and stop her. Her flight didn't leave for another hour. By now she was at the airport, though. It was too late for any last minute declarations.

"What the hell are you doing here?" Jack asked. "She's leaving. Go to the airport and tell her you don't want her to go."

"I can't," I said, my voice cracking.

"Bullshit. You've been such a pussy this whole relationship. I swear to God, it's like I have to shove you through every fucking door."

"She doesn't want to stay!" I shouted.

"You haven't even fought for her," he snapped. "You told her to go do what she needed to do."

"You agreed with me. You said I was right!"

"That doesn't mean you shouldn't have fought for her. How the fuck do you think she's going to know you want her if you haven't told her not to go?"

I didn't know what to do. But then Jack threw my jacket at me and grabbed his keys. "Let's go."

"What?"

"Do I have to drag you to the fucking airport? Let's go!"

I glanced at the clock again. "Her flight leaves in an hour."

"Then you'd better get your ass moving!"

"Yeah," I nodded, pulling on my jacket. I raced out of the station after him, not sure what I was hoping to accomplish. It felt like a fool's errand, but at this point, I was miserable without her and she'd only just left this morning. We got in the car and he hit the sirens, backing out of the parking space like a lunatic. He shifted into drive and pushed down the pedal. We were flying down the road like we were in the middle of a car chase.

"Which airport?" he asked.

"Uh...O'Hare."

"Fuck, that's gonna be crowded."

"How am I going to get past security? I'll never make it in time."

"Let me make some calls."

I drowned out his voice as I stared out the window and tried to come up with something brilliant to say to her. What could I possibly say to make her stay with me? I could beg her and tell her how much I loved her, but would that be enough?

The sirens of the car wailed loudly as we raced to Chicago. We were too far away. There was no way we would make it.

"Check her flight. See if it's still on time," Jack suggested.

I pulled out my phone, fumbling through the flights to find hers. I started panicking when I couldn't find her flight number, but then finally I found it and relief filled me.

"It's delayed," I said. "Only a half hour, but that at least gives me a chance."

Except as soon as we hit the Chicago traffic, that hope was diminished. Jack tried everything, even bypassing going through Chicago and taking the expressway instead. But the never-ending construction delayed us. When we finally arrived at the airport, I was met by two security officers who rushed me through the airport to her terminal.

I ran as fast as I could, leaping over luggage as someone knocked it over in my path. I didn't know if Jack was behind me or if he'd stayed in the car. My only goal was getting to Abby and keeping her here. But as I ran up to the gate, the flight had already boarded and was taxiing down the runway.

My heart caught in my throat as I watched her plane take flight, leaving me behind. The pain was so acute I felt it all through my body. She was gone. Jack's hand laid heavily on my shoulder as tears filled my eyes. I sucked them back, taking in a deep breath so he didn't see me break.

"I'm sorry, man."

I shook my head slightly. "There wasn't really a chance we would make it."

"You could still get a flight. You could meet her out there and…"

"No," I said, blowing out a harsh breath. "Maybe this is a sign."

"Since when do you believe in that shit?"

I huffed out a humorless laugh. "Since her." I turned to Jack and shot him the best smile I could muster. "Fate wanted her to go, so I just have to wait and see what her decision is."

I knew he wanted to argue with me, but he wisely kept his mouth shut. I walked back through the airport, nodding to the security guards that helped me in my wild race to get to her. When they saw me all alone, they nodded, knowing I'd missed my chance. Story of my life. Ace Magnets.

40

ABBY

This should have been the most exciting time of my life. I had a new job that would bring me adventure and new opportunities, but all I could think about was Carter. Had I made a mistake in leaving? What if I really loved this job? Would I be able to make the choice between him and my career? Granted, it wasn't like I was saving lives or anything, but this opportunity meant something to me. But Carter...I loved him so much, and even though things started out rocky between us, I had never been happier.

The apartment was amazing. It wasn't the one bedroom Cracker Jack box I thought it would be. It came fully decorated with modern furniture and pristine white walls. I should have been amazed by it all, but I missed the comfort of Carter's house. I missed my cats. How was I going to make it without them?

I spent the day unpacking, trying to make the apartment feel like home. When I was done, I walked down to the corner market and picked up some groceries. I grabbed everything I needed to make a big batch of muffins. I wanted to make a good impression on the first day.

Overall, the area was nice, but it wasn't like walking down the street at home. There was a homeless man that sat by the alley down the street from me. He smiled at me and even said hello. Feeling bad for him, I reached into my bag and grabbed him a banana. He thanked me, which lifted my spirits somewhat.

I spent the night mixing up dozens of batches of muffins. There were way too many and I knew it, but it was the distraction I needed. I was nervous about starting tomorrow, terrified I would royally screw up. But I wasn't driving a car and I didn't have the keys to anything at work, so I didn't have to worry about losing company keys. Still, my heart pounded out of control all night and I couldn't sleep.

Finally, when the first rays of light peeked through the window, I got up and prepared myself for the day. I dressed as nicely as possible, not wanting to make a bad impression on my first day. The butterflies in my stomach were so intense that I couldn't even think about eating, but I packed a few granola bars in my purse in case I got hungry.

Dressed and ready to go, I boxed up my muffins and was just turning to kiss Carter goodbye for the day when I realized he wasn't with me. I almost called him, but I was an hour ahead, and he would just be getting up. I decided to text him instead.

Abby: Just heading off to work.

Carter: It's early, isn't it?

Abby: I'm nervous I'll get stuck in traffic or the driver will get lost.

Carter: I don't suppose there are any big trees for reference.

My lips curved into a grin at his joke as I walked into the hallway and pulled the door closed behind me. I locked the door and made the conscious effort to slip my key in my purse so I wouldn't get locked out.

Abby: Keys are secure in my purse.

Carter: Finally! I don't suppose there's a way to find a sanitary cab. I know what the back of police cars are like.

Abby: As long as there are no spiders, I'm good. Besides, my driver is picking me up.

He didn't answer right away, so I headed downstairs to wait for my car.

Carter: I forgot about that. You'll look so important arriving in a town car.

Abby: As long as I don't fall on my face. I made muffins so people will like me.

Carter: You have no idea how jealous I am right now. Somebody else is getting my muffins. And you don't need to make muffins so people will like you.

I smiled at his text, wishing I could send him some baked goods.

Abby: I could make a care package, but I don't know how they'll taste by the time they reach you.

Carter: I would take your week-old muffins any day.

I almost started crying right then, but the car pulled up and honked its horn. I pulled myself together as the driver stepped out and walked around to open my door for me.

"Ms. Hall?"

"Call me Abby."

"Abby, I'm Carl. I'll be your driver while you work for Mr. Donahue."

Opening the container of muffins, I held them out to him. "Thank you. Would you like a muffin? I just made them last night."

He eyed the muffins with a devilish smirk. "I could get fat if you do this for me too often."

"I could always make you gluten-free," I grinned.

"I'll just get fat," he laughed as I slid into the backseat. He shut the door and ran around to the front.

I pulled out my phone, but Carter was already getting ready for the day, leaving me one final message.

Carter: I have to head in early. Have a great first day. I love you.

Abby: Thank you. I'll call you tonight.

The drive into work was quicker than I thought. Strolling into the office, I grabbed my badge and packet that was waiting at the front desk for me, allowing me up to the necessary floor. When I stepped off the elevator, I was shocked to see the receptionist was already in for the day.

She stopped typing as I walked in. "You're in early. We weren't expecting you for another hour."

She stood and walked around to shake my hand.

"Well, I was nervous and wanted to make sure I was prepared for the day."

"That's actually great. I can catch you up before Mr. Donahue gets in. He'll love that."

"Perfect." Remembering the muffins, I held up the container and opened the lid. "I made muffins for everyone. I have this weird thing about baking."

She smiled kindly, but grimaced at the muffins. "That's so kind, but I'm on a diet. I have to fit into my gown for this upcoming event," she whispered. "But put them in the break room. I'm sure they'll be gone by the end of the day."

I followed her back to my space outside Mr. Donahue's office.

"All of these offices are for Mr. Donahue's most executive employees. There are five floors below us that are also used by other members of the company. I'm the main receptionist for this floor, but there's a second receptionist that works with me, but she's more like my assistant and she comes in later."

I nodded, trying to remember all this.

"HR is on the fortieth floor, and you'll need to stop in there before the end of the day to make sure all your paperwork is in order. Also, Mr. Donahue likes everyone into the office ten minutes before the day starts, so make sure if you're running late you let him know."

We stopped by a very nice desk that was fancier than anything I'd ever seen before. I gawked at it like a kid in a candy store. There was an iMac sitting on the desk, along with anything I could possibly need to take care of things during the day.

"This is your desk, and in the packet you received, you'll find your keycard for anything on this floor. Mr. Donahue may need you to go into other people's offices at times to retrieve documents. They're all aware of this, so please don't freak out about invading their privacy." She glanced at her watch. "Right, I think you should head down to HR now. I'll phone them and let them know you're coming. After that, you can pull up his schedule and make sure you're ready for his day."

After waving goodbye, she headed back to the front. I stood there for a minute in awe before going in search of the break room. After finishing with HR, I went through his schedule and just finished taking notes on everything that needed to be done when he walked in.

"Ms. Hall, it's so nice to see you here."

I stood, shoving my chair back too much, sending it flying across the room. I ran after it, catching it right before it crashed into the wall not too far away. Biting my lip to keep from spewing apologies, I pushed the chair back to my desk and gave him a desperate smile.

"It's nice to be here. I want to thank you for this opportunity—"

"Please, you were the best candidate for the job. I'm very glad you're here. Have you been told about visiting HR?"

"I already went down there and took care of everything. Also, I was just going over your schedule for the day, so I'm up to date."

"Great," he beamed. "I knew I was right to hire you. Why don't you come into my office and I'll let you know what I'll need from you today."

He turned on his heel and headed into his office, so I snatched my pen and a notebook off my desk and headed inside. I was a professional. I could do this.

⚜

MY FEET WERE KILLING ME. I had been running errands all around the city for Mr. Donahue today. Thank God he gave me the car or I would be lost out there somewhere, still trying to figure out where the hell I was supposed to go. Now I understood why I needed my own car. I was already used to calling Carl for a ride and I'd only been here one day.

It was seven o'clock before Mr. Donahue was done for the day, and though he told me I could go home earlier, I stayed in case he needed something. We ended up in several meetings, with me taking notes and then calling around for various projects that needed to be updated. By seven, he was ushering me out from behind my desk and handing me my coat.

I swung by the break room to see how my muffins did, but I was disappointed to see them all still sitting there. Putting the lid back on the Tupperware, I took them with me. If no one else was going to eat them, I would eat them for dinner. I was too lazy to cook tonight anyway.

Carl was waiting for me by the curb and quickly drove me home. When I got out, I happened to look down the sidewalk and see the homeless man from yesterday still sitting there. I didn't really need all these muffins and since I didn't know when the last time he ate, I decided to give them all to him.

The closer I got to him, I noticed he barely had anything warm on, and his hat was threadbare to say the least. He had to be freezing. He hadn't shaved in a long time, his beard nearly touching his chest.

Heading over to him, I was determined to feed him. "Hey."

"Hey, Banana Lady," he grinned.

I laughed, hoping that wouldn't be my new nickname. "Yeah, that's me. Today, I have muffins, though."

"You don't have to bring me muffins."

I shrugged and handed them down to him. "I actually made them for work. It was my first day and I wanted to bring them as a treat."

"Then why did you bring them home?"

"Apparently, nobody wanted them. I don't know, I think everyone must be watching their weight or something."

He huffed out a laugh and took the container. "These are home-made?" he questioned as he looked at them. "You didn't buy them and stick them in a container to make it look like you baked them?"

"No, I'm not that clever."

He took one out and bit into it, his eyes closing as he chewed. "Damn, that's good."

"Thank you."

He slowly tilted his head up at me warily. "You really don't want these?"

"No, I stress bake, so if you stick around, you'll probably get a lot more muffins."

"I wouldn't say no to that."

Feeling a lot better after such a long day, I waved to him and said goodbye, then headed up to my apartment. It took me ten minutes to find my key in all my crap. I would have to buy something I could keep around my neck so I never lost them. This was ridiculous.

After setting down my purse, I pulled out my phone and called Carter. I was so eager to talk to him. Today was hard, but I didn't want him to think I was miserable, that I gave up everything for a job that I hated. I actually loved it. It was just a lot to take in one day. So, I needed to put on a happy face and make him think this was a great opportunity.

Taking a deep breath, I called him.

"Hello?"

"Hey," I said brightly, relieved to hear his voice.

"Hey, how was the first day?"

"It was really great. Everyone was so nice and I really loved the work."

"Yeah? Are you just getting home?"

"Well, Mr. Donahue worked late. He told me I could leave, but I didn't want to seem too eager to get out of there on my first day, so I stuck around. And then I ran into this homeless man on the way home and I gave him—"

"Wait, you ran into a homeless person in New York City, and you just decided to stop and talk?"

"Well, not exactly. I ran into him yesterday and gave him a banana, but he was sitting just down from my apartment, so I thought I would share my muffins."

"You shared my muffins with him?" he asked incredulously.

"They weren't your muffins," I laughed. "You're not here."

"You could have sent them to me," he grumbled.

"They would have been disgusting by the time they got to you."

"Still, you can't just go making muffins for another man. That's not fair."

"But he was hungry. Did you want him to starve?"

"That's another thing. We need to discuss you making friends with homeless people."

"Why?"

"Because you don't know him. You don't know if he's dangerous or not. He could drag you into an alley and rape you!"

I rolled my eyes at him, even though he couldn't see me. "Please, that's a very broad statement. That's like saying every broke person is going to scam you out of money."

"I'm not saying he's a bad person. I'm saying you don't know him. Big cities are dangerous."

"Well, if you had moved here with me, you could have protected me."

I knew it was a low blow the minute it was out of my mouth. He was quiet on the other end for a few minutes. It was just dead silent and I knew I had gone too far.

"Carter, I'm sorry. I know why you didn't want to move here."

"It's fine. Listen, I should go. I still have paperwork to finish up here."

"You're still at work?" I asked, frowning as I looked at the time.

"Jack wanted to get home early tonight, and it's not like I had any reason I couldn't stay."

So, it seemed that we were both taking shots at each other.

"I'll talk to you tomorrow," he said tiredly. "Have a good night."

"You too."

He hung up without saying anything else. I set down my phone and plopped down on the couch. Staring at the wall, I wondered if I had made the right decision.

🐾 41 🐾

CORDUROY

I slammed the door on my car and walked up to the animal shelter, ignoring the scathing look Antonio shot me as he opened the door and walked out.

"What are you doing here?"

"I came for my cats."

"What cats?"

"Abby had some cats brought here."

He nodded slightly. "I heard about her moving to New York."

He didn't say anything else, like *I'm sorry* or *That sucks*. But that wasn't his style, so it didn't matter.

"Is Jo inside?"

"Yeah," he grunted. "But you're only taking the six cats."

I looked at him strangely. "Yeah."

"Good, six is enough."

He stomped away. I didn't get it. Why would he be concerned about taking more than six cats? Wasn't six cats more than enough for any person? Shaking my head, I walked inside and rang the bell on the front desk. Jo came out of the back, grinning at me.

"Hey, Corduroy. What can I do for you?"

"I need to pick up the six cats Abby gave you."

Her eyebrows shot up. "You want all six cats?"

"Well…" I cleared my throat. "You know, she's not sure she's staying in New York, and there's no point in them staying here when they could stay at my house."

"But aren't you allergic? Abby said you had some really bad reactions."

"I'm fine with an antihistamine."

"Well, I already re-homed one of the cats."

I felt my heart race in panic. "Which one?"

"Yoda Bear."

"What? Why would you give that cat away!" I shouted, angry that Yoda Bear was gone.

"Well, he actually got a lot of attention. He was beautiful."

"That's besides the fucking point. Who did you sell him to?"

"I can't give away that information."

"Yes, you can," I stabbed a finger at her. "Open the damn book and give me a name."

"It's confidential!"

I leaned across the counter, getting in her face. "You listen to me right now. If you don't open that damn book, I'm going to get a subpoena for all the records in this place, and then I'm going to get a warrant and inspect this entire facility. I'll dig through this place until I uncover something that shuts this place down."

"You wouldn't!"

"Oh, you bet your ass I would," I shouted.

"What the fuck is going on in here?" I spun around to find Antonio standing in the doorway, looking at me like I was the crazy person. He was a fucking mountain man, but I was the insane one? "And why are you yelling at Jo?"

"She sold my cat and she won't tell me to who."

His eyebrows shot up. "You sold his cat?"

"It wasn't his cat," Jo snapped. "It was Abby's cat and she gave them to me to re-home."

"You should have asked me first. Those cats belong with me!"

"Antonio, will you explain to the deputy that I can't just hand over the name of a client?"

He winced. "I'm kind of on his side."

"Are you kidding me?"

He shrugged. "Sorry, but you sold the man's cat."

She tossed her hands up in the air. "Un-fucking-believable! I can't believe you're siding with him!"

"Tell her I need the name," I pleaded with Antonio.

"Oh, no," he shook his head. "No, I'm not getting involved with this. You're on your own."

"But you just said you were on my side."

"Just because I agree with you doesn't mean I'm going against Jo. Sorry, you'll have to call your buddy Jack for help."

"I'll save you the trouble," Jo announced, picking up the phone. "This is harassment. How do you think he's going to react when I tell him that you're threatening me?"

"I'm betting he'll be on my side," I yelled.

When Jack walked through the door twenty minutes later, he did not look happy to be here.

"Carter, what's this all about?"

I pointed my finger at Jo. "She sold one of my cats."

"One of *your* cats?" he asked, his eyebrows lifting in surprise.

"Yes, one of my cats. She just sold him."

"Which one?" he asked curiously. "Was it the horny one?"

"No, it was the furry orange one."

He grinned, nodding. "Yoda Bear. Yeah, he's a beautiful cat."

"Exactly, which is why I need to get him back."

"Carter, what do you want me to do? She sold the cat already."

"Tell her she has to give me a name."

"I can't," she shouted. "It's animal shelter...client privilege."

"That's not even a thing!"

"It is here," she growled. "I'm not giving you that name!"

I spun around and faced Jack. "You're gonna get me that name. I need that cat."

"Why? You're allergic."

"Because...because she's gone and those cats are the last piece of her I have," I said, my throat closing up. I could feel the tears in my eyes as I pleaded with him. Christ, I sounded like a sappy fucker. "She

called me the other night. She loves that job. She's not coming back."
My voice cracked and Jack's shoulders slumped.

"Aw, fuck, just give him the name," Antonio snapped, marching around us and behind the counter.

"Antonio—"

"No," Antonio said sharply, cutting her off. "I'm not going to stand here as a man breaks down because he just wants the one reminder of the woman he loves."

He gently shoved her aside and searched the computer, then looked up at me. "John Henderson."

"Chili Man?" I asked, surprised that he would even want a cat.

Antonio shrugged. "I don't know who that is."

"Wait," Jo frowned. "I thought Chili Man's name was Bob."

"I want the rest of my cats." I pulled out my wallet and tossed down my credit card. "I'll be back for them in an hour. Don't go selling any of them."

I turned and headed for the door, marching out to my car.

"Wait!" Jack shouted. "Carter, what are you going to do?"

"Get my cat back!"

"Fuck, why does it always have to be Chili Man?" I heard him mutter right before I slammed the door and took off down the driveway.

৯১৯

I POUNDED on his door for the fifth time. "I know you're in there, Chili Man! Open the door before I kick it down!"

"Would you stop threatening the man?" Jack asked. "This isn't how you get your cat back."

"You're right," I said, turning to head back down the stairs. "I should try the back door. He might have left it open."

He rushed down the stairs after me, catching me on the arm and spinning me around. "That wasn't what I meant."

I frowned. "Do you think I should wait until he leaves and then climb in the window?"

He punched me across the jaw. "What the fuck is wrong with you? You're a deputy!"

I shook off the pain and nodded. "You're right. I don't know what I was thinking."

He sighed and stepped back. "Maybe we can call him up and discuss a release."

I nodded. "You're right. Sorry, I lost my head there for a minute."

"Alright, let's head back to the station and see what we can do."

I started to follow him, but as soon as he was far enough ahead of me, I turned and ran for the back door, jumping over the fence and landing with a roll. I got up and sprinted to the back door as Jack shouted for me. I kicked in the back door without checking first to see if it was locked.

"Where are you, Chili Man?"

He appeared around the corner, holding Yoda Bear in his arms.

I started to run at him, but was tackled to the ground by Jack. My arms were yanked up behind my back as Jack slapped the cuffs on me.

"Goddamnit, Carter! You can't break into people's houses."

"Why not? You had people arrested for jaywalking!"

He jerked me upright, spinning me around just as I hissed like a cat at Chili Man.

"Christ, I have to get you out of here. John, I'm really sorry about this. Why don't you meet me down at the station?"

"Yeah, I'll be there."

Jack jerked me toward the back door and I grinned at the splintered door frame. I was so close to getting my cat back. I was shoved into the backseat like a criminal and Jack slammed the door. People were staring at me like I had gone insane, and maybe I had. I'd hissed at another man. Fuck, I was losing it.

"What the fuck is wrong with you?" Jack swore as he got into the front. "I'm arresting my own deputy for breaking into someone's house. How the fuck am I supposed to explain this?"

I glared out the window at Chili Man, who held up the cat like it was his prize. "Stupid fucker," I muttered under my breath. "No one likes your chili anyway!" I shouted.

"Would you shut up? You're not making this easier on yourself."

"Why the fuck does he have my cat? He wouldn't know how to take care of a day-old bowl of chili."

We roared down the street and Jack ignored me the whole time, refusing to listen to me bitch about Chili Man. When we pulled up to the station, a crowd had already gathered. Apparently, someone talked about it on the town page. Everyone had their phones up as Jack got out and hauled me out of the back seat.

"What happened?" Carrie asked. "Do you need me to go in there in case he needs to be talked down?"

"I've got this, Carrie," Jack said, holding up his hand to ward her off.

"Did he really lose it on Chili Man?"

"Was this because of a cat?"

"Is he still going to be the deputy? I could take his job!"

I ignored them all as Jack led me into the station and put me in a cell for the second time since I'd met Abby. Maybe this was another sign. Maybe I wasn't meant to be with Abby. Hell, that woman had a way of ruining me.

Jack took his seat and leaned back, staring up at the ceiling. "Explain to me how I let you keep your job when you just broke into someone's house."

I rubbed at my eyes as I took a seat on the bench. "Does it even matter at this point? The woman I love is gone and she's not coming back."

"So, you're just going to give up and become a vagrant?"

"What's the point in living?" I muttered.

"Oh, shut the fuck up. I don't want to hear that crap out of your mouth. She didn't die. She's in another fucking state, and if you weren't such a jackass, you would go tell her that you love her and want her to come home."

"She doesn't want me!"

"You don't fucking know that. You're just making excuses because this is another way out for you. Once again, you're fucking this up. She moved on, but you let her, and now you're blaming her for it. Are you going to blame her for getting thrown in jail?"

"Well, if she had bothered to ask me first, I would have taken the damn cats!"

"You're allergic!" he shouted. "Carter, you have to pull your shit together. This isn't like you. You're the calm and rational one. You're the jokester. You're the one that brings this town together, not tears it apart."

I knew he was right. God, I was a fuck-up. I would be lucky if he didn't take my badge from me, but what the hell was I supposed to tell the town?

"There he is," Chili Man shouted as he walked into the station. "I want that man arrested!"

Jack sighed. "John, he's already behind bars."

He frowned. "Oh, right. Well, I want him charged with battery and assault, and breaking and entering."

Jack stood and stepped in front of him so he couldn't see me. "John, maybe we can come to some sort of resolution on this matter. Look," he lowered his voice. "I didn't want to have to say this, but Carter's really struggling since Abby left. She broke his fucking heart when she walked out that door, and now he just found out that she's probably not coming back. The man had hope a few days ago, and now that's gone. Do you have any idea what that feels like?"

John was quiet for a moment, and then he nodded. "When I first moved here, I was in love with Adele, but she was already in love with another. I begged her to stay, but she had already made up her mind. They moved out to Portland and now they have three kids and a dog," he said, choking on a sob.

Jack nodded, patting the man on the back. "So, you know what he's going through. He didn't really want to hurt you. He just wanted the only reminder he has left of Abby. A woman can drive a man to do crazy things."

"I guess," Chili Man nodded.

I had to admit, Jack was doing a great job of getting me out of this, even if everything he was saying was technically true.

"What do you want me to do?"

Jack sighed, shoving his hands in his pockets. "Well, Carter could pay for the damage to your house, but that still leaves him without this piece of Abby."

"I could maybe part with Yoda Bear for five hundred dollars."

I made a noise of protest, but Jack held up his hand. "I think that's reasonable."

"And a chili cook-off. He held a bake-off for Abby. I think it's only fair that he give me this one thing."

"Of course," Jack nodded. He sighed heavily, pacing the office area. "There's just one problem. If I have to book him on breaking and entering, that's a felony. He'll go to jail, which will make it difficult for him to do the chili cook-off."

"What if I agreed not to press charges?"

Jack winced. "It might work, but then you posted that whole thing on Facebook. It's out there now. I don't know how I would explain that away."

Chili Man frowned, but then his eyes lit up. "What if we say that this was all a big ruse?"

"I'm listening," Jack said, crossing his arms over his chest.

"We could say that we were just having some fun around town. Like when the Cortell brothers went into the bank as kids and held it up. Everyone went along with that."

Jack ran a hand along his jaw, nodding in agreement. "It could work, but you could never tell anyone. It would have to be our secret."

"Of course. I completely understand."

"Then you have your chili cook-off."

"A big one," John stressed.

"The biggest one you've ever seen. I guarantee it."

"Alright," he said, shaking Jack's hand. Then he looked at me. "You can come pick up the cat when you have five hundred dollars cash. And don't break in my door this time."

42

ABBY

"Muffin Man!" I shouted as I ran down the sidewalk to him. He looked up from his spot on the concrete and frowned. "Muffin Man?"

Out of breath, I passed him the container of freshly baked muffins, bending over at the waist. "Yeah," I panted, "you know, because of the muffins."

He nodded slightly, looking at me like I was a total weirdo. "I have a name, you know."

"Yeah?" I tilted my head. "What is it?"

"Ms. Hall!" Carl shouted. "We need to leave now if you want to get to the office in time."

I waved at him and turned back to Muffin Man. "Sorry, I wanted to make you something really good, but I had all this muffin stuff and I needed to use it up."

"You didn't have to make me muffins."

"Well, it's not like I have anyone else to bake for. Besides, it makes me feel good to bake for someone that enjoys my food."

"Well, I do like it," he said hesitantly. Then he leaned over and grabbed my previous container. "Here."

"Oh, thanks," I said, tucking it under my arm. "Well, I have to run, but I'll see you tonight."

"What's tonight?" he called after me as I ran back to the car.

"Chicken casserole," I shouted over my shoulder.

I slipped into the back of the town car and we were off to the office. On the way, I pulled out my phone and started taking care of Mr. Donahue's emails. I was to sort through them and take care of any I could so he didn't have to deal with every small issue. When that was done, I called several people to confirm appointments. They didn't seem too happy that I was calling this early, but if I waited until I got to the office, I would never be able to keep up. Over the past week I had fallen into a routine with Mr. Donahue, figuring out his needs and trying to get them done before he asked.

I rushed out of the car, waving at the receptionist downstairs before taking the elevator up to my floor. It occurred to me right before I got off the elevator that I had become one of those New Yorkers in just a week. I was constantly on the go, always working no matter where I was. There was never any downtime, but I couldn't say I didn't like it either.

However, my time at the office was greatly interfering with my phone calls with Carter. Most mornings I just sent him a text. Last night, I actually fell asleep while I was on the phone with him. I felt terrible, and I was pretty sure that didn't make him feel too good either.

I quickly headed to my desk and got to work sorting through files in order of importance. When Mr. Donahue came in, I grabbed my notepad and headed into his office to get my notes for the day.

"We're leaving tomorrow at six o'clock for London," he said without any preamble.

I stopped and stared at him for a moment. "London?"

"Yes, I have a business situation that needs to be taken care of in person."

"Is there anything I should know?"

"You'll need to contact the London office and make sure they're prepared for my arrival. Also, I'll need you to make arrangements for our flight. All the contact information should be on your computer. You have a passport, right?"

"Um…yes," I said, still in shock that I was actually going to London. "How long will we be gone for?"

"Prepare for a week, but we may have to stay longer."

"Right, do you need me to take care of your laptop?"

"Yes, also, please call my house and ask my housekeeper Nancy to prepare for my travel. She'll know what to do."

"Of course."

He grabbed some files off his desk and walked toward the door. "I have a few meetings this morning that I'll need you to sit in on. After all arrangements are made and you're sure you have everything for the office, you should head home to pack."

I nodded and headed out of the room. I was so nervous. I'd never made travel arrangements before, especially not for a private plane. What if I screwed it up? I started sweating as I watched him walk down the hall. Grabbing my phone, I dialed Carter's number.

"Abby? Is everything okay? You never call me in the middle of the day."

"I'm totally freaking out!"

"Is this about a spider? Because I know about our dating contract, but I honestly don't think I could get there in time to kill it."

"This isn't about a spider," I snapped. "I'm leaving for London tomorrow morning and I have to make all these travel arrangements, and I've never made travel arrangements! What if I mess something up and he fires me?"

"He's not going to fire you," he said calmly. "Just take a deep breath and think about what you need to do."

I did as he said and then remembered what Mr. Donahue said. "Right, I need to look for the contact information on my computer."

"Okay, so take it one step at a time. You'll be fine."

"You're right. Thank you."

"So…how long are you going to be gone for?"

"I have no idea. He said a week, but it could be longer. And I have so much to get done. I'm sorry, but I can't stay on the phone."

"It's fine. Just call me tonight."

"I will. Thank you. Sorry I freaked out on you."

"It's fine. I love you."

Now that I was calm, I finally felt like I was ready to get to work. "Okay, I have to go."

I hung up and got to work, only realizing on my way home that night that I hadn't said I love you or said goodbye. I'd just hung up on him.

As I prepared the casserole to share with Muffin Man, I dialed Carter's number, but it went straight to voicemail.

"Hey, it's me. I'm just making dinner and then I have to pack. Sorry I was so flustered today. Call me if you get a chance. I love you."

While the casserole was baking, I worked on packing, trying to choose what to bring and what to leave behind. When the timer went off, I pulled the casserole out of the oven and set it on top of the stove. After pulling on my coat, I grabbed a towel to put under the dish and carried it down, hoping Muffin Man was still there.

I smiled when I saw him sitting in his usual spot. Sitting down beside him, I handed him a paper plate and fork.

"You were serious about that casserole," he grunted.

I glanced over at him, really looking at him this time. He was a tall guy, but I couldn't tell a whole lot more because of the gigantic beard covering his face. But as he looked at me, I could tell he had kind eyes. There was pain there, swirling in the depths. I wanted to ask him why he was here or what made him the way he was, but didn't think he would answer. I finished dishing out the food and leaned back against the wall to eat with him.

"Why are you doing this?" he asked, taking a bite of his food.

I shrugged. "You seem nice, and I don't have anyone else to eat with. I don't know anyone else in New York besides the people I work with."

"You don't know me. I could be a murderer."

"Are you?" I asked, taking a bite.

"No," he said quietly. "So, where are you from?"

"Indiana. I was originally from Indianapolis, but then I walked in on my boyfriend screwing my roommate, so I got out of there. I moved to a small town further north and lived there for about eight months."

"What made you move here?"

"A job." He nodded and kept eating. "I left someone behind." I laughed slightly, shoving my food around.

"A boyfriend?"

"Yeah," I sighed. "I'm not sure it was the right decision."

"Then why did you do it?"

"Because this was a great opportunity. I thought...I thought maybe this was my one chance to do something like this and I shouldn't pass it up."

"You sound like you regret moving here."

"Not really. I love my job. It's only been a week, but it's so great. But if I stay, I'm not sure how it'll work with Carter."

"Long distance relationships are hard."

"Yeah? Have you done it?"

He was quiet for a minute. His eyes drifted off like he was remembering something. There was a sadness to him, the way his whole body seemed to crumple in on itself. "A long time ago," he finally admitted.

I took a chance and asked him, even though I was pretty sure he wouldn't answer. "Why are you out here? What happened?"

He snapped out of his haze, looking over at me. "We were talking about your terrible decision-making skills."

I smirked at him. "I never said I was a terrible decision-maker."

"I did. If you got a great guy and gave him up, that just proves my point. Besides, who leaves a great small town to live here?" he asked, waving his hand around.

"I don't know, why are you here?" I turned the tables on him.

"See, I think you really liked where you lived, so it doesn't make sense that you would come to this big city."

I sighed, leaning back against the wall. "I did like it. It was really great. Everyone knew everyone else, and there was the town Facebook page where everyone posted everyone else's business. And the sheriff is really nice. He's Carter's boss and best friend."

"Your boyfriend is a deputy?"

I nodded.

"So, why didn't he transfer to be with you?"

"He didn't want to live in the city. He liked his small town and knowing everyone. He said he would hate it and end up resenting me."

"Well, if you want to know what Muffin Man thinks," he grinned, or at least I thought he did. It was hard to tell with all that hair on his face. "You should go be with him. A job is just a job, but finding a person you want to spend your life with is hard to find. You're missing out on a lot."

"I'm sure pretty much everyone in town would agree with you, including Plaid Man."

"There's a Plaid Man?"

I nodded, chuckling to myself. "And a Chili Man."

"Are these given names or is the town just insane?"

"They're all a little crazy."

He lifted his empty plate as a thank you. "You should go call your boyfriend."

Sighing, I stood and handed the casserole over to him. "Hang onto the dish for me. I'm leaving in the morning for a work trip."

"Sure, I'll stack it with my pots and pans."

I laughed and headed back down the sidewalk, pulling out my phone. I had a missed call from Carter. It must have been from before I came downstairs. As I went up to my apartment, I called him back, grinning when he answered.

"Hey, sorry I missed your call. I was having dinner with the Muffin Man."

"The Muffin Man?"

"Yes, the Muffin Man."

He was silent for a minute. "Does he live on Drury Lane?"

I frowned. "No, he's the homeless man on my street."

"You had dinner with the homeless man?" he shouted.

I pulled the phone away from my ear and winced. "It's not a big deal. He's really nice and completely harmless."

"How can you be sure?"

"He has kind eyes."

"Oh, is that how we're judging people now?"

I sighed in irritation. "Look, I don't have any friends here yet. I made a casserole, but since I'm going on this trip, I thought it would be nice to share it with him."

"You're going to get murdered in your sleep," he muttered.

"Because I shared a casserole?"

"Maybe not by this guy, but you're too nice. One of these days, that's not going to work out for you."

"Carter, I don't want to argue about this. I'm not getting any murdery vibes from him, and if I was, I wouldn't go near him."

"You've already sat and had dinner with him. You'll probably invite him upstairs for your next meal!"

"Maybe I will," I said indignantly. "And what are you going to do about it?"

"Apparently nothing, because you're halfway across the country!"

I took a deep breath and calmed down. "This isn't helping anything. If we're going to argue about this every time we get on the phone, this is never going to work."

"You're right," he muttered.

I checked the time and sighed. "I have to get to sleep. I have an early flight."

"Be safe."

"I will."

"And let me know you're alive."

"You know I will," I assured him. "I love you."

"I love you too."

I hung up and headed into my apartment. Maybe Muffin Man was right. Maybe this was the wrong move for me. Everything was tense between Carter and me. I just couldn't see how this was going to work if he was always so angry all the time.

43

CORDUROY

I woke up and couldn't see a damn thing. I fumbled around on the nightstand for my phone, knocking it to the ground in the process. I stumbled out of bed and searched with my hands for it, finally finding it under the bed.

"Siri, call Jack."

"Calling Josh Cortell."

"No," I shouted, clutching the phone in my hand. "Siri, stop."

I could hear it ringing on the other end. "Yeah?"

"I wasn't calling you," I snapped.

"Then who were you calling?"

"Jack."

"I'm not Jack," he said boredly.

"No shit. I need you to call him for me."

"Why?"

"Because I can't see anything!"

"Why didn't you just use Siri?"

"I did use Siri," I said in frustration. "She called you."

"I hate it when she does that."

"Can you call Jack for me or not?"

"Fine, what do you need?"

"Tell him to get over here with a giant bottle of Benadryl."

"Having an allergic reaction to the cats?" he grinned.

"I don't think my antihistamine is working anymore."

"Or," he said slowly. "It could be the fact that you're suddenly living with six cats."

"Would you just fucking call him?"

"Can you really not see?"

"No, my eyes are swollen shut."

"Are you sure it's not from crying?"

I leaned back against my bed and sighed. "Are you going to call him or not?"

"Fine, fine. I'll tell him to get over there."

"Thank you."

I hung up and got up and flopped back down on the bed. I wasn't moving until he got here with medicine. I started sneezing uncontrollably when Yoda Bear started rubbing up against me. I could tell it was him because of the long fur. I tried to shove him away, but he seemed to think I was playing with him and started swatting at my hand.

Finally, after what felt like lightyears, the front door opened and I heard Jack's footsteps walking through the house.

"Yo!"

"Where is he?"

"Aw, fuck," I muttered. "Who did you bring with you?"

"Josh. I thought I might need assistance." I could hear the grin in his voice as he walked into the room. "Christ, look at your face. What did you do?"

"It's the fucking cats, okay?"

"I can't believe you took them in when you have allergies."

"We can talk about my bad choices some other time. Give me the good stuff."

I felt him push the bottle into my hands.

"I already took off the cap for you."

"Thank God."

I started chugging the bottle.

"Whoa!" He grabbed it from me before I could drink the whole thing. "You're supposed to take one dose."

"Do you see my face?" I pointed at myself. "I need the whole bottle!"

"What you need is to get rid of the cats," Jack retorted.

"I don't know. I kind of like him this way. Say cheese."

I heard his phone camera click and then he was laughing. "This is going to be so good. Can we take him downtown and just let him walk around?"

"As much as I would love that, I think he's suffering enough right now."

"I'm so glad you two are having fun over my misery," I grumbled. "Jack, do me a favor and get the black notebook out of the nightstand."

"You want me to order you a hooker?"

"No, it's Abby's cat allergy remedies."

He didn't say anything for a moment and then huffed out a laugh. "The last time you tried one of those, you ended up in the hospital."

"I have no face!" I shouted. "I'll try anything right now."

"You know, we could take you to the doctor and have him prescribe something."

"Fine, whatever. Make me the appointment so I can see again."

"You really can't see anything?" Josh asked.

"Why would I lie about that?" I heard his chuckle as he moved across the room and then I heard rustling. "What are you doing?"

"Something in this room has just been down my pants."

"You're sick," I snapped. "Why would you do that to a blind person?"

"You're not blind," Jack muttered. "Just stupid."

Now I was afraid to touch anything in the room. I laid there as Jack made calls, but from the sounds of it, I couldn't get an appointment today.

"Okay, it looks like we're trying out the black book of allergy relief. What should we try? Ginger root? Cactus?"

"Is that really what it says?"

"I guess you'll never know," he laughed.

I felt something cold plop on my face and water dripped down my neck. "For your eyes. It should help with the swelling."

"This sucks," I sighed.

"Why don't you just let Chili Man take the cat?"

"Because I need them."

"I know you think that, but you can get them back when Abby comes home."

I stayed silent, not wanting to admit to them just how little faith I had in that happening. At this rate, I wouldn't even see her at Christmas like she had suggested.

"Or you could just pay Jo to keep them at the shelter," Josh suggested. "Hell, Antonio might take them in. I hear he got another cat."

"They're my cats," I argued.

"They're going to slowly kill you," Jack pointed out. "Just call Abby and find out when she'll be home—"

"She's not coming home," I snapped.

"I know you think that, but it's only been two and a half weeks."

"She's in London," I admitted. "She left a week and a half ago and I haven't heard from her once."

The deafening silence of the room told me all I needed to know. They didn't think that boded well for me either.

"The time difference is killer," Jack said, trying to make me feel better.

"You don't understand. All we do is fight. I don't..."

"You don't what?" Josh asked.

"When I tell her I love her...I don't hear it in her voice. It's just so blank, like an automated response. And now she's got this friend...the Muffin Man. He's homeless and she spends time with him."

"I thought she was in London."

"That's the last I heard. For all I know, she's home and just hasn't called."

"Have you tried calling her?" Jack asked.

"No," I said sarcastically. "I just decided to wait for her to call."

"Maybe you should go to London," Josh suggested.

"If she doesn't want me in New York, she doesn't want me in London."

"Wrong," Jack corrected. "She did want you in New York, but you didn't want to go."

"So this is my fault?"

"It's both of your faults," he said. "You could have gone with her and given it a chance. She could have realized that you didn't want to leave and decided to stay for you. Both of you are idiots."

"You know what? You can just fuck off," I muttered, laying back on the bed.

Jack sighed. "You might as well take the day off. You're no use to me if you can't even see."

"It's getting better," I grumbled.

"Not soon enough."

"Do you want me to send Carly over with some food?" Josh asked.

"No, I can manage. I can almost see a speck of light creeping in."

"Yeah, that sounds promising," Jack laughed. "We'll see you later."

"Yeah." I waved them off, laying back down on my bed. Was he right? Should I have tried to go to New York with her? I hadn't really tried. I'd just given up. But now that almost three weeks had passed, I knew I would have been miserable. She'd been on this trip for nearly two weeks. I would have been all alone for two-thirds of the time we were there.

I slept more of the day away, letting the medicine kick in. When I could finally see, I got up to take a shower. My eyelids were still swollen, but at least I could make out where I was going and what I was doing. I quickly showered and got out, letting myself drip all over the floor. When Abby was here, I was alway conscientious about things like water on the floor. She already had enough accidents. I didn't need her to have one in my house.

My phone rang in the bedroom and I ran to the door, desperate to get it in case it was Abby. I slipped on the floor, crashing to my hip. I bit back a groan and raced to the phone. Snatching the phone off the bed, I quickly answered.

"Hello? Abby?"

There was nobody there. I looked at the screen and sighed. One missed call from Abby. I immediately hit redial, but it went straight to voicemail.

"Fuck!"

I tossed down my phone, running my hands through my hair. How long could I put up with this? I loved her so much, but this was killing me. I'd barely spoken to her more than five minutes at a time when I used to spend my whole night with her. If I kept doing this, I would end up hating her. Maybe I needed to just end things. She had her new life, and as long as I hung onto hope that she would come home, I would never really be living.

44

ABBY

"Did you get ahold of him?" Mr. Donahue asked as we sat down on the jet.

"No, he didn't answer, but he was probably working."

"Well, you can sleep on the flight. We'll be home soon and maybe you can reach him in the morning," he said kindly.

Leaning my head against the headrest, I closed my eyes. I couldn't sleep, though. My stomach was churning with indecision. I loved this job, but not seeing Carter was killing me. I wasn't even sure what to think about our relationship at this point. I wanted to believe that we could make it, but I could feel the division between us growing every day. And every time we spoke, he started an argument with me.

He kept saying he would wait around for me, but what did that really mean? It felt the whole time like he was telling me to go for this job, but he didn't really believe we would make it. So, what was all that mushy stuff about always loving me? Was he trying to say goodbye in his own way?

At some point during the flight I finally dozed off. I was exhausted when we got off the plane, and thankfully Mr. Donahue gave me the day off. I didn't think I could function anyway. The trip had been so chaotic, I barely had a moment to myself. Every time I tried to call

Carter, it was always night and he would be sleeping. When Mr. Donahue said we would be working a lot, I didn't realize just how much that was. I loved the challenge of it all, but was this really what I wanted from my life?

Carl opened the car door after parking in front of my building. I smiled and thanked him for the ride and was just about to go upstairs when I glanced over to where Muffin Man was sitting. It was freezing outside and I didn't like the idea of him sitting out in the cold. Walking over to him, I waited for him to notice me.

"Hey," I rubbed my forehead tiredly.

"You were gone a long time."

"Well, I couldn't help that. Do you want to come upstairs?"

He looked at me funny. "Why would you offer that?"

"Because it's freezing out here."

"I chose to be out here," he said, giving away the first hint of his life.

"Okay, well, maybe you can come upstairs for something to eat and clean up a bit."

"I don't give a shit that I'm dirty."

"I wasn't saying you did. I just figured you might want to get warm."

He gazed at me in confusion for a moment before pushing himself off the ground. "You're very strange and you have no sense of danger."

I quirked an eyebrow at him. "Are you planning on murdering me?"

"No."

"Then if you'd like to come upstairs and warm up, I'd be happy to have you."

"I don't need any charity. I'm fine where I am, and you shouldn't be inviting strangers up to your apartment."

"But we're not strangers."

He sighed, running his hand over his beard. "You can't just walk up to people and invite them inside. It's not safe. It doesn't matter if you trust me or not. You don't know me!"

My phone rang in my pocket and I quickly pulled it out. "Carter," I said quickly, hoping I hadn't missed him.

"Hey, are you still in London?"

"No, I just got home. I'm just outside my apartment."

"Did you lose your key?"

"Ha ha. No, I'm trying to convince Muffin Man to come inside and get warm, but he's refusing."

"You're doing what?" he snapped.

"I'm trying to help Muffin Man," I said slowly.

"Abby, what the fuck? Get out of there now."

"Is he telling you to leave?" Muffin Man asked.

"What do you think?"

"At least he's a smart man. You need to go upstairs now."

"Is he telling you to leave?" Carter asked.

"Yes, but—"

"You should listen to him."

I growled in frustration. They were both talking over me.

Muffin Man grabbed my bag and started walking down the street. "Hey! That's my bag!" I shouted after him.

"He's stealing your bag?" Carter asked.

"No, he's forcing me to go upstairs by carrying my luggage."

"Thank God," Carter muttered. "But don't let him into your apartment."

"I'll let him in if I want!"

"I'm not going inside," Muffin Man said, pushing my luggage at me. "You're going to go upstairs and lock your doors."

"Yeah, what he said," Carter shouted over the phone.

"Would you two both shut up! I can make my own decisions."

"You invited a homeless man upstairs," Muffin Man snapped, showing the most anger I'd seen out of him yet.

"To keep you warm."

"He chose to be out there," Carter rumbled over the phone.

"Would you shut up?"

"Yeah, get in a fight with your boyfriend over a homeless man," Muffin Man griped. "Great way to keep that relationship afloat."

"Can you put him on the phone?" Carter requested.

"What? No, I'm not putting him on the phone."

"Let me talk to him," Muffin Man motioned for me to hand over the phone.

"I'm not giving you the phone!"

He grabbed it out of my hands and walked away. I raced after him, but then realized I was leaving my luggage out on the sidewalk. I didn't hear what they said, but then he was handing my phone back.

"You're going to go back upstairs and lock your doors, and I'm going back to my spot over there. You're not going to bring me any food. You're going to leave me alone and every other homeless person you see on the street. Are we clear?"

He didn't wait for me to answer. He just walked off and left me standing on the sidewalk.

"Abby!"

I finally realized that Carter was still on the phone and raised it to my ear. "What?"

"Excuse me?"

"Why did you have to do that?"

"Because you can't run around New York doing shit like that."

"And you can't tell me what to do."

"Goddamnit, Abby. I'm trying to protect you."

"Yeah, from another state. You're doing a great job."

He was quiet for a moment and then let out a harsh breath. "I have to go. Try not to get yourself killed."

I hung up and dragged my stuff inside, ignoring Muffin Man after the way he turned on me. I unpacked my things, angry about everything in my life. I tried to take a nap, but sleep wouldn't come. With nothing else to do, I went grocery shopping and made some dinner. When it was ready, I headed downstairs to sit with Muffin Man. When he saw me coming, he huffed in irritation.

"I kind of thought you would be gone by now."

"You saw me when you went to the grocery store."

"Yeah, but you still might have left."

He shook his head and patted the ground. "Might as well sit down."

"Thanks," I mumbled, sitting beside him and setting out our dinner.

We ate in silence, and when we were finished, I stared up at the night sky, but I couldn't see a single star. It was so sad.

"What did he say to you?"

Muffin Man turned to me and sighed. "He wanted to know you weren't about to get killed."

"Is that why you stayed here?"

He handed over his dish and plumped up his bag on the ground just inside the alley. "That day you gave me the banana was the first time I've stayed anywhere more than one night."

"But you've been here every night since then."

He nodded. "Goodnight, Abby."

He rolled over and ignored me, so I stood and carried my stuff upstairs. I kicked the door shut to my apartment and placed my dishes in the sink. Was Muffin Man staying down there to watch over me? Maybe I should be creeped out by that, but instead, I found myself smiling. And when I went to bed that night, I didn't have any trouble falling asleep.

45

CORDUROY

T wo more weeks went by. Two weeks where I barely spoke to her. I was going insane, barely sleeping and so drugged up on allergy medicine that I found it hard to focus most days. I spent all day waiting for a fucking phone call that half the time didn't come. And the only solace I had was that she had this Muffin Man looking out for her.

Something had to give. I had a hard enough time before she went on her trip, but it was almost worse once she got home. I should have had more time to talk with her, but instead, I found myself waiting on her phone calls almost every night.

As I drove into the station that morning, I found myself snapping at people left and right. Gone was the man that happily greeted everyone in town. The only person here was the shell of a man that just couldn't bring himself to do the one thing he knew needed to be done.

I shoved the station door open and stomped inside. Jack sighed and tossed his pen down on the desk.

"Still haven't heard from her?"

"Going on three days," I grunted, grabbing some coffee.

"Why don't you just go out there?"

"To talk to her door? No thanks."

"You could go to her office."

"And look like the desperate boyfriend?" I questioned.

"What the fuck does it matter if you look desperate? You love her."

I nodded, staring down at my coffee. "Do you know how many times I've called her in the past two weeks?"

"How many?"

"Every morning and every night. If she doesn't answer, I send her a text, telling her how much I love her or wishing her a good night. She's answered those texts twice. I've talked to her a total of six times over the past two weeks."

He winced, leaning back in his seat. "Ouch."

"No kidding." I sat down, my whole body slumping in defeat. "I can't do this anymore."

"You're breaking up with her?" he asked incredulously.

"I'm going to talk to her, tell her how I'm feeling. The rest is up to her."

"What if she decides to stay?"

"Then I guess we're over."

"You didn't give it very long."

"I gave it over a month. I get that I look like a pussy. I'm the guy that can't take his girlfriend being halfway around the country—"

"I wasn't going to say that."

"I just can't do this. I need more than a few short phone calls every few days. I need someone that wants to be with me at night. Deep down, I always knew this was the way it would end. I only tried this for her, but I'm beginning to think that was a mistake."

"How so?"

"Had I ended it when she left, I could have started to put it behind me. Yeah, it would suck, but dragging it out like this, hoping for something you know is never going to happen? That's just tearing my heart to shreds."

"When are you going to talk to her?"

"Tonight. If she'll answer."

"I hope it works out for you," he said sincerely.

I tilted my chin in acknowledgement and then got to work. I did everything to distract myself from the conversation I would have tonight. One way or another, this crap was ending tonight. When I finished up at the end of the day, I swung by the diner and grabbed some food. People talked to me, but I barely listened. I was too busy thinking about all the things I needed to say to Abby.

When I got home, I ate, despite my stomach protesting the food. I was way too nervous for this. I waited until after seven before I called her. I knew she tended to work late, so I waited until I had the best shot at her being home. When the clock struck seven, I dialed her number.

"Hey, babe!"

"Abby." It rushed out of me in a quick breath. Her voice was a balm to my aching heart, but a reminder that this may be the last time I spoke to her. "How was your day?"

"Not as bad as the rest of the week. I actually got off at five today."

I frowned. That was three hours ago by her time. "Why didn't you call me?"

"Well, you would have been working and I made dinner for Muffin Man. I lost track of the time and—"

"Abby!" I said angrily, barely containing my rage.

"What's wrong?"

"What's wrong? I haven't fucking talked to you more than five minutes at a time in two weeks, and meanwhile you're eating dinner every night with the homeless man on the corner."

"I was just trying to be nice."

"What about me?" I asked angrily.

"Carter, what is this about? Are you really so upset that I ate with a homeless man?"

"No, I'm upset because he gets all your free time. You're supposed to be my girlfriend, but instead, you're acting like he's the person you want to talk to."

The line went quiet and I sighed.

"I can't do this anymore, Abby. It's killing me every day that I'm not with you."

"I hate it too, but—"

"No," I interrupted her. I couldn't take any more possible scenarios that might work, or promises of better times to come. This was it. "Abby, we said we would try this, but honestly, it would have been easier if we had just ended things before you left."

"You don't mean that," she cried softly. "Please, Carter...don't do this."

"I need you, Abby. I need you so much. But you have to make a choice. Do you want your job or do you want me?"

"You can't just put me on the spot like that."

I closed my eyes as my throat swelled up. That was all the answer I needed. If the situation was reversed, I would be back by her side in an instant. I wouldn't need to think about it.

"Then that's my answer."

"That's not fair."

"Abby, you shouldn't need to think about whether your job means more than me."

"And what about you?" she argued. "You're not rushing out here to make this work."

"It's a different situation. We met here. I grew up here. It's where I want to marry my wife, raise my family, and die. You chose to move out there for a job. So, if that job means so much to you that you'd rather have it than me, you should stay."

I could hear her sniffles over the line and I wanted to make it better, but she was ripping my heart out right now. I knew this wouldn't work, but I also assumed that when I met the woman I wanted to spend my life with, there wouldn't be any questions about whether or not she wanted to be with me too.

"Carter, just give me some time. Please don't ask me to choose."

"You have to, Abby. I can't keep doing this to myself. I can't wake up every morning and wonder if this is the day you'll talk to me. I send you messages, hoping to just get a small reply from you, and I usually don't. Do you know what that does to me?"

"I'm busy!" she argued. "It's not like I'm ignoring you. I just don't have time to talk."

I leaned forward, resting my elbows on my knees. I ran my hand through my hair, tears pricking my eyes. I couldn't believe this was happening.

"Abby," I choked out. "This isn't a relationship. I'm not blaming you. I'm glad you love your job. I just wish it was me you wanted to devote your time to."

"Carter, please—" she sniffled.

"I love you, Abby, and I hope this job gives you everything you need."

"What do we do from here? Please don't say this is over."

"It has to be." I swiped at my nose with my sleeve, trying to hold it together. "I'm going to say goodbye and tell you I love you one last time, and then I'll hang up the phone. And tomorrow, it's going to suck so much, but I'm not going to text you to find out how you are. And I'm not going to call you at night, and you won't call me. And in a few weeks, it won't hurt so damn much."

"But..." She sniffled hard. I could hear her sobs through the phone and they were killing me.

"It's the way it has to be." I closed my eyes, letting the tears slip down my cheeks. Pain coursed through my throat as I sucked back the tears. "I love you so much, Abby. You made my life so much brighter, and I'll never forget that."

"Don't hang up, Carter," she cried. "Don't—"

I pressed the end button before I could hear her beg for me to stay any longer. When I tossed the phone down, I buried my face in my hands and the tears finally came hard. I wasn't sure if this was what it felt like when Jack lost Natalie, but I was pretty sure it came close.

❧ 46 ❧

ABBY

I didn't fall asleep until early this morning, and when I finally woke up, I was late for work. I already had five missed calls from Mr. Donahue. I quickly texted him an apology and told him I would be in soon. I looked like shit. My eyes were still puffy from last night and I hadn't had time to clean my mascara up as I rushed around to get ready. For the first time since I started working here, I just threw on some yoga pants and a t-shirt and ran out the door. I figured he would be happier if I was at work than if I was dressed properly.

Wrapping my burnt orange scarf around my neck, I ran to the car and jumped in, ignoring Carl as he shut the door. I pulled out my phone and started going through messages, but my concentration was shit. All I could think about was how Carter had broken my heart and then hung up on me without giving me a chance to say anything. What if I'd said I would come home? Would he have told me I was too late?

We pulled up in front of the building and I raced through the entrance, not remembering my ID badge.

"Ms. Hall, you can't go up without your ID," the security guard stopped me.

"I work here. I'm just running late this morning and I forgot it."

"Then you'll need to call up to get permission at the front desk."

"Are you fucking kidding me?" I shouted. "I work here every fucking day!"

"Ma'am, you're going to have to lower your voice or I'll have to escort you out."

"I have to get up to my office! Call Mr. Donahue! He'll tell you that he's waiting on me."

"Ma'am, like I said, you'll have to use the front desk to call up to him."

"Fine." I stomped over to the front desk and glared at the woman as she quickly picked up the phone and dialed, having already heard the exchange. After a few yeses, she hung up and waved me through. I turned around to the security guard and stuck out my tongue at him. It was childish, but I was not in the mood to be messed with today. Hell, I didn't even want to be here. For the first time since I arrived in New York, I hated coming to this building.

When I got off the elevator, the receptionist looked completely shocked at my appearance. I didn't care. I stomped right past her and headed to my desk. Mr. Donahue flung the door open to his office and frowned at my appearance.

"My office. Now!"

I followed him in, sure I was about to be fired. And why shouldn't he fire me? I was late, insubordinate, and dressed like a hobo.

"What is going on? Were you out drinking last night?"

"What?" I almost laughed at that. "No, I wasn't drinking last night, though I probably should have been."

"What are you talking about?"

"I'm talking about the fact that my boyfriend broke things off with me. Yeah, that's right," I said, my eyes wide and hands flying up in the air. Oh shit, I was losing it. "He called last night and asked me to choose, and the stupid woman that I am, I didn't immediately pick him. So, he ended things and I stayed up all night crying. And it's all because of you!" I snapped, pointing my finger at him.

"Me?" His eyebrows shot up in the air.

"Yes, you. Don't look so innocent. You work people to death. I have no life besides the homeless man outside my apartment. And the sad thing is, I spent more time talking to him than my boyfriend, because every time I talked to Carter, we started fighting."

"Who's Carter?" he asked in confusion.

My face shook and my body felt like it would explode. "My boyfriend!" I shouted.

He winced. "But I thought you broke up."

I narrowed my eyes at him. "You're arguing semantics now?"

"I'm sorry! I'm just trying to keep up."

"You know what? I don't think I want to be here today. I'm taking a personal day."

"But we have work to do."

"Do I look like I'm in a position to work? I have mascara dried down my face. My hair is ratty and needs to be washed, and I'm pretty sure these yoga pants have ketchup stains on them. I'll be in tomorrow," I snapped, turning my back to him and marching out the door.

I texted Carl that I needed the car and marched to the elevator. As I turned around and pressed the button, the receptionist stood, a slight smirk on her face, and started clapping just loud enough for me to hear. The doors closed and I fell back against the wall. Shit, I probably just lost my job, especially if other people in the office heard me.

The doors opened and I ran out to the street, racing around to the driver's side and snatching the keys from Carl.

"Ms. Hall!"

"I'm driving, Carl."

"You're not insured to drive!"

"It'll be fine," I said, getting in the driver's seat and slamming the door. He ran around the front and opened the passenger side door, barely getting inside before I roared into traffic.

"Ms. Hall, please slow down," he said, his voice quivering as I swerved in and out of traffic.

"No. You know what? I'm tired of listening to men. Why do men always get to tell women what to do?"

"Because this is my car!"

"And that's a valid reason?" I shouted, barely swerving around a car before I rear-ended it.

"Yes! You're not on the insurance."

"Right, it's all about protecting me! Why does every man in my life want to protect me?"

"I don't know what you're talking about," he gasped as I slammed on the brakes and jerked the wheel down the next road. I had no idea where I was going, but it didn't matter at this point. I just needed to drive.

"Just like Carter. He had to protect me from the Muffin Man."

"Who's the Muffin Man?" Carl asked, grasping the *oh shit* handles for dear life.

"He's the only man in my life that listens to me. Carter, he couldn't even bother listening to me before he broke up with me last night. I would have chosen him," I said, slamming my hand down on the steering wheel. "I just needed one fucking minute!"

Tears slipped down my cheeks as I started crying so hard I could barely see the traffic. I swerved down another street, barely hearing Carl scream over the sobs wracking my body.

"Ms. Hall, you're going the wrong way on a one way street!"

I swiped the tears from my face and screamed as I swerved out of the way of an oncoming car. "Why does this always happen to me?" I shouted, jerking the wheel again. I spotted an alley ahead and quickly turned down it, just hoping to get out of traffic. But the alley was too narrow and the car crashed into both buildings on either side of the alley. We came to a halting stop and my head just barely missed the steering wheel.

Heart thundering in my chest, I slowly peeled my hands off the steering wheel and leaned back in the seat. I looked over at Carl, who had his eyes closed and was taking deep breaths.

"Sorry about that," I whispered. "At least the airbags didn't go off."

"They should have."

"See? Now you'll take the car in to be looked at. I actually saved your life from a more deadly accident."

He slowly turned and glared at me.

"Should I...do you want to drive?"

He nodded and I shifted into park, then got out of the car and walked around to his side. He pointed to the back seat, not moving from his spot until I slid into the back. Grumbling, he took his seat in the front and reversed the car. I cringed as we pulled away and the bumper fell off the car. Carl didn't even stop to pick it up. I had a feeling he just wanted to get me home.

With swollen eyes, I leaned my head against the seat and tried to figure out my next step from here. I would just have to tell Mr. Donahue that I was done and hope that Carter took me back. We pulled up outside my apartment, and Carl got out to open my door, which really shocked me.

"Abby? What happened?" Muffin Man shouted, getting up and running over to me.

My face crumpled. "What didn't happen? Carter broke up with me," I cried. "I yelled at my boss, crashed this car, and now Carl hates me!"

"I don't hate you, but you're never driving again."

"Wait, did you say Carter broke up with you?"

"Yes."

"But he was just here."

My face jerked up to peer into his kind eyes. "He what?"

"He was just here. He just left!"

He pointed down the road where a cab was driving off in the distance.

"That's him?"

"Yes! He came to see you. I told him you were at work."

I jumped up and wrapped my arms around Muffin Man, hugging him tight. "Thank you!"

Kissing him on the cheek, I ran around to the driver's side, ignoring Carl yelling at me to stop. I got in and shifted into drive just as Carl got in the car.

"You are *not* driving this car!"

I spun the wheel and pulled a uey in the middle of the road. I clipped the car parked on the other side of the street, but gunned it as soon as I could. The cab was so far ahead I could barely see it. I pressed the gas down and hoped I got to him before I lost him in traffic. I ignored the red light ahead of me and zipped through traffic, narrowly avoiding the cross traffic. I only had two lanes to drive in and the people in front of me were driving really slowly.

"Don't these people know how to drive in New York?" I shouted.

"They do," Carl retorted. "You don't!"

There was a gap in the oncoming traffic. Making a split-second decision, I jerked the wheel into the oncoming traffic and raced around the cars in front of me. I swerved back into the right lane, shouting out when I saw his cab.

"That's him!"

I honked my horn, but it was drowned out by all the other people honking their horns too. Sirens sounded behind me as a cop car pulled up behind me.

"Shit! They're onto me."

"You think?" Carl asked, his eyes wide.

"Hey, I'm a good driver!"

"You're a terrible driver!"

I honked my horn again, ignoring the sirens behind me and all the chaos. The only thing that mattered was getting to Carter and winning him back. I sped through another light and headed into oncoming traffic again. I passed his cab, waving at him like a crazy person. I saw his jaw drop open in shock as I gunned the engine and pulled ahead of him. The traffic was clear up ahead, so I took my chance to stop this once and for all. I roared ahead, giving myself the appropriate amount of space.

I screeched to a stop and shifted into reverse. Putting my hand on the back of Carl's seat, I sent the car flying backward, gaining speed just like I was taught. I spun the wheel, pulling a J turn, right in the middle of New York City. As the car spun, I shifted into drive, but slammed into something behind me before I could take off. Pressing the gas down, I took off toward Carter, racing toward the man I loved.

I didn't get far before his cab stopped in front of me. He got out and was racing toward me as I unlatched my belt and jumped out of the car, noticing that it was still rolling forward. Water was shooting out of the hydrant I hit, spraying me with water.

I ran to Carter, slamming into him as he scooped me up in his arms and slammed his lips down on mine. I threaded my fingers through his wet hair, kissing him like I would die without him. I wrapped my legs around his waist and held on tight. The sirens and the honking horns were drowned out, and for this one moment, there was only Carter and me. I grinned as I saw him pull out his deputy badge and show it to the officers rushing toward us. They immediately backed off.

He pulled back and laughed as he brushed my wet hair out of my face. "Nice J turn."

"Well, I did learn from the best."

He laughed and kissed me again. I rested my forehead against his, my heart still racing out of control.

"You came for me," I whispered.

"I'll always come for you. I couldn't do it. It was like giving away a piece of my soul."

I squeezed him tighter to me. "Don't ever let me go."

We both looked up at the water pouring down from the spray of the hydrant. Laughing, he smiled down at me. I never thought I would see that smile again. Now I was back in his arms and everything was right.

"I think this is going to cause more paperwork."

He shrugged. "Yeah, but not for me."

And then he pressed his lips to mine again and everything else slipped away.

47

CORDUROY

I slid the key in the lock and took a moment to compose myself. She was home with me and my life was back on track. I wasn't sure what exactly inspired me to run out and buy a plane ticket. I was sitting there sobbing like a baby when it suddenly hit me that this didn't have to be the end. I couldn't let it be the end. She was everything to me and I had to fight for her.

I laughed every time I closed my eyes and saw her driving past me like a lunatic and then pulling that J turn in the middle of the busy street. She was insane, but it just showed me how much she really wanted me. Now she was out her license for the next six months, but it was totally worth it.

"Carter, are you going to open the door?"

I swung the door open and let her inside, stepping aside so she didn't miss the biggest surprise. She pulled her luggage in behind her and then gasped, getting down on her knees to see all her cats.

"Oh my gosh! You kept the cats."

She picked up Pteheste and snuggled against him. "Well, I couldn't let them go. They were part of you."

"But how did you keep them with your allergies?"

"Well, for a while I used antihistamines, but eventually they stopped working. I looked in your little black book and found something that worked."

"Really?" she smiled at me, standing up to wrap her arms around my neck. "It worked?"

I shrugged slightly. "Well, aside from the occasional rectal bleeding."

She shoved her face in my chest and laughed, her shoulders shaking hard. "I can't believe you did that for me."

I slid my hand through the hair at the nape of her neck and looked into those gorgeous eyes. "I'd do anything for you."

"Even live with a woman that's been to jail?"

"Well, I've been to jail a few times myself since I met you."

"Oh God, I don't even want to know all the trouble you've gotten into."

"You can catch up on the town page," I chuckled. "So, did you decide if you were going to stay with the company or not?"

"Well," she nodded her head from side to side. "I thought after what happened, it would be best if I just slipped away quietly."

"You did, huh?"

I nodded. I kissed her lightly on the lips, my own twisted up in a smirk. "And was this a mutual decision?"

"You know," she waved me off. "I told Mr. Donahue I wasn't coming back because I was leaving with you. He agreed it was for the best."

"Uh-huh."

"Because my focus was on you," she continued.

"Right, it had nothing to do with you yelling at him."

She pressed her lips to mine and murmured, "Maybe just a little."

I swung her up into my arms and carried her back to our room. We had been apart way too long to stay clothed any longer. I laid her down on the bed and shook my head slightly. "What am I going to do with you?"

"Well, the officer in New York did tell you to keep a close eye on me."

"I'll be keeping more than my eyes on you."

❧

AFTER SPENDING all night in bed with the woman I loved wrapped in my arms, I had to go into the station and do some explaining. Jack would probably kick my ass. I had run out with barely an explanation, though I did tell him to fuck off.

Abby was unpacking, putting her stuff in my closet where it belonged. I walked up behind her and wrapped my arms around her waist. "Good morning, beautiful."

"Good morning."

She spun in my arms and gave me a searing kiss.

"Is it good to be home?"

She sighed dreamily. "I can't imagine being anywhere else."

Kissing her again, I pulled myself away from her and started getting dressed for the day. She opened up another bag and pulled out a piece of paper. Unfolding it, she stared down at it, looking like she was about to cry.

"Everything okay, baby?"

"It's just the note..."

I walked up behind her and read it over her shoulder.

THANK YOU FOR EVERYTHING.

MUFFIN MAN

"A MAN OF FEW WORDS," I grumbled. "I like it."

She jabbed me with her elbow, sighing again. "I just wish I could have said goodbye."

"Baby, he was a homeless man that you had an obsession with. Frankly, I'm glad you're not around him anymore."

"Why?"

"Competition," I said with a wicked grin. "I can't have other guys getting more of your time than me."

"But he stayed on that street because of me."

"And then it was time for him to move on."

She dropped her head and stared at the note. "I just wish I could have helped him."

"You did, more than you know. You showed him kindness and gave him my muffins. I think you did more than enough."

She shrugged.

"Hey," I pulled her into my arms. "Do you want to head to the bakery with me? I thought maybe you could stop in and see Mary Anne."

"Why?"

"Well, she's looking for help," I said, then leaned in slightly, "and I have it on good authority that she would love to have you at the bakery."

"That's actually a really good idea. Just let me finish getting ready." She rushed into the closet to get dressed.

"You have ten minutes," I shouted after her, pulling on the rest of my clothes.

We headed into town, greeting people as we passed. Finally, I was back to the man I once was, only ten times better because Abby was back with me. When we walked into the bakery, I stopped dead when I saw Jack sitting in there.

"I've been waiting for you," he said, standing up and walking over to me.

"I had to go get Abby back."

"I know. Like I said, I've been waiting for you." He turned to Abby and actually hugged her. "It's good to have you back."

"Oh, well, thank you."

"Don't thank me. It was absolutely critical that you came back. This guy's been impossible since you've been gone. Did he tell you he hissed at Chili Man?"

Abby turned at me with wide eyes. "You did what?"

"I was desperate."

Jack winked at me, nudging Abby slightly. "It was all for show."

"What was for show?" Abby asked.

"Jack," I warned.

"You know," he grinned. "Carter kicking in Chili Man's door, hissing like a cat, getting arrested...it was all a show for the town."

Abby's mouth dropped open in shock. "I can't believe you!"

"I was..." I sighed heavily. "I was miserable without you. And he had Yoda Bear."

"You attacked him for Yoda Bear?" she said, her eyes welling up.

"A man will go the distance to get his woman's cat back."

She laughed at me, kissing me hard. I was so getting laid for that one.

"Oh, you're back!" Mary Anne said, rushing out of the back. "I'm so glad. We've made so many changes with the place since you've been gone."

I looked around, wondering what was different. She pointed in the corner where a TV hung.

"You got an upgrade," I nodded.

"And you're just in time for the preview," Jack patted me on the shoulder, stepping up beside me again.

I cocked my head at him as the TV turned on. It was news footage from a helicopter and down below was Abby in the town car, speeding through traffic in New York City as the police chased her down.

"Yep, got it all on the town Facebook page now. You two are practically famous. And Tyler's getting a lot of credit for that J turn."

I crossed my arms over my chest and watched as Abby got out of her rolling car and we ran into each other's arms.

"It's so beautiful," Jack said, wiping a fake tear from his face.

"It was fucking romantic as hell," I grinned, watching as we kissed in the midst of water pouring down on us.

"Nice one, pulling the badge."

I nodded. "I thought so."

ALSO BY GIULIA LAGOMARSINO

Thank you for reading Ace Magnets! I hope you all enjoyed Corduroy and Abby's story. Look for more from them in *Four Horsemen!*

Are you a new reader? See where it all began with the For The Love Of A Good Woman series. And continue with some of your favorite characters in the Reed Security series and The Cortell Brothers. Or follow the individual links down below!

Did you start in the middle? We've all done it! Find your place in the series and start from there! There's no need to question which book to start with. These books are best read in order. All books are available in Kindle Unlimited! For The Love Of A Good Woman:

Jack , Cole, Logan, Drew, Sebastian, Sean, Ryan

Not ready for those characters you love to disappear? You can catch them again throughout the Reed Security Series! These men and women are strong, sexy, and willing to fight for those they love. Sometimes, they fall right into love, while others need a little more convincing. Don't miss out on this exciting series!

Sinner, Cap, Cazzo, Knight, Irish, Hunter, Whiskey, Lola, Ice, Burg, Gabe, Jules, Sniper, Jackson, Chance, Phoenix Rising, Alec, Storm, Wolf, A Mad Reed Security Christmas, Rocco, Coop, TNT, Nightingale, Parker, GoodKnight, The Reed Security Relationship Manual

And don't miss out on meeting all of Derek's brothers in The Cortell Brothers:

Maintenance Required, Collateral Damage, Wanted Dead Or In Love, Textbook Approach, Priceless Ink, Tangled Web

A Good Run Of Bad Luck

Dead Man's Hand, Drawing Dead, The Dirty, Ace Magnets, Four Horsemen, The Nut Low, Big Slick

Printed in Great Britain
by Amazon

20451776R00185